ALSO BY ROSAMOND SMITH

Lives of the Twins
Soul Mate
Nemesis

SNAKE EYES

ROSAMOND SMITH

SNAKE EYES

A WILLIAM ABRAHAMS BOOK

DUTTON

DUTTON

Published by the Penguin Group
Penguin Books USA Inc., 375 Hudson Street, New York, New York 10014,
U.S.A.
Penguin Books Ltd, 27 Wrights Lane, London W8 5TZ, England
Penguin Books Australia Ltd, Ringwood, Victoria, Australia
Penguin Books Canada Ltd, 10 Alcorn Avenue, Toronto, Ontario, Canada M4V
3B2
Penguin Books (N.Z.) Ltd, 182–190 Wairau Road, Auckland 10, New Zealand

Penguin Books Ltd, Registered Offices:
Harmondsworth, Middlesex, England

First published by Dutton, an imprint of New American Library,
a division of Penguin Books USA Inc.
Distributed in Canada by McClelland & Stewart Inc.

First Printing, February, 1992
10 9 8 7 6 5 4 3 2 1

 REGISTERED TRADEMARK—MARCA REGISTRADA

LIBRARY OF CONGRESS CATALOGING-IN-PUBLICATION DATA:
Smith, Rosamond.
Snake eyes/Rosamond Smith.
p.   cm.
"A William Abrahams book."
ISBN-0-525-93404-9
I. Title.
PS3569.M537967S58   1992
813'.54—dc20
91-25843
CIP

Printed in the United States of America
Set in Janson
Designed by Steven N. Stathakis

PUBLISHER'S NOTE

This is a work of fiction. Names, characters, places, and incidents either are the
products of the author's imagination or are used fictitiously, and any resemblance to
actual persons, living or dead, events, or locales is entirely coincidental.

for Dutch Leonard—
il miglior fabbro

IT HAS BEEN SAID UNTO YOU, AN EYE FOR AN EYE, AND A TOOTH FOR A TOOTH: BUT I SAY UNTO YOU, THAT YOU RESIST NOT EVIL.

MATTHEW 5.38–39

ALL JOURNEYS HAVE SECRET DESTINATIONS OF WHICH THE TRAVELER IS UNAWARE.

MARTIN BUBER

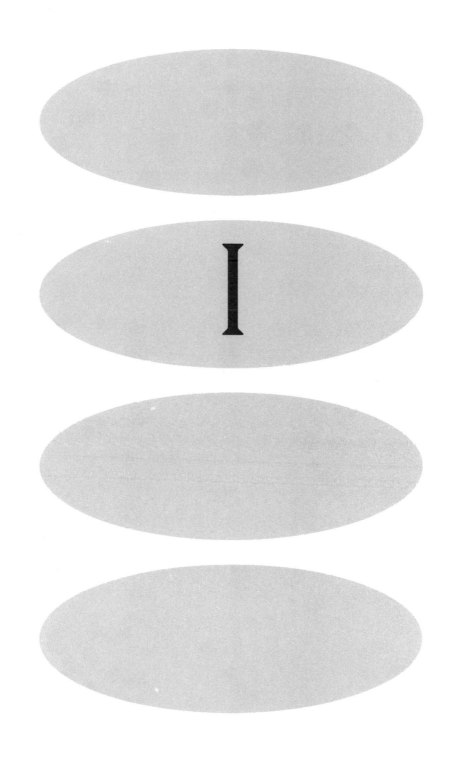

I

Lee Roy Sears had only a single tattoo, on his sinewy left forearm, but it was a masterpiece. He'd designed it himself and had it executed by a Filipino tattoo-artist, in Manila, where he'd been sent on leave near the end of his Vietnam tour of duty, as it was then called. This was late 1971.

The tattoo challenged all conformist standards of "ugliness" and "beauty." It was so ugly it turned beautiful before your eyes.

In fact, the tattoo was hardly a mere "tattoo"—a trick of dyes stippled into living human flesh—but an actual presence, alive in itself. You had only to contemplate it for a few minutes, with no distractions, to understand that.

Lee Roy Sears, who had been visited by "dream visions" since earliest boyhood, had transcribed it out of a fever-dream in a Vietnam jungle: a tensely coiled snake, oily black, gold-spangled, with a bony humanoid head. Its small forked red tongue protruded between tusklike fangs that dripped venomous saliva, and its strangely gleaming gold eyes were pricked with tiny black pupils like pulsing ink spots. Even before Lee Roy Sears did the trick with his forearm muscles, giving the impression that the snake was twitching to life, about to spring and strike, about to sink those fangs into warm flesh, your instinctive reaction was to shrink away.

Uncoiled, the tattooed snake would have measured only about eight inches. But you'd remember it as much larger—life-sized.

You might not even remember it as a tattoo, exactly.

LEE ROY SEARS WAS not ashamed of "Snake Eyes" (which was his pet name for the tattoo)—Lee Roy Sears was not ashamed of anything to do with Lee Roy Sears save infrequent lapses of strength and will—but, of course, being no fool, he knew to cover it for what could be called formal occasions. When conformity to bourgeois society's customs might be strategic. Like the hearing before the five-member State Board of Pardons at the Connecticut State Prison at Hunsford, on the morning of May 11, 1983, thirty-six hours before Lee Roy Sears was scheduled to die in the electric chair in an adjacent wing of the facility, on a charge of first-degree murder.

There, subdued, watchful, erect, the condemned man sat, listening as strangers debated his fate, his "case," before him. In his spotless prison khakis. Sharp-creased trousers, long-sleeved shirt discreetly buttoned to the wrist.

"It *is* sad, I suppose. He has such haunted eyes."

It was the eve of May 11, 1983. In their white colonial house on Glenway Circle, Mount Orion, New Jersey, Gina O'Meara was speaking to her husband, Michael, scheduled, the next morning, to attend the hearing at Hunsford and to speak on behalf of the convicted killer Lee Roy Sears—who, of course, so far as Gina could gather, Michael did not necessarily think *was* a killer. She was peering at a small, smudged photograph of Sears stapled to one of the numerous photocopied documents in Sears's file. Such a strange, intense, brooding face! Like one of those ugly-exotic masks from Polynesia, hanging on the walls in that sinister-dark wing of the Metropolitan Museum of Art—mere holes for eyes, but *were* they mere holes, and not, somehow, *eyes* capable of seeing?

Michael O'Meara rarely told Gina about his *pro bono* legal work for The Coalition because Gina had a habit of challenging him, in her coquettish yet sharp-witted way, like a rival lawyer. Her

wifely attitude was that so hard-working and so dedicated a person as
Michael O'Meara should always be paid for his labor, though she did
not like to say so since this sounded—didn't it?—as if *she* wanted to be
paid. So she struck a more ideological note, an objectively philosophical
note, as she did now, frowning. "I know I probably don't understand,
the law is a game you can't really play without knowing the rules, but,
Michael dear, isn't the crucial thing whether this man *is* a murderer or
not? Not whether he received a fair trial, or there were inflammatory
things said, or this—what is it—'prosecutorial'—"

"—'discretion.' "

"Yes, that. Well?"

"But, in our criminal justice system, as it is today, the prosecutor
can misuse his power," Michael said earnestly. "He dictates the terms
of the case from the start, first to the grand jury, then at the trial. It's
his prerogative to offer plea bargains, to coerce frightened and sometimes even mentally incompetent men and women into entering pleas
of 'guilty' when, if they were tried, the charges against them might not
be proved. Then again, if they dig in, and insist upon a trial to clear
their names, like Sears, they can be punished."

"But—*is* Lee Roy Sears a murderer, or not? Doesn't anyone
know?"

Michael sighed. He had told Gina only the rudiments of the
complicated case, glossing over Sears's earlier brushes with the law
and certain unsubstantiated charges, later dropped, of kidnapping
and rape. He believed he could hear, in his wife's ingenuous voice,
an underswell of numberless voices, incredulous, demanding, claiming a wish for knowledge without the good faith to receive it. Yet,
one must try. "Sears insists he didn't fire a shot; two 'witnesses' say
he did. There were others on the premises who had guns. The State
so argued its case, five years ago, and the defense so bungled its case,
the verdict went against the defendant. That's all we—I mean we
outsiders—really know."

Gina said, lightly chiding, "You make it sound as if the trial
was a lottery."

"It was. Trials are. Especially for the indigent in America."

"But some of these accused people *are* guilty, aren't they? Even
if the public defender bungles the case?"

Michael tried to smile and squeezed Gina's fine-boned hands, with their carefully polished nails, in his. He was a man of only moderate height, five feet nine when he stood very straight, but his frame was affably stocky, his shoulders wide, hands and feet big. A bearish sort of man, at least as bears are commonly perceived: there was something both boyish and anxious about him, a characteristic look of appeal, a squinting sort of grin, that endeared him to both men and women; especially to women, at least initially. He was not handsome, neither was he ugly. His eyes were without luster, rather a drab muddy brown, but warm, direct, candid. His fair, curly, red-burnished hair had begun to recede sharply while he was still in his twenties, but its crest remained springy, like a rooster's comb. His handshake was brisk, even fierce; his touch unfailingly gentle, as if, conscious of his strength, he feared giving hurt inadvertently. By contrast, Gina was slender, even thin; fashionably thin; very feminine, with high, delicate cheekbones in a classically oval face, and large seagreen eyes like gems, and ashy blond hair always stylishly cut—at present, swinging level with the graceful line of her jaw, so that her lovely neck appeared to advantage. Where Michael O'Meara was outspoken, curiously without subterfuge for one trained in the law, his emotions showing raw and unmediated on his face, like a child's, Gina was all ambiguity, subtlety, calculation. There was something Oriental in her mannerisms, though in her values as in the stamp of her femaleness, she was thoroughly American: if you were a man you were enthralled by her, yet very possibly annoyed, irritated, for was the woman flirting?—or was she slyly making a fool of you? Now twenty-nine years old, three years Michael's junior, she'd been, not quite a decade ago, a popular Philadelphia debutante; in Michael's admiring eyes she looked scarcely older, or more mature, than she'd looked upon the romantic occasion of their first meeting, when, in a Delancey Street brownstone, a private home with an elevator, the elevator door had opened and he'd found himself staring at a girl of dazzling beauty in a black shimmering-silk cocktail dress. *There. Oh God.*

In a sense, their courtship still continued, perhaps in part because Gina had yet to become pregnant. Thus she remained virginal in a sense, not completely won. From the first Michael had felt a subtle yet powerful erotic tug between them in which he, the man, thus *manly*, must conquer her, the surpassingly feminine woman, who is after all not so easily conquered. "Gina, darling," he said, stroking her hands, which were cool, dry, a bit restless in his, "that isn't the point. There are always degrees of guilt, as there are degrees of intention. For crime to be crime, traditionally speaking, there must be *mens rea*—literally 'evil mind,' or criminal intent, as opposed to 'accident.' Also, you certainly know that our criminal justice system favors the well-to-do. Look at a bastard like ——" naming a Manhattan socialite tried for, and acquitted of, attempted murder of his heiress wife, for years in a comatose state. "Defendants who can afford private attorneys invariably receive a kind of justice poor defendants don't. Lee Roy Sears was a poor man. I know only the outline of his background, but—"

"He's Indian, is he? Is that what you said?"

"He claims he's one-eighth Seneca, from upstate New York. He—"

"But, wait—he *could* be guilty, even if he has been discriminated against. Isn't that so?"

"Look, Gina. Of the appalling number of murders committed each year in the United States—forty-eight thousand, I read the other day—how many are solved by police?—how many perpetrators are arrested, indicted, brought to trial, found guilty, let alone sentenced to death?—how many of them, like Lee Roy Sears, wind up spending years of their lives on death row?"

"What are you saying? I wish you wouldn't raise your voice."

"I'm not saying, honey, I'm asking."

"But," Gina persisted, "maybe they *should* be!"

Michael laughed sharply. "Should be—what? Sentenced to death?"

Gina hesitated. Her lips, coral pink, curled in a small smile, then pursed, soberly. "Found guilty."

"Yes, and then?"

"And then what?"

"And then—what should be their punishment?"

"*I* don't know, for heaven's sake! Let's go to bed," Gina said, laughing. "*You're* the lawyer in the family."

"I'm only trying to suggest, Gina, how relative the concept of punishment is, in any society. There's the old, primitive *lex talionis*— 'an eye for an eye.' There's the new, revolutionary concept, developed by the Quakers, of rehabilitation. It's the outrageous inequity of Lee Roy Sears's sentence we've been protesting, not the issue of his actual guilt."

"So you, Michael O'Meara, don't know, any more than anyone else does, if the man is a murderer or not. If, even, he committed other murders and was never caught before."

"Gina, what a thing to say!"

Michael was genuinely shocked, which made Gina laugh—he *was* an endearing man, and at such moments, at least when they were alone together in their comfortably furnished house, and there were no distractions—no other more striking, more romantic-minded men—she did love him, very much.

Impulsively, seeing the hurt and disapproval in his eyes, Gina kissed the knuckles of one of Michael's hands; big, hairy-backed knuckles; and detached her own from it. She ripped the photograph of Lee Roy Sears from the document to which it was stapled and brought it to the lamplight, frowning thoughtfully, biting her lower lip with her perfect white teeth. Finally she said, as if this were all that might be said, to put an end to the discussion, "Your man doesn't look very Indian, does he?"

MICHAEL O'MEARA'S SECRET, THE engine, as he thought of it, that drove him, and that probably accounted for his professional success, was his sense of guilt.

An obscure guilt, a seemingly sourceless guilt.

More than that, a sense of having done wrong in some specific way; and of being unable to remember what the wrong had been, or upon whom it had been perpetrated, or when—years ago perhaps, when he was a child?

Guilt lay like a shallow pool of dark, rancid water at the base of his skull. So long as he kept himself occupied he scarcely knew it was there, but of course, yes, it *was* there. It hadn't been possible for Michael to make such inquiries of his father, but he'd tried several times to ask his mother—had anything happened in his childhood, had he done something for which he'd been severely punished, or, perhaps, insufficiently punished?—had anything upsetting or myste-rious happened back then that had never been explained?

Michael's mother was a sociable woman, with many friends; a

shrewd bridge-player; but easily wounded, and quick to take offense
if it seemed to her that she was being criticized even in the most
oblique of ways. She'd laughed nervously, and, Michael thought, a
bit angrily, at his earnest questions, denying any bad memories of
the past—"Up until your father's death we were all so happy." Michael's father had been a very successful retail furrier who had died
of stomach cancer when Michael was a sophomore at Williams College. "So happy," she said again, conclusively.

Nor had Michael's sister, Janet, five years his junior, been any
more helpful. Janet now lived in Manhattan and worked for CBS-
TV in a sub-subordinate position, as she called it, and she'd acquired
a cheery, brassy, fast-talking manner in which all personal history,
including family history, was best served by being translated into
rowdy capsule-anecdotes of the kind one might hear on television
talk shows. She spoke of Michael in rounded generic terms, saying
he'd been the ideal older brother when they were growing up, sweetly
protective of her, smart, helpful, even, in his own idiosyncratic way,
good-looking, so he'd become a model for the other boys and men
in her life—"Unfortunately!—since, set beside Michael, most men
today are bastards, or gay, or *both.*" And Michael's young sister
would throw back her head and laugh with crackling-canny laughter,
of a kind he'd never heard before in her.

Michael's boyhood in Darien, Connecticut, certainly seemed to
him, from an adult perspective, both very American and uneventful.
He could recall no memorable traumas, hurts, disappointments; he'd
never been snubbed in high school; in fact he'd been a popular guy,
a football player of slightly above average ability, an officer in student
government, a very good but not exceptional student. His anxiety
about being guilty of something obscure and unnameable surfaced
from time to time, but was readily banished. And then he went off
to Williams, aged eighteen, and entered a new world—not that, in
the late 1960s and early 1970s, Michael O'Meara was radicalized,
like many of his contemporaries, by anti-Vietnam War agitation, but,
being an idealistic and sympathetic young man as he was, he'd been
profoundly moved, spiritually engaged, by the example of an activist
clergyman, a "renegade Christian" as the man called himself, who
had been publicly censured by his church for his politics. So, after

college, Michael intended to become a clergyman too: it scarcely mattered which denomination, in this era of ecumenical feeling.

The O'Mearas, two brothers, had emigrated from Dublin, Ireland, early—in the 1840s. Apparently, with surprising alacrity, they'd cast off their Roman Catholicism and become assimilated into New England; they and their children married where love, or perhaps business interests, guided them. Michael's mother's family was Protestant, but not very decisively—to Michael's mother, such subjects as God, redemption, "soul" were as embarrassing to speak of as physical intimacies and maladies. Michael's father had had no formal religion at all but referred vaguely to himself as Christian, as if to set himself apart from Jews, his fierce rivals in the fur trade.

Though it wasn't the Word of God so much as the Spirit of God Michael O'Meara hungered for, he'd enrolled in a distinguished, indeed very famous, seminary in New York City, with the intention of becoming a Protestant minister who was also (about this, Michael was vague) a teacher. Immediately, however, he was overwhelmed by the seminary's requirements and expectations of its students, in such contrast to the amiable Bachelor of Arts curriculum he'd taken as an undergraduate: ancient Greek? Latin? Hebrew? His introductory courses forced upon the twenty-one-year-old the paralyzing fact that he had no idea what *religion* meant, let alone what *God* meant these were mere words, word symbols, concepts, political/historical/sociological/geographical phenomena, ever-shifting and evolving—or devolving. (Michael had been certain he'd known who Jesus Christ was, but, exposed to a critique of the New Testament, he quickly came to see that the Jesus Christ of His time was not the Jesus Christ of subsequent times; nor was the Jesus Christ of His time altogether consistent in His teachings or His behavior.) The Bible, subjected to dissection, turned out to be not the Word of God—hardly!—but a ragtag anthology by diverse hands, compiled, not altogether fastidiously, over a period of centuries; in short, a work of fictions, some very weird indeed, containing competing ideologies and even religions. The Lord God Yahweh, so jealous, threatening, and unpredictable, was traced back to humble sources— he'd begun as a volcano god somewhere in the ancient world! Like a mediocre local politician who ascends to extraordinary heights not

by merit but virtually by chance, this volcano god somehow ascended to the highest throne of all, *and now cannot be dislodged.*

Of course, Michael O'Meara's teachers at the seminary did not
say such things directly, nor even simply. It is not the intention of
scholarship to say things directly or simply; for then, and very
quickly, the game might be up.

Michael was also forced to consider what he'd only vaguely
realized in the past—that Christianity, in fact the Judaeo-Christian
tradition as it was called, was but one tradition among many, and
by no means the most enduring. The world was layered with religions extinct, near-extinct, living, flourishing, freshly seeded, like the
very Earth itself, layered geologically in time. Each religion was divinely
chartered, and each religion had its savior, though more usually saviors;
there were holy books, and holy men; miracles, mysteries, authorities;
rites and rituals; sacrifices; sacraments; demons; heavens and hells and
points in between; every variety of punishment, every variety of childish
wish given form. As in a budget-conscious stage production in which a
few actors played many roles, the gods of one sect were the devils of
another. If love for one's neighbor was preached, hatred for one's enemies was practiced. The most pacific-minded people could be galvanized
into becoming the most bloody warriors, once their god bade them act,
and their priests blessed their swords.

None of these revelations was new. But all were new to Michael O'Meara.

Dazed and demoralized but unwilling to give up, for, after all,
there was the example of the activist-clergyman who had been a very
intelligent and reasonable man, but had nonetheless believed in Jesus
Christ, as there were similar, numberless examples, through history,
of men who had managed somehow to accommodate both intelligence and faith, Michael had saturated himself in a purely intellec-
tual study of philosophy and theology. Some of it was coursework,
some of it his own meandering research, amid the millions of
volumes (most, unfortunately—or was it fortunately?—in languages
Michael did not know) in the seminary library. Xenophanes, Des-
cartes, Voltaire, Plato, Pascal, St. Augustine, Martin Luther, Nie-
tzsche, St. Thomas Aquinas and many others, in a jumbled
chronology; Tillich on God-symbolism, Eliade on myth, Kierkegaard on fear and trembling, Tolstoy on Christ's teachings, Dostoy-

evsky's Grand Inquisitor; the significance of the Dead Sea Scrolls; Barth, Buber, Maritain, Schweitzer, Weil; papal encyclicals—Pius IX, Leo XIII, Pius XII, John XXIII. There was the flashing, glamorous weapon of structuralism, there was the laser-ray of semiotics, there was the audacity of Freudian psychoanalysis, there was the ray of hope of Jungian "individuation." There was of course anthropology, pitiless as a surgeon's scalpel, laying bare brains, blood vessels, nerves. There was even an interlude of Ingmar Bergman films, austere, chill, beautiful, which Michael and some of his new friends at the seminary saw frequently, obsessively. Near the end of his third viewing of *Through a Glass Darkly* Michael O'Meara broke down and began to cry and stumbled out of the movie theater into the sulphurous haze of early evening on Bleecker Street. For some frightening seconds he truly didn't know where he was, still less why.

Where had it gone, he wondered, that quicksilver leap of certitude he'd had only a year or so before, that almost rowdy happiness pulsing in his veins, that conviction in his heart that drove out all absurd shadows of guilt, that there *was* a living God, a communal spirit to be experienced, if not understood?

"Too late have I loved thee, thou beauty of ancient days"—these words of St. Augustine's, disembodied as the lyrics of a popular song, ran through his head.

Was it too late?

Unshaven, underweight, hoarse with a bad cold, in a visibly desperate state, Michael made an appointment to confer with his adviser at the seminary, a man who had studied with Tillich in the 1940s and who was highly respected in his own right as a New Testament scholar. Michael asked bluntly, "I just want to know—*is* there a God? And if so, what are we supposed to do?"

It was determined, during the course of the conference, that Michael O'Meara was perhaps not suited for seminary studies; nor for scholarly pursuits in general.

Following that disaster, Michael became a student again, in order to prepare for medical school. He was all afire with the idea that, to do good, whether God exists or not, is after all the aim of men (and women) of good will: but, in order to do good, one must be trained to do a specific *good.* He reasoned, and in this he was very like many of the pre-med students he befriended, that there was no other more direct opportunity for helping others than being a doctor.

Michael was admitted to a less-than-prestigious medical school in upstate New York, at the mature age, as he thought of it, of twenty-four. Here he was to last an even shorter period of time than at the seminary, where he had been able to finish out the year.

It was not to be the numbing rote memorization that defeated him—Michael had always been the kind of eager student, unburdened with an excessive imagination, cooperative rather than rebellious, to whom the memorization of even dull unrelated facts came easily. Nor would it be the protracted hours of sleep deprivation, for which medical school was notorious—Michael was the bearer of that sort of metabolism, common in muscular endomorphs, that allowed him to remain awake for long hours but granted him too, virtually at will, the ability to take quick, wonderfully refreshing catnaps, sometimes as short as a single minute, anywhere he found himself. What defeated him was gross anatomy: his first cadaver.

Michael O'Meara, even as he'd made out application forms for medical school, had known, but had not wanted to think about it, that he would be required to dissect a cadaver at some point in medical school. He had known, but had not wanted to think about it, that this task might give him trouble. (In her carelessly entertaining anecdotes of her model older brother, Janet O'Meara often spoke of Michael's excessive sensitivity and empathy—"He's the kind of person who wouldn't hurt a flea, and I mean an actual *flea.*") He had not quite understood that he would be confronted with a cadaver on the very first day of classes, however. "Are they serious?" he asked a second-year student, and was told, "Are *you* serious?"

Upperclassmen at the school were amused by first-year students and condescending in their advice, which was, regarding the inevitable cadaver, not to get stuck with one that had been dead too many years.

The dreaded dissection lab was preceded, early Monday morning, by an introductory lecture; after approximately half an hour a cadaver was wheeled into the amphitheater, with no ceremony, no theatrical flair, as the professor of anatomy continued his lecture, and everyone continued, or tried to continue, taking rapid notes. Michael, seated in the fourth row of the steeply rising seats, close to one side, fumbled with his pen, dropped it and snatched it up again, his eyes blurred with tears and his nostrils assailed by a sudden acrid odor. The body on the gurney was discreetly draped in white; a human body in outline only; when the professor's assistant pulled aside the white cloth, at the professor's bidding, there was childlike relief in the amphitheater—the cadaver was covered with an opaque plastic sheet. And beneath this sheet, as it turned out, was another protective layer, this one in gauze; beneath the gauze, yet more gauze that protected the hands and the head. By this time, Michael had relaxed slightly, like most of the others around him. The cadaver's face—his identity—would not be revealed. Not in the lecture.

Still, Michael stared entranced at the mummylike form, so utterly motionless. The anatomy professor was an energetic gray-haired little man, speaking in measured cadences, pausing to allow the taking of notes, his eyes moving quickly yet mechanically about the large room: how alive *he* was, as unlike the dead body on the gurney as he was, in his aliveness, unlike the gurney itself. Michael was thinking how uncanny a thing, to be in the presence of a . . . corpse; a being like ourselves, once possessed of a personality, an identity, a soul; but no longer. A guilty sensation washed over him, a taste as of bile at the back of his mouth. How evil you are, Michael O'Meara. How evil, and never to escape it.

He swallowed, he roused himself to full wakefulness. The anatomy lecture was concluding; the cadaver, now harmless, a mere object, was being covered up again, wheeled out of the amphitheater. Michael thought, This is nonsense. I'm strong. I'm motivated. I know what I'm doing, and why.

Since his disillusion with formal religion, and with the galaxy of ludicrous competing gods, he wasn't even certain he believed in "evil."

Immediately following the lecture was the anatomy lab, a two-hour ordeal, into which a powerful surge of adrenaline carried Michael, determined not only to get through the first dissection experience but to excel in it. He was smiling vacuously, and noticed that some others were smiling too, though their eyes were somber, scared. Michael O'Meara's characteristic response to situations of crisis—a response he was to retain all his life—was that of a quarterback of limited ability but visionary dreams: there was a heavy-footed grace about his stocky, affable body, an air of control, and enthusiasm in control. Since the age of thirteen, since summer camp in the Adirondacks, he'd discovered himself looked to by others as a natural leader; the kind who does not seek leadership, may in fact be embarrassed by it, but accepts it, at least some of the time, because others so wish. So, in the, dissection lab on that Monday morning in September 1975, in that nightmare of a room, stinking of phenol, in which, on twenty-five tables were twenty-five cadavers, each covered with an opaque plastic sheet, Michael assumed an air of equanimity and smiled and nodded as one of the graduate instructors spoke, and, as the class divided into groups, each assigned to a table and to a cadaver, he smiled too, encouragingly, at his teammates—three very sallow-skinned young men who were clearly waiting for Michael to position himself at the head of the table, and to be the one to uncover the cadaver.

The table to which Michael's group had been assigned was near a tall window, thank God, and the cadaver to which they'd been assigned did not somehow look full size. (Several of the cadavers in the lab looked enormous.) Was this good, or was this bad? Even as he was smiling at the others, as if he'd done this sort of thing many times before, Michael was gripped with a sudden sensation of horror: what if their cadaver was not an adult, but a young person?—a child?

The instructor was still lecturing, and, as they were bid, the students opened their dissection kits, examined scalpels, scissors, a hacksaw. (A hacksaw?—for sawing through the skull?) Dissection was a technique one learned as one learned any technique. The human body was a body, a model of anatomy. Michael nodded, as if in absolute agreement. The instructor had already noticed him, seemed to be speaking to him, as teachers frequently did. Michael O'Meara the intelligent, capable-looking young man with the strong face, the alert unwavering eyes, the fair red-burnished hair that, on his head and thinly and fuzzily covering his bared arms, gave him a faintly singed look, as if he'd been forged of some material sturdier and more reliable than that of the others who surrounded him.

At last the lecture ended, and it was time for the cadavers to be undraped.

Michael stared down at the form directly before him. His three teammates did not look at the form at all, but were watching Michael, intently. Beneath the plastic sheet there would be gauze—

wouldn't there? Head and hands, at least, wrapped mummylike in protective layers of gauze?

The instructor repeated his command, since no one in the room had moved. Michael, his senses blurred, was but dimly aware of the nightmare of tables, draped forms, students uncomfortably crowded together, breathing in the vile-smelling preservative that would become, from this day onward, a routine fact of their lives. The surge of adrenaline had ebbed; he felt now without strength, defenseless. Yet he must move, he must take command, others were looking at him expectantly, he had no choice. How evil you are, to have done this. And never to escape.

Elsewhere in the room sheets were being lifted, timidly. Michael O'Meara lifted the plastic sheet covering the cadaver before him—in a daze pulled it aside—one of his teammates murmured, "Oh!" and another clenched his fists—and Michael blinked and stared seeing, before him, *a naked corpse.* Only the hands and feet were wrapped in gauze, the rest was exposed, *naked.*

Somewhere distant the instructor's voice rang out assuringly. They were being told to pick up a scalpel, to begin, to begin with a leg, two people on each side of the body, yes, now it's time to begin, to begin, no going back you must make the first cut, you must utilize each second of lab time, it's precious time, you'll learn how precious since you must keep on schedule through the semester you must be finished with your dissection in twelve weeks. Elsewhere in the lab tentative movements were being made, scalpels lifted. Michael too had a scalpel in his badly trembling hand but he had little awareness of it, little awareness of anything save the corpse stretched out before him, a young male, Caucasian, very pale in death, skin the sickly hue of bleached mustard, bruised eyes shut but seemingly about to open showing a thin crescent of bluish-white beneath the lids, nose somewhat bumpy at the bridge as if it had been broken, fair red-brown hair, thick on the head and sprouting like wires on the well-developed chest, belly, pubic area, arms and legs. Michael O'Meara was staring in horror seeing a cousin, a brother, a twin battered and disfigured and even discolored in death, no mistaking it, the dissection lab had been so arranged as to bring him to this, this unspeakable horror, everyone was watching covertly as he, Michael, stood trembling above his victim, who was Michael

too, the one still living, with a deadly weapon in his hand, his eyes
rapidly blinking, a mottled flush in his face and his skin covered in
icy sweat, unmistakable symptoms of guilt, here's the guilty man,
here's the guilty boy, this time we see you, this time you can't escape,
and now the cadaver's lips drew back tightly from his stained teeth
in a supercilious sneering accusing expression as he peeked beneath
his eyelids at Michael, *How evil, how evil, you, you're the one, did
you think you could escape it?*

Someone spoke. Someone, the lab instructor perhaps, called
out. Michael had stepped backward, or had he slipped, or been
pushed, and the floor had opened up behind him, a pit, a sheer drop
into utter blackness, into which, no longer conscious, and not at all
resisting, he fell.

FOLLOWING THIS DISASTER, AFTER a six-month recovery period, Michael O'Meara went to law school, in Philadelphia, and did exceptionally well. His mother was vastly relieved and many times told
him so. Law school, with a specialization in corporate law, was exactly what his father had wanted for him, after all.

HE FELL IN LOVE at the age of twenty-seven, idyllically in love,
passionately in love, and his old feelings of guilt began to surface
again, like bubbles in heated tar, for he wasn't worthy of such a pure,
beautiful young woman as Gina, was he?—how could he be?—*he?*
Yet Gina seemed to love him; her parents, her entire family, seemed
very fond of him; it was by way of his prospective father-in-law,
a Philadelphia banker, that he was hired by Pearce Pharmaceuticals, Inc., of Newark, New Jersey, the largest manufacturer of antipsychotic drugs in the United States.

Michael's position at Pearce was a very junior position, amid a
legal staff of thirty-five men; but it was very highly paid, with the
promise of raises, promotions, for good work.

On the eve of his wedding to Gina, lovely Gina, Gina whom
he loved far more than his own life and would love forever, Michael,
always the stronger, the more reasonable, the less emotional and
impulsive of the two, astonished the young woman by confessing
there was something about him she didn't know but should know:
but, when Gina asked what it was, Michael laughed strangely and

ran both hands through his hair and said, "Well—I don't know. I feel it, Gina, but I don't *know.*"

"But, Michael dear, if you don't know, what is it you *feel?*"

He had not yet told Gina in much detail of his failure in the seminary and his failure in medical school—though not out of subterfuge exactly: Gina became visibly nervous, and changed the subject, when anything mildly disagreeable arose between them—and he knew that now, with the wedding close at hand, was not the time. So he told her about the guilt, simply—the obscure, nagging, sickening sense of guilt he sometimes felt; not often, certainly not constantly, but sometimes; as if he'd committed an evil, wicked act and had never been punished or even discovered. Gina listened wide-eyed, tremulous. Did she fear some hideous, irremediable confession?—did she fear, all evidence to the contrary, that her lover, her fiancé, was not a heterosexual but—how Gina disliked the very word!—"gay"? So it was, as Michael continued, haltingly, miserably, saying that it was a mystery to him but it was part of him, he'd hoped to outgrow it but had not thus far, saying that, for all his outward accomplishments, and manner, he felt inwardly inadequate, unworthy, a fraud, Gina grew increasingly relieved, and the light came back into her eyes, and a smile played about her lips. She was a girl who loved to tease, and who was at her best, teasing; her most characteristic response was a high, delighted laugh, a girlish giggle as of icicles breaking. When Michael somberly recounted an incident from his undergraduate days—he'd been elected senior class president at Williams, and he'd wanted to confess in his acceptance speech that he'd deceived them, somehow—if they had known who Michael O'Meara really was, they would not have voted for him—Gina bit her lip to keep from laughing and quite astonished her lover by slipping her fragrant arms around his neck and murmuring moistly in his ear, "Oh darling Michael!—I feel the same way exactly! *Everybody does!*"

ONCE THEY WERE MARRIED, and very happily married, living in the suburban village of Mount Orion, New Jersey, Michael O'Meara ceased to acknowledge his moral weakness, as he'd come to think of it; he rarely shared his moods with Gina, who, in turn, rarely inquired after his interior life, as if—and this was, oddly, flattering to Michael, as a man—he had no interior life.

The life he'd come to believe in, and to put his trust in, was almost wholly exterior—a world of other people, whom, like Gina, he loved, or, like his superiors at Pearce Pharmaceuticals, he worked for, or, like men and women generally, his Mount Orion friends, his associates in the various organizations to which he belonged, he served. His legal work, for instance, at Pearce (Pearce Pharmaceuticals, Inc., was forever being sued!) took up much of his time—a minimum of sixty hours a week. Then there was Michael's community activity, his citizenship as he called it—for Michael as an adult took both pride and satisfaction in his identity as an American citizen: soon after moving to Mount Orion he became involved in the campaign to save the old Mount Orion library, housed in a historic eighteenth-century building; he found himself on the board of the local YM-YWCA; a recruiter for the Northern New Jersey Citizens for a Clean Environment; a member of the Democratic party, and an active participant in Mount Orion township meetings; he volunteered his services as legal counsel for the reform-minded Coalition (a large, heterogeneous, frequently divided citizens' group concerned with such issues as civil rights infringements and the death penalty).

And then there was friendship, and social life—under the expert orchestration of Gina, who had immediately locked into, and flourished happily amid, an élite circle of primarily older couples associated with such prestigious organizations as the Mount Orion Country Club, the Mount Orion Tennis Club, and the Mount Orion Friends of the Museum (a county historical museum housed, like the library, in a beautiful old Georgian mansion ideal for cocktail receptions and five-hundred-dollar-a-plate benefit dinners). Michael came to like his friends very much, and the friends of friends; he was himself gregarious, delighting in companionship and laughter; giving the impression, in any social setting, of being at the center of it, or very near the center. Yet parties did tire him, and weekends, far from being restful, quickly became ordeals from which it might require most of Monday to recover. Once, Michael observed to Gina, with a smile, and a caress, to indicate that he meant no serious criticism, that she had certainly made them popular here in Mount Orion; and Gina replied tartly, with that dead-certain air with which she'd lately learned to return serves on the tennis court, rushing to the net, slamming her racket at the ball, sending the ball into her startled opponent's lap, "Not at all, Michael dear. It's you who's responsible—I'm just 'Mrs. O'Meara.' "

Which Michael knew was not true in the slightest, but—he had no wish to provoke a quarrel.

The old sensation of guilt, banished from daylight, surfaced now and then in dreams, which bore no relationship whatever to Michael's waking life. At such times he woke in the middle of the night more astonished than frightened, stunned by something he'd seen, or experienced, but could no longer recall, though he'd been in its presence only seconds before. Occasionally the dreams slid into classic nightmares, in which, helpless, he was caught up in an agitation as of dark, swirling, sucking water; he was both himself, and not himself; in a child's frenzy struggling to free himself of someone or something that was bearing him down, down, *down*. A band—was it arms?—another's arms?—tightened around his chest, choking off breath as he thrashed, pummeled, kicked. He screamed for help but, opening his mouth, he could not speak, for his very mouth was filled with that dark water. He panted, sobbed, tangled his feet in the bedclothes, as, waking, he saw the dream rapidly fading, *saw* it fade before his eyes, like an image projected upon the screen as the lights come up.

And wasn't there too, just faintly, a smell of something harsh, dry, astringent . . . the preservative phenol?

With the swift passage of years, once they had survived a somewhat difficult early period of six or so months, Gina, sweet Gina, had learned to sleep through all but the worst of her husband's nightmares. She was in the habit of alluding to herself, to their friends, as an insomniac; certainly she *was* highly sensitive, even at times cryptesthesiac; yet, lying beside poor Michael as he struggled in his sleep to keep from drowning, Gina floated free and was spared. Michael would begin to breathe heavily, and twitch, and writhe; he would fling out an arm, and kick at the bedclothes; he might, at last, sit up in bed to stare wildly and blindly into the dark, coughing, choking, whispering words that, not quite intelligible, might have been, "—who? *Where*—?" Gina, a slender figure on the far side of the king-sized bed, turned away from him, would drowsily murmur, without opening her eyes, "Yes, darling, that's right," and, "Yes, good, we'll talk about it in the morning."

Of course, they never did.

* * *

IN BED, MANY NIGHTS, Michael lay awake wondering whether *he* should father children?—not knowing what it was, imprinted deep in his soul, that he might have done, for which he should be punished.

Gina, for her part, seemed to want a baby, or babies. Or believed that she did. Or spoke as if she did. She was nearing thirty: an age that shimmered before her, dreadful, inescapable. This beautiful young woman, so very American, trained virtually from the cradle to be a *girl,* and supremely successful and happy as a *girl;* if *girlhood* must be surrendered, might *motherhood* be a face-saving substitute?

She said, longingly, with a mild undertone of reproach, "We should, you know. Soon. If we are going to, at all."

And Michael would say quickly, "Yes, of course. When?"

Which question always deflected further discussion.

Michael recalled his own father so awkwardly formal, so resistant, in the role of *father.* A painful creased expression on his face as, with apparent reluctance, he'd stooped to pick Michael up in his arms. Murmuring to Michael's mother, "But what if I drop him?"

Michael's father had spent most of his waking hours at his store, amid exquisitely beautiful, and expensive, fur coats, jackets, stoles. *O'Meara's Furs of Distinction.* That templelike place on Main Street of Darien, Connecticut, with its broad show windows, its coolly lit plush-carpeted interior, numberless mirrors, luxury, in which, it scarcely needs be said, the O'Meara children were not welcome. Mr. O'Meara was a successful businessman if success meant making profits, and making them with regularity, yet he appeared to his family as driven, perplexed, forever impatient and irritable; whenever anyone spoke to him, he responded with a look of barely contained outrage, as if an urgent conversation inside his skull had been rudely interrupted. What remained of his ancestral Irishness— a certain wry combination of features, muddy green eyes, somewhat pug nose, cleft chin, russet brown curly hair—had, like his ancestral religion, Roman Catholicism, ebbed, faded, to be replaced with— what? He'd soon come to hate his merchandise: the words *fur* and *furrier* sounded harsh in his mouth, like expletives. He seemed to have no friends, only business acquaintances who were forever letting him down—thus Mr. O'Meara's bemused quip, "What are people for, except to let you down?" Only years later, as adults, did Michael and Janet realize that the quip was not a common saying, like "A stitch in time saves nine," or, "A rolling stone gathers no moss."

What are people for, except to let you down?

No, this was wisdom Michael O'Meara decisively rejected.

Beyond Jerome O'Meara the furrier of Darien, Connecticut, was Michael's paternal grandfather, a merchant too, whom Michael could recall only dimly (he had died when Michael was very young) as a bemused taciturn old man whose predominant grandfatherly quality was his custom of slipping his grandchildren five-dollar bills on birthdays and holidays, like clockwork. The bills were both blessings of a kind and dismissals. Expressions of gratitude—"Thank you, Grandfather!"—were waved aside as if recognized, perhaps accurately, as mechanical too.

Beyond this chilly old gent was the only legendary O'Meara— Lucas Quincy O'Meara, of Oxblood, New Hampshire. He had been a lawyer, and then a judge, with the local reputation of being a "hanging" judge, and was one morning near Christmas 1889 discovered in his courthouse chambers, savagely stabbed and beaten, his very blood and brains smeared on the walls. Numerous suspects were questioned, for the judge had many enemies, but the murderer, or murderers, was never found. There existed, evidently, a local rumor, of which the O'Meara sons, seventeen and twenty years old at the time, were perversely proud, or about which, in any case, they were defiant, that they themselves had killed their father!

Such family secrets, Michael O'Meara naturally did not care to share with Gina.

NOR HAD HE WANTED to tell her much about his involvement with The Coalition; and with the case of Lee Roy Sears, who, having been found guilty of first-degree murder five years ago in Hartford, Connecticut, was scheduled to die in the electric chair on the night of May 12, 1983.

Sears, the quintessential American victim: the victim-turned-outlaw.

Michael O'Meara was not an expert in the Sears case, as others, representing the American Civil Liberties Union, had become, in their zealous but futile efforts to have his conviction overturned

by the state supreme court; but all that he'd learned outraged and
sickened him. It seemed probable that Sears was innocent of the
charge for which he'd been found guilty, yet, apart from that, apart
entirely from the issue of the man's guilt, was the issue of capital
punishment itself. What more lurid perversion of the state's power—
the power of "The People" (as the prosecution calls itself)—than
putting a human being to death in the interest of justice! Years ago,
as an idealistic undergraduate, Michael had read Albert Camus's
"Reflections on the Guillotine," and it had made a powerful impression upon him, substantiating inchoate convictions of his own.
Since that time, Michael had grown to believe that it is a society's
collective guilt that sends individuals to their deaths in the name of
justice. The "guilt" of the convicted individual is only partly a factor.

Sears, never before indicted on murder or manslaughter charges,
had been found guilty in late 1978 of the shooting death of a Hartford man known to be associated with drug dealing, and subsequently sentenced to death in the electric chair. The verdict was
clearly unjust: witnesses gave conflicting testimonies at the trial, and
were in any case unreliable; evidence linking Sears to the shooting
was circumstantial; the likelihood had seemed to be that an accomplice of Sears's, an older man long involved in the drug trade, had
actually done the shooting, but was in turn shot down by police
shortly afterward, fleeing the scene of the crime in his car, and leaving Sears behind. Sears had fled on foot, going to the home of a
neighborhood woman, apparently an acquaintance, friend, or lover
of his, and convincing her—or, it may have been forcing her—to
drive him out of Hartford; he was subsequently caught by police the
following day, badly beaten while "resisting" arrest, jailed and in
time convicted of first-degree murder though he insisted upon his
innocence and had twice passed a lie detector test. (The results of
such tests are not admissible in court.) Like all criminal cases, this
was more complex, and more mysterious, than a brief summary
makes it sound. For one thing, there were said to be numerous others
in the murdered man's apartment during the course of the night, in
addition to Sears and his accomplice; and these others Sears may
have been protecting out of fear of retribution, or misplaced loyalty.
(One of the apartment walls had been—so very oddly, the coincidence fairly took Michael O'Meara's breath away!—smeared with

the murdered man's blood, an act of deranged vengeance entirely at odds with Sears's having fled the scene of the crime as desperately as an eyewitness claimed he had.) In another puzzling aspect of the case, Sears was at first charged with having kidnapped, raped, and abused the woman who drove him out of the city, as well as abusing the woman's twelve-year-old daughter, for some reason taken along on the wild ride; these charges were later dropped, when the woman failed to press them, defied the district attorney's office, and later, apparently with her daughter, disappeared. Sears claimed that he and the woman had had voluntary sexual relations, as they had had several times in the past; it was only after Sears's arrest, and after police had questioned her at length, that the woman initially agreed to file charges. Most damaging to the prosecution's case was the fact that witnesses could not agree on what they'd seen, or at what time. Sears might very well have been confused with another man, or men; he might have been deliberately tagged for the killing, since one of the witnesses was a relative of the murdered man who was also an acquaintance of Sears, and who might very well have ordered the killing himself, or committed it himself; another witness was a well-known police informer who, happening to share a holding cell with Sears after his arrest, shrewdly negotiated a deal for early release with police in exchange for testifying that Sears had boasted of the killing. For some reason, the public defender assigned the case had not very thoroughly cross-examined these witnesses. He had even counseled his client to plead guilty to the district attorney's offer of a reduced charge of aggravated manslaughter, with a sentence of twenty years in prison and a mandatory minimum of ten—though Sears had insisted he was innocent.

Reviewing the case, Michael O'Meara, though no expert in criminal law, was dismayed by the presiding judge's apparent indifference to the quality of the police work and the prosecution's case; most of all, the slapdash defense provided Sears by the public advocate's office. It was as if—and this angered Michael—everyone, all the officers of the court, and the twelve jurors, had made up their minds beforehand not only that Lee Roy Sears was guilty but that his very life was of no special worth.

The trial had lasted only three days, and the jury had been out only two and a quarter hours. Guilty! Guilty as charged! The verdict was outrageous, particularly in light of the defendant's prior record and his having served in Vietnam, yet, at the time, it passed unnoticed by the press. (No doubt, there were other highly publicized outrages at that time, claiming the public's attention.) Had Lee Roy Sears died on schedule, he would have been the youngest man executed by the State of Connecticut since World War I.

In all, there would be five years of appeals to the state supreme court, stays of execution, hearings, delays, postponements; and now this final-hour hearing, an appeal to the Board of Pardons to commute Sears's death sentence to life in prison. Michael O'Meara rose early, before dawn, and drove up into Connecticut, both eager and apprehensive, suffused with a sense of purpose, yet dreading what might happen. It was his first direct involvement with any of the unhappy clients whom The Coalition defended. Lee Roy Sears was the first "condemned man" he had ever seen in person.

Thinking, chilled, What must it *be*, my God!—to be *him*.

For a prisoner on death row, Lee Roy Sears, at the age of thirty-one, was unexpectedly young-looking, though alarmingly thin. His arms and legs were long and gangling; his head seemed too narrow for his shoulders, as if it were squeezed together, or had not fully matured. And he was short—no more than five feet seven or eight. When he entered the crowded hearing room, limping, eyes straight before him, escorted by two burly prison guards, everyone stared at him, and there was a moment's startled silence—*That's* Lee Roy Sears?

Despite his limp Sears carried himself with a measure of dignity. Head stiffly high, shoulders very straight, and stiff too, he limped to the chair reserved for him and lowered himself into the seat with exaggerated care. The maneuver was awkward: he was handcuffed. At once the buzzing in the room resumed, with an undercurrent of embarrassment. It seemed to have struck everyone at the same time, Michael O'Meara included, that here was the sole man for whom the liberal issue of "Lee Roy Sears" was not theoretical in any way. If the Connecticut Board of Pardons could not be persuaded to set aside his sentence, Sears would be dead by midnight of the next day.

Sears, in his immaculate prison khakis, creased slightly baggy trousers and long-sleeved shirt primly buttoned to the wrists, did not much resemble the swarthy, smudged photograph Gina had studied the night before. His skin was grainily pale, his bony forehead oddly prominent, with a vague reptilian cast. If you believed him to have Indian blood, his features might have suggested it—his hair very black and lankly straight, his nose long, thin, and aquiline, with prominent nostrils. His hair had been severely trimmed, shaved up the sides and the back, so that his waxy-pale ears stuck out, with a look of schoolboy innocence. Certainly he did not look like a killer. Nor like a man whose existence was such a grave threat to humanity that he must be executed within thirty-six hours.

By 10:20 A.M., when the hearing finally began, the atmosphere in the room had grown tense and combative. There were more than sixty people, the great majority of them men, crowded into the low-ceilinged, harshly lit room; some latecomers were standing at the rear and along a wall of barred windows that overlooked damp concrete walls shutting out the sun. At the front, at a rectangular table, sat the five-man Board of Pardons, facing outward; far to one side was Sears, as if his physical presence were irrelevant to the proceedings. The opening remarks were formal and summary, read off by the chairman of the board, who frowned at the sheet of paper in his hand as if he had never seen it before. He was a man of late middle-age, with a thick suety body, a bald-gleaming head. All of the gentlemen of the Board of Pardons were middle-aged, and Caucasian; two lawyers, a penologist, a psychologist, a university professor; men of no evident distinction except that they held another man's life in their hands.

Next, a young assistant prosecutor rapidly reviewed the state's case. Lee Roy Sears stared off stonily into space, beyond the room's foreshortened horizon. Maybe he thought of himself as a dead man already. He'd lived through five years of this sort of thing, after all.

Suddenly nothing seemed to Michael O'Meara more important than that Lee Roy Sears's life be saved. He began to feel adrenaline pumping erratically through his veins, quickening his heart.

Since Sears had been incarcerated in Hunsford in late 1978, he'd been granted three stays of execution; his most recent appeal to the state supreme court, in March, had been rejected, and his death sentence set a fourth time. Since that time, however, his defense had managed to launch a protest; articles began to appear, letters and telegrams were sent to the governor of the state, there were public officials beginning to speak out on his behalf. An article appeared in the *Boston Globe* in which Lee Roy Sears was discussed along with a number of other Vietnam veterans-turned-criminals who were believed to be suffering "post-traumatic stress disorder" and neurophysiological impairments associated with the highly toxic defoliant Agent Orange. An essay by a celebrated American male novelist appeared in the April issue of *The Atlantic*, "On Dying in the Electric Chair," which named Lee Roy Sears and some others as "martyrs" to the corrupt criminal justice system. Both these publications had aroused a good deal of comment and controversy. The very fact that so many people had converged upon Hunsford State Prison in this rural corner of the state was an encouraging sign.

Yet, here was, again, repeated by the state's representative, the case against Sears. His criminal record, his troubled background. His dishonorable discharge from the army. His heroin addiction and his involvement in drug dealing. The "particular brutality" of the murder of which he'd been found guilty—the "wall smeared with blood." The abduction of a woman and her twelve-year-old daughter, charges of rape, abuse, threats . . . That these last-named charges had never been substantiated was glossed over in the telling.

Sears's lawyer rose hastily to protest, there was muttering on all sides. A current ran through the room—Michael O'Meara felt it like an electric shock—the instinctive male dread of female accusations; the unspoken brotherhood of men at risk with women.

In his seat Lee Roy Sears gave a sudden convulsive movement. His face crinkled like an infant's. The two burly guards standing behind him were comically galvanized to alertness, stepping closer.

Sears murmured hoarsely, "She lied! It's all a—lie!"

The young prosecutor concluded his statement by snidely challenging the defense's "sentimental" claim for Lee Roy Sears as a victim. There was no real proof, for instance, that Sears had the slightest trace of Senecan Indian blood, since his birth records were lost and he seemed to have no relatives at all in Watertown, New York—"Sears" was the name of his first foster parents. There was no absolute proof, upon which medical experts agreed, that he, and numerous other claimants, suffered from either "post-traumatic stress disorder" or the effects of Agent Orange. These were mere fashionable defenses, excuses for criminal behavior, which Sears's jury in Hartford, in December 1978, had wholly rejected.

Most alarming, the prosecutor said, was the fact that, since his crime, Sears had shown no remorse whatsoever—"Additional proof, if proof were needed, that the man is a dangerous, psychopathic killer."

At this, there were numerous protests. From the rear of the room a man—a radical lawyer whom Michael O'Meara recognized, with a media-familiar face—called out derisively, "How the hell can a man show remorse when he isn't guilty?" Others joined in. The chairman had to rap his gavel to restore order. By the time the young prosecutor sat down his face was damply flushed. He'd been feeling the tide of popular sentiment in the room running against him, and he did not like the feeling.

Michael stared at this young man, a fellow lawyer; a careerist. For the first time he saw such people, functionaries of the state, white-collar executioners, as the enemy: as Lee Roy Sears must have seen them.

Your enemy is my enemy too. I pledge myself to save you.

THE FOCUS OF THE hearing now shifted to the defense, and Lee Roy Sears was subsequently presented in very different terms. a victim, indeed, of a complex of social circumstances, a man whose criminal activities must be interpreted in the context of his background. He was abandoned by his teenaged mother when less than a month old, discovered wrapped in a filthy blanket, inside a plastic garbage bag, on the steps of the county welfare office in Watertown. He became a ward of county institutions for the next sixteen years—foster homes, juvenile detention facilities. He was poorly educated, a discipline problem. Expelled from school at the age of fifteen. In the Veterans Administration hospital in Hartford, where he'd gone for therapy for his injured knee, he'd been diagnosed as dyslexic, which had surely contributed to his problems in school, but of course no one had known, or much cared, what might have been troubling him. (According to school records, Sears sometimes scored far above average on I.Q. tests, and sometimes far below.) He'd been abused by institutional authorities. He'd been severely beaten, at least once, by

Watertown police. In 1969, at the age of eighteen, he joined the army, to serve two and a half years, two of them in Vietnam, where, in jungle combat above Ban Phon, he was exposed to the highly toxic Agent Orange. He was wounded, hospitalized. Acquired a heroin addiction. Ended his army career in the stockade, for having gone berserk and assaulting an officer. Dishonorably discharged, 1972. In the States he worked at a succession of low-paying jobs— dishwasher, janitor, taxi driver, construction laborer—in Manhattan, Jersey City, Danbury, New Haven, Hartford. His first arrest was in 1974, in Hartford, for drug possession; following that he was arrested several times, on varying charges, ending with the 1978 arrest for first-degree murder. During a previous jail term—Sears had been jailed twice before, for brief periods—he'd been described by authorities as an emotionally troubled man who kept to himself unless provoked; hardly a model prisoner, but yet not a troublemaker. Other inmates respected him and kept their distance. He'd even signed up for courses, in remedial reading and art therapy, offered by volunteers associated with a local V.A. hospital. In these courses Sears was described by his teachers as "eager" and "exceptionally motivated"—at least initially.

A Hartford social worker, a woman, spoke of Sears's disadvantaged background in greater detail. His "ethnic identity," which had been denied him; his probable neurophysiological condition, which contrary to those "experts" who denied its existence, is suffered by as many as 200,000 Vietnam veterans, or 12 percent of all Americans who had served in the war. There was a stirring of sympathy, shared outrage. The members of the Board of Pardons appeared to be listening attentively. (Michael scanned their faces with his shrewd lawyer's eye. He knew that, unlike juries of more representative citizens, such professional panels are often constituted by people who know beforehand how they intend to cast their ballots.) A Boston penologist spoke; a lawyer from the Connecticut Civil Liberties Union; a woman sociology professor from Wesleyan. Then it was, abruptly, Michael O'Meara's turn.

Michael had stayed up until two in the morning preparing a statement that would, in assiduous lawyerly fashion, focus upon technical details having to do with Sears's trial; but this statement, gripped between his fingers, he now forgot. As soon as he got to his feet and felt dozens of eyes swing upon him, he was overcome by a ballooning sensation, as if he were dangerously afloat; suffused with a sudden urgent energy, and purpose. *He had to move these people. He had to save Lee Roy Sears's life.*

Michael O'Meara was not a smooth, practiced, articulate public speaker—given his personality, his very physical type, he'd never dared try for such a style—but, when deeply moved, speaking from the heart, he was wonderfully persuasive. He was one of those guileless and unpremeditated men, whom some politicians cannily imitate, who declare themselves candidly, spontaneously, with an earnest air of discovering truths even as they share them with others. So, now, he told the gathering, these fellow professionals with whom he felt an uneasy but unmistakable kinship, that, this morning, what overwhelmed him most was the simple, obdurate, terrible fact that, as they debated the issue of whether Lee Roy Sears's sentence should be commuted, they were in the presence of a man condemned to death; this fact should take precedence over everything else. "Only think of it— *condemned to death.* And on such slender, controversial evidence!"

Michael paused, breathless. He'd begun to perspire profusely inside his clothes. He continued, for another two or three minutes, speaking haltingly, saying that while, for most of them this morning the hearing represented a forum of a purely legal and ethical sort, for Lee Roy Sears it was his very life. "There's an irony in this, something grotesque, even tragic, that people like us—middle-class, white, educated, 'professional'—people who have lived with privilege since birth, breathing it in like oxygen—should find themselves sitting in judgment of Lee Roy Sears, who has been disenfranchised from America since birth. His death would be a meaningless sacrifice—of what, to what, I don't know. Once in history the death penalty, for all its cruelty, had a sacred meaning. It was part of a religious tradition. The condemned man's soul was to be redeemed by his physical death—ideally. But now, in our time, there is no redemption. There is just—death." Michael paused again. He was aware of utter quiet in the room. A sea of blurred faces, grave expressions, here and there a frown, a quizzical half-smile, a grimace of embarrassment—or was it startled sympathy? No one had addressed them in this way, so openly, so from the heart, and they did not know how to respond.

Lee Roy Sears too had woken from his trance and was staring

at Michael O'Meara. His skin glowed as if a fierce muffled light illuminated it from within.

With that gesture that so exasperated Gina, running a hand distractedly through his hair, Michael rapidly summed up his brief on Sears's behalf, speaking of the egregious technical flaws in the criminal justice system, one day, soon perhaps, to be remedied, that had resulted in Sears's conviction—"Just let's hope Lee Roy Sears is still living when these reforms become law."

His voice trembled with anger. He sat down, abruptly. A long moment followed of absolute stillness, silence, as if his audience expected him to continue; then, unexpectedly, a number of people, with a particular concentration near the rear of the room and along the wall, burst into spontaneous applause.

"Quiet, please!" The chairman cleared his throat, rapped tentatively with his gavel, and the hearing continued.

But its tone had changed, quite palpably. From this point onward there was an air of hope, of uplift, even of triumph in the room: a sense that something deathly had been confronted, surmounted, passed.

AT THE END, LEE Roy Sears was himself invited to speak if he wished. Everyone leaned forward expectantly.

For an uncomfortable, protracted minute or so Sears sat stiff and unmoving, as if unhearing; then, slowly, with an air of subtly wounded dignity, like a defiant child, he got to his feet.

Since Michael O'Meara had spoken, Lee Roy Sears seemed to have lost his pose of stoicism and indifference; he'd been looking out at the spectators, particularly at Michael, peering from beneath his heavy dark eyebrows as if trying to figure out the connection between them. His arms were stiff at his sides, elbows oddly akimbo, wrists at about waist level where the handcuffs linked them; distractedly, not knowing what he did, he tugged at the wristbands of his khaki shirt, pulling the sleeves down, again as a child might, so that the cuffs covered part of his hands. A tic animated his left eyelid so that it looked as if, so very inappropriately, he were winking.

And how unexpected, the man's voice, raw, near-inaudible, both shy and reckless, as, suddenly, words tumbled from him: "—I don't know if my life is worth saving!—I mean, I never did know—from

the time I was a kid—they tell you you're shit, so how d'you know?—
you don't know anything except what somebody tells you and God
is mostly silent so—so I don't know!" He smiled, showing discolored
chunky teeth; his eyes shone with tears. His voice was becoming
higher-pitched, like an adolescent boy's. In the face of his listeners'
utter astonishment he continued, his eyelid twitching as if keeping
time with his words, "—the main bad things I did, the true evil I
repent of, I did in the war—I did because I was told to—I don't
remember exactly because I got sick but I know I did them or somebody
right around me because who else, y'know?—*I* was in the uniform—
and you can't get out of it just have to keep going forward to the
end—till you're dead too, and they send you home. So, like now, this
hearing, I thank you kindly for your words and for your concern for
me like I'm not just shit but I have to say I don't know, truly—if God
has new plans for me—I *am* innocent of taking another's life—except
in uniform—but—I don't know what God wants me to be—whatever
it is—that's up to I guess God?—and I guess you?—"

Abruptly, Sears ceased speaking; though, for a few seconds, his
mouth continued to work. Then he sat down. His movements were
jerky, spasmodic. By this time tears were streaming over his cheeks, but
he seemed oblivious of them, a small fixed smile stretching his lips

Michael O'Meara's final vision of Lee Roy Sears—Michael was
certain it *was* to be the final vision—was that of the prisoner being led
away by the guards who towered over him, back to his cell on death
row.

It was a four-hour drive back to Mount Orion, New Jersey, from
Hunsford, Connecticut. When, exhausted from the drive, and the emotional strain of the day, Michael O'Meara entered his house, he was
surprised to be so ecstatically greeted by Gina, who rushed at him,
slipped her perfumed arms around his neck, kissed him full on the lips;
and informed him, eyes bright and sly, that he was to telephone a certain
number immediately—the message was on his desk.

Michael stared at Gina's animated face. This was a woman who
rejoiced in success. "Is it?—Sears?" he asked excitedly.

Gina pressed a forefinger against Michael's lips and smiled.

"Call, darling. And see."

The message was from one of the A.C.L.U. organizers of Lee

Roy Sears's defense, and, when Michael called, he was informed that, forty-five minutes after the Hunsford hearing was adjourned, the Board of Pardons had voted unanimously to commute Lee Roy Sears's death sentence to life imprisonment.

By the time Michael hung up he'd begun to cry—laughing, and crying. So happy!—so damned relieved!—and tremendously grateful!—as if his own life, or, better yet, the life of someone he loved above his own, had been spared.

Gina, delightful Gina, who had so resented Michael's involvement in this time-consuming *pro bono* work, insisted that they celebrate: before Michael could reply she informed him that she'd already telephoned their closest friends in Mount Orion, another couple whom they saw regularly; she'd already made reservations at Le Plumet Royal, Mount Orion's distinguished French restaurant. "It isn't every day that my husband saves a man's life!" she said.

Michael laughingly protested that he had certainly not saved Sears's life: it had been a collective effort on the part of dozens of people, over a period of years.

Gina said carelessly, caressing his cheek, "*I* don't believe that, *I* know you."

That evening as they were dressing to go out, Gina approached Michael, hesitantly, and, her eyes locking with his in a bureau mirror, said with uncharacteristic shyness, "Michael, will you forget that man, now? And move on to—other things?"

Michael, who was knotting a tie around his neck, stared at Gina in the mirror. Her ashy blond hair lifted from her face in an artful sweep, her eyes were large and grave, her small high breasts, framed in the intricately woven lace of her black silk slip, rose with her breathing, in tremulous apprehension. Michael's heart kicked.

He whispered, "Oh, yes. My darling."

THINKING, INTERMITTENTLY DURING THE days that followed, until at last he did begin to forget, poor Sears, poor bastard—his life saved but only to be lived out behind bars, behind those particularly grim, ugly, mildewed-looking cement walls of Hunsford State Prison.

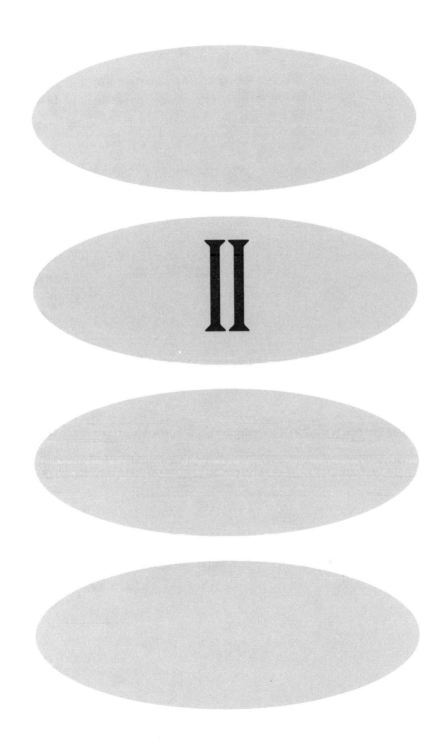

II

TIGHT-COILED, OILY BLACK AND spangled with gold, Snake Eyes slept. Hidden deep inside the jungle. Hidden from the glaring tropical sun.

Was Snake Eyes sucking out of the depths of the earth his powerful venom?—Lee Roy Sears pondered.

Of this, Lee Roy Sears was fearful sometimes. Not all the time but sometimes.

He was innocent, now he had his mission in life.

Now he had his mission in life, he mostly rejoiced. God forgives a smiling grateful face and so does Man.

Bare your teeth in just the right way, it's a smile.

For, Lee Roy Sears had been spared. Out of justice and mercy and compassion and American bounty. He'd surrendered himself to Death having seen in a dream vision his naked body dumped back into that garbage bag like shit; then, to his astonishment, he'd been spared.

Some visions, you never forget.

Some people who intervene on your behalf, you never forget.

Your enemies, you make a vow to forget.

You make a vow to forget your enemies those fuckers who hoped to squash you like they'd squash a cockroach under their heels and grind it flat the fuckers who don't deserve to live who deserve to be whacked off taking it full in the face but these enemies of yours you make a vow to forget.

For, now, spared and reprieved from Death, Lee Roy Sears was a new man, and he was embarked upon a new life, and he was determined to be good.

He had a mission. He was fired with his mission. To bring light into the darkness. To bring light where no light has ever shone. To help other men, Vietnam casualties like himself. To show them the way to deal with their nightmares and bad memories, through *art*. To fulfill his, Lee Roy Sears's, own God-given talent as an *artist*.

Was the man sincere, yes certainly he was sincere, his voice quivering with passion. Just look into his eyes. His damp slightly bloodshot slightly hooded dark eyes.

As he told the prison chaplain, maybe if you've never been condemned to death in the electric chair then reprieved by the grace of God and Man you can't know what it is to REJOICE.

At first, for many weeks, the chaplain was suspicious of Lee Roy Sears—there's an aura, distinct as a bad smell, that clings to an ex-death row prisoner—then he came to believe. Came to believe that Lee Roy Sears was a purer Christian than he himself was—now was that true, or was that a lucky error?

2

"Oh Daddy !"

"—Daddy!"

He lifted his head at once, startled.

The voices, bell-like, clear, thinly soprano, might have been a single voice and its immediate echo, they were so alike: identical. And, in their childish urgency, with its undercurrent of excitement tinged with mild apprehension, unexpected. So deeply absorbed in his muscle-straining labor was he, Michael O'Meara had lapsed into one of his characteristic fugues of obliviousness, and for a fraction of a second—these curious pleats in memory still occurred, after seven years—he'd virtually forgotten he *was* a father and that, at any time, he might hear the cry *Daddy!*—and its echo.

For there they came, running. His sons.

His heart flooded with love of them: Joel and Kenny.

Kenny and Joel: the O'Meara twins.

"Daddy, here's something—"

"—something for you—"

Michael, who had been working for several hours shoveling sediment out of the pond behind his house and hacking away at overgrown cattails and rushes, wading in rubber hip-boots he'd borrowed from a friend, waved at the boys, and started for shore. He tried never to disappoint his sensitive sons by failing to fall in with their moods: Joel and Kenny were still of an age when so much was exciting, even crucial, especially if it allowed for a legitimate intersection of their lives with their parents' lives. To be the bearer of important news makes children experience themselves as important: Michael O'Meara could recall claiming, or trying to claim, his own distracted father's attention, years ago.

"Daddy—!"

"Dad*dy*—!"

Michael had been about ten yards from shore, in muddy-churned water up to his thighs. It was difficult walking purposefully, trying to keep his balance, in the damned clumsy boots, which seemed to be leaking. Soft black muck sucked lewdly at his feet; he sank, in treacherous spots, up to his ankles. It was a prematurely warm April day and his face smarted with sunburn. His gloved hands were throbbing with pain of which he was just now conscious and there came a sharp warning twinge between his shoulder blades. Was he so badly out of condition, for a man of only forty?—who prided himself, however modestly, on his general fitness? He had certainly underestimated the task of dredging out some of the accumulated sediment from the pond and clearing away the excessive cattails and rushes that were choking it at one end. Seemingly small, self-contained, and shallow, seen from the house above, the O'Mearas' pond was in reality more than one hundred yards in circumference and, though shallow near shore, deceptively deep, over a man's head, at the center. Overhung by full-grown willow trees, bordered by wild azaleas, water iris, and cattails, the pond was exquisitely beautiful, if a bit neglected, and for years Michael had intended to clean it up. Despite his best efforts, however, and his stubbornness, the work was really too much for an inexperienced man; as Gina had several times suggested, he should have called in a professional. Even Joel and Kenny, who had been helping him earlier, delighted at the rare opportunity to be in their father's company out-of-doors, had grown restless and bored with the repetitive work, and had drifted, without exactly announcing their departure, back up to the house. To read, or to write (the boys were composing a comic-strip epic jointly, which neither Michael nor Gina had yet been allowed to see), or to watch television: they had no friends their own age in this semi-rural suburban neighborhood, miles from the village center of Mount Orion, where spacious houses were built on three-acre wooded lots, and there were no sidewalks, and Glenway Circle was not a through street but a graveled, idyllically winding cul-de-sac.

Michael tossed the spade he'd been using down on the bank and heaved himself up, grunting, hip-boots streaming water. "Okay, guys, what are you bringing me?" he called. The boys were racing downhill more recklessly than he liked to see, showing off for Daddy, Joel waving an envelope importantly—or was it Kenny?—the twins so closely resembled each other that, at such times, when they were animated and breathless, it was virtually impossible to tell them apart.

It was a letter for Michael O'Meara, and it had come special delivery, and Gina, up at the house, had signed for it. A thick packet, an official-looking letter with a return address of the Connecticut State Parole Board in Hartford, Connecticut.

Michael stood frozen, staring at the envelope for a long moment before moving to open it. Even then, his numbed fingers moved stiffly.

"Daddy, what's wrong?" Joel asked anxiously.

And Kenny, at once, "—what's *wrong?*"

Michael said, smiling, "Why, nothing." He opened the envelope, and scanned the letter addressed to him, and merely glanced at the photocopied material, and, smiling, more emphatically now, said, "It's good news, boys. You've brought me good news. So, guys, *thanks. Thanks a lot.*"

Michael O'Meara's tone with the twins was nearly always hearty, happy, upbeat, brisk.

Wasn't that the way to do it?

ALWAYS, HE WOULD REMEMBER that moment: that hour: that day: Saturday, April 13, the day following his sons' seventh birthday.

Not that there was any connection between the two dates, the two events. Not even coincidence.

HE WOULD LONG REMEMBER, too, with a pang of both guilt and defiance, Gina's reaction.

"So, you've been making these arrangements for this man, this Sears, this"—her eyes flashed with incredulity—"murderer, behind my back? You've helped him get paroled, you've helped him get a job, and—he's coming *here*? To Mount Orion?"

Gina was speaking rapidly, more puzzled than angry: she knew that Michael adored her, that he could never behave in any way contrary to her best interests; thus, whatever foolish, generous, charitable thing he did *was* in her best interests, somehow. But how?

Michael said, "Gina, no. Darling, I never did anything behind your back, believe me! I just didn't trouble you, as I don't trouble you with any number of things that seem unimportant. Since nineteen eighty-three, when his sentence was commuted, Lee Roy Sears has written to me a few times, strange, very short letters—just notes, really; basically thanking me for helping to save his life. He exaggerated my part in it, and I tried to tell him that."

"You've been corresponding with that man? You didn't tell me *that*."

"Then, about eighteen months ago, I received a call from the director of the prison rehabilitation program at Hunsford, telling me about the work Sears had been doing. On his own initiative he began an art-therapy program, working with the Vietnam veterans mainly, and it's been extremely successful. The director sent me slides of Sears's own art, and while none of it struck me as very talented, some oil paintings, clay figures, I was impressed that he had such sensitivity—after all, remember his background. Here was a man who'd had nothing, no advantages, no education—"

"And—?"

"And what?"

"And what did you do, then? How did you reply?"

"Then?—at that time, I didn't reply at all. Except maybe to comment that, yes, Sears did seem to have a mission, and it was fortunate that the prison system allowed him to exercise it." Michael frowned, running both hands through his hair. "I have to admit, honey, I *am* surprised that the board paroled him so early. But—"

"Surprised?" Gina's voice lifted shrilly. "You knew all along! Here"—she tapped his chest with the letter—"the board is thanking you for your assistance!"

"Please, Gina. You must understand that naturally I wrote on Sears's behalf to the board, as positively as I could, while stressing the fact that I wasn't personally acquainted with him. I was hardly the only person they contacted—there must have been dozens. In any case, I assumed the hearing was *pro forma*—"

"Skip the Latin, will you, Michael?—you aren't in court, trying to impress other lawyers."

"—just perfunctory, a matter of form. Because I'd been certain the board would probably reject his application as premature."

"Yes, why *is* he getting out after eight years? He was sentenced to life imprisonment, wasn't he?"

" 'Life' is just the maximum sentence; the parole board determines the actual sentence. If a prisoner behaves, as Sears seems to have done, in exemplary fashion, he's credited with ten days 'good' time for each thirty served. That works out to one-third of the maximum sentence." Michael spoke quickly, seeing, as he often did when presuming to give Gina information, her eyes begin to glaze over. "And there are other factors involved—the art-therapy program, which greatly impressed the board, and Sears's participation in religious activities in the prison, and courses in remedial English he'd taken, and his interviews with prison psychologists, social workers—"

"But—eight years! Did you and the others in The Coalition expect him to be paroled so soon?"

"That wasn't an issue."

"Wasn't an issue?" Gina laughed incredulously. "Aren't you all lawyers, aren't you supposed to know the law?"

Michael winced, wanting to say that he wasn't a criminal lawyer, as Gina well knew; he could not have endured a career in criminal law. Instead he said, defensively, "We were protesting Sears's death sentence. We were protesting the barbarism of capital punishment. It was a principle of justice we were pursuing."

Gina persisted, eyes shrewdly narrowed as if she'd caught him

in a lie. "But you went farther than that, Michael. You seem to
have gotten Lee Roy Sears a position at the Dumont Center, right
here in Mount Orion—didn't you? How then can you claim you're
surprised he's been paroled? There's a contradiction here."

Michael said, keeping his voice level, "I was asked if I knew of
any community service centers where Sears, with his interest in art
therapy, might work at least part-time, so naturally I gave them
Clyde's name. Yes, of course, I spoke with Clyde first." Michael
paused. Clyde Somerset was a friend of the O'Mearas, a locally
prominent citizen active in community affairs, and director of the
Dumont Center; he and his attractive wife, Susanne, were an older
couple, central to Mount Orion's élite, whose good opinion meant
much to Gina. Michael understood, though he was far too tactful
to suggest it, that Gina's exaggerated concern about Lee Roy Sears
was primarily social— yet, for that, no less crucial to her. He must
take her doubts seriously, and he must, with a lover's solicitude, and
a husband's sense of propriety, protect her from knowledge of her
own less than noble motives. He said, meaning to placate, as Gina
continued to stare at him doubtfully, "I didn't get Sears the job at
the Dumont Center, he got it himself on the strength of his creden-
tials. You know Clyde—Clyde isn't sentimental, and he isn't a
fool. In any case Sears has another job, in a parking garage in Putnam, that will provide most of his income. And he'll be living in
Putnam, in a halfway house for parolees. He'll be reporting to his
probation officer weekly. He won't be living in Mount Orion."

Putnam was a working-class town, a suburb of Newark, a half-
hour's drive along the traffic-clogged New Jersey Turnpike from leafy
Mount Orion. But Gina said, "He'll be your responsibility in Mount
Orion, Michael—people will see it that way. And that means my
responsibility too."

Gina spoke so harshly, so in disgust of him, Michael's sunburnt
face stung. He'd had a glimpse of himself in a mirror and had winced
at his clownish reddened nose. Every year, a premature dose of the
sun, every year virtually the same thing!—Gina would laugh at him,
and kiss him, and rub Noxema into his flamey skin. Except, today,
with this unexpected news between them, she had no kiss for
him, nor even a few fond words of commiseration. Indeed, she gazed
at him as if, in his solid stocky ex-athlete's body with its comfortable

ring of flesh around the waist, graying-red hair disheveled and streaks
of mud on his clothes, he were a stranger, an uncouth intruder, in
their attractively furnished bedroom.

Yet, for all her bristling animosity, how beautiful Gina was!

They were to go out (to Michael's disappointment: he'd forgotten) that evening, and Gina had shampooed her blond shining
hair; she wore a brilliant green silk kimono dressing gown, bought
for her by Michael on a recent business trip to Tokyo, the wide sash
tied tight, as if to emphasize her elegant thinness. Her cameolike
beauty was a rebuke to him, and to the clumsy erotic yearning he
felt at such times.

Michael spoke forcibly, but gently. He hoped to entice from
this woman, so stiff in opposition to him, a small smile.

He said, reaching for her hand, "Gina, don't you feel sorry for
Lee Roy Sears? Just a little? Here is a thirty-nine-year-old man, no
wife, no family, not much education, his youth wasted first in Vietnam, in a filthy, pointless war, then in prison—not eight years, as
you've been saying, but thirteen, since he'd been in prison five years
before his sentence was commuted. Think of it, Gina—five years on
death row! When he gets out of Hunsford on Monday morning
he'll have less than one hundred dollars in his pocket, probably, and
nowhere to go except to"—Michael hesitated, about to blunder into
saying "to us"—"except to Putnam, New Jersey, to a halfway house.
And you, Gina, who've never known an hour's want or deprivation—would you deny the man so very little?"

Gina laughed unexpectedly. That bright brittle laughter as of
icicles breaking that so roused Michael O'Meara's desire.

"Yes! Oh for Christ's sake *no!* Oh leave me alone, will you!"

Michael winced at Gina's harsh voice. He worried that, though
they were upstairs in their bedroom, the door shut, and Joel and
Kenny were far away downstairs in the family room watching television, the derisive sound might carry. As Gina was in most ways
closer to the boys than Michael was, so too she was conspicuously
less careful in shielding them from matters that might upset them;
she did not consider them nearly so sensitive as Michael did. Yet,
from time to time, mysteriously, and to Michael disturbingly, the
boys seemed aware of things not told them directly by either of their
parents.

What Michael O'Meara most wanted to protect his sons from was premature knowledge: growing up too soon.

Gina was angry, and Gina was on the verge of tears, and Michael simply went to her, risking a slap, or her small hard fists pummeling him, and put his arms around her. He said, "You don't mean it. You're much too nice to mean it."

"Am I!"

Gina stood very still in Michael's embrace, neither resisting him nor exactly giving in. Their quarrels, which were infrequent, frequently ended in this way. Michael buried his burning face in Gina's fine coolish hair and caressed her gently, almost shyly, reverently. Her slender curving buttocks that were so tense, her narrow waist, her ribcage, her small high breasts . . . he held her as he would a rare prize, feeling himself unworthy, yet exulting in possession, as her husband: the father of her children.

They were silent for some seconds. Overhead a jet passed.

Gina said, "I know you're right. Of course you're right. You make me ashamed of myself, I'm so selfish and stupid. You really should be married to someone else, Michael. Someone worthy of you."

Did that mean, *I should be married to someone else. . . ?*

Michael protested, unthinking, "But, Gina, I love *you!*"

ANXIOUSLY JOEL ASKED, AS Michael was about to switch off the bedside lamp between the boys' beds, "Daddy, is somebody coming to live in our house?"

And Kenny, at once, breathlessly, as if the words had been pent up for many minutes, "Daddy, is it a *bad man?*"

Michael, who had noticed that his sons had been unusually subdued as he'd tucked them into bed, chatted with them a bit, kissed them goodnight, was nonetheless taken by surprise, and said, hesitating only a moment, "Why, no. Of course not. Who on earth told you that?"

He stood tall and protective above them, smiling, he hoped not uneasily, smiling hard, a bit baffled; considering and then rejecting that, for some whimsical reason of her own, Gina had gone ahead and told the twins about Lee Roy Sears. But of course she hadn't. Somehow, they simply knew.

Michael looked with loving concern at Joel in his bed, at Kenny in his, screwing up his face like a television daddy to suggest honest perplexity and the silliness of the boys' fears. He asked again who had told them, but the little boys pursed their lips tight and said nothing, just gazed up at him, each with a tiny convulsive shiver despite the warmth of the room and the bedclothes drawn up to their chins. Joel in "his" bed, on the left; Kenny in "his" bed, on the right. True, the beds were identical, they were "twin" beds, but Joel's bedspread was navy blue with cartoon nautical symbols, and Kenny's bedspread was hunter green with cartoon farm animals. Joel's pajamas were lightweight flannel with blue and white stripes, Kenny's pajamas were lightweight flannel with beige and white stripes. Joel's new sneakers were aqua and white, Kenny's red and gray. Joel's newest good trousers were dark brown, Kenny's dark blue. Over Joel's desk, on his side of the room, was a glossy poster of E.T., and over Kenny's desk, on his side of the room, was a glossy poster of those mutant turtles whose metamorphosis, from television animation to Hollywood "acting," had so alarmed Michael O'Meara when he'd taken his sons to the movie.

Looking from one silent boy to the other, Michael said, "There's no 'bad man' coming to visit us, but there *is* a man, new to us, you might possibly meet next week. He isn't coming to live in our house, though. He won't be around here much at all. No more than"—Michael paused, searching for the perfect analogue, which eluded him "—the oil delivery man."

But this was lame and unconvincing. Joel and Kenny, big-eyed, hours from sleep, continued to gaze up at their father. What is it about a child's smooth forehead creased in anxiety that so pierces the heart! Michael tried to smile, more cheerfully. "Remember your birthday—your birthdays— yesterday? Wasn't that fun?"

Gina had arranged for eight of the boys' classmates to come over in the late afternoon, following school; Michael, who customarily stayed at the office until six o'clock, had not come home in time for the party, but he'd been told, by an exhausted Gina, that it had been a great success. And, following Gina's discreet suggestions to the other mothers, two or three of whom were her friends, there had been no "twin" presents—matching toys, clothes, games, books, videos.

For while it was obvious that Joel and Kenny were identical twins, thus bearing identical chromosomes, it did not follow—and on this point Michael was particularly adamant—that either child's personality should be subordinated to the other; or to the fact, essentially accidental, of *twinness.*

The boys nodded and smiled wanly, yes the party had been fun, yes the presents were okay, but their apprehensive mood was not so easily dispelled. Joel said shyly, "I guess that letter had bad news, Daddy?" and Kenny said, with childish vehemence, "Mommy made us bring it to you, Daddy—it wasn't *us.*" Joel joined in, nodding vigorously. "It wasn't *us.*" Both boys' knees bobbed and quivered beneath the bedclothes.

Michael said, "Oh no, guys—not at all. The letter had good news, really. Very good news. But, to Mommy, maybe, it was sort of surprising news." He hesitated, not wanting to say anything further about Mommy that might, even in playful man-to-man terms, seem critical; even when Gina's nerves were on edge from the children, and she didn't trouble to disguise her emotions, Michael took care never to speak a critical word about her in their sons' hearing. (How he wished that Gina, impetuous quick-tempered Gina, would do as much for him—but that was another story.) He said, "But everything is fine now, guys. Mommy and I are going out but we'll be home by midnight. Marita is here—you remember Marita, don't you? You like Marita, don't you?" The boys nodded wanly. Marita was the latest in a succession of helpers whom Gina hired and oversaw, whose task was to care for Joel and Kenny when their parents were otherwise engaged. Michael scarcely knew her himself.

Michael said, smiling, "Tomorrow is Sunday. We'll go over to The Islands, maybe, if the weather is nice. Just the three of us, maybe. Okay?" The Islands was a wildlife sanctuary with hiking trails, footbridges linking small islands, canoeing. The boys' eyes usually widened with excitement at the prospect of being taken there, on a rare outing with their busy father, but, now, their enthusiasm seemed only polite. Kenny jammed a thumb into a corner of his mouth, saying, "Daddy, is Mommy mad at *us?*" Joel shivered, whining, "Daddy, it wasn't *us,* it wasn't *our fault.*"

"Of course, nothing has been your fault, and Mommy isn't mad at anyone, don't be silly. It's bedtime. I'll turn off your light, and"—Michael stooped to the light, but the boys protested shrilly, kicking at their covers.

"Daddy, no!"

"Daddy, *don't!*"

"Daddy, don't go! *Daddy—*"

"*—don't go yet!*"

Michael laughed, startled. "Hush, boys. Joel, Kenny—be good! Hush!"

He gripped the boys' flailing legs through the covers and held them still. At once, like captive animals, the boys ceased to struggle. Yet they were panting, and their eyes, delicately lashed as Gina's, and of that same striking seagreen hue as Gina's, flared up in frightened defiance. Joel asked, "Who is it! Who's coming to visit next week!" Kenny chimed in, "Daddy, *who!* Tell us *who!*"

Michael hesitated. He'd never been a competent liar; in fact, he virtually never lied. It was a matter of principle, but, had it not been principle, it would have been of necessity. As a stammerer learns to avoid syllables that exacerbate his stammer, so Michael had learned, over the years, to avoid occasions that forced him to lie. Yet, now, his two young sons staring avidly up at him, he was at a loss for words.

Finally he said, meaning to end the discussion, "Lee Roy Sears is just a—human being. A man like me. And now it's bedtime."

" 'Lee Roy—' "

"—'Sears'?"

"*Is* he a bad man?"

"Daddy, *is* he?"

Michael laughed, exasperated. "I've told you *no*, boys. He is *not* a bad man. Daddy wouldn't have anything to do with a bad man, you know that. Where did you get such an outlandish idea?"

The boys giggled, glancing at each other at the same instant; as, in the grip of such a childish mood, they often did. As if their communication with each other were wordless, visceral. As if a single leaping thought galvanized them both.

Kenny sputtered, his thumb jammed deeper into his mouth, " 'Cause he's been in *jail.*"

Joel said, giggling daringly, " 'Cause he killed somebody, I bet!"

Kenny echoed, "I bet, I bet!"

This set them off—giggling, squealing, squirming, kicking off their bedclothes. It took all of their father's patience to calm them down. "C'mon, c'mon, Joel, Kenny! Be good! Cut it out! You don't want to behave like silly little babies, do you?—when you're seven years old?" Michael's sunburnt face smarted with irritation; he *was* exasperated; yet there was something of the boys' mother in their naughty behavior, an undercurrent of puckishness, even of coquetry. And they were such beautiful little boys, with their fair, fine, wavy hair, their big eyes, their perfect skin. Not once in seven years, not even at their rampaging naughtiest, had Michael been able to chastise them with anything more forcible than words.

What Michael most wanted to protect his sons from was physical injury: his own, or another's, wrath.

Judging that they'd gone far enough for the evening, and that Daddy was serious in his displeasure with them, and maybe, in his own complicated adult way, hurt, Daddy whom they adored and whose love they cherished, the twins decided, in the same instant, to stop being rowdy; to settle down and be good; to listen to Daddy, and believe him, when he said that the man who was coming to visit the next week was *not* a bad man, and certainly *not* a murderer, but someone they might like—"At least, you should give him a chance. Isn't it only fair, Joel, Kenny?—to give Lee Roy Sears a chance?"

Joel and Kenny mumbled, "Yes, Daddy."

"You're good boys," Michael said, with such sudden passion that Joel and Kenny were embarrassed, as they were when their mother cursed in their presence, or burst into tears. "You're sweet, and you're kind, and you're generous, and it's only fair, isn't it, to give Lee Roy Sears a chance? A man who, when he was your age, had none of the advantages you have?"

Again they mumbled, in a single voice, "Yes, Daddy."

Michael briskly adjusted their pillows and disheveled bedclothes, and tucked them in another time, and stooped over them to kiss them, in turn, goodnight. He switched off the bedside lamp but sat with them in the half-light (the bedroom door was open a few inches, a hall light was on) until they fell asleep. It was an old custom of Michael's, begun when the boys were babies, of which Gina did not approve, to comfort them when they were overly excited or troubled or had wakened from bad dreams. He said, gently, "Everything's okay. Daddy's watching over you."

What difference might it have made in his life, he wondered, had his own father taken the time to sit with him like this, many years ago.

So fastidious was Michael regarding his sons' feelings, so scrupulous about never betraying the smallest gesture of favoritism, he wasn't sitting on the edge of one of their beds but on a stool he'd pulled over. He understood that Joel and Kenny, more keenly than ordinary siblings, were aware of such things.

By degrees the boys' breathing grew rhythmic, regular, deeper. Michael watched their faces as they sank into sleep: their shut eyes, their slightly parted lips, their small perfect noses . . . He felt a sensation of love so piercing, he could barely contain it.

Yet his old guilt rose in him at such times, like stagnant, lapping water. For he felt that he did not deserve these beautiful young sons, as he did not deserve his beautiful wife. His very happiness, his very identity as Michael O'Meara—he did not deserve.

And why, because he wasn't worthy of them. Their love and trust. And why wasn't he worthy of them, why not worthy of their love and trust, because they didn't know him. They knew nothing of him. If they knew, they would not love him. Still less would they trust him.

Michael's guilt regarding his sons was obscure, but regarding Gina it was pointed—she'd had a difficult pregnancy, and their marriage had been severely tested. Though he knew it was primitive reasoning, Michael couldn't help but feel he'd inflicted a dangerous pregnancy upon his unsuspecting wife.

At first, newly pregnant, in the summer of 1983, Gina had been overjoyed. She'd hugged and kissed Michael a dozen times a day; her sarcasm and short temper vanished immediately; like an adoring child she telephoned his office simply to whisper to him, "I love you so." She'd gone to New York City with her closest Mount Orion friend, Tracey Deardon, to buy maternity clothes at Bloomingdale's. She'd talked and laughed on the telephone for hours with her mother, her married sisters, old college roommates, while Michael, puzzled, but happy for her happiness, waited for dinner, or sometimes ate alone, forced to think (and the insight had the weight

of a profundity!) that, until now, Gina must have felt herself deprived; excluded from the company of women who were truly
women.

At first, too, Gina had been radiantly healthy. Her skin lost its
porcelain pallor and acquired a warm, rosy glow. Her eyes lost their
sharpness, that glisten of sarcasm, and shone. She gained weight in
her hips and breasts, and regarded herself with wonder. Eagerly she
decorated and furnished the nursery. Eagerly she interviewed poten-
tial live-in helpers. (There was no question of Gina taking on the
task of baby-rearing by herself.) She studied baby books, nutrition
books, popular psychology books. *(The Care and Feeding of Expectant
Husbands* was one amusing title.) Taking Michael with her, she began
attending natural childbirth classes at a Mount Orion women's center. (Michael was enthusiastic about the classes, but Gina quickly
lost interest—if childbirth was meant to be natural, why was it such
work? Gina's delivery was to be cesarean, like most of her friends'.)

Once Gina learned that she was pregnant with twins, however,
everything changed. Her health. Her attitude toward Michael. She
began to suffer the symptoms of classic morning sickness—nausea
and vomiting. She had trouble sleeping. She wept at the slightest
provocation, or at no provocation at all. Like Michael she'd professed
to be overjoyed by the news—the young couple insisted that they
were "twice as happy"—but like Michael she was stunned. *Twins.
Identical twins. Where one baby had been expected.* When well-
intentioned relatives and friends congratulated the O'Mearas, Gina
bit her lips in silence.

When Michael went to embrace her, she pushed him gently
but emphatically away. She couldn't bear to be touched, she told
him. Not by anyone.

She contemplated, or terrified Michael by seeming to contemplate, having an abortion.

For Michael, this wretched period ironically marked the first
time he became conscious of how he was regarded in Mount Orion.
Until then he'd scarcely given it a thought—he wasn't the kind of
person to contemplate his own popularity, his reputation among
others. As soon as news of the young couple's pregnancy made the
rounds, however, numerous friends, acquaintances, and business associates congratulated Michael; when it was learned that twins were

expected, people laughed, remarking, "How like Michael O'Meara, to father *twins!*"

Michael was mystified, bemused. Did people consider him a model of virility? A fount of tireless energy?

Gina fled Mount Orion and the white colonial house on Glenway Circle, and, for three terrible weeks, during which time Michael had no choice but to continue with his busy outward life as if nothing were wrong, she stayed with her parents in Philadelphia. Her body was becoming grotesquely misshapen, her beauty swallowed in sallow, puffy flesh. She insisted that Michael could not possibly love her since she was loathsome, disgusting; in his place, she could not possibly love herself. What had they done, to bring such misery upon them! "Of course I love you, Gina," Michael pleaded over the telephone. "I would give up my life for you." Gina said, weeping helplessly, *"I'm giving up my life for me—for this!"* In the end Gina allowed Michael to drive to Philadelphia to bring her home, resigned to her fate.

Michael had consulted his mother—was there a history of twins in the family?—her family, or in his father's? Mrs. O'Meara, wintering in Palm Beach at the time, sounded as far away as the equator, her normally curt, crisp voice yet more impersonal over the telephone, saying, "Michael, pregnancy is always difficult for women, you'll have to be very understanding about Gina," and Michael said, "Oh, yes, Mother, I think I have been, I've tried to be, I love her desperately and I want to be the best possible husband in these circumstances and the best possible father"—and Mrs. O'Meara said, her voice overlapping with his, "For a woman, having babies seems like the answer to a riddle but, in fact, it turns out to be part of the riddle," and Michael said, raising his voice because the connection had begun to crackle with static, "Yes, Mother, but what about *twins?*—is there a history of *twins* in the family?" and Mrs. O'Meara said, her voice now remote, "I know nothing of twins. I know nothing." Shortly after, the connection was broken.

In its bloody physicality, childbirth turned out to be less arduous than the months preceding. Gina's labor began, lasted approximately seven hours, and came to an end. It was Heaven, Gina said. Meaning to be free: to be *delivered.* Or, euphoric with drugs, and the delight of being presented with two perfect baby boys, one weighing six pounds four ounces, the other six pounds one ounce, Gina found it so. How happy she was, and how happy, and relieved, Michael was! For weeks afterward Gina smiled and smiled, a new dazzling-white lovely smile, as if she were dazed, overwhelmed, yet in bliss. She could not nurse Joel and Kenny and happily gave them up to formula. She could not deal with their crying and happily gave them up to their father or to Rita, the live-in helper. She fussed over them when visitors came, kissed and hugged them, posed to have her picture taken with them, was clearly delighted with them, beautiful little Joel and beautiful little Kenny, yet, when she was out of the house she seemed almost to forget them: it was others who reminded her. How did it feel, Gina O'Meara was repeatedly asked, to be the mother of identical twins?

Gina bared her lovely white teeth in a smile and said, "It feels like Heaven!"

Since that time, as the boys grew, Gina experienced periods of intense satisfaction with motherhood and her place in the world— for, however unfixed her basic identity, she *was* now a mother, and that was undeniable. She could speak expertly of private schools in the area, pediatricians, children's clothes, toys, and television programs, and she could respectfully seek advice from older mothers in their Mount Orion circle. She had made her parents proud, doting grandparents. She could bask in her husband's unstinting adoration (in Mount Orion, Michael O'Meara's devotion to his wife was much envied by other wives) and feel not the slightest twinge of guilt at sometimes—almost—betraying it.

For Gina, like many beautiful American women, was intensely romantic: which is not to say adulterous, precisely. In their many years of marriage Gina had had no adulterous affair, but she'd had, and fully intended to continue having, romantic friendships.

Alternating with these blissful periods were others less clearly defined, yet unmistakable. So far as Michael could judge, poor Gina simply felt cramped, overwhelmed by the three males in her family— thus short-tempered and prone to sarcasm, wounded feelings, tears, silence. Recalling those terrible weeks (to which, in fact, neither Michael nor Gina ever alluded) when Gina had left him to live in Philadelphia, Michael was careful never to make things worse for Gina: he gave in to her requests readily, and usually cheerfully; he consented to a round of social events, a ceaseless self-perpetuating round, that sometimes left him breathless; he allowed her certain costly indulgences (membership in the prestigious Mount Orion Tennis Club, for instance, and tennis lessons with the resident pro) as if they were but her due as Mrs. Michael O'Meara, which perhaps they were. He may have sensed from time to time her emotional dependency upon her romantic friendships, but really he knew nothing about them, and he never made inquiries. He wasn't a jealous husband. He was a gentleman to his fingertips. He knew too that Gina was not a physically passionate woman; thus it was unlikely she would ever betray him *in that way.*

One of the twins stirred in his sleep—Joel, since he was in Joel's bed. Michael looked to Kenny, and saw, to his relief, that Kenny was sleeping deeply, oblivious of his twin, and of his father sitting a few feet away. In the dim light from the hall, the boys' faces were angelic, and identical. Michael knew that Joel was a pound or two heavier than Kenny, that Joel was usually just perceptibly quicker, more impatient than Kenny, that Joel's hair whorled gently to the left at the crown of his head, while Kenny's hair whorled gently to the right. They were "mirror twins"—a term their father did not like, and never used. This meant that, though identical to the casual eye, they were yet characterized by subtle asymmetries, mainly facial, so that, standing side by side and slightly facing each other, they gave the impression—eerie, or charming, depending upon your taste—of being a single child contemplating his mirror image.

Now Kenny stirred, sighed, raised his already damp thumb to his mouth, moaned slightly. Michael would have liked to ease the thumb away—seven years old was far too old for thumb-sucking—but he didn't want to disturb the boy.

It *was* Kenny, wasn't it? The little boy sleeping in Kenny's bed.

(Once in a while, though not often, since Daddy so disapproved, the twins changed places—identities. Just to confuse others. A teacher, some of their little friends. Mommy too, sometimes. *She* thought it was funny and called them little devils. If Daddy was home, the trick was riskier. If they did it, they had to really *do* it, and stay with their switched identities for as long as Daddy was around. If he found out, he wouldn't laugh and scold, like Mommy, he would stare at them as if they had betrayed him, and he would be hurt, and since they loved him they did not want to hurt him, not their Daddy, not *hurt*. But still, sometimes, it was so *funny*.)

Since the twins' birth, the primary factor in the O'Mearas' marriage was, for Michael, that Gina concur in rearing them as if they were merely brothers, and not twins. For Michael, who believed in the unique worth and dignity of the human soul (and whether God existed to sanction this belief, Michael neither knew nor cared, at age forty), there was something subtly debasing about the very idea of *twinness:* the duplication of one's chromosomes in another. Something subtly disturbing about *mirror selves.* (Michael O'Meara had been less effective than he should have been, as a quarterback on his high school football team, somehow thrown off stride, worried by his own aggression, regarding his opposite number on the opposing team.) Gina hadn't entirely understood, but she hadn't opposed Michael in his child-rearing notions, seeing he was, in this instance, adamant, and it gave her pleasure to acquiesce to him in matters that seemed to her insignificant. Therefore, even when they were infants, she dressed Joel and Kenny differently: no cute twin outfits, thank you! Friends and relatives were firmly instructed not to give the boys twin presents, nor even to indulge in "twin talk" with them. Teachers were firmly instructed to treat the boys like individuals and to seat them far apart if they were assigned to the same classroom. Like most normal children, the O'Meara boys took their cues from others' responses to them, and, so far as Michael O'Meara could determine, these responses were to them as brothers, not as twins. At least, when Michael O'Meara was present.

Yet Daddy couldn't always tell Joel and Kenny apart—he had to admit. If the playful little boys wanted to deceive him there wasn't much Daddy could do except try to make a game of it, and not be hurt, or angry. Gina, who took it all less seriously, was harder to deceive: she had only to swoop down upon the twins, laughing, clamping a hand down on each boy's shoulder, crying, "Joel, behave! And Kenny! *I know which one of you is which!*"

It must be, Michael thought, gazing at the sleeping boys, that a mother *is* closer to children than a father. Than even the most loving and concerned of fathers.

Joel stirred, sighed, his eyelids fluttered but did not open. In a vague groping gesture he jammed a thumb into a corner of his mouth.

Michael was nearly dressed for the imminent dinner party (at the Trimmers', was it?—or the Deardons'?), had only to quickly knot a tie around his neck and put on his suit coat, but he seemed to have forgotten the time, so lost in contemplation of his sons. It *was* uncanny how closely they resembled each other. Why did it make him uneasy? If it did not disturb them, why should it disturb Daddy? Michael tried to see an advantage of twinness: one was, at least, not *one* in the world, in a very literal as in a more poetic sense, but *two*. One's being was doubled in the world. Thus, one could not be so readily erased.

(Twins! When Michael related to his sister, Janet, their mother's odd reaction to the twins—both to the announcement that Gina was expecting twins and to their actual birth: Mrs. O'Meara had not flown up to see them until they were four months old—Janet had said, hesitating, "Yes, there's some mystery about our childhood, or about Mother and Father, but you can't ask her about it, you can't even approach asking, I've tried." Michael had been astonished at this casual revelation, but skeptical. He'd laughed and said, "Mystery? Are you serious? *Us?*")

He was thinking, for no reason he could have named, of Kierkegaard; of Kierkegaard's classic essay *Fear and Trembling* which he'd read twenty years ago. The story of the biblical Abraham and his twin sons. A nightmare parable out of Genesis, when we, the human species, were so newly and precariously human, we might be asked to sacrifice our own children to ravenous Yahweh the Volcano God.

Abraham had journeyed to Mount Moriah, commanded by God to sacrifice his twin sons, not knowing until his arrival that this was a test of his faith and that a sacrificial ram would be provided—fortunately! Abraham the patriarch and his beloved son Isaac and—. What was the other son's name? Try as he could, Michael could not remember.

Michael did remember, distinctly, reading the Kierkegaard essay in a single ecstatic sitting in the library of the seminary, and being powerfully moved. Ah, yes! Kierkegaard had written passionately of the "infinite resignation" that must precede true religious faith: the leap of the Absurd: the leap over the abyss.

At the age of twenty-two, Michael O'Meara had opened his heart boldly to such notions. To some extent, he *had* believed. But he had not been ravished by religious certitude. At the core, he remained the same person, unmistakably.

Though who that person was—he didn't quite know.

Wryly Michael thought, You can leap with all good faith and yet fall *into* the abyss.

Surely, in human history, that was happening with ever greater frequency?

"Michael—?"

Gina had come up behind him to lay a tentative hand on his shoulder.

Michael woke from his reverie to see Gina, in high heels and a dress of some pale silky material new to him, leaning over him with a vexed expression. A cool sweet scent as of narcissus wafted about her.

She led him out into the hall, whispering, "I've been looking for you, it's *late.*"

At the door, Michael cast a final yearning glance at his sons. They slept as before, undisturbed. Joel in his bed, Kenny in his. Michael felt again that pang of exquisite helpless love.

He slipped an arm around Gina's stiffened body. "I'm sorry, honey!—I was waiting for them to fall asleep, and I must have lost track of the time."

Gina was regarding him with thoughtful eyes. "Yes. It seems to happen so often."

"DON'T BRING UP THE subject of this—ex-convict protégé of yours tonight. Please."

"I wasn't intending to."

"Word will get out quickly enough in Mount Orion."

"Gina, honey, don't you think you're exaggerating this?"

They were on their way to the Trimmers' and were already twenty minutes late. Michael was driving the newer of their cars, a sleek white Mazda with a sun roof, and Gina, beside him in the passenger's seat, cast him one of her fierce sidelong looks. "Don't you think *you* are?" she asked.

IRONICALLY, AS SOON AS Michael and Gina entered the Trimmers' vast living room, escorted by Mrs. Trimmer, Clyde Somerset, one of the guests, called out in his booming voice, "Michael! Hey! Isn't it great, how this Lee Roy Sears"—the name sounded distinct on his tongue, as if it were a foreign expression—"is coming *here?*"

Michael glanced at Gina, who, after the smallest fraction of a moment's hesitation, smiled happily at Clyde Somerset.

Naturally everyone within earshot was curious to know who Lee Roy Sears was, and what was his connection with Michael O'Meara and Clyde Somerset and the Dumont Center: so the story came out piecemeal, much abbreviated, in Clyde's grandiloquent telling. Lee Roy Sears emerged as an unjustly imprisoned young man of American Indian extraction who had been saved from the electric chair, by the actions of Michael O'Meara and a few other vigilant citizens; he was a Vietnam veteran suffering from "post-traumatic stress" and the after-effects of Agent Orange; most importantly, from Clyde's perspective as director of the Dumont Center, he was a gifted artist, a bold, iconoclastic sculptor, whose proposal of an art-therapy program for "physically wounded" Vietnam veterans like himself was already drawing a considerable amount of attention.

Clyde Somerset was a stout, ruddy-faced, bluntly handsome man in his mid-fifties, the kindest of men, a civic leader and booster, and he and his wife, Susanne, had been very friendly toward the O'Mearas, yet, hearing the self-congratulatory tone of his words, Michael felt his face burn with embarrassment. What would Lee Roy Sears think, if he heard! The worst of it was, Clyde directed his remarks at Michael, as if the two men were having a public dialogue. "Of course it's risky," Clyde said ebulliently, "taking on a man like this, with his background. It's experimental in every sense of the word. But the Dumont Center has been overly conservative in its programs, and, as I told the trustees the other day, now is the chance for us to do something radically different." He raised his glass in a salute. "Thank you, Michael O'Meara."

For most of the half-hour preceding dinner, Michael was plied with questions about Lee Roy Sears. Gina, drink in hand, observed without interrupting. If she was upset in the slightest, she gave no sign: she was far too socially poised, and too vain. And, indeed, she was seeing again, hardly for the first time, how, in public, her husband *was* an attractive figure: guileless, transparent in his idealism, an overgrown boy with shining eyes and a flushed, sunburnt face.

His laughter was immediate and generous; his smile was a smile to win votes. (In fact, Michael had recently been elected to the Mount Orion Township Council, and Gina gaily fantasized him soon running for mayor, then for a seat in the House, why not the Senate?) Now he was, at the relatively young age of forty, chief legal counsel for Pearce Pharmaceuticals, Inc., with a considerable staff at his disposal, and a considerable yearly income; his formerly irritating modesty had acquired a glamorous tone: Michael O'Meara was a man to whom Gina might have been irresistibly drawn, had she not already been his wife, thus immune to his charm.

Susanne Somerset murmured in Gina's ear, "Your husband is so *sweet*, Gina! Clyde and I are both so fond of him."

Gina smiled, somewhat mollified. She murmured in reply, "Why, thank you!"

It wasn't so far-fetched, Michael's running for mayor of Mount Orion. Just the other day Dwight Schatten, one of the local Democrats, had made just that suggestion to Gina, at the conclusion of a romantic luncheon at the Far Hills Inn.

Once everyone was seated at dinner, and other more scattered conversational topics were taken up, Michael was able to relax; to sip his wine, which was a very good red wine; to allow his eye to move restlessly over the gathering. It was a long, elaborately laid table, for Pamela and Jack Trimmer were very well-to-do and took entertaining seriously, as Gina did. (Nothing made Gina so happy as receiving invitations from socially important people—unless it was sending out invitations to socially important people.) Fourteen men and women were seated at the table, all of them friends of the O'Mearas', or, in any case, friendly acquaintances. (With the painful exception of Marvin Bruns, a prominent real estate speculator, whom Michael frankly disliked, and who he knew disliked him.) They basked in the glow of one another's regard and respect as around a common fire, and their faces were warmly illuminated by this fire, animated with pleasure. How happy Michael O'Meara felt among them, how blessed, as if one of them!

Yet he felt a tinge of guilt too. Poor Gina!—maybe he had not been altogether truthful with her, about his recent efforts regarding Lee Roy Sears. Yet he knew he'd done the right thing, and he did not regret it.

(It was true, as Gina thought, that since the birth of the twins, Michael had been relatively inactive in The Coalition. There simply wasn't time. He gave money, he signed petitions, that was about all. He'd even forgotten about Sears, as, after the first flush of triumph, we are likely to forget the reasons for our having cared so much about winning. And then Sears had written, a brief, crude little note, thanking him for what he'd said at the hearing. And Michael had written back—very briefly too. And, after a year or so, Sears had written again, another note, simple yet enigmatic: *This is just to say how your words lodged in my heart & undeserving as Lee Roy Sears is he hopes one day to SHAKE YOUR HAND IN BROTHERLY LOVE.* In all, there had been seven letters, over eight years. Michael had saved them all, hidden away in a file in his desk at home.)

There sat Gina, chastely beautiful by candlelight, clusters of tiny pearls gleaming in her ears, her nails pinkly polished. She loved such occasions, she was most herself at such times: caught up, as now, in a spirited exchange with Jack Trimmer and Clyde Somerset, with Marvin Bruns looking on. Was Gina aware, Michael wondered, of how *intensely* Bruns stared at her?—as, it occurred to Michael suddenly, the man so often did. (Last Sunday at the Rathskills' brunch. The week before, at a cocktail reception at the Dumont Center.) Michael was not a jealous husband, but it abraded his nerves to see another man so regard his wife: that look of sly admiration, or more than admiration, held in check by Bruns's sardonic curl of a smile. Bruns was dark, sleek-headed as a seal, with sallow yet flushed skin, playful derisive eyes. He was always expensively dressed. He carried himself with a certain pride. And that maddening little smile!—he'd flashed it at Michael like a taunt a few weeks ago, when, after a turbulent meeting of the Mount Orion Township Council, Michael had privately accused him of having manipulated votes in order to break a zoning regulation, to the advantage of Bruns and his real estate partners. Bruns had denied it at first; then, suddenly, with that smile, he'd laughed in Michael O'Meara's face and said, "So?—this isn't the Boy Scouts, pal."

Subsequently, when the men encountered each other, they were civil—barely. No one knew of their animosity. Michael had decided not to tell Gina because he knew it might upset her, or, worse yet, fail to upset her, much.

Michael ate his superbly prepared rack of lamb and sipped his tart red wine, and talked, and laughed, and enjoyed himself as he always did at such times, yet he was thinking of how the only really abiding focus of his life was his love for Gina and their sons, beside which everything else—his work for Pearce Pharmaceuticals, his professional "identity"—paled, vanished. So long as he had them, he had everything.

Yet, disturbingly, he did not truly know the degree to which his family loved *him*. In fact, whether they loved *him* at all.

Did Daddy even know with absolute certainty whether Joel was Joel, or Kenny Kenny!

His attachment to Gina was passionate, erotic—never, before meeting and falling in love with her, had Michael O'Meara had such powerful feelings. He knew he could never have them again. Yet, should the circumstances of their life together shift, Gina would divorce him and take away their sons—it would be "painful" for her, it would be "devastating," it would be "tragic," and yet—.

As for Joel and Kenny, who loved Daddy, well, *he*, Michael *(was* his name Michael?), had been a son too, once. So he well knew how such filial bonds, seemingly so deep, so permanent, forged in love, can be ruptured, overcome. And good riddance.

Guilt. Why the hell *did* he feel guilty? He'd bet that Marvin Bruns, who was duplicitous if not openly dishonest, unethical if not overtly criminal, and who was known to have been unfaithful to his wife (an attractive, aging woman from whom he was now separated), had never felt an instant's pang of guilt. The bastard.

Now Bruns was talking with Gina, and Gina was laughing, that high cool delicious laughter that sounded always just slightly mocking. Whatever they were talking of, Michael couldn't hear.

Michael was himself engaged in a lively conversation at his end of the table. Pamela Trimmer had asked him about Pearce Pharmaceuticals, in which the Trimmers had stock—evidently sales were up an astounding 30 percent in the past year? Michael laughed wryly, and said yes, but lawsuits were up too. "But that's good, isn't it, Michael, for *you?*" Susanne Somerset asked. Michael said, "I don't think my bosses would see it that way." This led to a discussion of neurophysiological medicine, in which Pearce, Inc., was one of the world's leading researchers, having isolated some of the brain's most

subtle biochemicals in order to duplicate them or to produce drugs
to bind with them in the brain. Since the basis of neurophysiological
activity was chemical, only chemicals could restore the ailing brain
to normalcy: there were ingenious new drugs to block anxiety, and
drugs to block depression, and drugs to block obsessive-compulsive
behavior. "Of course," Michael said wryly, noticing how everyone
at the table was listening, "there *are* problems, sometimes."

This in turn led to a discussion, for some minutes quite heated,
about medical technology, malpractice suits, the ethics of "interfer-
ing" with human lives; the role of such companies as Pearce, Inc.,
in helping patients, or exploiting patients, or, from a certain objective
perspective, both helping and exploiting them at the same time. Jack
Trimmer announced that *he* would never take any drug so powerful
it would control his very brain, and Valeria Darrell, a divorcée in
her mid-forties, rather heavily made-up this evening and a bit drunk,
interrupted to say that *she* would, and in fact had—"Nobody dares
say a word against these drugs who hasn't suffered from depression.
I know what I'm talking about." There was a moment's silence, since
no one cared to refute Valeria, still less did they want to provoke
her into further disclosures (which, in any case, everyone had heard
before); then Clyde Somerset asked, in a mock-scandalized way, how
they could all let Michael say, deadpan, that the basis of neurophysiological behavior was only chemical, and this led to Michael's mild
defense of his remark—he was paraphrasing Pearce, Inc., not speaking for himself, his own belief was that human beings were far more
than merely biochemical mechanisms. Then Tracey Deardon, who
was very fond of Michael O'Meara, and often asked him such questions at such times, called down the table to ask about obsessive-
compulsives—she was sure, she said, *she* was one. As everyone
laughed, Michael paused, feeling a bit uncomfortable, for wasn't it
wrong to be amused by others' pathologies; wasn't there something
morbid, both voyeuristic and masochistic, in taking an interest in
medical case histories? Yet, made garrulous by wine, seeing too how
Gina was smiling in his direction, Michael could not resist telling
his friends of a case study he'd read the other day, an otherwise
normal man—"most obsessive-compulsives are presented as 'otherwise normal' "—who had to repeat everything he said, first in a
normal voice and then in a lowered voice. There was another oth-

erwise normal man who sorted out things in sevens; another who could never look anyone in the eye; a woman who had to brush her teeth a dozen times a day and had destroyed her gums. There was a woman who'd plucked out most of her hair, including her eyelashes and eyebrows. There was a man under a compulsion to examine every room he entered for "spiders and filth." One man was under a compulsion to touch his genitals repeatedly, another could never bring himself to touch his. There were eating compulsions, which sometimes resulted in death. There were compulsions governing sleep, and compulsions involving violence. In fact, Michael said, virtually any compulsion you can imagine, no matter how grotesque, someone has made the center of his or her life—"It's like God, gone wrong."

Michael paused, as if he'd said something wicked, but no one noticed, for now came a flood of anecdotes, mostly of a light, comical nature, centering upon his friends' personal obsessions. Though Michael smiled and laughed with the others, his face had grown very warm; and, in truth, he was ashamed. He'd been instructing his sons in the importance of never laughing at others' weaknesses, still less at their afflictions, and here Daddy was doing it, himself.

He hoped too that no one in this lively company would toss out a barbed query asking how he, a man of presumed integrity, could make his living defending a billion-dollar drug manufacturer against charges brought it by unhappy men and women—for he had no ready answer.

Then Marvin Bruns was speaking, raising his voice to be heard over the rest. There was a seriousness in his tone that Michael could not recall having ever heard before. "An obsessive-compulsive is a desperately unhappy person," he said. "I speak from personal experience, since my father was one. No, I won't go into details, it's still too painful, and embarrassing, and, in the end, it killed him. The French have an excellent term for it—*la main étrangère*. It refers to my father's particular sort of behavior problem, in which a person repeatedly does things without 'knowing' that he is doing them, while at the same time 'knowing' very well that he *is*. A kleptomaniac is in the grip of *la main étrangère*, for instance, but that wasn't my father's problem—his was worse! And if there had been medication to help him, he would have taken it, gladly—as I would, in his place, knowing what I do." Bruns glanced down the table in Michael's direction, as if, so unexpectedly, aligning himself with him. "Pearce, Inc., is doing a great job, that's what I think. Sure, things go wrong occasionally, there is always a chance of side-effects with any medicine or medical treatment, but you can't have progress otherwise."

Michael O'Meara took a great gulp of his wine, in confusion. With a pang of guilt he wondered if, these many months, he had misjudged Marvin Bruns?

AND GINA: HAD HE been misreading her too?

On the way home from the party she rested her head against his shoulder, as she had not done for years, chattering happily of the evening, how wonderful their Mount Orion friends were, how fortunate they were to have such friends; how handsome Michael had looked in his new spring suit, with the Pierre Cardin necktie she'd bought him—"And how brilliantly you talked: I was fascinated."

And, as they were undressing for bed, Gina surprised him yet more by rubbing Noxema into his reddened forehead, cheeks, nose, as tenderly as she'd ever done; on her tiptoes she stood to kiss his mouth, and to gaze languidly into his eyes, her own dilated by wine, both sleepy and erotically inviting. "My God, Gina!" Michael said. Greatly excited, he lifted her in his arms and carried her to their bed.

Where, after making love, Gina cradled herself against him and murmured drowsily in his ear, "Darling, promise me just one thing?" and Michael prepared himself for a belated reference to Lee Roy Sears, but, no, yet another time Gina surprised him, her head gently nudging his, "You *will* call in a professional to clear the pond, and not try to do it yourself?"

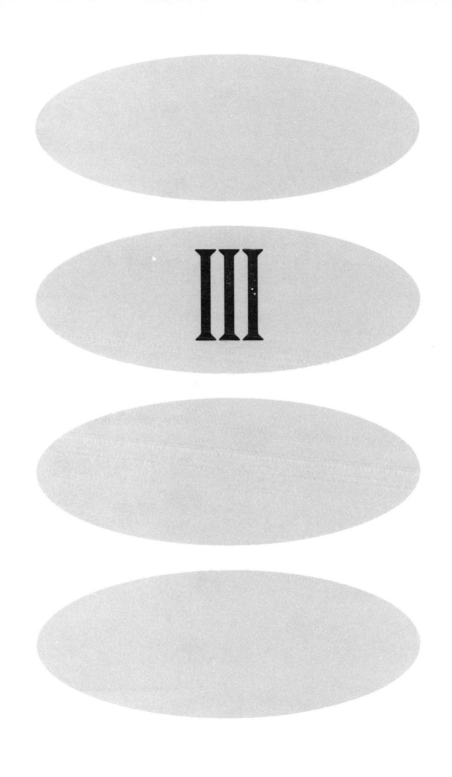

III

IT WAS THE FIRST morning of his new life.

Don't forget medication on this special day!—no he sure wouldn't.

He was a man with a mission burning inside him fierce as a laser beam, you would not want to impede, frustrate, deny, or challenge him.

Yes but he smiled. Sweetly.

Ducked his head, shifted his skinny shoulders inside his new cheap white Dacron shirt. Black garbardine trousers too, but no belt. He'd buy a belt tomorrow. A mud-green necktie the chaplain had given him. And his own brown shoes with the cracks and water stains from maybe fifteen years ago.

You know what you look like, Lee Roy, ha ha!—one of them whatdayacallit Moron guys goin door to door sellin fuckin Bibles haha!

Yes but you would not want to stand in his way.

Yes he did, and yes he will. Two tablets daily, at meals: big white chunky tablet of Chlonopramane. A crap-floury coating and inside a bitter taste, it burns going down. A danger in gagging.

He has the papers, to prove it. Release papers, I.D. papers, letters from the probation office, from Mr. Sigman (in Putnam, New Jersey), from Mr. Somerset (of the Dumont Center for the Arts and Community Services, Mount Orion, New Jersey), from Mr. O'Meara (of 17 Glenway Circle, Mount Orion, New Jersey).

Nobody asks. People don't ask. Inside the smile the tongue pokes pink and moist, snaky-quick. And the eyes.

Lee Roy Sears made the men laugh, his quiet-quivering voice— I stand outside the Caucasian race.

Don't you laugh at me you fuckers I'll tear out your throats with my teeth. *But no he did not utter a word*, this was Lee Roy Sears's principle of behavior.

He was a man with a mission. The parole board took heed.

And afterward he wept. On his knees Oh Jesus the man wept like he was five years old again and his foster father name now forgotten ceased walloping him with that chunk of firewood crumbling in his hands and asked, Was he sorry? was he sorry? was he sorry he'd been born?

No. Because he was a man with a mission bringing light where no light shone.

He was not ashamed of his strength, it was weakness of which he was ashamed. But tears are strength, sometimes.

Eight A.M. Monday. In the jolting prison van marked CONN. CORRECTIONAL FACILITIES. Ninety dollars in his wallet. Carrying his old suitcase, a duffel bag one of the guys had given him, a cardboard box tied together with twine. They'd drop him off at the bus station, that was their policy.

In the cardboard box: carefully rolled-up canvases and posters (acrylics), carefully wrapped-in-newspaper clay sculptures, bundles of sketches of works of art yet to be executed.

The sky was very big—he hadn't remembered it, so big.

He wasn't going to look.

You could get lost in that bigness. Out-of-doors. Your head drops back and mouth drops open—Oh Jesus! So *big!*

Except: two tablets daily Chlonopramane and he had 'script for three refills. Remember, Lee Roy, to take the tablets only at meals for otherwise they will dissolve in the stomach's acids and pass through the stomach's lining too quickly, will you remember?—yes he will.

The V.A. pays. At least, the fuckers pay.

His bad knee they won't pay for claiming it was not a legitimate war wound.

They eyed him coming in. A swarm of eyes like killer bees.

Oh Jesus lookit that one: ex-con written all over him, haha!

Crouching sort of walk and hair shaved up the back and sides of the head and skin rough and pale as puke, and those clothes, haha!—and his eyes snatching around like a dog's like a dog waiting to be kicked, you can always tell them.

The woman at the ticket counter was nice, though. She was very nice.

A ticket for Hartford, and in Hartford he'd buy a ticket for New York City that would take him to the Port Authority and there he would buy a ticket for Putnam, New Jersey. He fumbled with the bills and the change, but the woman was patient. She knew.

A dog that's waiting to be kicked, it's waiting to be kicked so it can bite. That's what teeth are for.

He was not nervous, the Chlonopramane coursed peacefully through his veins. Still, he shut his eyes against the big white sky.

He shut his eyes leaning his head, his greasy hair, Indian-black greasy hair against the bus window. Sitting alone. At the rear. Where none of them could get behind him.

Yes but he smiled so sweetly. The young woman wearing glasses, from the probation office, stared at him liking him. And the young woman who was Mr. Somerset's assistant though you could see she was scared, never been in a prison before, there in the visiting room just staring and swallowing and Lee Roy Sears was a gentleman intent upon reassuring *her*.

Once, how many years ago, before the U.S. Army, in that clinic in Springfield, Mass., he'd broken into the doctor's office looked swiftly through the files saw SEARS, LEE ROY and pulled out the folder to read *paranoid-schizoid dysfunctional/requires medication/responds well to therapy.*

Through Ashford, Conn., through Manchester, through Hartford (where he changed buses cringing and near to puking, *so many people*), through Waterbury, through Bridgeport, along I-95 into Manhattan into the Port Authority (where he *did* puke, on his own shoes—*people staring/smiling/laughing/holding their noses*), changing buses and a grizzled-gray young-old man bumped into him and his suitcase was knocked to the filthy pavement and the young-old man bared his teeth in a grin and said, Ooops!—'scusa me!—and as Lee Roy Sears stared the young-old man walked off with his suitcase *walking fast* like a man in a movie and Lee Roy Sears was *rooted to the spot* unable even to call out for help!

The Port Authority cops eyed him with derisive grins. You can always tell them, lookit the poor fucker's clothes. His dropped-open mouth.

He isn't a Caucasian, lookit his hair lookit his beak-nose lookit his eyes.

Stinking of puke, wiping it off with wet paper towels won't help much. There's a stink of death row that never goes away.

From Manhattan to Putnam, New Jersey. Lookit his hands shaking!

It's a black man selling tickets here, and he isn't friendly.

Tear out your throat with my teeth. Fangs.

Safe on the bus, at the very back, Lee Roy Sears unbuttoned his shirt cuff, pushed up his sleeve—yes, Snake Eyes was sleeping.

One eye open, maybe. That gold-glaring eye.

Snake Eyes twitching in his sleep. Itchy sensation on Lee Roy Sears's forearm.

He was innocent, riding eyes shut to Putnam, New Jersey. To his new life.

They tried to deny his identity saying he was not of *Seneca Indian blood*, no family on the reservation would acknowledge him trying to stamp him out scrape him against the pavement like a cockroach.

It wasn't a tattoo. Well it was, but it was more than a tattoo.

Not just the big sky and not just the people watching him like the bus driver like the guy in the opposite corner of the back seat not just the jolting bus smelling of exhaust not just the unexpected noises and smells different from the ones to which he'd become accustomed for thirteen years but—*he was free.*

He was free and that scared him 'cause, shit, you hear of guys, they go off their heads go to Florida, go to Alaska instead of reporting to their parole officer, right away they're picked up and taken back to prison. Some guys, they do worse.

He was free and the fuckers better know it, he had some scores to settle, Snake Eyes had some scores to settle, but maybe not, Oh Jesus no, Lee Roy Sears was a man with a mission he *was*.

He was an artist, the flame burned within.

He still had his duffel bag and he had his box of artworks as they were called. His reputation was based upon these artworks. Already men and women spoke of them in words of awe.

He was free but *He was smart* and *He had plans* and *He would make no mistakes this time* and *Best not to stand in his way* but *There was no danger with medication twice daily* and *No danger long as Snake Eyes slept*.

The bus was stopped on the side of the road, Route One. A cop was going along the aisle checking guys, another cop at the front and they singled out only certain persons, you could see prejudice operating clearly, of the many passengers on the bus only five or six were singled out, all of them men in their thirties or forties traveling alone, the cop stared at Lee Roy Sears sniffing like he smelled something bad. Okay, buddy, let's see your I D.

Yes officer.

He's shaky-handed and scared but smiling. That practiced smile where you stretch your lips over your teeth so as not to expose the greeny-straggly teeth to smirking eyes.

His long-sleeved shirt is buttoned to the cuffs.

A white shirt, and black trousers newly laundered, and the mud-green necktie around his neck. A necktie never fails to make a positive impression in America.

Proud to show the fucker: he is Lee Roy Sears who has a place to go to where they are expecting him and where he will be gainfully employed. And where they will respect him as a human being. As an artist.

These documents: release papers from Hunsford, I.D. (including U.S. Army discharge, Veterans Administration card), letters from Mr. Harold Sigman parole officer in Putnam, New Jersey, and Mr. Clyde Somerset of the Dumont Center for the Arts and Community

Services, Mount Orion, New Jersey, and Lee Roy Sears's friend Michael O'Meara of 17 Glenway Circle, Mount Orion, New Jersey.

Frowning, the cop examined Lee Roy Sears's documents. Paused over the release from Hunsford State Prison. Looked at Lee Roy Sears like Lee Roy Sears was shit. Said, Hey Lee Roy, this is your first day out?

Lee Roy Sears was sitting quietly in his seat his bony-knuckled hands clasped on his knees, his eyes a little hooded, watchful, his lips smiling thin over his chunky teeth.

His voice was higher-pitched than he'd meant, like a girl's, or a scared kid's. He said, Yes officer. It sure is.

MICHAEL O'MEARA ADVANCED UPON Lee Roy Sears with a smile,
hand extended for a brisk friendly handshake. "Hello! How are you!
Good to meet you, Lee Roy, at last!" Descending the steps into the
basement of the Dumont Center, preparing to meet Sears, Michael
had shifted to his gregarious social manner, sunny smile, shining
eyes, warm voice, long since cultivated at Pearce, Inc., to put junior
associates at their ease and to mask Michael's own nervousness. Poor
Lee Roy Sears, more diminutive than Michael recalled, blinked at
him as if a dazzling light were shining into his face, and, awkwardly,
for he was holding what appeared to be a mound of clay (it *was* clay,
he'd been modeling a small humanoid figure), managed to extend a
shy, tentative hand to Michael. His fingers were dry from the clay
but noticeably cold, and seemingly without strength. Like a fearful
child the parolee mumbled, "H-H'lo, Mr. O'Meara." He smiled
with thin-stretched lips and the glisten of his very dark, hooded eyes
had something feral about it.

It was 5:20 P.M. of Wednesday, April 17. No one could have guessed, from Michael O'Meara's genial manner, how excited, how anxious, how intensely hopeful he was, meeting Lee Roy Sears in his studio at the Dumont Center.

By this time, Lee Roy had been free only two and a half days. He'd checked in at the halfway house in Putnam in which he was obliged to live for six months, and he'd had his first meeting with his parole officer, and he'd begun work (the night shift: 11 P.M. to 5 A.M.) at the Putnam Municipal Parking Garage; he'd checked in at the Dumont Center, where he was to be "artist-in-residence" and "adjunct instructor" under the joint auspices of the Dumont Foundation, the New Jersey Council of the Arts, and the Veterans Administration. And now Michael O'Meara, his friend and benefactor, had come to take him home with him, to meet his family and to have dinner.

The men stared at each other, and Michael O'Meara continued to smile, his cheek dimpling with the effort. He said, gently, "Please call me 'Michael,' Lee Roy, will you?"

In a hoarse murmur Lee Roy Sears said, "—'Michael.'" The word sounded unconvincing.

Clyde Somerset's assistant, Jody, who had escorted Michael partway down the stairs, now said goodbye and started briskly back up, and Michael found himself alone with Lee Roy Sears and tried to think what to say. He'd dreamt of the man the night before, he was sure—very likely, he'd dreamt of him a good deal—and Sears had been much on his mind since the news of his parole—but, so very oddly, Sears, in person, seemed not quite the man Michael had expected.

To cover his confusion, Michael continued as before, warm, welcoming, genial, his voice just a little loud, "And how *are* you, Lee Roy?—you're looking fine."

Lee Roy Sears crumbled bits of clay off his fingers and stared at Michael O'Meara as if the question were preposterous. In Hunsford State Prison, did guards inquire of inmates how they were?—did inmates so inquire of one another?

Sears mumbled, in the same low, hoarse, hurried voice, "I'm—real well, Mr. O'Meara." He paused. A tic began in his left eyelid. He gave off a dank commingled odor of hair lotion, clay, turpentine.

He smiled again fleetingly. Added, "—I'm great." Paused. With a sudden high-pitched giggle added, "—'Michael.' "

Again there was silence. Elsewhere in the Center people were talking, a telephone rang. There was traffic outside, at a short distance. (The Dumont Center, one of Mount Orion's newer, eye-catching buildings, had been constructed just north of the two-acre village green.) The thought came to Michael, not that he'd made a mistake helping Lee Roy Sears get paroled, but that he'd made a mistake in insisting to Gina that he bring the man home for dinner.

Michael had cautioned Clyde Somerset, and others at the Center, that they should keep in mind that Lee Roy Sears had been incarcerated for thirteen years, five of them on death row. His transition to the outside world could not be easy. They should keep in mind—and Michael would have to remind himself, too, frequently—that Sears was hardly a typical staff member at the Center, nor even a typical patron.

The Dumont Center had been designed by a well-known Japanese-American architect. Its style was postmodernist, with amber-tinted glass, sweeping planes of concrete and aluminum, and warm pink granite; from a short distance, it looked like a three-tiered wedding cake. The rooms of its upper floors were high-ceilinged and flooded with light, and, until now, Michael O'Meara had never been in the basement, where the space was very different—functional, unglamorous, with humming fluorescent light and an odd smell of earthen damp and disinfectant. Yet, Lee Roy Sears was delighted with his studio, which he showed to Michael with childlike pride and enthusiasm. At Hunsford, he'd had only rudimentary art supplies; here, he already had a small treasure of sketching pads, charcoal and pastel crayons, acrylic paints, a half-dozen brushes, sculpting clay, unframed canvases, an easel, a workbench—"It's, like, I'm *dreaming* this, I'm in the jungle burning up with fever dreaming *this!*"

There was a simplicity and directness in Sears that touched Michael's heart. Indeed, he reminded Michael of his sons, chattering excitedly of their birthday presents the other day, showing them to Daddy.

As Sears showed Michael his "new work"—pages of smudged charcoal sketches, some small, clumsily executed humanoid figures in clay—Michael observed him out of the corner of his eye. Lee Roy Sears!—was this the man whose life he'd helped save?—the man with whom, off and on, he'd corresponded? In his imagination, Michael had been envisioning Sears as a sort of brother—well, not a brother exactly, that was a bit far-fetched, but a sort of—disadvantaged cousin; a distant relative of his approximate age who'd had bad luck even as he, Michael, had had good luck. (It was in the nature of "luck," the very principle of luck, that it is undeserved. This, Michael O'Meara fervently believed, even as he believed yet more fervently in our ability to remake ourselves; in the principle of free will.) Yet, though Lee Roy Sears was thirty-nine years old, only a year younger than Michael, he looked much younger; with his sallow, slightly blemished skin, his dark damp shining eyes, his narrow shoulders and hips and keyed-up mannerisms, he might have been a precocious teenager, a street kid, battered, but hopeful.

No doubt about it, Sears *was* ugly. The waxy-pale bony planes of his forehead, with its suggestion of something reptilian; his long thin nose with its oversized nostrils; the teeth oversized too, as if there were too many for his narrow jaws, with a perceptible bituminous stain—ugly, yet in a way curiously appealing, even attractive. Perhaps it was his energy—his wiry, tensed-up body, seemingly small-boned, yet with hard tight compact little muscles. Even his slight limp—Sears favored his left knee, injured in the war—gave him a rakish off-balance charm.

To meet the O'Mearas, Lee Roy had dressed up a bit, and combed his lank lusterless black hair with a pungent-smelling oil; he'd shaved with an uncertain hand, scraping the underside of his jaw in a half-dozen places. He wore a white shirt that needed laundering, and a pumpkin-and-brown plaid Dacron jacket; a necktie of some greasy green material, inexpertly knotted at his throat; nondescript brown-gray trousers that hung baggy at buttocks, knees, ankles. His brown shoes had not been polished in years and were cracked and waterstained, yet sported tassels. His fingernails were ridged with dirt and clay, yet he wore a signet ring on his left hand, onyx, or plastic resembling onyx. Michael winced, thinking of Gina. She had a habit of cruelly, and irrevocably, dismissing people on sight, if they were not the right sort of people.

"This one, *he's* gonna be real important, I got a strong feeling, but he isn't exactly born, yet," Lee Roy Sears was saying earnestly, holding out for Michael's appreciation one of the misshapen humanoid figures, meant perhaps to depict a man, a wounded soldier?—contorted in agony. "If he's born too soon he won't last."

Michael stared at the clay figure, smiling, admiring, not certain what was expected of him. As with his sons, who frequently showed Daddy their drawings, schoolwork, ingenious little inventions, Michael expressed unqualified enthusiasm; but, with Sears, he had no questions to ask. He was thinking of the evening ahead.

Sears laughed harshly, baring his teeth, and said, in a tone that sounded almost warning, "Yah. Like, if he's born too soon he won't last. None of 'em do, Mr. O'Meara."

Again he paused, and again there came that sudden high-pitched giggle, "—I mean t'say, 'Michael.' "

"MUST YOU BRING THIS 'Sears' home, Michael?" Gina had asked, pronouncing the name as if it were a rare disease; and Michael had said, "It's just this once, Gina, I promise." And Gina had said, with her usual keen, yet somehow misplaced, logic, "But, why, really?—if it's 'just this once,' what difference can it possibly make to the man?"

Michael had said, "I want Lee Roy Sears to feel that someone cares for him, that he isn't completely alone."

"He has his parole officer, doesn't he?"

"Really, Gina!"

"—and Clyde, and the staff at the Center?"

"Clyde won't have time for him, you know that. He'll chat with him a few times, and for publicity's sake he'll pose with him, but—you know Clyde."

"I know that he's a busy man. And so are we all—busy." Gina poked Michael playfully, yet a bit roughly, in the soft flesh at his waist. "So are *you*, especially."

"Not so busy I don't have time for crucial matters."

"If you took Lee Roy Sears out to dinner sometime to a nice restaurant in Putnam—not in Mount Orion, he'd feel awkward I think, but Putnam—wouldn't that do just as well?"

"Gina, honey, I want Lee Roy Sears to meet you and the boys—my family." Michael paused. He was reluctant to tell her, for

fear of seeming absurdly vain, or sentimental, that he wanted Sears
to have the experience of seeing a normal, happy American family;
he wanted Sears to realize that such normalcy and happiness were
well within his own reach.

As if reading her husband's mind, and, as on the tennis court,
leaping slyly ahead, Gina said, "Next, you'll be wanting to introduce
Lee Roy Sears to a 'nice girl.' You'll be wanting *me* to arrange it."

Seeing the expression on Michael's face, Gina laughed, and
sighed, a charming sign of surrender in her, saying, as if this had
been the issue all along, "Well, I won't have time to cook on
Wednesday, I have a luncheon meeting, then a tennis lesson. If you
and your guest won't mind, I'll just pick something up at ———"
naming Mount Orion's premier gourmet food store, where, in any
case, Gina shopped at least once a week.

Michael thanked her and kissed her. He'd known she would
come around: she always did.

THE FIRST ODD THING: as Michael O'Meara and Lee Roy Sears left
the basement area, ascending to a door at the top of a flight of stairs,
Sears stopped dead in his tracks, and waited for Michael to open
the door; belatedly, Michael realized that Sears had forgotten he was
no longer in prison, and had to wait for Michael, his guard, to
unlock the door!

A painful moment, but Sears didn't seem to notice.

The foyer of the Dumont Center was airy and spacious, with
tall amber strips of glass, and portable white walls upon which were
hung photographs by a local photographer; a half-dozen people stood
about looking at the exhibit. As Sears crossed the foyer with Michael, his limp became more pronounced and he seemed to be
shrinking in upon himself, head bowed, shoulders hunched, a hand
raised in front of his face as if to shield it from the curious glances
of strangers—who, were it not for Sears's peculiar behavior, would
never have taken note of him.

Two or three of the visitors were acquaintances of the O'Mearas,
and Michael exchanged cheerful greetings with them, while not
slackening his pace, indeed making an effort not to embarrass Sears
by stopping to talk. He sensed how desperately the parolee wanted
to get away.

Yet, outside, in the warm, waning light, Sears flinched; blinked rapidly; his hooded eyes darting about, like those of a nocturnal animal thrust into the light. He fumbled at a pocket and withdrew a pair of wire-rimmed sunglasses which he fitted nervously into place. In the parking lot, he started as a car gunned its motor nearby; in Michael's gleaming white Mazda, as Michael turned the key in the ignition, he was frightened by the sudden mechanical action of the shoulder belt as it swung up and onto him—"Jesus! What the hell!"

Michael said quickly, "It's all right, Lee Roy. Just the safety belt—federal regulations."

Sears adjusted his sunglasses, which had been knocked askew by the belt. He joked, lamely, his face coloring, "Huh!—thought it was a *snake.*"

Several times during the brief drive to Glenway Circle, Lee Roy Sears flinched and froze in his seat, though Michael, always a careful driver, was exceedingly careful tonight, and there was no question of an accident. His reactions reminded Michael of the "startle reflexes" normal in an infant, and he tried not to be annoyed. He understood Sears's condition, which was as much neurological as psychological: after so many years in a limited and controlled environment, Sears's brain was struggling to monitor the barrage of stimuli of the ordinary world. Pearce Pharmaceuticals manufactured drugs to block excessive stimuli, thus to diminish the anxiety such stimuli evoked, but it was far better to confront them naturally, as Sears was presumably doing.

As they turned onto Glenway Circle, and Michael slowed his speed even more, driving now at no more than twenty miles an hour, Sears made an effort to relax, and murmured, embarrassed, "Guess I haven't been in a car in a long time."

Michael said, with an ebullience that surprised him, "You'll get used to it—you'll get used to everything. In a few months, maybe you'll be driving again, yourself."

Sears only grunted, a vague doubtful assent.

Then it was Michael O'Meara's neighborhood that intimidated Lee Roy Sears: this splendid semi-rural suburban landscape of custom-designed homes, each on a large, wooded, sloping lot, partly hidden from the graveled road and worth, even in the deflated market of spring 1991, above five hundred thousand dollars. So long had Michael lived on Glenway Circle, so typically preoccupied were his thoughts as he drove this familiar route, he'd long since ceased to see his neighborhood at all, let alone to gaze at it with eyes of admiration, astonishment: why, he lived *here!* he, Michael O'Meara, a man of no exceptional intelligence or talent, in his own severe estimation at least, a man who surely did not deserve such a reward—*he* lived *here!* The O'Mearas' handsome white colonial was at the end of the gracefully curving cul-de-sac, set atop a hill and surrounded by a virtual forest of evergreens and tall newly budded deciduous trees; the sky beyond was a rich pellucid blue, as in a Renaissance painting. *How beautiful! How was it possible!* As Lee Roy Sears stared as if struck dumb, hunching his head down between his shoulders like a turtle trying to retract into its shell, Michael O'Meara seemed to be seeing his property through the other's awed eyes. He felt a thrill of intense emotion: joy, triumph, guilt.

He murmured apologetically, driving up the lane, "It *is* a bit large, for a family of only four."

Lee Roy Sears simply stared.

AND THEN THERE WAS Gina.

"Why, hello!"—as if, smiling her dazzling white smile, lovely eyes widened in welcome, she were genuinely surprised to be meeting *him:* a hostess's flattering attitude, so finely bred in Gina as in most of the women of her social circle as to constitute not hypocrisy but instinct.

Michael introduced Lee Roy Sears to Gina, very much relieved that Gina had decided to be nice; and tactfully ignored, in the flurry of first exchanges, Sears's gaping stare—at Gina, at the beautifully furnished living room, at the view from the glass wall at the rear, at Gina.

It *was* a gaping stare, both comical and touching: Sears's lower jaw had dropped.

But Gina handled the situation masterfully, drawing Lee Roy Sears forward, asking would he like to have a seat (on the curving oystershell sofa facing the rear, with its view of trees, shrubs, the pond below), would he like a drink?—wine, perhaps?

Sears blinked at Gina for several seconds, as if trying to interpret her words. He removed his wire-rimmed sunglasses and fumbled

slipping them in a pocket. "Thank you, Mrs. O'Meara, but I"—
and here his voice dropped in shame—"I can't drink. I mean, I'm
not allowed." He paused, stretching his lips in a woebegone smile.
"I mean—as long as I'm on parole."

"Really!" Gina exclaimed, as if she'd never heard of such a
thing, and shared Lee Roy Sears's discomfort. "They can dictate to
you whether you're allowed to drink or not?—in the privacy of a
home?"

Sears nodded glumly. He shifted his narrow shoulders inside
the gaudy pumpkin-and-brown plaid jacket. "Sure can, ma'am. That's
one of the conditions of my parole."

Gina looked at Michael, incensed. *Is* that the law, Michael?"

Michael said, "I suppose it is, if the"—he paused, delicately—
"parolee has a history of alcohol abuse, substance abuse, that sort of
thing. Lee Roy, can I get you something else? Ginger ale, club soda?"

Lee Roy Sears mumbled, "Yah, that's fine. Anything's fine.
Thank you."

Sears limped to the sofa and swung himself around, sitting with
excessive care. His skin was mottled as with hives. How the
O'Mearas navigated the first phase of this excruciatingly awkward
visit neither would be able to recall afterward: it seemed to have
been Gina's valiant effort primarily, which then inspired Michael,
as, on the stage, when something has gone wrong, one supremely
capable actor or actress can inspire the rest, and the scene is saved.

So, Gina chattered; and Michael joined in. Lee Roy Sears replied to their friendly questions in monosyllables, now and then
interrupting himself to cast a floundering look about, and to mum-
ble, "—real nice of you, *real* nice—"

And, "—never set foot in a house like *this*—"

And, "—*real* grateful for your kindness, Mrs. O'Meara, Mr.
O'Meara—uh! I mean 'Michael'!"

At which Gina smiled another of her dazzling smiles, insisting,
"Yes, Lee Roy, but, you know, you must call me *Gina*. 'Mrs.
O'Meara' is my mother-in-law, who lives in Palm Beach."

This graceful remark, poor Lee Roy Sears did not grasp at all.

Gina went off to fetch the twins, bringing them back with a
flourish: she rarely looked more radiant than when introducing her
beautiful little boys to company. "Lee Roy, here's Joel—*is* it Joel,

mmm?—Joel, say hi! to Lee Roy Sears. And this is Kenny—come *on*, honey, say hi! to Lee Roy Sears." The boys stumbled reluctantly forward, big-eyed, unsmiling. Gina chided gently, "Joel, Kenny, this is Daddy's friend Lee Roy Sears, please can't you say he*llo?*"

But Lee Roy Sears stared as silently at the boys as they at him. Where with Gina he'd seemed overwhelmed by her beauty, with Joel and Kenny he seemed genuinely alarmed, frightened. His hand holding the glass of ginger ale visibly trembled.

The sudden thought came to Michael O'Meara, as if out of the other man's very consciousness, *He has killed children this age, has he!—in Vietnam.*

An absurd thought, which Michael immediately rejected.

He urged the boys forward, to shake hands with Mr. Sears, and so they did, shyly, yet sweetly; and the painful moment passed, or seemed to. The boys did their best to smile at Daddy's strange-looking friend, who was so very different from Daddy's and Mommy's other friends, and Lee Roy Sears made an effort too, to overcome his discomfort. He stretched his pale lips in a ghastly smile, hunched forward, saying, "You're—uh—twins?—that's fun, I guess?—yah?—like at school, screwing up your teachers, huh?—"

Joel giggled suddenly. Kenny, whose thumb had crept into the corner of his mouth, giggled too.

Gina said, chiding, "Boys, don't be *silly.*"

Michael said, "They hardly think of themselves as twins, just as brothers. That's the main thing."

"They were seven years old, just last week," Gina said proudly. "Weren't you, fellas?"

Lee Roy Sears looked from one child to the other. Joel to the left, Kenny to the right. Joel wore a blue shirt, Kenny a green plaid shirt. Joel's hair whorled clockwise, and Kenny's counterclockwise— or was it precisely the opposite?

"*I* was a twin, I'd have a helluva time!" Lee Roy Sears said crudely. He glanced at Gina, and at Michael, and sensed that he'd made a blunder. Quickly he amended, "I mean—when I was a kid. Not *now.*"

As if she'd only now thought of it, Gina exclaimed in a childlike voice, "Oh, I know: let's all go outside, while it's still light. Dinner won't be ready for a few more minutes. I bet Lee Roy would enjoy seeing our pond, wouldn't you, Lee Roy?"

"Yes, ma'am!" Lee Roy Sears said with undisguised relief.

Michael unlatched the sliding door to the terrace, and they all went outside, Lee Roy Sears limping, the twins running ahead, the elder O'Mearas hand in hand. Michael had had a quick glass of wine and was feeling rather festive. "It's strange for me, on a week-day, to be home so early," he said, and Gina said quickly, as much for Lee Roy Sears to overhear as for Michael to hear, "Yes, it's a shame—you never get home before seven. So *this* is an occasion."

It was a clear, fresh, fragrant day, smelling of last year's leaves underfoot, a sodden, earthen odor, delicious to the nostrils. Lee Roy Sears limped along energetically, blinking and staring at the tall trees, the many shrubs, the flowerbeds, a pair of white wrought iron chairs set picturesquely above the pond; and at the pond itself, brimming from recent rains, dark, lustrous, its surface relatively clear of leaves and other debris. Sears paused to draw in a deep shuddering breath. He murmured, as if to himself, "—*Real* nice!"

The boys were running ahead, a bit wildly, giggling and nudg-ing each other. Michael watched them closely, with a father's pride, seeing them through the prism of Lee Roy Sears's eyes: his sons.

His, and Gina's.

And there was Gina, lovely Gina, slender in her aqua print Laura Ashley dress, a rope of amber beads around her neck, her pale hair shining. She wore high-heeled alligator pumps whose nar-row heels sank into the soft earth, so she had to lean on Michael's arm, glancing up at him with a sly inscrutable smile not meant for their guest to see. That afternoon, at the club, Gina had played tennis on an outdoor court for the first time this season, mixed doubles with a friend (had it been Dwight Schatten?—Michael couldn't recall whom she'd mentioned), and others.

Sometimes, after a siege of serious tennis, Gina was distracted and irritable; today, she was in high spirits. The games must have gone well.

Lee Roy Sears drew a deep shuddering breath, and said, "The air here is sure *nice.*"

"Is it!" Gina exclaimed.

Lee Roy Sears cast a wistful sidelong glance at her, which Michael couldn't help but notice.

As they descended the hill, the pond opened out before them horizontally, as if mysteriously, considerably larger than it appeared from the house. Underfoot, the earth was increasingly marshy. Red-winged blackbirds broke from cover. Jays cried in the near distance. Joel and Kenny explored the farther side of the pond, peering into the water, grabbing at broken cattails and rushes. There was a curious, not entirely agreeable wildness in the boys, down here, which Michael had noticed in the past: as if the very smell of the pond, that dark, brackish, sweetly sour odor, set them off. "Joel, Kenny—be careful," Michael called. "Don't get your feet wet."

In a single murmurous voice the boys said, "Okay, Daddy."

Lee Roy Sears was marveling at the pond, in such simple terms—"real nice"—"*real* pretty"—he was sounding a bit simple-minded.

Was the man simple-minded?—had drugs, or alcohol, or his traumatic past, taken their toll?

Michael stood on the bank of the pond, his pond, and cast his eye about his property, back up to the house, *his* house—and felt again that surge of powerful emotion, part gratitude, part guilt. For how had *he* come to be here, and not, for instance, Lee Roy Sears?—whose mother had abandoned him as an infant and who had no family at all?

It was late afternoon and the sky was rapidly fading. The pond's surface had become a perfect mirror, dark, and opaque; you could not see beyond it. Michael had years ago stocked the pond with ornamental carp, gold, gold-spangled, black, pale orange, but they had bred in such a way that black took precedence: only a few specimens of lighter colors remained, amid a quick-darting school of bladelike black fish, rarely visible except in the most intense sunlight. At the moment, there was not the slightest hint of life below the surface of the water. The weedy bottom might have inches below, or many feet.

Michael was standing on the bank beside a willow tree, grasping a limb, leaning over the water, musing at his reflection. He wore his weekday clothes: a suit, a necktie, a good shirt. But his head looked round and foolish in the water, his face ruddy as a pumpkin.

The water trembled, rippled, his reflection seemed about to dissolve. Lee Roy Sears limped over to stand beside him, and there appeared suddenly his reflection too, bobbing beside Michael's. His head was not so round as Michael's and his face not so ruddy, in fact a lurid waxy white, his eyes black as mere holes. Yet he was smiling— grinning. "How deep is it, Mr. O'Meara?—you-all swim in it?"

Michael said, "It isn't a pond for swimming, it's too shallow at shore, and weedy. See those cattails?"

This inspired Gina to tell the story (already it had become a comical anecdote, of the kind relayed at Mount Orion parties) of how poor Michael had tried to clear the pond himself and had nearly broken his back. "Can you imagine!" Gina laughed, stroking Michael's arm. Her manner was an invitation for Lee Roy Sears to laugh with her, but Sears was only puzzled, looking from Gina to Michael. He quite touched Michael's heart by saying, naively, "You want me to help you dredge it, Mr. O'Meara?—just say when."

Michael said, "That's very generous of you, Lee Roy, but—"

"Nah, it's nothing," Lee Roy said vehemently, "c'pared to what you did for *me.*"

"—I've already arranged for a professional crew to do it, next week."

As if he had not heard this, or hadn't absorbed its meaning, Lee Roy Sears announced importantly, for Gina to overhear as well as for Michael to hear, "Yah, I'm pretty good with my hands, doing jobs like this. Maybe I don't look it, I guess I look sorta runty right now—but I *am!*"

OF THE REMAINDER OF that initial visit of Lee Roy Sears to his house, Michael O'Meara would afterward remember only isolated moments.

For instance: the twins were to eat their dinner in the kitchen, overseen by Marita, and as they were about to leave the company of the adults Gina hugged them, and coaxed them prettily, "Okay, fellas, say goodnight to Mr. Sears," and shyly the boys murmured, in near-unison, "G'night, Mr. Sears," each peering up at Sears through his eyelashes, as Sears, smiling lopsidedly, said, "Yah, g'night, great to meet ya!" It would have ended at that, but suddenly Joel— unless it was Kenny: Michael wasn't sure—piped up shrilly, "Mr.

Sears, how come you were in *jail?*" and his twin giggled wildly, and
Gina exclaimed, "Joel! Kenny! Boys! For *shame!*"

Marita appeared and led the boys off. Gina and Michael apologized, both quite profoundly embarrassed, but Lee Roy Sears
shrugged and said, "Hell, it's a good question, wish *I* knew the
answer."

Then, as Gina finished preparations for the meal, and Michael
and Lee Roy moved about the living room with fresh drinks (they
were too restless to sit down), Lee Roy's attention leapt to the
O'Mearas' art, which he had not noticed previously. There were
several oil paintings, some pastel drawings, a half-dozen lithographs,
two small but striking bronze heads on the mantel. Lee Roy plied
Michael with questions that were both naive and shrewd: who were
the artists? were they famous? were they alive, or dead? how much
did the works cost? Michael was bemused at his companion's tight-
jawed intensity and answered as best he could.

"Most of these works are Gina's acquisitions," he said. "She
knows people in art—in Manhattan and Philadelphia. I trust to her
judgment. *I* only know what I think I like."

"D'you like *this?*" Lee Roy asked derisively, of a large abstract
canvas of dense, swirling, muted colors on a white background. The
oil painting was by a prestigious American, only recently deceased;
Michael had always suspected that Gina had paid its considerable
price because others in Mount Orion collected the artist, and because this particular canvas harmonized so well with the living room
furniture. "—too fucking *soft,*" Lee Roy muttered.

This was the first time Michael had heard Lee Roy Sears speak
in quite that tone. He was glad that Gina was out of earshot.

"I like it well enough," Michael said, an edge of irony in his
voice. "You'll find, I'm not hard to please."

AND THEN THERE WAS dinner.

A swift, tattered meal, as it turned out, for though Gina had
bought a delicious beef bourguignon, Lee Roy Sears ate nervously
and compulsively, turning his head to one side as he chewed, like a
voracious animal. He seemed to know that he was being offensive,
for he several times murmured, "Sorry!—forgot my table manners!"
and "Sorry!—so *hungry!*" The O'Mearas glanced at each other, with

neutral expressions—had their guest not had a decent meal in thirteen years?—or longer?

Gina, with her usually infallible hostess's instinct, tried to draw
Lee Roy out in conversation, asking him questions of a kind that
might not embarrass—how did he like his fellow tenants in the halfway house, for instance?—but Lee Roy merely mumbled or grunted
answers. An oily film coated his forehead, his eyes shone with moisture. He panted as he ate. He paused mid-meal to swallow down a
large white capsule with a mouthful of water. (Medication? Michael
wondered. An antipsychotic, or merely a tranquilizer?) When he
wasn't avidly eating, Lee Roy compulsively adjusted his plate, his
water goblet, his cutlery, the tiny silver salt and pepper shakers before him; even, though they were scarcely out of alignment, the
silver candleholders Gina had placed in the center of the table.

"Sorry!—*sorry!*" Lee Roy muttered.

Gina, whose appetite was fickle at the best of times, seemed to
have lost all desire to continue eating, in the presence of Lee Roy
Sears's appetite, yet, nonetheless, as if out of a female martyrdom,
politely offered her guest more: more beef, more rice, more vegeta-
bles, more bread. "Thanks, Mrs. O'Meara!" Lee Roy panted. He
seemed incapable of stopping himself from heaping his plate with a
trembling hand, and from beginning to eat anew. But a minute later,
in the midst of vigorous chewing, he paused, with a stricken expression, hunched toward the table, and softly moaned; and again the
O'Mearas exchanged a glance—Michael pained and apologetic, his
face reddening; Gina quite inscrutable.

Lee Roy gasped, "Oh!—God!—excuse me!"

He had eaten too much, and too fast; his shrunken stomach
could not accommodate such a quantity of rich food; he staggered
from the table like a dying man, bent nearly double, a hand to his
mouth, face deathly white. Michael tossed down his napkin and
dealt with the emergency by hauling Lee Roy to the guest bathroom
in the hall—not a moment too soon.

When Michael returned to the dining room, fighting down a
pang of nausea himself, he saw Gina sitting with her hand over her
eyes, utterly still.

He said, "Gina, my God, I'm so sorry! I'll get rid of him as
soon as he's well enough to leave."

Gina looked up at Michael, startled. Her lovely forehead creased in worry. "But, poor Lee Roy! He's so *sweet*, and he's so *helpless!* He isn't our age at all, he's just a *child! What will become of him?*"

Now it was Michael O'Meara's turn to stare in amazement at his wife. Of all the remarks he might have expected from her, these were the least likely.

THOROUGHLY EXHAUSTED, THOUGH IT was not yet nine o'clock in the evening, Michael drove Lee Roy Sears to his residence in Putnam, New Jersey: since Sears had no idea of his surroundings, and could give Michael only the street address of the house, Michael got lost several times and had to ask directions. Beside him, limp, giving off a breathy stench of vomit, the parolee moaned, "—sorry, oh God!—" but was of little aid otherwise.

A child. What will become of him.

Finally, Michael located the halfway house, which was of shabby yellow brick, in appearance rather like a flophouse, and in a district of taverns, pool halls, all-night diners, pawnshops.

He helped Lee Roy Sears out of his car and walked him up the rickety steps of the house and into the dim-lit foyer. Sears swayed like a drunken man. He was sick, but not too sick to fix his benefactor with damp doggy pleading eyes and to seize his hands in both his hands. "Thank you, Mr. O'Meara! Oh God! Jeez! From the bottom of my heart!"

Michael gagged at Sears's breath and discreetly extricated himself from his grip. "Goodnight, Lee Roy!"

Out on the sidewalk, eager to escape, he heard, from inside the house, the other's faint, apologetic cry, "—I mean *'Michael.'* "

3

"Oh!—it's so sad. Those *eyes.*"

Gina O'Meara was staring at the gnomish little humanoid figure Lee Roy Sears had given her, a bit reluctantly, to examine; and,
to be truthful, Gina did not know what to make of it. She prided
herself upon having a natural eye for art, and she had many times
been complimented on her exquisite taste, by gallery owners who
had sold her overpriced works, but—*this?* This misshapen little thing
with the pop eyes?

It was meant to be a man, about eight inches long, twisted as
if in agony, with a crude, distorted face, gaping mouth, arms and
legs spread, a shallow cavity where his insides should have been;
fortunately, there was no groin at all. Made of still-damp, funky-
smelling clay, it was oddly heavy, and nasty somehow. But Gina
continued to smile.

Lee Roy Sears stood close by, breathing nasally, flexing his clay-
covered fingers, eager and expectant. Gina had come to fetch him

for their afternoon of shopping and errands, but he'd seemed at first to have forgotten she was coming, so absorbed had he been in his work—this "sculpting."

(The ugly little figure, so inexpertly fashioned, was, Gina saw, one of a dozen similar figures, lying about like discarded fetuses on Sears's workbench. Variations on a theme, but what clumsy variations, and what an unpromising theme!)

"—yes, those *eyes*. Remarkable!"

Lee Roy Sears, face mottled as if in extreme embarrassment, took the figure from Gina's hands and set it with exaggerated care among the others. He mumbled something Gina could not decipher—she hoped it wasn't that tiresome refrain of his, *"Sorry—!"*

"Well!" Gina said briskly, smiling her dazzling smile generally about the room—why on earth hadn't Clyde given this poor man one of the upstairs workspaces, with some decent light and a view of the sky? "We'd better go, Lee Roy, it's getting late. I have to pick Joel and Kenny up at three-thirty, you know, at their school—"

Washing up at a tiny sink in a corner, Lee Roy Sears said, not for the first time, "I sure don't want to trouble you, ma'am—"

Gina laughed, "—'Ma'am'?—*what?*"

"—Mrs. O'Meara—"

"I told you, Lee Roy, 'Mrs. O'Meara' is my mother-in-law, and she lives, not very happily I'm afraid, in Palm Beach, Florida."

Lee Roy made an effort to laugh at this remark, but it sounded more like coughing.

"I told you too, Lee Roy, that it isn't any 'trouble.' I'm happy to do what I can, to help you"—she paused discreetly—"adjust."

She added, "And it's 'Gina'—!"

Running water at the faucets, Lee Roy Sears probably didn't hear, so Gina let it pass. There was something elevating and even dramatic about the parolee calling her "Mrs. O'Meara" with that look in his eyes of helpless adoration, respect, awe.

Which, of course, Gina tactfully pretended not to see. Or, in any case, did not acknowledge.

Disdainfully, Gina wiped her hands on a damp paper towel, hoping the funky smell wouldn't accrue. She was eager to get out of this depressing basement and into the bright clear spring air; she was eager to get into those Mount Orion stores where she felt so much at home.

Amateur efforts at art embarrassed her, in any case. She had gone through a brief phase when Joel and Kenny were small and she'd been hungry for independence, self-expression, a "creative" outlet for her pent-up emotions, during which time she had signed up for the popular ceramics course at the Dumont Center. For a while it had been delightful, and challenging, yes and *fun* ("Art should be fun!" their bearded instructor claimed)—Gina and the other novices had not fashioned pots out of clay, of course, but had merely busied themselves applying colored glazes to factory-made greenware, which their instructor then fired, dramatically, in a kiln. He'd assured Gina that she had genuine talent for ceramics, he'd seemed truly impressed with her work, but, unfortunately, Gina's busy social life intruded, and an intense romantic friendship with a Mount Orion physician, and she'd had to drop out of the course.

Her three or four efforts, all bowls, were prominently displayed in the house. Visitors frequently complimented Gina on them, especially if they were told that Gina had done them.

So Gina held in reserve, as in a secret compartment of her handsome Gucci purse, the promise of "art"—someday, when the twins were older, she might very well try again. Not glazing greenware, but real art, like Georgia O'Keeffe, or Helen Frankenthaler, or, what was that sculptress's name, the one with the turban and the false eyelashes?—Louise Nevelson.

For the moment, however, Gina O'Meara would content herself with making the rounds of the Mount Orion stores.

FIRST, GINA TOOK THE parolee to The Village Beauty Salon, where she asked Nikki, the unisex hair stylist who did Gina's own hair, if something could be done with Lee Roy's—"Just look, his hair is so sort of chopped-looking, and shaved-up-the-back," Gina said, "like a Marine recruit from the Ozarks!" As Lee Roy Sears, stony-faced, flushed, sat in the stylist's chair, staring at himself in a three-way mirror flecked with gold, Nikki fussed, and frowned, and made dramatic swipes with his steel comb, but came to the conclusion, more disappointing to Gina than to Lee Roy, that, until his hair grew out a bit, nothing much could be done—"Bring him back, Mrs. O'Meara, in maybe three weeks."

It was a measure of Nikki's extreme sophistication—he'd come to Mount Orion from a West Broadway salon—that, though he stared at Lee Roy Sears with clearly repelled fascination, he did not inquire of Gina who he was.

Only once did the men's eyes chance to lock, in the gold-flecked mirror, and, seeing something in Lee Roy Sears's eyes that must have impressed him, Nikki looked quickly away.

As Lee Roy Sears limped out to the street, Gina pressed a twenty-dollar bill into Nikki's palm. "We'll be back in three weeks," she said.

With a strained smile, Nikki returned the bill to Gina. "Until then, thank you, Mrs. O'Meara."

Next, The Boulevard Men's Shoes.

In this plush-carpeted gentlemen's store, amid numerous mirrors and displays of highly polished, beautifully designed shoes, Gina oversaw the purchase of a new pair of shoes for Lee Roy Sears, black-leather, Italian-made, expensive—despite Sears's faint protest that he could not afford new shoes right now, let alone shoes that cost $95.98. Gina seemed not to hear, giving instructions to the youngish salesman: "Very good, we'll take these, they seem to fit perfectly. And—would you dispose of the old ones, please?"

Lee Roy Sears opened his mouth to protest further, but the salesman had already tossed his old brown shoes into a shoebox and was carrying them off.

Warmly, Gina said, "Now we're on our way!"

Outside, Lee Roy Sears limped along beside her, self-conscious in his gleaming new shoes, which contrasted so dramatically with his baggy work pants and plaid jacket; he tried to tell Gina that, with his low-paying part-time work at the Putnam Municipal Garage, and so many unexpected expenses, he didn't know when he would be able to repay her. Gina said quickly, as if embarrassed, that there was no hurry—"Whenever you can, Lee Roy. The important thing is that you feel comfortable in the world. That, you know, you look as if you *belong* in the world." She paused. She was hoping that Lee Roy Sears would understand that he need never repay the O'Mearas, but she hesitated to say so. She supposed that the parolee, for all his humility, had his pride. He might not want outright charity.

There followed then in quick succession The English Shop, Carlisle's Clothiers, and The Esquire, where Michael O'Meara, under Gina's expert guidance, bought most of his clothes; then they went to Henle's, Mount Orion's opulent department store, where virtually every salesclerk knew Gina O'Meara; then, since it was on their way to the car, The village Art & Photographics Supplies Company. Then, suddenly inspired, Gina said, "We should make appointments for you to have check-ups too—with a doctor, a dentist, maybe an optician?" and Lee Roy Sears said, "They take care of that kinda stuff in prison, Mrs. O'Meara, that's one thing they do do," and Gina said, skeptically, "But public health practitioners can't be trusted, can they?"

Fortunately, it was time for lunch.

A fashionably late lunch, at two—in Mount Orion, only working men and women ate at noon, and few of these could afford typical restaurant prices. "You'll love The Café," Gina said, "—I go there all the time." When Gina entered, with Lee Roy Sears in tow, quizzical glances flew in their direction from numerous tables, but, though Gina O'Meara happily acknowledged her friends and acquaintances, she made no effort to introduce her odd-looking companion to them. She asked for a table in an alcove, with a tinted glass wall and potted ferns, from which vantage point she could sip a glass of white wine and gaze into the interior of the restaurant, or out into the street, and not be seen. What bliss!

Tactfully, she seemed not to notice the haste with which Lee Roy Sears swallowed down one of his white capsules, as soon as a waiter poured ice water into his glass.

Nor did she allow herself to be annoyed by his nervous mannerisms, as he read, or tried to read, the menu; shifting his shoulders inside his jacket, and peering from beneath his heavy eyebrows, as if anxious that he was being watched. Again, he compulsively straightened his plates, his cutlery, his water glass; he fussed interminably with his chair, moving it in tight little jerks close to the table, so that, finally, he was squeezed uncomfortably against the edge of the table, his narrow shoulders ramrod straight. Gina supposed he had not been in a restaurant for thirteen years—had not

been in a woman's company, perhaps, for thirteen years. She was
sympathetic, she wasn't about to judge. Her heart opened to this
poor, sad, deprived man, a cast-off, a veteran, a victim; even, of all
injustices, an American Indian, repudiated, it seemed, by his own
people. She said, laying a hand on his arm, her pink-polished nails
startling against the cheap fabric of his jacket, "Lee Roy, order anything you like, please!—this is a celebration."

He said, in his nasal, high-pitched voice, "Uh—maybe you
could order for me, Mrs. O'Meara?"

It was to be a strained hour, Gina O'Meara's lunch with Lee
Roy Sears, in The Café.

Gina chattered and asked questions; Lee Roy answered in monosyllables, or not at all. He continued to fuss with his plates, his
chair. He drank several glasses of water in succession, as if he were
burning with fever, or in the grip of a manic attack. He alternated
between gobbling his food and not eating it at all—laying his knife
and fork chastely across his plate, and waiting. Beads of sweat formed
on his forehead. His darkly bright eyes, the eyes of a nocturnal
animal who has ventured into the light, fastened themselves helplessly upon Gina O'Meara, who basked in such attention even as,
with a part of her mind, she found it a bit unnerving.

She managed to extract from Lee Roy Sears the fact that, before he'd arrived in Putnam, his suitcase had been stolen from him
in the New York Port Authority: thus he'd badly needed the clothes
and other items Gina had bought for him. (Surely he needed more?—
socks, underwear, toiletries, that sort of thing. Gina made a mental
note.) She learned too, though clearly he did not want to expand
upon it, that he'd been wounded at a place called Phu Cuong. (Of
which Gina had never heard, though she nodded sympathetically, as
if the very sound of the words evoked a common cause.) She learned
that, though he'd been arrested, tried, and sentenced to death for a
crime he had not committed, though, in prison for thirteen years,
he'd been abused, beaten, humiliated, forced at times to eat filthy
food crawling with beetles, he did not harbor any bitterness—why,
none at all.

Because he had his art.

Because he had his God-given talent.

Because he knew his destiny.

Because he believed in God. *A God Who exacted justice from man, in the end.*

Gina, wide-eyed, sipping white wine, murmured breathily, "Oh yes, oh *yes!* That's so."

Lee Roy Sears took up his fork again, and chewed, and swallowed, and ate hungrily, even as Gina, who never ordered anything other than light salads for lunch, and rarely finished these, picked about in the leafy greens on her plate. She was feeling—ah, what *was* she feeling? That delicious, innocent elation that comes of sipping white wine on a near-empty stomach, in the tiniest, most measured of sips?

She noted that Lee Roy Sears's hands were shaking, more visibly now than when they'd first sat down. Impulsively she said, "Have a little of my wine, Lee Roy, please!—no one will see."

Lee Roy looked up at her, startled. "Uh—no thanks, Mrs. O'Meara."

"Oh, don't be silly, this is a celebration, come *on.*"

"Thank you, but—"

"They say—I mean Michael says—I mean I've heard him say—in brain research—they've discovered there's a sort of mechanism in the left brain that makes up theories, stories—you know, reasons things happen the way they do, and why we do things we do—and so," Gina said, gaily, giddily, scarcely knowing what she said except that Lee Roy Sears had again laid his fork down across his plate, and was sitting ramrod straight, listening, with the most intensity she'd ever seen in any man, "and so, we might as well just say, let's *do* what we want to do, and make up the reason later!"

Lee Roy Sears was shaking his head, saying, embarrassed, "Well, uh—it isn't just the parole violation, it's this medication I take—"

Gina pushed her wine glass in Lee Roy Sears's direction, with a sly conspiratorial smile. "It's just dry white wine, very low in calories," she said, giggling.

And: "You've paid your debt to society, what the hell."

"I'M AFRAID I CAN'T see you after all this afternoon," Gina O'Meara was saying into the telephone receiver, her voice husky with regret, "—something has come up. I'm so *sorry.*"

The man's voice at the other end of the line, deep, husky too, had that edge of abrasiveness to it that, these past few weeks, Gina had come to anticipate. It made her uneasy, it frightened her a bit.

Made her smile.

Saying quickly, "—a friend, a friend of Michael's actually, a favor I seem to have to do for him, yes it's a *him*, no he's no one you know, I didn't anticipate how long it would take—" She paused, and listened. She nodded. Frowned. "—Oh yes, darling, I know you're leaving for Tokyo in the morning, I know we won't see each other for a week—*two* weeks? Oh!—"

A group of men was passing by, one of them raised a hand in greeting, and Gina pursed her lips in a kissy sort of smile, and waved back: Jack Trimmer with some businessmen.

"—Oh but I *do*, you must know that I *do*, it's just that life is so complicated, and—I have more shopping to do this afternoon, and I have to pick up the boys at school, and—"

Gina had taken her gold compact out of her purse in order to inspect her lipstick, her mascara, the condition of her face powder: she was so skillfully made up, with a fine, reliable foundation, and a feathery-light loose powder, she looked, to the undiscerning eye at least, scarcely made up at all.

And much, much younger than her age.

Not that Gina O'Meara dwelled upon age. You are as old as you look, it's as simple as that.

Yes but she needed lipstick, so she applied it. Frowning, listening to the voice at the other end of the line. "—Oh that's unfair!—that's cruel!—'deliberately'?—now, 'deliberately'?—are you accusing me? I don't do *anything* deliberately!—" Seeing with a tiny thrill of satisfaction that her tube of lipstick was nearly depleted, which meant she was obliged to drop by Hélène's Cosmetics after they left The Café. And next door to Hélène's was Henri Bendel's.

Certainly Lee Roy Sears wouldn't mind, the man was so sweet.

It was time to hang up the phone but how to hang up, the voice at the other end was so unexpectedly emotional, so demanding, odd how others' emotions, especially over the phone, can leave us so unmoved, "—yes I *do*—I do feel the same way—but—life right now *is* so complicated—I'd like to say yes, but—I can't—I mean I can't promise—Oh! what! how *dare* you!"

And if, after Henri Bendel's, she dropped in at Bergdorf's (not drop in so much as cross through: the parking lot was on the other side of the store), if she was five minutes late picking up the twins, would it matter?—it would *not*. When Mommy's late you play in the playground.

Supervision at the Riverside School was absolutely reliable: children were never allowed to leave if they hadn't an adult to take them home.

"—I don't see how you can say that, in fact you hardly know me at all—you only *think* you do! Just like my husband!"

Sighing, pouting. Listening. As her gaze drifted to the interior of the restaurant, the familiar setting of hanging plants and hardwood floors and attractively dressed patrons and waiters in white uniforms, that pleasant buzzing-bustle, and, in a corner, Lee Roy Sears with his very dark, Indian-black hair, sitting alone and brooding.

At least, at this distance, it looked as if he were brooding.

At the other end of the line the voice droned on. Gina, the most gracious of women, was forced to interrupt, saying, with sudden vehemence, "—If that's how you feel, then—good*bye!*"

Tears brimming dangerously in her eyes, her heels staccato on the floor, Gina returned to the table; as incensed as if she'd truly felt the emotions she'd simulated. There, Lee Roy Sears was sitting staring at her as she approached, his face flushed too, damp mouth ajar. He'd drained not only Gina's glass of wine but the carafe as well.

"Let's go!" Gina exclaimed. "It's a lovely, lovely day!"

A QUICK VISIT TO Hélène's, and Henri Bendel's; across the street then to Bergdorf's; and, since it was so close, Xavier's Men's Clothing, for some Calvin Klein underwear, for Lee Roy Sears. And a Dior necktie, midnight blue silk. (To replace that hideous mud-green thing he insisted upon wearing.) You would think that by this time of the afternoon Lee Roy would be more relaxed, but no, poor man, to Gina's bemused exasperation he stood self-conscious, stricken, and mute, face oily with sweat, as Gina chatted with salesmen and -women. She introduced him as an artist-friend of hers and her husband's—"In fact, Lee Roy is artist-in-residence at the Dumont Center. He's primarily a *sculptor.*"

So stiff and forbidding was Lee Roy Sears, none of the sales-clerks proffered to shake his hand.

They must have made an odd pair, Gina O'Meara with Lee Roy Sears in tow, making the rounds of the better Mount Orion stores that day. Gina was in her element, glowing with pleasure. In such stores, as in similar stores in New York City, Gina was known by name; if not precisely by name, then by her species. She was the exemplary American woman shopper, not enormously wealthy, but well-to-do; educated, but not so educated as to cripple her enthusiasm; no longer, at the age of thirty-five (or was it thirty-six?), young, but strikingly young-looking; and fashionably thin. And how Gina put her trust in a litany of names, as her ancestors might have put theirs in a litany of saints' names: Gucci, Dior, Calvin Klein, Bill Blass, Yves Saint Laurent, Christian Lacroix, Princess Marcella Borghese, Lancôme, Estée Lauder . . . she was an avid subscriber to, if not an assiduous reader of, *Vanity Fair, The New Yorker, Town & Country, House & Garden;* her favorite novelist was Tom Wolfe.

As she told a dazed, punchy Lee Roy Sears, she'd long ago vowed not to be a vain, neurotic, self-absorbed woman, like so many; even when she was feeling a bit melancholy, she did her best to disguise it.

By this time they'd finished their shopping and were headed back to Gina's car. Lee Roy Sears was carrying most of Gina's purchases and limping badly, as if, though he had not uttered a word of complaint, his handsome new Italian shoes were hurting his feet.

Gina chattered on, reflectively, as if thinking aloud, "—I have a sort of negative model in my mother-in-law, of how I don't want to be, ever. I think of Michael's mother as 'the other Mrs. O'Meara': she's an attractive woman for her age, she's financially secure, her two grown-up children love her, yet there's something wrong with her. I'm sure she drinks too much; there's some hurt, or wound, or old trauma in her life, a sort of bleak shadow over her life. Brrrr!" Gina said, shuddering. "I surely don't want to be like that!"

Lee Roy Sears made a grunting sound, of sympathy, or assent, but had nothing further to contribute on that subject. He was watching Gina O'Meara in a wistful, sidelong way, head tilted, eyes doggily bright in their sockets.

* * *

"GINA?—WAIT!"

They were crossing Laurel Street, Gina briskly in the lead, her ashy-pale hair flashing like a helmet, Lee Roy Sears limping gamely behind, when a man's voice sounded: deep, baritone, just perceptibly accusing: and Gina turned, already smiling, and saw not the man she'd half expected to see, but another man: Marvin Bruns.

Marvin Bruns in a navy blazer with gold buttons, a sort of raffish nautical look, and his handsome slightly flushed face, wide-set quizzical eyes—he was out of breath, having hurried after Gina from a gallery up the street. (The Laurel Gallery, Inc., was one of a number of upscale Mount Orion properties with which Marvin Bruns was in some way associated, as owner, or co-owner, or investor; as creditor or debtor.) He shook Gina's hand in greeting, and held it; smiled hard at her, and slowly; glancing indifferently, rather coolly, at the odd-looking stranger who stood a few feet off staring at him with the prickly, agitated air of a dog undecided whether to be cowering or belligerent.

Gina knew that Marvin wanted very much to speak to her in private; thus, mischievously, she introduced the two men, bemused by the sudden tension between them.

As if they were rivals?—but for whom?

Marvin managed a tight, disdainful smile, but pointedly did not offer to shake hands. "—'Sears'? Yes, Clyde Somerset was telling some of us about you. I believe it was you?—going to teach a course at the Dumont Center?"

So flatly stated, the parolee's miraculous position, and the dignity that accrued to it, was revealed as not much, after all. At least Marvin Bruns with his curl of a smile and his cold shrewd assessing eyes did not appear to think so.

Marvin adroitly drew Gina off to say he'd been hoping he might see her soon. He'd called several times, but she seemed never to be home, and he hadn't wanted to leave a message on her answering machine.

Innocently, smiling, Gina inquired, "Why on earth *not*, Marvin?—that's what answering machines are for."

Marvin's smile tightened. "I'd prefer not to, Gina dear, that's all."

Oblivious of Lee Roy Sears as if he were a lamp post, standing a few yards away, shifting his weight from one foot to the other and making a quiet snuffling sound, as if trying to clear clogged sinuses. Gina and Marvin chatted: laughed together: discovering, to their mutual pleasure, that they were both invited, not only to the same dinner party on Friday night, but to the same dinner party on Saturday night too. Perhaps ten minutes passed, no doubt very swiftly for Gina O'Meara and Marvin Bruns, who'd grown wonderfully animated in each other's presence—Marvin's handsome, slightly flushed face grew ruddier, Gina's eyes positively glittered; then Marvin thought to ask would Gina like a drink?—Gina, and, of course, her companion?—but Gina declined, glancing worriedly at her wristwatch.

She said, a bit agitated, "Oh God!—the boys have been waiting for me for half an hour."

"Another time, then?" Marvin asked.

Backing away, Gina said, "Yes. Maybe."

Marvin persisted, "Yes, or maybe—?"

Gina laughingly said goodbye, and she and Lee Roy Sears hurried off, leaving Marvin Bruns to gaze after them. At the intersection close by Gina couldn't resist glancing back, seeing, with a tiny pang of satisfaction, that he was still standing there on the sidewalk, smiling vaguely, and stroking his chin.

Dear Marvin! There were Mount Orion women who spoke reproachfully of him, but Gina O'Meara never would. *She* wasn't worried.

SINCE THE CAFÉ AND that hour of seeming intimacy, since, above all that glass or two of dry white wine, Lee Roy Sears had been behaving somewhat differently, but, in her vivacity and general cheeriness, Gina O'Meara had not noticed. She was one of those women who delights in being observed, admired, desired; one of those women who wants, not lovers, but admirers. She would have had to ponder hard to see that, unlike a mirror in which our images so irresistibly float only when we are before it, a man, an admirer, a man aroused by desire, is after all *living*—and may continue to see, to stare, to desire, even when the object of his interest is no longer aware of him.

Or, in fact, interested in him, in the slightest.

So, as Gina was starting the car, not the Mazda, but a handsome metallic gray Honda hatchback, she was basking in a glow (not erotic, but indeed *very* romantic) that had less to do with Marvin Bruns than with the idea of Marvin Bruns, and, beyond him, the idea of being admired, desired, yes and adored, as in a Platonic realm of the spirit in which the very body is but a pretext for such supplication; so she scarcely paid any heed, nor probably even clearly heard, Lee Roy Sears timidly yet boldly clearing his throat, to say, "Mrs. O'Meara,—I—I never met anybody like you ever—I was dead and you gave me life and—"

Backing out of her parking place (damn! she'd parked at an angle, was within a fraction of an inch of scraping the lipstick red Toyota to her left), Gina was all business now, a decided frown between her perfect eyebrows, her lovely lips downturned at the corners, murmuring, as one might to a distracting child, "Oh!—isn't that sweet of you, Lee Roy! Why, thank *you*."

And the Honda hatchback was clear and aimed for the street.

GINA APOLOGIZED FOR NOT having time, right now, to drop Lee Roy off at the Dumont Center "I know you must be anxious to get back to your sculpting!"—but she *was* late: already swinging around to Riverside Drive, and to the Riverside School, to pick up Joel and Kenny on the playground: never more obviously twins, and identical, as now, having sighted Mommy's car and racing to it, two small-boned blond boys with strikingly beautiful faces, the one (Joel?) in a green shirt, the other (Kenny?) in blue. How they ran, ran!—overjoyed to see Mommy at last!—slowing only when they saw, seated beside Mommy, *that* man.

That man Daddy had brought home with him the week before. For a reason, but *why*?

Guardedly the boys climbed into the rear of the Honda hatchback as Gina leaned around, happily as always, to kiss and hug them. "You remember Mr. Sears, boys, don't you?"

Somberly, they nodded.

Gina said, "Say hello, then!—where are your manners?"

Joel mumbled, "H'lo, Mr. Sears," eyes downcast, and Kenny mumbled, "—'lo, Mr. Sears," and Lee Roy Sears mumbled, "H'lo," too, smiling a slit of a smile, his eyes glaring. But Joel and Kenny, shivering, did not smile back.

The O'Meara twins weren't sullen from waiting so long for Mommy, in fact they were overjoyed, and relieved, to see Mommy, but, no, they weren't going to smile at Lee Roy Sears, the black man, they just weren't.

Not that Mr. Sears was *black* really. Not his skin, or his features, or anything about him really, except his hair.

Only seven, Joel and Kenny were too young to bend to the social obligation to smile, or even to appear to smile, when their hearts weren't in it.

And Mr. Sears's face was strange, even stranger than before, a queer coarse waxy-white, and his eyes damp, glassy, hard, and *staring:* as if there was some secret between them and him, or was meant to be.

Though, *he* smiled. He was trying to be friendly wasn't he?

As always when she was late picking them up Gina peppered the twins with questions as she drove. "You weren't waiting for Mommy too long, were you?" she asked brightly, smiling at them through the rearview mirror, and, shy in the black man's presence, Joel mumbled, "No, Mommy," and Kenny, a bit louder, *"No,* Mommy."

"Were you playing with some of your nice friends, in the playground?"

"No, nobody!"

"Oh, now, I'm sure you *were!*—weren't you?"

Gina swung her car along Crescent Avenue, and so back to Mount Orion Street, which would have been a direct route back to the Dumont Center except, as if impulsively, she turned right on Highland Street, sped up the hill, and braked to a stop in front of a handsome brownstone office building. Prominent on the building was a brass sign reading DOBERMAN & SCHATTEN, ATTORNEYS AT LAW.

"Excuse me, I'll be right back!" Gina cried breathlessly.

Gina left the car keys swinging in the ignition and hurried up the walk. In her wake, in the car, there was a profound and embarrassed silence, and the airy sweetness of her perfume.

Lee Roy Sears in the front seat, in an attitude of sheer surprise, and Joel and Kenny in the back, blinking, puzzled, staring after Gina

O'Meara, who would be gone, somewhere in that brownstone building, for a mysterious half-hour.

AT FIRST, THE PAINED silence prevailed.

Then, an odd whispering began.

It wasn't the twins—it must have been Lee Roy Sears.

He had not turned to face them, but he was leaning over to
the left, to peep at them through the rearview mirror, so that, looking up to see him, those eyes, those dark-glassy staring eyes, they
felt a single shiver pass over them, from Kenny to Joel, and from
Joel back to Kenny. But was it a game?—for Lee Roy Sears made
his eyes bug out a bit, to be funny, and wriggled his eyebrows (which
were almost a single eyebrow, growing dark and tangled over the
bridge of his nose), and the twins couldn't help but giggle, in surprise
and mirth.

And, still not facing them, Lee Roy Sears giggled too, a high-
pitched hissing sound. And this made the twins giggle all the more,
as if they were being tickled.

Then, suddenly, as if it were coming from all sides, there was
a hoarse whisper, "—Hey li'l fuckers, hey hey *hey* li'l fuckers," and
Joel and Kenny froze, jamming their fingers into their mouths and
watching the black man in the little mirror, who was watching them,
only his eyes were visible, shiny like the surface of the pond behind
the house when the light was fading and the water was black, black
and opaque, not like water at all but like something else.

The boys were wondering if they'd heard right?—"Hey hey
you li'l fuckers you wanna see something?—a secret thing nobody
else can see?—yah?"

Joel stared blinking at the eyes in the mirror, and Kenny stared.

The black man in the mirror.

Was it a game, meant to be funny?—the whisper that was urgent, teasing, threatening, playful?—they shivered again, side by side
in the back seat, arms pressed tight together.

"Li'l fuckers wanna see a secret, huh?"

Shyly the boys nodded, nodded in the same instant, as if mesmerized, oh yes.

"It's a *secret*, though—got it? Like, it's *death* if you tell anybody,
no Mommy and no Daddy, got it, li'l fuckers?"

Lee Roy Sears drew a forefinger swiftly across his throat. Joel giggled shrilly, and Kenny giggled shrilly.

So Lee Roy Sears swung around to face them, and he *was* smiling, unbuttoning the left sleeve of his shirt, and rolling it up to show them something on his forearm, smacking his mouth as if chewing gum, "Hey hey hey better not look, li'l fuckers, if you're scared!"

And he held it out toward them.

A snake: black and gold-spangled, and glaring gold eyes, and a forked tongue, and fangs—coiled, preparing to strike.

The boys lost control and threw themselves backward, screaming, panicked (the snake *was* wriggling, it *was* alive), Joel clutching at Kenny, and Kenny half-sobbing clutching at Joel, until Lee Roy Sears coaxed them in a daddy's voice to calm down, calm down: "Nah—Snake Eyes won't bite, kids. Won't bite *you.*"

Lee Roy Sears glanced worriedly outside, hoping no one had seen.

Hoping their mother wouldn't suddenly appear, hurrying back to the car.

He saw the little boys were scared, as scared probably as they'd ever been by anything, Snake Eyes *was* pretty scary when you were unprepared, and who could be prepared, the first time, for Snake Eyes?—but he saw too that they were hoping to be told *not* to be scared.

He saw (and this was a theme he wanted to portray in his art) that the seven-year-olds, like fully grown men and women, wanted to be coaxed out of fear even while knowing that there was reason, and good reason, to be scared shitless. So he said, chuckling, like an uncle or somebody, somebody they could trust, "Nah, Snake Eyes ain't gonna bite *you*, ain't gonna sink his fangs in *you*, don't bite anybody unless I give the signal."

So, after a few minutes, the twins were able to examine Snake Eyes, still apprehensive, wide-eyed, as Lee Roy Sears told them a little about Snake Eyes, how Snake Eyes had come to him in a dream-vision in the heat of a jungle far, far away from the United States and Mount Orion, New Jersey—so far away it might as well be in another world. 'He don't show himself, much. I mean, there's reason for him to stay hid."

Summoning up his courage, Joel asked, "Is he a tattoo, Mr. Sears?" and Lee Roy Sears laughed and said, 'He is, yah, and he isn't, y'know why?" and the boys shook their heads in wonderment, and Lee Roy Sears said, tensing his muscles so it looked again as if Snake Eyes was on the very brink of striking, and the boys couldn't help but shrink back, "—'cause Snake Eyes possesses the power of life and death over all persons in his vicinity, that's why."

Lee Roy Sears was pleased with the O'Meara twins' reaction; he saw that they respected Snake Eyes, and they respected him, and that was good.

All his life, and especially since being sent away to Nunsford, and now, as a "parolee" accountable to authority not his own, Lee Roy Sears raged in his heart that he was not respected *as was his due.*

A man requires dignity, and self-respect, and he cannot be blamed for his actions *should such be denied.*

He *was* enjoying himself, showing Snake Eyes to the boys, basking in their fearful attention, but he had to be careful (he was keeping a sharp eye) that *she* didn't come out and discover them.

Someday, maybe, he'd reveal Snake Eyes to *her*, but only at the proper time.

Gina O'Meara: the bitch: teasing him as she'd done, and knowing it: ashy blond cunt *he knew the type.*

And right now she was in there (he knew, he knew!) fucking some guy, she'd be breathless and apologetic returning, and they'd have to swallow it, that shit, Lee Roy Sears and her own kids, *he knew the type.*

You can fuck and fuck and fuck them and they scarcely take heed so it's more than just fucking the bitches require, yes but she *was* nice to him wasn't she, and kind, and generous, don't forget how generous, her and Mr. O'Meara both, like saints they were, no matter they were rich and could afford to be generous and Lee Roy Sears was shit on their shoes, the point is that Lee Roy Sears was a man with a true mission, an artist, already recognized and rewarded for his artistic talent. The precious flame that burned within must be maintained, *he would make no mistakes this time.*

So he rolled his shirt sleeve back down, and buttoned his cuff, warning the boys that it was a secret and it's death if you tell and they certainly weren't going to tell, oh no! oh no! so he was feeling pretty good, relieved too, thinking how these American-blond kids were nothing like the native kids he'd blasted away.

The first glimpse he'd had of the O'Meara twins, he'd flashed onto the native kids, but that was erroneous: *they* were dark-haired, and chinky-yellow-skinned, sort of like rats there in the mud, half-drowned, and in any case Lee Roy Sears hadn't meant to blast them, he'd meant just the adults, but he'd lost control, and anyway he had not been the only guy to lose control, the hell with feeling bad.

He'd had enough of feeling bad. There was a shimmering moment when *feeling bad* turned inside-out to *feeling good* he'd have to concentrate on. That meant his *art.*

The promise too was *no danger with medication twice daily* except: what if the dosage had to be increased without Lee Roy Sears being informed?—you had to trust the doctors, who didn't give a shit.

One of the twins asked, "Mr. Sears?—did you ever kill anybody?" and the other giggled, and Lee Roy Sears laughed too, though a bit surprised by the question, and by the sobriety of the question, and he said, innocently, "Nah—not *me!*"

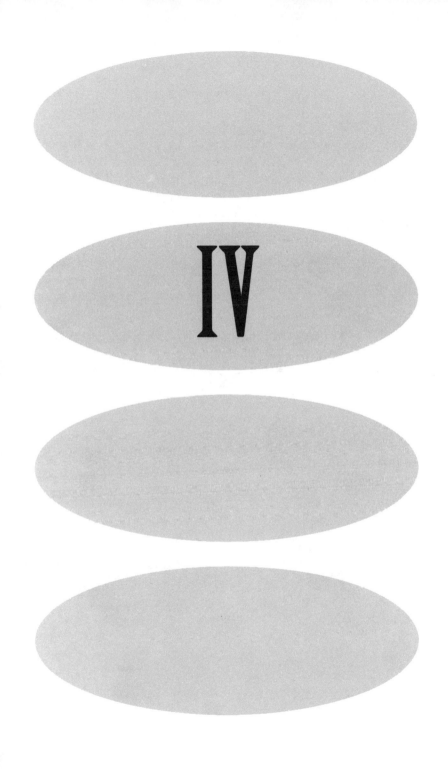

IV

1

Said Janet O'Meara, smiling, raising her voice to be heard over the genial buzzing of the crowd, "Isn't it a delightful coincidence, that CBS should send me *here!* That, on this beautiful June day, I should find myself *here!*"

The occasion was a cocktail reception for the Friends of the Dumont Center, on June 21, at which Lee Roy Sears and three of his art-therapy students were being honored. Michael O'Meara was taking Janet around and introducing her to his friends and acquaintances not as his sister, or not as his sister primarily, but in her professional role as television interviewer and filmmaker. She had been assigned to do a documentary piece on Lee Roy Sears for a CBS series titled "Community Watch," which was broadcast on Sunday mornings, and, in her ebullient, cheerful way, she was making much of the coincidence that she, Michael O'Meara's sister, should have been assigned a story on a subject so close to Michael's heart; a story that, in fact, owed its very existence to Michael's efforts. "Of course," Janet said, "it's an absolutely irresistible subject for television, and for 'Community Watch' in particular. 'Death Row inmate saved from execution'—'prison rehabilitation'—'Vietnam veteran'—'therapy through art.' It's upbeat and encouraging and it happens to be *true*."

Michael said, trying not to sound reproving, "Yes, Janet, but we don't want to overwhelm Lee Roy with attention, so soon—we don't want to appear to be exploiting him. He's already been interviewed by local papers."

" 'Exploiting him'?—what on earth do you mean?" Janet asked, smiling quizzically at Michael as if he'd said something preposterous, and glancing at others for corroboration. *"He* wants his story told. He's a man with a mission, he's remarkable."

"Well, yes," Michael said uneasily, "but all this is happening so quickly. I wonder why you didn't wait a few months, for your program? Until Lee Roy was a little better adjusted, and he and his students had more work to exhibit."

Janet spoke breathlessly, laying a hand on Michael's arm to forestall further comment from him. She'd pushed her glasses with the large round maroon-tinted lenses up on her head, the wire frames hooked around her ears, and this underscored her look of youthful vigor and impatience. "Of course, Michael, ideally, *yes*—I agree, and so does the show's producer. Except—one of our competitors would beat us to the story. And the art Lee Roy and the others have produced so far is, well—*striking*. The segment will only be twenty minutes long so we wouldn't have much time for that aspect of it anyway; the focus is on Lee Roy Sears's situation, his courage, his *resolve*. I know, with your busy schedule, you never watch television, Michael"—this uttered in a wry, mildly reproachful tone—"but 'Community Watch' highlights people who have overcome obstacles, primarily. They needn't be geniuses, or 'successful' in conventional terms. I would think that you, of all people, would be enthusiastic—your friend Mr. Somerset is!"

Why, now that Janet had grown up, now that she clearly was, not Michael O'Meara's adoring young sister, but a woman of some achievement, and much ambition, did she seem so frequently to misunderstand him?—why, when they saw each other, did Michael fall into a pattern of defending himself? He said, maintaining an air of affability, as if that hand on his arm wasn't a bit insulting, "I'm enthusiastic, Janet, of course. It's just that I wish we could all go more slowly. Lee Roy has certainly made progress in the past eight weeks or so, but it hasn't been easy, adjusting to—"

"But that's part of what we *discuss*. We talked about it yesterday, and we'll talk more about it now. A parolee's re-entry into society. Into *our* world, which we take for granted, as if it were the *only* world. We have two hours of footage already; Lee Roy told us some frank, fascinating things, about having been a 'casualty of institutions.' Once he gets talking, he *talks!*" Janet squinted toward Sears and his students, on the far side of the crowded lobby, where blindingly bright lights were shining; the camera crew was nearly set up. "You'll see—you'll all be amazed, I think—when the program is broadcast."

Janet was moving away, and Michael called after her, "—*Two* hours? And you're going to do more? For only twenty minutes of television time?"

Janet called back, as if this were an answer to his question, "The interview will be edited, of course. That's what film is all about—skillful *editing.*"

MICHAEL FOLLOWED JANET'S BROAD shoulders and high-held head across the crowded lobby, as much to avoid conversations with certain of his friends as out of genuine curiosity about the interview. He was feeling, this Saturday evening, unusually tense; yet tired too, for it had been a long week—a malpractice suit, delayed for years, had at last come to trial, and if Michael O'Meara and his assistants did not argue their case persuasively, Pearce Pharmaceuticals might be liable for as much as $10 million, payable to the widow of a thirty-year-old man who had crashed his speeding car on the Garden State Parkway after taking twice the dosage of tranquilizers his prescription indicated, and drinking hard liquor. (The suit was absurd, the widow's claim unjust, yet Michael could not help but feel sorry for her; and he worried that others, for instance the jury, might feel sorry for her too.)

So many people, attractive men and women, crowded into the marble-floored lobby of the Dumont Center!—a blooming buzzing confusion of the kind that, these past few years, had begun to weary

Michael O'Meara, though, as he told himself, he *liked* his friends;
and quite understood the necessity of such large celebratory occasions. Like many gregarious souls Michael imagined himself a re-
cluse, in his innermost being—he might have said, vaguely, that he
did not feel he deserved the company of others. He had work to do,
he had serious thinking to do, yes and repenting too, if only he
knew what it was, and how to discharge it.

That old throbbing wish, edged with guilt, yet the satisfaction
too of guilt, that he be elsewhere—anywhere, but elsewhere!

But there was this reception to get through (it was only seven
o'clock: another hour to go), and, afterward, the O'Mearas were
having Lee Roy Sears to their home for dinner; and Janet would be
joining them, since she was a house guest. Though Michael truly
looked forward to the evening, thinking of it, hopefully, as a sort of
family evening, he did feel uncharacteristically tense, and he did feel
tired. Drinking wine wasn't a good idea in such circumstances, he
knew, especially this strong red wine that was sure to give him a
headache, yet he found himself draining his glass and cheerfully
accepting another from a uniformed waiter who came by with a
tray.

And where was Gina?—Gina in her new raw silk purple sheath,
with the stylishly short skirt, and the very sheer mauve stockings?
She'd been at Michael's side earlier, with Janet, and had then drifted
off, as she did at such gatherings.

Michael scanned the room, but did not see her.

Unless—was that Gina, in a farther corner, laughing with a man
who resembled Marvin Bruns from the rear?

No. Not Gina. Another woman.

Not that Michael O'Meara was seriously looking for his wife:
he wasn't.

That would be demeaning, and he wasn't.

For he had no reason to be jealous, any more than Gina had
reason to be jealous of him.

What a pleasant surprise it had been, Gina's hospitality to Lee
Roy Sears!—not only had she volunteered to take him shopping two
or three times, helping him to buy clothes and other necessities; she
had even made appointments for him with a doctor, a dentist, an
optician; she'd even taken him to her hair salon to have his crudely

cut hair restyled. At first, Lee Roy had been frightened of virtually everything: riding in a car, walking on the street, crossing at traffic lights; talking to salesclerks, buying things, ordering food from menus in restaurants. "It's as if the poor man really had died, and has come back from the dead," she'd said, with a happy little shiver.

Michael too kept in contact with Lee Roy Sears, of course, and made it a point to drop by the Dumont Center at least once a week when Sears was in his basement studio. He persuaded Gina to invite Lee Roy to dinner once a week, usually on Friday evening; this meant cutting back on the O'Mearas' social life, but Gina had not strenuously objected. Like Michael, she'd come to think it important that Lee Roy Sears get to know a normal, happy American family, after all he had suffered of lovelessness and deprivation.

Even the twins, shy of strangers, and not very comfortable with the O'Mearas' friends generally, had come around to liking "Mr. Sears" as they called him.

And Lee Roy Sears, in his awkward, tongue-tied way, seemed fond of *them*.

Michael was making his way through the festive throng to the far side of the high-ceilinged lobby where, amid a display of their art, and against the murmurous background of the cocktail party, Lee Roy Sears and the three other Vietnam veterans were blinking dumbly into the bright television lights. One of the men, Mal Bishop, sixty pounds overweight, was in a wheelchair; the others stood, each rather crookedly, like waxwork figures that have begun to melt in unexpected ways. How self-conscious they looked, how out of place!—as if they too were on display, objects of curiosity. Janet O'Meara, tinted glasses perched atop her head like a second pair of blank, shiny eyes, was speaking with them, focusing her attention on Sears, who appeared both anxious and belligerent, wiping his nose repeatedly on the cuff of his pumpkin-plaid jacket, and nodding impatiently, as if eager to get the interview underway.

Janet had tried to inveigle Michael to be part of the interview, at least for a few minutes, but he'd firmly declined—he had already been interviewed, with both Lee Roy Sears and Clyde Somerset, for the *Mount Orion Courier,* and he'd winced to see his remarks in print.

Clyde Somerset, however, was delighted with the publicity. It seemed that anything favorable to the Center, thus to his director-ship, was of immense value to him. Far from refusing to let the CBS cameras in for this evening's reception (as, in fact, Michael had con-fidentially urged), Clyde had been eager to accommodate the visi-tors. Until the advent of Lee Roy Sears, no one outside Mount Orion had known, or cared, about the Dumont Center.

The cameras were on. The interview had begun. Janet was asking Lee Roy Sears a question about his course at the Dumont Center, holding a microphone up to his mouth, and Lee Roy Sears was doing his best to answer, still blinking, like a man in a daze, and grinning; beside him, the other men stared stonily, awaiting their turns. Mal Bishop, Ned Fiske, Andy Scarf. A semi-circle of curious onlookers had convened, drinks in hand; one of them, her expression rapt, was Valeria Darrell. Michael felt a stab of embarrassment and annoyance. He'd asked Janet why she wanted to include footage of a cocktail party, what on earth that had to do with her subject, and Janet had had a ready, airy reply—"But that *is* part of our subject, Michael—how Lee Roy Sears has been *assimilated* into Mount Orion, how *friendly* everyone is to him!"

It was hardly true that Lee Roy Sears had been assimilated into Mount Orion society, for virtually no one at this gathering knew him personally: they had perhaps read of him, in that article in the *Courier,* and heard gossip of him. But Michael despaired of convinc-ing his sister of anything she didn't want, for her own purposes, to believe.

Now she was on camera, exercising a warm, seemingly effort-less authority, talking with Lee Roy Sears as if this were, indeed, a casual conversation. Janet O'Meara seemed altogether in control—a true professional. Her voice was carefully modulated, her manner candid, direct. She was not a beautiful woman but, in her mid-thirties, she had acquired a mature attractiveness: wheat-colored hair and eyes, the O'Meara snubbed nose, a wholesome face suggesting health, vigor, intelligence, *optimism.* Michael knew, in outline rather than in detail, that Janet had been badly hurt by a failed love affair of several years before; he knew that, even more than he, no doubt because she remained single, Janet was troubled by their mother's aloofness, her distance, her air of melancholy and reproach. Yet, to

hear Janet speak, to see her smile, you would never guess that she
had a problematic inner life at all.

Several times, since Janet had gone to work for CBS, Michael
and Gina had made it a point to watch her on television, on documentary programs that, like "Community Watch," were aired at
odd, marginal hours, and they'd both been impressed by her; yet
perplexed too, for, capable as Janet was, *why* wasn't she more successful? It seemed so sad, so unfair. (Said Gina with a sigh, "It's the
competition, of course. In the damned performing arts, a thousand
times worse than in *life.*" Before they were married, Gina, with her
thin, wavering soprano voice, had hoped vaguely for a professional
career as a singer.)

Janet had learned, as an interviewer, to put nervous subjects at
their ease; or, at least, to deflect their nervousness into on-camera
intensity, drama. Only a fellow pro, Janet said, could detect her own
anxiety—"Being in control is only an illusion, but, if others accept
it, it's an illusion that *works.*"

It seemed to be working now, to a degree. Lee Roy Sears was
speaking more coherently; the others had begun to participate, at
Janet's encouragement. ("And what do you think, Mal?"—"And
what do you think, Ned?"— "Andy, do *you* agree?") Most of what
the men were saying into the microphone, earnestly, with such intensity you would think they were addressing a vast, rapt listening
world, struck Michael's ear as predictable, banal, but certainly heartfelt—"Being an artist is my way of coming to grips with the Vietnam
nightmare inside me," Mal Bishop stated, and Ned Fiske nodded
vehemently, and Andy Scarf said, spittle gleaming at the corners of
his mouth, "Yeah, man, that's *it.*"

Janet O'Meara's voice lifted in simulated wonder, "And you've
discovered a means of *expressing yourselves*—of *communicating with
others*—unavailable to you previously?"

"Yeah! Man that's *it!*"

The men began to talk more forcefully, interrupting one another, and, as they spoke, one of the three cameras drew back to
pan the crowded lobby, where, oblivious of the veterans, well-dressed
patrons of the Dumont Center clustered in gay conversational groups,
densest near the bar and the long, lavishly set table of hot and cold
hors d'oeuvres; another camera panned the display of the veterans'

art, some twenty works, paintings, drawings, Lee Roy Sears's clumsily executed clay figures, set against a white backdrop. (*Were* these
works art? Michael O'Meara wondered. But what *was* art? To his
layman's eye, much of modern and contemporary art hardly satisfied
the definition of "art.")

Of the four veterans, Lee Roy Sears looked the youngest, and,
oddly, the most commanding. His position as artist-in-residence at
the Dumont Center clearly made a difference in his sense of self. In
the past month he'd gained perhaps ten pounds; he'd mentioned to
Michael that he was working out at a gym in Putnam, lifting weights,
"rebuilding" his body, and it was clear that his shoulder muscles and
neck had grown. His hair was longer, thus more attractive, swept
back from his forehead in a stylish crest, very black, with an eerily
iridescent sheen, as if slick with oil. His sideburns were prominent,
hook-shaped. His mouth looked fleshier, his teeth chunkier. His eyes
seemed larger, more alert and intense. Typically, he'd had some bad
luck a few weeks ago—most of his new clothes had been stolen from
his room in the halfway house, and never recovered, so he was forced
to wear the pumpkin-plaid sports coat, and his old baggy trousers;
but the thief had overlooked the midnight blue Dior necktie, which
he wore this evening, resplendent and silky. And the highly polished
Italian shoes. (When the O'Mearas learned of the theft, they had
naturally offered to buy Lee Roy Sears replacements; that is, to spare
the man's pride, they had offered to lend him money, so that he
could buy the replacements himself. But Lee Roy had been surprisingly adamant in refusal. He didn't want charity, he said. Pretty soon
he'd be making enough money to pay his own way; and maybe, just
maybe, he'd find out who the bastard was who'd taken his things
from his room and get them back. "Mightn't that be dangerous?"
Gina had asked, concerned, and Lee Roy had said, blinking, "Huh?
For who?")

The other men, in their forties, looked middle-aged, battered.
Casualties of war. "Veterans." Michael O'Meara would have recognized them had he glimpsed them in the street: those whom life
has damaged. Mal Bishop in his wheelchair, both legs amputated
beneath the knee, spine twisted, his upper body bloated and his
small close-set eyes glittering, piggish—Ned Fiske, thin, gaunt, grim,
wearing thick lenses, legally blind in one eye, a perpetual tremor in

both hands—Andy Scarf, flush-faced, bald, smiling, smirking, a much-decorated ex-bomber pilot who, since the war's end, nearly twenty years before, had been unable to hold a steady job, or even live with his family. Michael O'Meara gazed at the men, as others did, beside him, sipping wine, feeling guilty, helpless; embarrassed. Regardless of Janet's enthusiasm and the self-importance the television interview seemed to give them, what was there to say to these men, or of them?—not only had they been damaged by life, they had been left behind by life.

But Valeria Darrell seemed to be feeling differently, for, in a characteristic gesture, leaning close to Michael as if to speak in hushed confidence, she murmured, her breath sweet in his ear, *"Aren't* they brave! And your friend Mr. Sears most of all!"

In her wholesome, uplifted interviewer's voice, Janet O'Meara was asking Lee Roy Sears whether his experience as a death row inmate had been more traumatic than his experience in Vietnam, and Sears shrugged, and laughed, a harsh, barking laugh, as if there were nothing more to say. But Janet continued, " 'American institutions'—how have they shaped you, Lee Roy Sears?—can you tell us?"

Sears said, "You mean foster homes?—detention homes?—jail?—the U.S. Army?—the U.S. Army stockade?—*what?"*

"Which made the most impression on you, in your estimation?"

"They all do, while you're in them, 'cause you never think you're gonna get *out."*

"Could you be more specific, please?"

"Huh? 'More specific'—how?"

"Which has left the deepest memories?"

Sears laughed again, drawing his sleeve roughly beneath his nose. There was a manic gleam to his eye, exacerbated by the television lights, which Michael O'Meara had never seen before. "In the homes for kids they treat you like shit, in jail they *really* treat you like shit, in the U.S. Army you *are* shit."

Janet paused, then said, her voice dipping conspiratorially, almost sensuously, "You did say, Lee Roy, you acquired a drug addiction?—in Vietnam?"

Sears said carelessly, "Yah, sure, I did lots of shit, we all did, mainly heroin, but I'm clean now. Wanna see?" He made a bravado gesture as if to roll up his sleeves, to show his arms to the television camera; fortunately, it was only a gesture. "You think I should be ashamed, or something?" he asked belligerently. "Okay, yah, I *am*, lady, and I am *not*: I *am* 'cause any dependency is weakness, and I scorn weakness, and I am *not*, 'cause ninety percent of the fucking U.S. of A. is addicted to something, alcohol, smoking, drugstore shit, you name it, lady!" Mal Bishop, Ned Fiske, Andy Scarf were looking on slack-jawed, their expressions neutral, like children watching one of their playmates sliding toward an abyss.

Janet persisted, daringly, "Now, Lee Roy Sears, you were sentenced to Hunsford State Prison in Connecticut, on a charge of first-degree murder, and this charge you claim was—?"

"Lies! Fucking lies!"

"But could you tell us how your service in Vietnam might relate to your years in prison, *is* there any connection?"

"Nah! Whatja think!"

"There is no connection?"

"Whatja think, lady, I'm asking *you!*"

"No, Lee Roy Sears," Janet said, her voice deep and tremulous, as if this were a kind of flirtation, "—*I'm* asking *you*. Is there any connection?"

Sears bared his teeth in a frustrated smile, his teeth like yellowed ivory, shook his head as if to clear it, said, "Look! They trained me to kill! I lived up to my training! I'm on recon right now! I'm on recon all the time! I don't forget! I learned all they had to teach me! And more! I learned more! I didn't do it for the U.S. of A., or for South Vietnam, to save 'em from the Vietcong, I did it 'cause I wanted to, I did it for *me.*"

Sears had reached out, quick, snakelike, to close his fingers around Janet's holding the microphone, and to bring it closer to his mouth, and Janet flinched away. Her stylish glasses slipped from her head, and fell to the floor. Both she and Sears released the microphone at the same instant, and the microphone fell too. "Oh!— excuse me!" Janet murmured, clearly quite frightened.

On that painful note, the interview ended.

* * *

MICHAEL O'MEARA WAS THINKING, Yes, it *will* have to be edited.

AS THE GROUP DISPERSED, led by Clyde Somerset's effervescent assistant, Jody, to the hors d'oeuvre table, Michael lingered behind to examine the art exhibit. Why was *he* trembling?—*he* had not exposed his soul.

. The paintings by Mal Bishop and Andy Scarf were crude, eye-catching, sensational as comic book art, with brushstrokes thick as feathers and acrylic-shiny as plastic. Helicopters careened through the steamy jungle air; tanks exploded in swaths of flame; mannequins in United States Army uniforms fired enormous phallic weapons. There were oversized suns, mad-glaring moons. There were lumpy fallen figures with yellow "Asian" faces. Raw emotion, spilled on the canvases' surfaces, unabsorbed, unassimilated—Michael thought it, yes, "striking," as patrons had been murmuring all evening, but it was embarrassing too. Ned Fiske's charcoal drawings were more skillfully executed, more subtle, yet marred, as if deliberately, by smudges, erasures, tears in the paper. His human figures (Americans, Vietnamese) had disproportionately large heads; his landscapes of tangled vegetation were flat as wallpaper. Michael wondered how, with his badly trembling hands, the man managed to draw at all. *That* was the remarkable thing.

But it was Lee Roy Sears's work that most attracted the eye: six clay figures displayed on white columnar pedestals, humanoid creatures, naked, bestial, with contorted faces, misshapen bodies, gashes for mouths. One was eyeless. One had only stumps for limbs. The smallest was about the size of a man's hand, the largest about ten inches long, and, arranged from left to right, they became increasingly larger, more human and defined, yet their suffering was, if anything, more acute. The final figure lay on its back in a posture of frozen agony, his mouth a wide gash, his abdomen torn open to reveal a tangle of guts—snakes?—as in the most lurid of hallucinations.

For some minutes Michael O'Meara stood staring at Sears's sculptures, his forehead gravely furrowed. The work was a riddle to be decoded—but how? And what was the connection between this art and Lee Roy Sears himself? (The man himself, so far as Michael could judge, did not seem capable of such work, unless he was hiding his truer, deeper self. At the moment, Sears was in a state of extreme excitation, encircled by several Mount Orion matrons, including the glamorous Valeria Darrell; his face was very pale, and oily with perspiration, his eyes sharp and manic, and, even as he spoke, he was eating hors d'oeuvres greedily from a paper plate held up close to his mouth.) Michael was so intensely involved with the work that friends of his, about to approach him to start a conversation, changed their minds and kept their distance; he was vaguely aware of them at the periphery of his vision, but did not turn. Though he could overhear them—Tracey Deardon murmuring, "You can see this means so much to Michael!" and a man, very likely Jack Trimmer, replying in his amiable way, "Yes, but what, do you think, *does* it mean? Michael was no more in Vietnam than I was."

If he's born too soon he won't last, none of 'em do.

Then came Clyde Somerset, smiling and genial as a master of ceremonies, with an art historian friend from Boston to introduce to Michael. Freeman was his name—Freedman? Michael was annoyed at being interrupted, but smiled and shook hands, distrusting Freedman at once, for the man had an air of professorial self-importance, quick-darting bemused eyes behind the lenses of his glasses, as he took in—"took in" was exactly what he did—the exhibit, and, in response to Clyde's query, said in a slow, ponderous voice, as if knowing that his judgment was final, thus must be rendered with tact, "Well. Yes. 'Art therapy.' I can see that these things are authentic, they are certainly 'from the heart,' but"—and here he paused, sucking in his lips, considering, as, elsewhere in the crowded room, the tinkle and babble of voices continued, given an eerie, booming amplification by the lobby's high, vaulted, glass-and-aluminum ceiling and its marble floor. Clyde Somerset said quickly, yet expansively, "The men have worked *hard.* Lee Roy Sears has been able to inspire them to open their hearts. None of them, including Sears, I think, has had any formal training; they're amateurs—primitives. Therein lies the interest. The"—he too paused, searching for the right word—*"poignancy."*

Michael asked, "What about Sears's work?—it looks good to me."

He realized he'd sounded a bit belligerent. Which was unlike him, especially at Mount Orion social gatherings.

Freedman nodded, but rather doubtfully; even disdainfully. He poked at the largest of the figures, the one with the bellyful of—was it snakes?—and said, again tactfully, "Well. yes. Quite—interesting."

Michael felt his face sting. "Only—'interesting'?"

Clyde Somerset seemed not to hear this question, but, glancing about, as if fearful of being overheard, said, in a lowered voice, with an air of bemusement and chagrin, "It's the paintings that are a bit, well you might say amateurish. Weak. Frankly awful, eh?—a sort of nightmare combination of George Grosz and Grandma Moses." When Freedman laughed, Clyde continued zestfully, for Clyde was one who loved to tell such anecdotes, with himself as the hapless protagonist, beset by ironies, "At least the most offensive, the most truly obscene, aren't here. That poor, deluded man in the wheel-chair—Bishop—he's a racist, a genocidist!—what's worse, he has come to think he's Picasso. He did several paintings in which Vietnamese figure, and they're the ugliest, nastiest, most inept caricatures you'd ever want to see, and most of them are dead. Mutilated, gory, *dead*. Just comic book stuff, yellow faces and slanty eyes, like monkeys—dreadful! So I told Sears that this sort of thing won't do, the Dumont Center can't hang 'art' like that in any public place, we can't coun-tenance, or even seem to countenance, the sensibility behind it, and Sears said, 'Is this censorship, Mr. Somerset?—you gonna censor us already?' Imagine!"

Clyde had mimicked Sears's speech, fairly accurately, and Freedman laughed again. Michael said, "Well, Clyde, it *is* censor-ship, isn't it?"

Clyde continued, with a droll face, "Then I spoke with Bishop, quite reasonably I thought, for, after all, the exhibit has to be selec-tive; it can't contain any more then x pieces by each artist. And Bishop too challenged me, asking if I wanted to 'stifle his creativity.' My God! I tried to explain that the Center is partly funded by the New Jersey Art Council, as well as by our endowment and by pri-vate donors, and we can't afford to, in fact we don't want to, offend the community. There are Asians in Mount Orion, in fact there are several Japanese-Americans who are donors, and they're here to-night—very fine people, and *very* generous. We can't hang art that depicts Vietnamese as freaks, I told Bishop, and d'you know what he said, 'That's what the gooks look like, Mr. Somerset. *I* was there.' "

Freedman laughed explosively, for it *was* funny; Michael winced, and said, "Clyde, the exhibit itself is premature. This entire event tonight—I thought from the first it would be premature."

"But it's for fund-raising purposes," Clyde said vaguely, as if that were an answer. He was wiping his eyes with a handkerchief, he'd been laughing so hard at his own tale. "Also, the CBS coverage—it's too good an opportunity to pass up."

Freedman said dogmatically, "Your program is very well-intentioned, and I'm sure it has already had some beneficial effect upon the veterans. I don't at all mind my tax money used for such purposes. But, you must know, the very term 'art therapy' is oxymoronic: while real art may be 'therapeutic,' that aspect of it is incidental, or accidental; therapy, however, can never be 'art.' Because therapy by its very nature is pragmatic and for a purpose, and art transcends mere purpose. It simply *is.*"

Freedman spoke glibly, as if concluding a lecture. Michael asked, his voice edged with anger, "How can you be so sure?—who is to judge?"

Freedman laughed, saying, as if playfully, "Why, *we* are to judge."

"And who the hell is 'we'?"

Michael O'Meara's tone was so uncharacteristically adversarial, his friend Clyde stared at him blankly; and Freedman, smile fading, drew back just perceptibly. Elsewhere, near the bar, laughter erupted; it was nearing the time when the first guests would begin to leave. Michael understood that he was exaggerating the situation, making a fool of himself, and for what reason?—he scarcely knew. Later that evening Clyde would remark to Susanne that Michael O'Meara must be under some strain. By the end of the week it would be all through Mount Orion.

Michael said quickly, as if relenting, "I suppose I want Lee Roy Sears to be a real artist, since I can't be one myself."

It was the first time such a thought had entered his mind. But now he'd uttered it, and Clyde Somerset and his friend Freedman seemed to accept it, it sounded just right.

THERE, SEEN AT AN angle, reflected lewdly in a vertical panel of gleaming aluminum, the couple was embracing surreptitiously, in a

doorway on the far side of the mezzanine. So unexpected and shocking a sight, above the crowded lobby, that Michael O'Meara, just
leaving the men's room on the mezzanine, froze where he stood, and
stared.

A blond woman in a purple dress that fitted her slender figure
snugly. A man, just her height, black-haired, in an orange plaid coat.
They were standing very close—intimately close.

Reckless in their behavior, no doubt a bit drunk, confident that
no one would see them, up on the mezzanine.

Who were they?—kissing, mauling each other, the man squeezing the woman's breast?—and she laid her hand against his chest to
push him away, and he responded at once with a low laugh gripping
her buttocks in the expensive purple fabric tightly, yes and rudely,
no gentlemanly nonsense about him, pressing her against him groin
to groin.

The two of them swaying together as in a lewd clumsy dance.
And that peal of high tinkling laughter like shattering glass.
Like a woman in sudden, unexpected orgasm.

Yet, when Michael O'Meara unthinkingly turned, it was only
to see his wife, Gina, and his friend Lee Roy Sears talking together,
not in a doorway, but at the top of the stairs; Gina stood on the
landing, and Lee Roy Sears, a curious abashed defiant look on his
face, a step or two below. They were not touching. They were
chastely apart and gave no evidence of having been touching, let
alone embracing as Michael had seen, or had thought he'd seen.

Michael blinked, shook his head, as a dog might shake its head,
to clear it in some comically literal way. *What* had he seen?—only
Gina talking with Lee Roy Sears, as they quite frequently talked, in
Michael's presence.

He looked back at the aluminum panel—but there too, in its
gleaming, just slightly distorting surface, the blond, purple-clad figure and the man's figure, in pumpkin-orange plaid, were not touching—one could see inches of space between them.

Later, Michael O'Meara would tell himself, as a doctor might
tell a worried patient, or, indeed, as Michael O'Meara himself, in
an avuncular tone, might counsel one or another of the junior legal
staff at Pearce who sometimes came to him with their problems—

*Too much to drink, on a nearly empty stomach. Too much excitement.
The pressures of the job. The pressures of the life.*

A MOMENT LATER, SEARS had turned to descend the stairs, limping
briskly along; and Gina, seeing Michael, who was now approaching
her quite openly as if nothing were wrong (nothing *was* wrong—
obviously), called out to him in the voice of a hurt, angry little girl,
with such vehemence Michael's first thought was that he must be to
blame, "Oh Michael, you won't believe this: Lee Roy isn't going to
have dinner with us after all! After he'd said he would! Valeria Darrell has talked him into driving into Manhattan with her, so that,
as she says, she can introduce him to 'powerful contacts' in the art
world! *The bitch!*"

UNAVOIDABLY, LEE ROY SEARS'S absence from the O'Mearas' household that evening, the more emphasized by Janet O'Meara's zestful
presence, was the primary theme: which Gina, in that way she had
of sometimes spoiling occasions for herself, thus for others, refused
to let go. Had Lee Roy betrayed his friends, his only true friends in
Mount Orion?—or had he been abducted, by that man-hungry ridiculous woman?

Michael was embarrassed that Gina should speak so hotly, in
Janet's presence, complaining of Valeria Darrell—"And I'd thought
that woman was a friend of mine!—of *ours!*"

As if innocently, yet with her interviewer's instinct for the provoking query, Janet asked Gina about Valeria: what was her background, how long had she been divorced, was she a woman likely
to have reckless love affairs, was she truly interested in art?—which
led poor Gina to utter remarks that, Michael was sure, she would
not have uttered, nor perhaps even thought, otherwise.

For, so far as Michael knew, Gina had always liked Valeria
Darrell, who, though older than Gina by some years, was nonetheless one of the most vivacious and attractive women in their circle.
She had sympathized with Valeria's predicament as a woman of no
particular talent or abilities save an assured social manner, living in
a large, expensive house in Mount Orion, New Jersey, as if waiting—
ah, so many American women *are* waiting, married or single!—for
something to happen.

Calmly, laying a hand over Gina's as if to restrain her, Michael said, "Gina, please be reasonable. It's only natural, now Lee Roy is settled more into his life, he should start to make friends of his own and not always be associated with *us*."

"Yes, but Lee Roy *is* associated with us," Gina said, withdrawing her hand like a spiteful child. "He wouldn't be at the Dumont Center, the object of so much attention, if it hadn't been for Michael O'Meara." She paused, frowning: two quite distinct lines showed in the smooth skin between her brows. "He wouldn't be walking on this earth if it hadn't been for Michael O'Meara. He'd be dead. *Electrocuted.*"

"But, Gina—"

"He wouldn't have any underwear and socks, a decent shirt, decent *shoes*, if it hadn't been for *me!*"

Janet, nodding gravely, as if sympathetically, nonetheless could not resist, "Lee Roy Sears did strike me, when I interviewed him, and still more when I was just watching him, as a fundamentally *unknowable* person. An enigma. Someone you might imagine you know, perhaps even mistake as a little simple, but, in reality, as you one day discover—you don't know him at all." She paused, shivering. By candlelight, Janet's fair, open, moon-shaped face, with its hint of fleshiness beneath the chin, looked youthful, guileless. "The Ted Bundy type, y'know?—though not quite so attractive as Bundy."

Gina stared at Janet blankly. "Ted *Bundy?* The mass *murderer?*"

"Serial murderer, to be precise. Bundy was electrocuted by the State of Florida for having killed as many as thirty girls and women. He wasn't psychotic. He just wanted to kill. People who knew him claimed he was a 'nice guy.' "

Gina looked at Janet as if trying to gauge whether her sister-in-law, whom she did not know well, but had always liked, was being deliberately provoking; or whether, in her rawboned, headlong way, she hadn't any clear sense of what she said and how it might be interpreted. Gina laughed, though annoyed, saying, "Janet, that's ridiculous. Michael and I *do* know Lee Roy, really! He's sweet, he's naive, he's impressionable. He'll be putty in Valeria Darrell's hands."

It was late, past ten-thirty. They were sitting at the dining room table, Gina and Michael and Janet, languidly finishing a second bottle of wine. The twins had been put to bed hours ago and the house was quiet—unnervingly quiet, to Michael's ear. (Or did he hear his sons, far away upstairs?—laughing together, moving about when they were supposed to be asleep? Of late, they'd been behaving unpredictably.) After the reception at the Dumont Center, Janet had helped Gina serve a belated dinner, and a sad dinner it turned out to be, though Gina had intended something very different. No one had seemed to have much appetite, despite the delicious gourmet food (from a Mount Orion caterer); Gina in particular had only picked at it, in that fastidious, disdainful, self-punishing way of hers, which worried Michael. She did drink, however: several glasses of red wine.

Gina and Janet continued to speak, not quite quarreling, of Lee Roy Sears. Michael smiled, watching Gina. Should she turn suddenly to him, in appeal, he *was* smiling.

Had Michael O'Meara seen anything in that aluminum panel on the mezzanine of the Dumont Center?—he had not.

Or, having glimpsed something, he would soon forget; had in fact already forgotten what he'd seen—that is, what he had *not* seen.

"Would you pour us a little more wine, Michael?" Gina asked, pursing her lips, "or is that bottle empty?"

"It's almost empty."

"Then—would you open another? Please?"

"Another? Now?"

Gina lifted both her and Janet's glasses, in a gay drunken gesture, as if offering twin toasts.

"Another, darling. *Now."*

"I don't think I should, Gina. We've all had enough."

" 'Enough'? What is 'enough'? Who is to say, what is 'enough'?"

Gina faced Michael boldly. She was in a state in which emotion coursed through her like electricity. Her hair was disheveled, the pupils of her eyes very black. She was still wearing the purple silk dress, but she'd kicked off her shoes and had drawn one leg up beside her, awkwardly, yet in her own way rather gracefully, on her chair. Michael smiled at her, smiled hard. He'd been drinking intermittently for hours but he wasn't drunk, alcohol had very little effect upon him, but he *was* tired, and distracted, and not in a mood to get into a quarrel with Gina, especially with his sister so pointedly a witness.

Janet said, rousing herself, "Oh, Gina, thanks, but *I* really don't want any more. I—"

"Yes, but *I* do," Gina said. "Michael, go get another bottle, will you?—*will* you? Since Lee Roy isn't with us, we'll celebrate in his absence."

There was a moment's pause, a moment's distinct silence, then Michael rose from the table, and went into the kitchen, to fetch a fresh bottle of wine. He uncorked it in the kitchen, rather clumsily, partly crumbling the cork, spilling wine on the counter. He knew he wasn't drunk but his fingers were oddly numb, distant from the thoughts that directed them. *Skillful editing is required. If he's born too soon he won't last.* He hadn't been able to force himself to eat much though he was hungry, in this wayward, undefined mood, in which faint nausea contended with a powerful erotic yearning he could not comprehend.

When, bearing the wine bottle like a prize, he returned to the dining room, it seemed to him that Gina and Janet, speaking earnestly together, lowered their voices at his approach. The candle flames flickered.

"Thank you, Michael darling! *Aren't* you a darling!" Gina cried.

Michael poured wine, in three glasses.

(Hearing, or imagining he heard—what? Someone approaching the house, along the driveway? Footsteps overhead?)

Whatever the women had been speaking of in Michael's absence was adroitly dropped. Gina asked Janet about her television work, and Janet, taking the cue, spoke animatedly, and at length, with an underlying air of mild complaint. She was after all a woman of thirty-five, unmarried, childless. Her career was her life, but what *was* her career? Michael was concerned for her, living alone as she did in New York, yet he knew that, should he speak along such lines, he would be rebuffed at once; should he ask if she was "seeing anyone," Janet might flush in indignation at the question, as an invasion of her privacy.

Once, years ago, when Janet was newly out of college, Michael, her well-intentioned older brother, had asked casually if she was "seeing anyone," and Janet had replied tartly, "If you mean am I sleeping with anyone—no, no I'm not, at the moment. Okay?"

Okay.

Janet went on to speak of family now, cousins of hers and Michael's whom neither had seen in years, and then Janet was speaking, more urgently, of their mother, whom Michael telephoned every two or three weeks, with an adult son's cheery-dutiful obligation. Janet said, stubborn as always when she took up this subject, "There *is* a mystery of some kind in Mother's life, I'm sure of it. But—" Her voice trailed off, vague, irresolute.

Michael merely shrugged. It was an old topic, and he had no thoughts on the subject.

Gina said, with an air of excitement, "Oh, yes, I've always thought so too, Janet. The way she looks at me sometimes—so sort of pitying, *tragic*. The way she looks at Michael, and at the boys." She paused, nodding. "The boys, especially."

"But she doesn't talk to you, I suppose?—confide in you?"

"Me?—her daughter-in-law? Certainly not," Gina said. "Why would she? After all these years I don't dare call her anything other than 'Mrs. O'Meara.' Imagine calling her 'Mother'!"

"Well," Janet said, giggling, suddenly tearful, wiping at her nose, "I thought just possibly, since Mother never talks to *me*, she might talk to *you*."

Gina leaned forward, elbows on the table. "Did she talk to your father, ever? Did he talk to *her*?"

Michael listened, or half-listened, bemused, restless. Was he insensitive?—typically and crudely male? For the life of him, he was puzzled by such conversations, which women seem to seek out, as if family relations were so very crucial. Why, for instance, did Gina and Janet care so much about the elder Mrs. O'Meara?—*did* they care, really? Or was such maudlin talk, exacerbated by the wine, the lateness of the hour, the absence of Lee Roy Sears, simply the sort of talk women of a certain class, education, and background drift into out of an unexamined notion that, yes, one's mother *is* important, no matter her insignificance in the larger world; and the most banal deficiencies in her character might be transposed into *mystery*.

Gina said sharply, "Michael, why are you laughing?—what's funny?"

Michael said, "I'm not laughing."

But he guessed he'd been grinning. The lower part of his face ached with strain.

Janet said defensively, "Oh, it's an old story. Michael is convinced that I exaggerate, about Mother. About our parents. He thinks I'm imagining—whatever it is."

Michael said, meaning to be kind, "Janet, I think you love Mother very much and are wondering how to make her happy; or less unhappy. When you can't seem to succeed, any more than I have, you attribute it to a specific cause. Whereas I—"

"Oh, hell, you're a lawyer!" Janet said, laughing.

"—tend to interpret it as a matter of character, of heredity, genes—"

"—a lawyer for a pharmaceutical company!"

Janet laughed, and, as if she'd uttered something witty and not, to Michael's way of thinking, something simply fatuous, Gina burst into laughter too. High tinkling glittery laughter. Michael, blushing, looked from one woman to the other, perplexed.

Janet sobered, and said, "Oh, God. I'm just remembering. Mother once took me aside, I can't think why, and said, 'Having babies—you think it's the solution to the riddle of what to do with your life, when you're a young woman. Then, once the babies are born, you see that the riddle has only begun.' "

Gina gave a little shriek and nearly upset her glass of wine. "Oh, God!—she told me that too! When Joel and Kenny were born!"

Michael sighed, knowing that Gina and Janet would pursue this subject for many minutes. He had known that his mother had told Gina that cryptic aphorism, but he'd long since forgotten and could not think why it had any particular significance, now.

No more significance than his father's cryptic aphorism: *What are people for, except to let you down.*

Michael was stacking plates at the table when he happened to catch a glimpse of a face floating in the doorway between the dining room and the darkened hall beyond—it was small, ghostly pale, indistinct in the shadows. He stared past Gina's shoulder, and the expression on his face must have frightened her, for she turned, quickly, to see what it was, just as the face vanished into the darkness. "Michael, what is it?" Gina asked.

Michael could not speak. The hairs on the back of his neck quite literally stirred.

Then a second pale face appeared, bobbing in the shadows, and now Michael heard muffled laughter and a sound as of something scraping against a wall—"Joel! Kenny!" he called out. "What are you doing out of bed?"

The boys fled. There were rapid footsteps in the hall, a sound as of skidding on a loose rug, more muffled laughter, high-pitched and frantic, as if nothing could be more hilarious than Daddy's wrath; then, as the adults sat staring toward the doorway, there came a sound of mischievous giggling close behind them at the doorway to the kitchen, where Joel (or was it Kenny?) poked his head, and then Kenny (or was it Joel?) poked his head, both boys squatting low so that their heads bobbed unexpectedly close to the floor. What impudence! With identical grins Joel and Kenny demanded in identical piping voices, "Where is he?—Mr. Sears?" and "Where is he?—Mr. Sears!"

Gina laid her hand against her breast, as if her heart were beating very hard. Her eyelids fluttered. She said, breathless, scolding, "What on earth, you two!—scaring us like that!"

Michael was on his feet. "That isn't funny, Joel!—Kenny! You know better!"

This set the twins off giggling harder. In near-unison they cried, "Where is he?" and "Where *is* he?"

Michael advanced upon them even as they ran off, colliding with each other, shrieking and laughing, through the kitchen where they knocked something over (a chair?) and into the rear hall and so up the back stairs, their bare heels pounding on the steps as if they were, not seven-year-old boys, but much older, heavier. The cry "Where is he!" and its echo "Where! is! he!" resounded through the house.

As if this were a familiar nighttime game, not a singular act of defiance, Michael stood in the hall, hands cupped to his mouth, calling, "Back to bed, you two! C'mon, now! Back to bed!" He dreaded his sister judging him as a father unable to control his sons.

From upstairs came the sound of jarring footsteps and the

mocking cry "Back to bed!" and its echo "Back to bed! to bed! *bed!*"

After a brief while there was silence again upstairs. But it was the kind of silence, increasingly familiar in this household, that Michael O'Meara could not trust.

Gina finished her glass of wine and set it down on the table rather hard. She cut her eyes at Janet, meaning to be amusing, but her voice came out hoarse, cracked, "So!—d'you think you'd like to be a mother?"

"Oh yes," Janet said emphatically, "—oh *yes.*" In that lilting television voice that, candid, direct, sincere, was wholly unconvincing.

In their bed, at last, after this lengthy, distressing, exhausting day, Michael O'Meara gently kissed his wife's eyelids, which were damp with tears of hurt and frustration; gently eased the straps of her silk nightgown off her shoulders, so that he could kiss her breasts. Ah, lightly!—reverently! He was careful to hide the sexual desire he felt, knowing that such desire, at this time of night, and in such circumstances, might have been distasteful to Gina; at the very least, it would have embarrassed her.

Gina's lovely breasts!—small, very pale, oddly cool, with a delicate tracery of bluish veins, the roseate nipples as seemingly untouched as those of a young girl!—and unbruised, so far as Michael could see by lamplight, betraying no telltale signs of soreness.

Asleep but not sleeping. Trapped in sleep but not of his own volition. He was struggling to wake yet shrewd, canny in struggle, tensing his body, muscles rigid as in combat, a fight to the death, though the voice came jeering *Michael was no more in Vietnam than I was* and suddenly he saw, as if a gauze wrapping were removed from his eyes, what was keeping him there, wrestling him down, trying to choke his oxygen supply: the humanoid figure, a misshapen dwarf with a gaping hole in his abdomen, roiling snakes for guts, glaring eyeless sockets and a grinning gash of a mouth.

And that smell! Sickening!

A stink as of phenol, or was it chlorine!

Michael wrestled the hideous dwarf down, hands closing around his throat. Down, down! Leave me alone! *Die!* At the same time he managed to thrash himself awake, and woke, sweaty, shivering, not knowing for several confused seconds where he was. Beside him, Gina, his beautiful wife, who had been sleeping a deep, stuporous, wine-sodden sleep, murmured, scarcely able to hide her annoyance, "Yes darling, yes, fine—we'll talk about it in the morning."

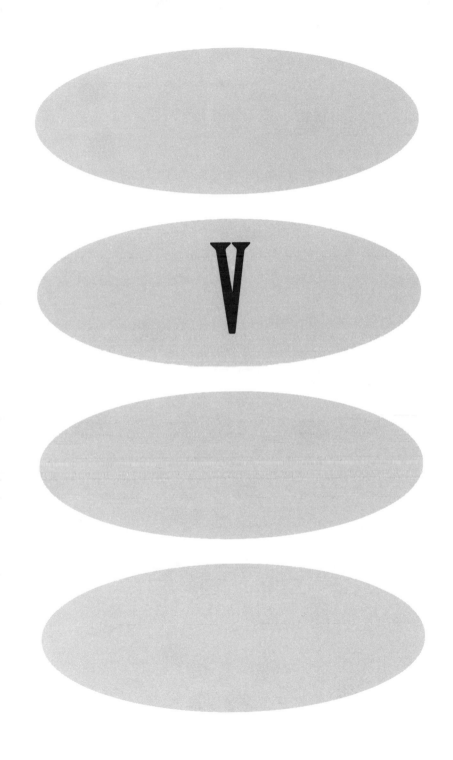

V

1

WHERE WAS HE?—HE WAS in the Free Fire Zone.

Through the months of that summer, in the Free Fire Zone.

Sculpting clay. His hands groping, kneading. Gouging fingers. Working in a trance a hazy sweaty trance, they knew better than to interrupt Lee Roy Sears in the Free Fire Zone.

Even climbing the stairs to the parole office on Twelfth Street, entering H. Sigman's office, he was in the Free Fire Zone.

Even at the Putnam Municipal Parking Garage working for chump money doing shitwork by night pushing a giant broom picking up trash by hand he was safe in the Free Fire Zone.

(First week of September, he'd quit. Tell the assholes go fuck. Take his chances with H. Sigman, who was impressed—the asshole *should* be impressed!—with Lee Roy Sears's rich friends and supporters over in Mount Orion.)

In the Free Fire Zone, Snake Eyes twitched asleep with his eyes open. Poised tight-coiled ready to strike if an enemy came too near.

Yah but *he* was safe: wore long-sleeved shirts when he was in Mount Orion, sometimes even at the gym working out with barbells, weights, he figured it's to his (and Snake Eyes's) advantage.

Oily sweat running in rivulets down his face, his body.

In the Free Fire Zone, that's okay. He could handle it.

Not even requiring medication, some days. As the summer wore on.

Figuring the doctors, the psychiatrists, paid to scare you, what do they know?—shitheads don't know shit. Don't know Lee Roy Sears. Nah not *him*.

Telling them yah for sure he was taking the Chlonopramane, twice daily, with meals. Told them he was clean—no drugs, no alcohol, not even cigarettes. Swore to H. Sigman regarding him with eyes of utmost sincerity, Lee Roy Sears cleanshaven and softspoken and respectfully dressed in coat, white shirt, tie. Following the printout PROCEDURE FOR PAROLEES, yah for sure, *he* wasn't ever going back to prison again.

One thing *was* certain, as Lee Roy Sears inwardly vowed: he would never be an addict again. Never heroin, that shit, ever again—heroin's for losers.

Okay, he might do a little coke, have a few drinks, in secret. In the Free Fire Zone where it's safe. (If Valeria Darrell was paying. Rich cunt so eager to *pay*—wild!)

In the Free Fire Zone, like in Nam, where you can do anything you want, or need. To anybody, to anything. The power deep within.

If he'd had it then. If he'd known of it then. Thirty years ago. His foster father beating him with a mop, a filthy wet mop, the other kids standing laughing at Lee Roy Sears peeing his pants and his foster father (no-name: pale puffy face, bulging outraged eyes) the more incensed, slamming pounding poking with the mop handle trying to gouge out Lee Roy Sears's eye. And everyone laughing.

If he'd had his power, then.

Snake Eyes twitching, yearning to spring to life.

Years ago, before Hunsford, before Nam, when he'd first gone into the army, Lee Roy Sears had had a lean, wiry, muscular body— he hadn't been one of those freak bodybuilders, still less one of those bleached-hair fags, but he'd looked good, he'd looked tough, musculature is armor, the only way for a man to get respect from other men. (A knife or a gun will get temporary respect, but you're still a punk once you're disarmed.) Now, forty years old, he was systematically regaining that body, squeezing the poisoned blood out of his veins drop by drop, the weakness of which he was ashamed.

In the Free Fire Zone, there is neither weakness nor shame.

Three workout sessions per week at the squalid little gym near the halfway house in Putnam. Taking it slow. Nothing fanatic. Biceps, triceps, quadriceps. Pull-ups, barbell rows, deadlifts, low pulley rows. Squatting. Leg-press. Stretch and squeeze. Shoulder-press rack. Deltoids, pectorals. Dumbbells. Shocking the muscle—galvanizing it into life.

Into *resistance*, thus into *life*.

In April, just out of Hunsford, Lee Roy Sears had weighed one hundred thirty-two pounds.

By September, Lee Roy Sears weighed one hundred sixty-three pounds.

Showing it most in the neck, shoulders, upper arms. Looking taller, too. Proud. His manhood confirmed.

Snake Eyes had grown, too. Tight-coiled on Lee Roy Sears's left forearm, his gold-spangled length shimmering with muscle.

Mostly, Lee Roy Sears refused to discuss his physical regimen. Did not encourage prying questions about his gain in size and weight.

He was an artist, art was his calling.

(Shit, but he had to laugh!—the way people were beginning to look at him, wary, guarded, with respect. Like his "students" at the Center—Fiske, Scarf, Bishop—that fatass Bishop in particular—staring at Lee Roy Sears when they thought he wasn't aware of them. Not daring to ask, though.)

(And the O'Mearas. He'd gone for supper the other evening, the first time he'd seen them in weeks, they'd been away "at the seashore" as they said, Lee Roy Sears *not* invited, but, hell, he didn't blame them, he loved them, the O'Mearas were his closest friends on earth, *his* family, and the twins were crazy about him if maybe just a little scared of him but Snake Eyes won't bite *you*, nah no need to worry he ain't gonna bite *you*. And he'd been lifting the twins in play, a little boy in the crook of each arm, and Gina O'Meara had happened to see his shoulder muscles swell, and she'd blinked, and stared, and said in a faint, breathless, wondering voice, a voice he'd never heard in her before, "Why, Lee Roy—what has *happened* to you?" So he'd mumbled something about "working out"—"lifting weights"—giving a clear sign he didn't want to pursue the subject, out of modesty. Michael O'Meara was a witness to this exchange but said nothing, respectful as he was of Lee Roy Sears's privacy.)

"I STAND OUTSIDE THE Caucasian race"—he'd told them, more than once he'd told them, over the years, and now since coming to his new life in New Jersey, but the bitches seemed not to comprehend. Just because Lee Roy Sears looked white didn't mean he *was* white.

Last time he'd said it, one of them—was it Valeria?—or Somerset's assistant, Jody?—or Janet, the hot-shit TV interviewer?—*was it Gina?*—had looked at him as if she was about to laugh in his face, then changed her mind quick seeing what was in his face.

Pressing her hand, glittering rings, polished nails, bones Lee Roy Sears could crush in his fingers in a second, against her throat, murmuring *Oh!*

Always, they did so. The bitches. White bitches.

Gazing into Lee Roy Sears's Rasputin eyes, their smiles fading.

Feeling the heat and pulse of Snake Eyes though they could not see him in the living flesh.

Except: the Darrell cunt the other night, at her place, million-dollar house she'd gotten in a settlement from some chump ex-husband, and Lee Roy Sears was undressing and she saw Snake Eyes good and clear for the first time, high on coke, drunk, yah but seeing Snake Eyes she got sober fast, blood draining out of her middle-aged face leaving the makeup crust exposed, a sickly sallow orangish color like dried puke, and she's standing flat-footed in her stocking feet not in her fancy high heels so she's foreshortened, dumpy, and her dyed russet hair synthetic as a wig, staring mesmerized at Snake Eyes there on Lee Roy Sears's forearm hot and ready to strike—"Oh God, what is that, Lee Roy!—is that a *snake!*"

And he's laughing at her grinning with his teeth holding Snake Eyes out to her, flexing his muscles so Snake Eyes is twitching, and she's stumbling backward, and he's following, Jesus he has to laugh seeing the rich cunt's face, eyes like tiny pinwheels spinning, "Nah, sweetheart, he ain't gonna bite you. I got something else for *you.*"

* * *

SHE'D MOANED AND WEPT, hot stinging tears that embarrassed him, makeup smeared all over her face and her lips pale and fleshy drawn back from her teeth, she was saying she loved him, oh God she loved him, never anybody like him, never before in her life running her fingers over Lee Roy Sears's back where an old scar ran slantwise like a zipper, fifteen inches long, tiny puckers in the skin she'd assumed was a Vietnam wound and he didn't set her right, fuck it it was nobody's business that scar from a beating he'd had as a kid of seventeen when a guard at the Youth Detention Center, Watertown, New York, had laid into him with a length of barbed wire.

Afterward she'd pressed a cloth soaked in cold water against her nose to staunch the bleeding. He hadn't meant to hit her—had he?

Nah not *him*.

HE NEVER MEANT TO hit them, but sometimes it happened.

How the fuck was *he* to blame?—sometimes it happened.

In the Free Fire Zone especially, sometimes it happened.

EARLY MORNING OF A wet-glaring day in September, in the fourth month of Lee Roy Sears's parole, there he was in his studio in the Dumont Center, alone, working in clay, his fingers rapid and supple, grabbing kneading gouging sucking in wet clay, Jesus he's feeling so good he's flying high in the Free Fire Zone where none of you fuckers can follow.

This is the morning following the night he'd quit his job at the Putnam Municipal Parking Garage. Got into a fight with the manager shoving him backward the heel of his hand against the son of a bitch's chest, hadn't known Lee Roy Sears was so strong, eh?—so there's panic in the guy's eyes, Okay Lee Roy Sears is going to be hearing about this from his parole officer but he's confident he can handle it, he's got these rich friends in Mount Orion, he's got Michael O'Meara a renowned attorney, right now he's flying high shaping clay as it has never been shaped before in the history of the world, he hasn't slept since the day before or was it the day before yesterday?—fuck it, who cares.

In the Free Fire Zone, you don't need sleep.

Slapping clay, kneading, gouging—it isn't one of his male figures emerging but this time a female, a woman, a young girl, yah Lee Roy Sears remembers her, precisely her, flat Asian face and delicate folds of skin at her eyes, she's still alive inside his hands, lying crooked on her back, legs spread wide, wide so they're almost broken, a jagged gouged-out hole between her legs, and her head thrown back in agony.

He hadn't done it to her, with the bayonet. He hadn't even seen clearly who had.

THEN IT BEGAN.

He would say, afterward, when the nightmare had at last dissipated, and his life as Michael O'Meara was restored to him, that it began on this day: a Friday in mid-October: when his secretary entered his office, interrupting a meeting, to tell him that Mrs. O'Meara was on the line wishing to speak with him—"She says the matter is urgent."

Michael politely excused himself, to take the call in another room. His colleagues might have observed that, in even the exigency of the moment, he maintained his composure and betrayed no obvious anxiety.

An ideal lawyer!—the warmest and most friendly of men, yet, beneath it all, so *composed*.

But he picked up the receiver in the adjoining office with trembling fingers, for not within recent memory, since the turbulent days of her pregnancy, had Gina insisted upon interrupting a meeting of

Michael's; she well knew the pressure he was under, and that it was surely to her advantage, as his wife, to distract him as little as possible. The chief legal counsel of Pearce Pharmaceuticals, Inc., could afford few distractions.

The fleeting prayer came to Michael, *Don't let it be our boys.*

Michael asked Gina what was wrong, and Gina told him, in a flood of words, emotional, agitated, yet querulous too, so that he understood at once that the news could not be devastating. Nor was it domestic, thank God: something about Clyde Somerset calling Gina, with a complaint about Lee Roy Sears.

Gina was saying breathlessly, "—Clyde is terribly upset, Michael, he wanted to talk to you personally, you know how he can be sometimes—that patrician air of his that's really a pose, how it dissolves if it's challenged!—apparently Lee Roy Sears challenged him this afternoon at the Center, they had quite a quarrel, and Clyde got hold of me demanding to speak to you, asking for your private number there but of course I wouldn't give it to him. I did say I would call you, though, and I promised him"—here Gina's voice dropped, as if guiltily, so that, for some seconds, background noises made it difficult for Michael to hear her"—that you would drop by the Center this afternoon, on your way home from—"

It was absurd for Gina O'Meara to be saying such a thing, for, of course, the Dumont Center would long be closed and darkened for the night by the time Michael returned home from work. Gina knew this, and Michael knew that she knew it, yet he understood her position, for, clearly, she had not wanted to further antagonize Clyde Somerset; nor had she wanted to suggest to Michael that he should interrupt his afternoon, drive to the Center, and then return again to Pearce—an outrageous suggestion, on the face of it. Michael would be obliged to think of this solution himself.

He said, "Yes, Gina, but what is it?—more of the same, with Mal Bishop?"

About twelve days before, Mal Bishop had caused a commotion at the Dumont Center, rolling in his mechanized wheelchair into Clyde Somerset's office to charge his former teacher, Lee Roy Sears, with theft: Bishop had several paintings of his to show Clyde, and masses of charcoal sketches, meant to substantiate his claim that certain of his ideas had been plagiarized by Lee Roy Sears for his clay figures. (Bishop had dropped out of the art-therapy program over the summer. Fiske and Scarf had continued, joined in September by six others.) Clyde had listened courteously to Bishop, a blustering egomaniac, as he thought him, but dismissed his charges as untenable—unprovable. He'd told Michael O'Meara that both the men's art was pretty hard to take.

Gina was saying hurriedly, "No, this has nothing to do with that awful man, I'm afraid it's more serious. You know Julia Sutter of course"—Julia Sutter was the widow of a wealthy Mount Orion philanthropist, a woman in her mid-eighties, who had donated hundreds of thousands of dollars to the Dumont Center since its inception—"well, Julia and some of her women friends are taking a ceramics course at the Center, and they visited the art-therapy studio and were terribly upset by something of Lee Roy's they saw there—one of the women nearly *fainted*. (Clyde has described the work so graphically, *I* know *I* don't want to see it!) So naturally Julia went to Clyde to complain, and she's demanding that the work be removed from the Center, she claims it's obscene, and Clyde went to investigate and *he* was shocked and disgusted. So he talked to Lee Roy, and Lee Roy refused to cooperate, and—"

So the comical little tale unfolded. Michael listened, his pulse quickening as if he, and not Lee Roy Sears, had been insulted.

Wasn't this just like Clyde Somerset!—to boast of having created a space for troubled men to exorcise their demons through art, and then to take the sides of the philistines who objected to that art. Michael interrupted Gina, asking, "What am I supposed to do, Gina? Does Clyde seriously expect me to talk Lee Roy Sears into being *censored?*"

In a bright yet evasive voice, as if her attention had, for a moment, shifted elsewhere, Gina said, "Darling, I don't know, but you must do something—you must mediate between Clyde and Lee Roy. Clyde is actually threatening to revoke Lee Roy's residency at the Center! He says that Lee Roy spoke rudely to him and to Julia Sutter, that in fact he has been rude to the Center staff quite a bit lately, that he's uncooperative in general, and never did listen to Mal Bishop's accusations. You know, Lee Roy *does* have a temper sometimes, like a child. But of course Clyde is probably exaggerating—"

In the background as Gina spoke there was a wash of sound,

surflike, blurred, as of many voices, punctuated by higher-pitched noises like metal clanging against metal. It was unlike Gina to have a television set on during the day, and if Marita was cleaning house, Gina would hardly be making a confidential call within her earshot. Or had Joel and Kenny brought classmates home to play?

Michael finally asked, "Gina, what's going on there? Why is it so noisy?"

There was a moment's pause, then Gina said, "I'm not at home, I'm calling from a hotel."

"A hotel?"

"I mean, a hotel *lobby.* I've been having a lunch at the Hyatt"— as if, under these rushed circumstances, Gina had not time to substitute another place, a restaurant or a club, closer to home. (The luxurious new Hyatt-Regency was eleven miles away, in the suburb of Green Ridge, New Jersey.)

Michael said, puzzled, "But I thought Clyde called you."

Gina said, at once defensive, "He *did.* He had me *paged.* Is this a cross-examination, darling?"

Had he more time, and had he been able to think more clearly, Michael O'Meara might have pondered this curiosity, that Clyde Somerset, wanting to speak with Gina, should somehow know to have her publicly paged at the Hyatt; unless—was this more likely?— he'd had his staff place calls at any number of area restaurants and hotels, with the assumption that, on a weekday, Gina would be lunching in one of them.

And with whom?

But Michael never gave this another thought, for, hanging up the phone with a promise of hurrying to the Dumont Center, to set things straight between Clyde and Lee Roy Sears, he had so much else to think of. A wave of sickish apprehension, dread, excitement swept over him. *Philistines. Enemies. Insult.*

AFTERWARD, HE WOULD GRIMLY recall this day, the start of the trouble: Friday, October 18, his eye catching the date on a calendar as if to memorialize it. He would not have wished to think that perhaps the trouble had started years ago, on that bright May morning in 1983 when, at the hearing at Hunsford, he'd first laid eyes on Lee Roy Sears.

In his office, Michael poured himself a quick drink, an inch of Scotch in a tumbler; he swallowed down a tranquilizer—the small, pale green pill Liloprane.

Told his secretary he had to hurry home on a domestic matter—"almost, but not quite, an emergency"—but that he expected to be back in the office within ninety minutes. (It was now 2:50 P.M.)

Got into his Mazda and drove. Back to Mount Orion.

Calming somewhat, on the Parkway, as the Scotch and the Liloprane, warmly meshing, coursed along his veins with a soothing hum.

(It should be noted that Michael O'Meara rarely took drugs. He was one of those Americans who stoically refuse even aspirin. Most of the time.)

(It should be noted that, strictly speaking, he had no prescription for Liloprane, but, as one of Pearce Pharmaceutical's most profitable psychoactive drugs, it was readily available at Michael's office. What harm, a single pill?—under these trying circumstances?)

(In any case, the mild tinge of guilt he felt at taking the Liloprane, and the Scotch, was almost immediately assuaged by the Liloprane, and the Scotch. For such was the purpose of the Liloprane, and the Scotch.)

For the past six weeks, it seemed that Michael O'Meara had been working even harder than usual for Pearce, Inc. The $10 million malpractice suit had been settled in Pearce's favor; but, only the previous week, preliminary papers had been served against the company by the family of a Memphis factory worker, who, under treatment for depression with Pearce's anti-depressant Peverol, had gone berserk and killed seven people, including himself, with an AK-47 assault rifle. Lawyers for the dead man's family were arguing that Peverol, popularly billed as a "wonder drug" in the cure of depression, in fact triggered, in certain individuals, mania, obsession with suicide, and violent behavior . . . This time, Pearce, Inc., was being sued for $50 million in punitive and compensatory damages.

Unfortunately, the Memphis coroner's report concluded that drugs the dead man had been taking at the time, including, but not restricted to, Peverol, may have influenced his behavior. Thus, to refute this allegation, Michael O'Meara and his team of lawyers would proceed by—

"But why am I thinking of that *now?—now* isn't the time, surely!"

He was driving along the Garden State Parkway, on his almost too-familiar route, fifteen miles above the speed limit, yet with his customary skill and tact. The alteration of his brain's chemistry had been minimal, and entirely to the good. Though he saw that he'd been gripping the steering wheel so tightly, his fingers were white, like bone.

An artist. Art is his calling.

If he's born too soon he won't last.

Thankfully, Janet O'Meara's television interview with Lee Roy Sears had turned out quite respectably—admirably, in fact. For some reason the network had delayed its broadcast until August, and scheduled it for a Sunday at noon, but the O'Mearas had seen it at their summer place on Cape Cod, at their rented summer place. (Joel and Kenny had seen it too, greatly excited watching their friend Mr. Sears on television.) As Michael had supposed, the controversial footage had been edited out. Lee Roy's intemperate outburst might never have occurred, and most of the conversation between him and Janet was briskly upbeat, and blandly general. ("Do you think that art is a good, healthy, normal outlet for all men and women, not just those who have suffered traumas?" Janet had asked, and Lee Roy had nodded vaguely, then more emphatically, like a trained dog, baring his crooked teeth.) The coverage of the veterans' art was brief and perfunctory, which was probably just as well. Clyde Somerset had been pleased with the publicity: *"very* pleased" with the publicity.

What worried Michael was that, in the months since, Janet had returned several times to Mount Orion, for the ostensible purpose of writing a freelance article, a "print piece," as she called it, on Lee Roy Sears. She hadn't been at all satisfied with the interview—television, she lamented, is so *limited.* Twice, she had stayed with the O'Mearas, but she'd been in Mount Orion once or twice more without so much as calling them. Was she interviewing Lee Roy at length?—was she researching his past? The prospect left Michael uneasy.

Gina said slyly, "If I didn't know your sister, and respect her intelligence, I'd almost think she was pursuing Lee Roy."

"Pursuing? How?" Michael asked, appalled.

Gina merely smiled. *"If* I didn't know her."

The last time they'd spoken together, Michael and Janet had nearly quarreled over the issue of Janet's having lent Lee Roy money. Michael strongly advised against it—"Being in prison so many years has made him dependent, he has to become independent." Michael did not mention that, in all, between the two of them, he and Gina had "lent" Lee Roy hundreds of dollars, which it was unlikely he'd be able to pay back in the near future. Janet said defensively, "I'm not lending Lee Roy Sears money, still less am I giving it. Lee Roy Sears isn't a man to accept charity. What I'm doing is *investing* in his future as an artist." Janet, for all her native shrewdness, seemed somehow convinced that a New York gallery was going to represent Lee Roy Sears's work soon, and that his career as a new American artist would be launched.

Not that Michael O'Meara did *not* believe in his friend's talent, but—!

This fantasy of a New York gallery, and all it promised of fame, money—Michael knew to trace back to Valeria Darrell, who had tirelessly pursued Lee Roy Sears over the summer. She claimed that she was "mesmerized" by him, but she denied any "romantic attachment" to him—the man was an ex-convict, after all. All of Mount Orion pondered: were the two lovers?—did Lee Roy Sears reciprocate the older woman's interest?—or was Valeria simply being kind, including Sears in her highly active, and not highly discriminatory, social life? Or was all of this rumor, without foundation? Lee Roy was gentlemanly, or guarded, in speaking of Valeria; in fact, he never spoke of her unless, obliquely, taking care to show not the slightest sign of jealousy or disapproval (for in truth he felt neither), Michael inquired after Lee Roy's "other" Mount Orion friends. Gina simply refused to inquire.

She *was* jealous, and she *was* disapproving. Though Lee Roy Sears was clearly in awe of her, often tongue-tied in her presence, she was not placated. "I will never forgive Valeria for stealing Lee Roy away that night," Gina said, with an angry little smile, "and Valeria well knows it."

As for Lee Roy himself, Gina had forgiven him long ago. He was naive, and he was a man; he could not be expected to understand the protocol of Mount Orion social life. "He stands," Gina said thoughtfully, "outside the Caucasian race."

"THE MADMAN HAS BARRICADED himself in the studio, and refuses to talk to anyone!—he thinks I'm going to have him forcibly ejected. Did Gina tell you?"

Clyde Somerset was speaking loudly, and angrily, as if Michael O'Meara was to blame; Michael, astonished, had never seen the older man so agitated, and seemingly at a loss. Beside him, stiff and self-conscious, grim, irresolute, stood the Dumont Center's sole security guard, a gray-haired man in his mid-fifties, smartly uniformed but unarmed.

"Gina told me something of the—circumstances."

"About Julia Sutter?—and Marian Parrish?—poor Mrs. Parrish nearly had a heart attack, I do mean an actual heart attack, when she realized what it was she was looking at, in the studio. Her eyes aren't good—she had to get up close. I had no idea what he was up to, damn him! Utterly revolting—disgusting—obscene *things!*"

"His—clay figures, do you mean? What are they?"

"The 'art' is obscene by Mount Orion community standards, and it's obscene by *my* standards. Sears knows this, certainly—his kind of 'artist' knows exactly what he's doing. Of course, I tried to explain to Julia that this was new work, and it wasn't on exhibit, it isn't in a public place, but Julia said, and of course she's right, that Sears *is* on the staff here; he's our 'artist-in-residence'; his studio is on our premises, and he works with supplies we buy. His stipend for the twelve-week course he's teaching is five thousand dollars, which is *very* generous, by anyone's standards!"

"You say Lee Roy is *barricaded* in the studio?"

"Yes, and I've told him I will call the police if he doesn't open the door. I've warned him! I will! I don't give a damn about the publicity, if the safety of my staff is threatened!"

Clyde Somerset's normally affable, ruddy face was heavy with blood; his eyes were faintly bloodshot; his impeccably tailored three-piece suit, with its British affectations, looked rumpled. The Dumont Center itself, this splendid postmodernist building with its vaulted glass-and-aluminum ceiling, its open lobby, spotless marble floor, had about it this afternoon a jarred, dazed air, as if it had been taken up, violently shaken, and set down again. But how was there any threat? A few visitors were walking through the first-floor exhibit, "Autumnal Visions by the New Jersey Watercolorists Society"—the exhibit itself looked quaint and almost comically incongruous, in the light of Clyde Somerset's intensity.

Michael said, calmly, "Clyde, I seriously doubt that anyone's safety is threatened. Why don't we go downstairs? I'll see if he will listen to me."

Michael felt a tinge of pleasure: taking charge: assuming responsibility: as he'd felt, so many years ago, in the dissection lab in medical school.

The three men went downstairs, Michael O'Meara in the lead. Clyde said, less vehemently, "I suppose the man is simply a bit—rattled. When I went to speak with him, Julia insisted upon coming along; she was excitable, as women of her age who are used to having their own way can be. Accusing Sears of 'misogyny'—as if he'd be likely to know what the word is!" Clyde laughed, and dabbed at his face with a monogrammed handkerchief. "I spoke quite reasonably with Sears, I thought, suggesting that he simply remove the new work from our premises, take it home with him, wherever. But he turned stubborn. Wasn't even embarrassed about this trash of his. The way, you know, he hadn't been embarrassed by seeming to have plagiarized from what-was-his-name—that pathetic man in the wheelchair. No, your Lee Roy Sears can't be embarrassed, I'd say!—or shamed!"

Michael said, "But Lee Roy *hadn't* plagiarized—that was just Mal Bishop's accusation. There was never any proof."

Clyde said carelessly, "Oh, hell—that's what they all say."

"What who says?"

"Plagiarists. Thieves."

"But why take Bishop's word over Sears's?—Lee Roy told *me*, Bishop had stolen from *him*."

"Well, naturally," Clyde said, with a spiteful laugh, "that's what he would tell *you*; that's what *you* would want to hear."

Michael, offended, had not time to pursue this subject, for they were at the door to the studio, in a fluorescent-lit corridor with a distinctly subterranean air. The security guard immediately pressed

his back against the wall, arms outstretched, in a posture of naive
vigilance, as he had perhaps seen television policeman do, in similar
circumstances; Michael simply knocked on the door. "Lee Roy?—
it's me, Michael." He tried the doorknob. "Will you let me in,
please?"

There was no sound from inside.

Michael knocked again, not hard, but firmly; spoke as before,
in a slightly raised voice. The thought struck him, with a pang of
horror, that Lee Roy, in a sudden panic, overwhelmed by circumstances he could not control, might have killed himself.

Of all things Lee Roy Sears most feared being sent back to
prison—he'd told Michael and Gina that he would rather die.

He'd told them too, the other evening, speaking boastfully, a
bit wildly, that he would die for what he believed in—now he *had*
something to believe in.

"Lee Roy?—it's Michael. Please unlock the door."

There was a long pause; Clyde began to speak, but Michael
signaled him to be still; then came the sound of the door being
unlocked.

Michael pushed the door open—of course, there was no barri-
cade.

The studio's overhead lights were off, but waning light came
through the long horizontal window that ran the length of a wall,
near the ceiling. Lee Roy Sears was quickly limping away, to a corner
of the room, as a shamed child might, hiding his face from Michael.

Clyde Somerset and the security guard remained in the corridor, and Michael went inside, partly closing the door behind him.
He greeted Lee Roy warmly, yet cautiously. "Thanks for opening
the door, Lee Roy. How are you?"

Lee Roy, his back to Michael, now squatting, made no reply
that Michael could hear.

"Clyde has told me there's been a misunderstanding? I'm sure
it's nothing that can't be cleared up."

Again, no reply.

Michael approached Lee Roy, slowly. He wasn't afraid of his
friend but he was fearful of further disturbing him—he could tell,
by a rank, animal odor in the air, and by the other man's pronounced
breathing, that Lee Roy was in an extreme emotional state.

"Lee Roy?—I'm sure it's nothing that can't be cleared up."

Lee Roy was squatting on his heels, his back to Michael. He appeared to be contemplating, or guarding, a number of clay figures scattered on a ragged newspaper at the base of the wall. In the half-light, Michael could not make out details, but he recognized Sears's characteristic work. Humanoid figures in odd postures, the largest about eight inches long. And other, smaller objects.

Squatting as he was, his legs and thighs straining, Lee Roy was trembling; quivering; like a vibrating mechanism. His breath was rasping and erratic, as if he were climbing a flight of stairs, or lifting a heavy weight. His hair had grown shaggy, and greasy, but, with his head bowed and chin creased against his chest, the back of his neck was exposed, and Michael could see how thick it had grown—how muscular. And his arms, and shoulders, straining too inside his white shirt! The gangling, emaciated-looking Lee Roy Sears whom Michael O'Meara had first known was gone—where?

As Gina had said, the other night, in bed, as if reading Michael's thoughts, "I hope we don't lose him." Michael had not needed to ask Gina of whom she spoke.

For several minutes Michael spoke to Lee Roy, quietly, placatingly, as if addressing one of his sons, or a demoralized junior lawyer at Pearce, Inc. He assured Lee Roy that he would not be forcibly ejected from his studio; nor would he be dismissed from his position. (Was Clyde Somerset listening, at the door? Michael hoped so.) He was standing behind Lee Roy, at a respectful distance of two or three feet. Cautioning himself, Don't startle the man, don't upset him further. If this were a prison situation, he could erupt under pressure. Michael seemed to know that Lee Roy was under a powerful psychoactive drug—which should help.

Was it possibly Chlonopramane, Pearce, Inc.'s highly profitable "wonder drug" for the control of mania, obsessive thoughts, and violent behavior?—of course, Michael would never have been so tactless as to ask his friend.

So pressed for time had he been in recent weeks, Michael had not visited the studio since the fall term had begun, and he was surprised at its disorder, and the pungent odors of paint, clay, turpentine, human sweat and effort. The large space was also the art-therapy classroom: various works by Lee Roy and his students were on display, in a jumble of colorful images, like psychedelic cave drawings. Crude cartoonlike sketches in charcoal and crayon; swaths of acrylic color on sheets of construction paper taped to the walls. How primitive, how exposed!—art's rawest impulses, without the strategies of art.

From where, Michael wondered, struck by pity, did this impulse spring?—and why?

At last, sullen, mumbling, Lee Roy responded to Michael's questions, though still without looking up at him. Squatting on his heels in front of the clay figures, arms tightly folded, head bowed, Lee Roy put Michael in mind of a snake—queerly upright, yet coiled. He said, "—ain't got no right, calling me names. Saying things about me like I'm an—animal." Michael said quickly, "Lee Roy, no one thinks of you that way. There has been a little misunderstanding, that's all. If we could—" Michael stepped cautiously closer, looking down on the top of Lee Roy's head; seeing, for the first time, that Lee Roy's thick, shaggy black hair was in fact slightly thin at the crown; a bald spot the size of a silver dollar was defining itself, like a sly, secret thought unfolding in darkness. Lee Roy drew the edge of his hand roughly beneath his nose, saying, "—no 'misunderstanding,' Mr. O'Meara! Nah!" He glanced up at Michael, his eyes damp, dark, shiny, and his forehead creased. His ordinarily boyish, expectant look was replaced by an expression of scarcely controlled fury; his lips were drawn back from his teeth. As Michael blinked down at him he mumbled something further that sounded like "Fuck it!"

Michael switched on the overhead light, and, seeing the objects at Lee Roy's feet, stared in silence, appalled.

Even through the mellow haze of Liloprane, Michael O'Meara *was* shocked.

The most prominent were humanoid figures, like Lee Roy's earlier work, but these were female, and more grotesquely mutilated. They were naked, lying on their backs or sides, heads flung back in agony, with gashes for mouths and lurid gouged-out spaces between their legs. One figure's legs were twisted out from her body almost perpendicularly. Another's legs, spread, were broken at the knees. There were eyeless sockets, noses mere holes. Breasts were attached to bodies by flaps of skin, or torn off altogether. One figure's abdomen had been opened, and a fetus removed, entwined in spaghetti-

like coils meant to represent intestines. The smaller objects on the
newspaper did not bear close examination—they were eyes, fingers,
genitals, interior organs.

Of the six figures that were complete, four were Asian; the
other two, Caucasian. All were young, mere girls.

Michael thought, My God!

Michael thought, They *are* obscene.

There was a long, painful silence, broken only by Lee Roy's
harsh breathing and, from outside, a sound of traffic, voices—jar-
ringly ordinary. Michael felt faint, yet, at the same time, determined to take this in stride. He whistled thinly through his teeth
and said, "Well." A pause. *"Well."*

Hunched over, his face masklike with tension, Lee Roy squinted
up at him.

There was nothing to do but plunge forward: so, in lawyerly
fashion, his face burning, Michael explained to the silent Lee Roy
Sears that, though he understood, and sympathized with, the auton-
omy of the artist, there remained the fact that the community has
rights too, and has customarily exerted pressures enforceable by law.
When, in particular, a sexual taboo is broken, and when the community in question is financially supporting the artist—

Lee Roy made a derisive grunting noise, shifting his weight on
his haunches. He was still squinting up at Michael, in that strained,
quivering, reptilian pose. His bony forehead was prominent. The
smell lifting from him more pronounced.

Michael bravely continued, trying to speak reasonably, as a
professional man to a friend, explaining that, since its inception, the
Dumont Center had depended solely upon private donations and
public funding; with an emphasis upon private donations. In Mount
Orion, there were a number of generous, civic-minded people, many
of them women—older women—like Julia Sutter. And so—

"All Clyde Somerset is asking, I think, is that you remove these
pieces from the premises. You could take them"—Michael paused,
not certain that the word *home* exactly applied to the rundown halfway
house in Putnam where Lee Roy lived—"home with you. Couldn't
you? I'll help you, I'll drive you, right now. What do you say?"

With a curious shrugging gesture of his shoulders, as if his shirt
were too tight, Lee Roy grinned up at Michael. His eyes were

unnaturally shiny. "You're on their side, huh, Mr. O'Meara!" It was not a question so much as a statement, an accusation.

"It isn't a question of sides, Lee Roy. It's a question of how best to proceed. If you refuse, your future at the Center may be jeopardized. If you compromise—"

"—said I was 'obscene.' Said I didn't deserve to be here."

"Who said that? I'm sure you misheard."

"They did. *They* did." Lee Roy jerked his head in the direction of the door.

Out in the corridor, at a discreet distance, Clyde Somerset and the uniformed guard stood, cautiously watching. With his back to the doorway, Lee Roy Sears could not see them but very likely knew they were there.

Under his breath he muttered, "Fuckers!"

Michael had to resist the impulse to touch Lee Roy's shoulder, to quiet him.

He would have liked too to squat down beside Lee Roy, as if they were equals: but feared seeming condescending.

He said, "Lee Roy, you must know that you have created some very extreme images here. When an artist, or anyone, violates a taboo, offends what's called 'community standards'—" As he spoke, Michael was uneasily aware of both Lee Roy's derisive expression and the clay figures at his feet: the mangled, mutilated female bodies, the outspread legs, back-flung heads, severed body parts. The clay was even the color of raw meat; and its texture suggested a damp stickiness. Michael felt dizzy, disoriented. *Why am I here, appealing to a madman?—am I mad myself?* Yet he dismissed the thought, a thought shared by any number of lawyers, certainly, during the course of their careers; he continued speaking reasonably as before, confident that, in another few minutes, he would win over Lee Roy to his side. (If he left the Dumont Center soon, and drove Lee Roy to Putnam, he could swing around to the Parkway just east of Putnam, and be back at Pearce, Inc., within forty-five minutes.)

He saw that Lee Roy's white shirt, his so characteristic white shirt, was encrusted with clay and other stains, and that the sleeves were rolled up partway to his elbows, cuffs flapping loose. And was that a tattoo on his left arm?—Michael had only a glimpse of a

corner of something black, spangled with gold. He'd never known
that Lee Roy Sears had a tattoo.

Michael said, suddenly, almost reproachfully, "Lee Roy, you
wouldn't want Gina to see these, would you?"

Lee Roy ducked his head guiltily. He rocked on his heels. "She
don't need to, then," he mumbled.

"But she might, if she came here, to visit your studio. What
then?"

Lee Roy shrugged.

"Don't you think Gina would be shocked, seeing these? Perhaps
even *hurt?*"

Lee Roy mumbled, "They're what came out."

"What do you mean, you didn't shape them yourself?—with
your own hands? Who did, if you didn't?" Michael asked skeptically.

He had surely not intended to get into an argument with Lee
Roy, particularly in these volatile circumstances, yet, as it happened,
he seemed scarcely aware of what he was saying, still less what he
might be precipitating. He would think, afterward, with a kind of
baffled shame, *That isn't like me at all. 'Michael' is the one who never
objects.*

Lee Roy gave a sound of anguish, or was it anger—choked,
guttural. His face was an aborigine's, dark with blood, the eyes shiny,
manic. Again he mumbled, "They're what came *out,*" the word
"out" elongated, a low wail.

"For God's sake, Lee Roy—"

Lee Roy seized one of the clay figures and held it up to Michael, as if offering it to him. (And how grotesque, how ugly the
thing was!—a broken female, vagina gouged out, one couldn't help
but imagine Sears's fingers plunging, scooping.) Seeing the look in
Michael's face of disgust, disdain, Lee Roy said, *"You* hate me too,
huh! *You,* and *them!"*

To Michael's astonishment, Lee Roy began crying; sobbing; muttering to himself. Quite deliberately he broke the clay figure in two and
flung the parts down. He picked up another, and this time broke it
fiercely into bits, flinging them down, now out of control, sobbing like
a broken-hearted child. A child in the throes of a tantrum.

"Yah?—this? This? *This? Yah this?"*

He snatched up figures, shook them at Michael, and broke

them. As Michael stood over him, too surprised to act, or, perhaps, fearful of trying to stop him, Lee Roy crawled on his hands and knees on the outspread newspaper taking up and breaking the figures, smashing them, grinding them to bits with his fingers. Now he was in a paroxysm of destruction, sobbing, laughing, "Uh! uh! uh!"

"Lee Roy, no—"

Lee Roy scrambled to his feet, hunched, panting, his eyes wild in his mottled face, and went for the charcoal sketches and paintings taped to the walls, tearing them down, tearing them into strips, he seized canvases resting against a wall and tore and kicked at them, with a violent wave of his arm he sent jars, bottles, cans, paintbrushes, a ceramic bowl flying off the workbench—all before Michael dared try to prevent him, dared even to touch his arm. And when Michael did touch Lee Roy's arm, Lee Roy shoved him away—like a rabid dog turning against his master he actually bared his teeth at Michael.

"You hate me too!—you think I'm shit!"

Then, sobbing, Lee Roy Sears ran out of the studio.

In the corridor, several staff members had gathered, with Clyde Somerset and the security guard, to watch what was happening in the studio; when Lee Roy rushed out, everyone scrambled aside, to give him passage. Afterward it would be recounted (not by Michael O'Meara: by the others) that Lee Roy Sears had gone berserk—no other word for it but *berserk*.

AND WAS HE TO *blame. Who was to blame.*
Who to blame.

Though greatly upset, needing in fact to swallow down a second pale green pill, even as he was making his way weaving skillfully through traffic on the Parkway, Michael O'Meara managed to return to Pearce, Inc., by 4:30 P.M.; worked until 6:30 P.M.; put all thoughts of Lee Roy Sears and of what must be done (what he must do) out of his head, until he was once again free, and again navigating the Parkway westward for the final time that day.

That day!—Friday, October 18. How long it had been thus far, and how much longer it would be!

He was seeing as in a kaleidoscopic jumble the ugly, obscene humanoid figures and organs—for they *were* obscene: why prevaricate?—and he was seeing Lee Roy Sears's crouched tremulous form;

hearing Lee Roy Sears's heartrending sobs, and that accusation, which Michael O'Meara believed he would never forget, for the remainder of his life.

You hate me too. You think I'm shit.

Yes, and there was Lee Roy's contorted face, an infant's face. Glistening eyes. Mania. The sharp sweat-smell of mania. Who to blame? Had Michael only been thinking more coherently, he would have realized that you don't attempt to reason with, thus end up arguing with, a distraught man, a man recently paroled from a maximum security prison, a man who fought in, and was wounded in, Vietnam, a man who was exposed to the toxic Agent Orange, a man with a history of emotional instability. You don't.

What must be done, what *he* must do.

If he could not salvage Lee Roy Sears's residency at the Dumont Center, he could at least prevent the poor man from being returned to prison.

For prison, for Lee Roy Sears, would be a death sentence.

Michael's thoughts leapt ahead in swift lawyerly fashion. He would speak with Clyde Somerset, and he would speak with Julia Sutter, and he would speak with Marian Parrish—whom he did not know, but whom Gina knew slightly. He would argue on Lee Roy Sears's behalf. But he would not put them on the defensive: he would explain, apologize. Appeal to these good people. For they *were* good people, generous, and charitable, and kind. They were not vindictive, were they?—far better to forgive.

He would arrange to see them all tomorrow. Thank God, tomorrow was a Saturday.

He had work to do for Pearce, Inc., which he'd brought home, but he could do that early, he'd get up early, at dawn. And there was Sunday.

He'd vaguely promised Joel and Kenny he would take them to The Islands, but the promise had been vague, and maybe, just maybe, they wouldn't remember?

The following week, he would probably speak with H. Sigman, Lee Roy's parole officer. The man was a thorough professional, hardly idealistic, yet not cynical; beyond cynicism, you might say. He wanted simply to do his job, to get it done. How many parolees he had in his charge, in his files, Michael did not know, but he sus-

pected quite a few. When Lee Roy Sears had walked off his job at
the parking garage, and the manager had accused him, falsely, with
no witnesses, of having threatened him, Michael O'Meara had taken
the time to meet with Sigman, in his cramped office, and that had
seemed to flatter him, Michael's very presence had seemed to flatter
him, let alone Michael's sincerity. Here was a successful corporation
lawyer from Mount Orion, well-dressed, down-to-earth, making it
a point to speak to H. Sigman who was nobody. About an ex-con
named Lee Roy Sears who was nobody too.

Sigman should be persuaded, this time too.

WHAT A DREARY, DEPRESSING place!—Michael ascended the creaking
stairs quickly, glancing neither to the left nor to the right, trying not
to breathe too deeply. He was not by nature an overly sensitive
man—Gina frequently chided him for his imprecision in identifying
smells—but the odor here, a nightmare admixture of rancid food,
grime, dried vomit, urine, Lysol, brought tears to his eyes. He could
not imagine how Lee Roy Sears bore it.

Unless prison had been worse?

Of course, prison had been worse.

Michael knocked on the door to 12B, which was Lee Roy's
room: seeing no light beneath the door, and suspecting, in any case,
that Lee Roy would not be in. He saw that the door was scraped
and battered, as if gnawed upon. The corridor was dimly lit, the
walls stained and layered with dirt.

Michael knocked again, and, for the second time that day, said,
cautiously, "Lee Roy?—it's me, Michael."

He had not spoken loudly, but a door opened at once behind
him, and a paunchy squinting man in an undershirt appeared, asking
something in Spanish that Michael could not comprehend. He believed he heard the name "Sears," but he might have been mistaken.
"Yes, thank you," he said, stammering, "n-no, thank you," retreating to the stairs, confused, sick at heart, blinking genuine tears out
of his eyes. The man in the undershirt questioned him again, in
Spanish, more belligerently. Michael waved vaguely, hurrying down
the stairs. "No! No thanks! It's all right! Never mind!" For one so
heavy in the stomach, the man moved with startling swiftness, to
the stairway railing, and, now shouting in Spanish, leaned over and

spat out a great gob of mucus that landed on the right sleeve of
Michael O'Meara's navy blue pinstripe suit.

MICHAEL WAS TOO SHOCKED, and too frightened, to protest. He half-
ran out of the building and to his car parked close by. He imagined
he heard laughter in his wake. Had others in the rooming house
been watching too?—did they recognize him, somehow?

He might then have fled home, to Mount Orion; to Gina. But
he wanted so badly to talk to Lee Roy tonight . . . to see that Lee
Roy was all right, and to give him counsel.

Yes, he had to talk to Lee Roy. Simply had to.

He'd failed to protect Lee Roy, as he might have. He knew it,
and Lee Roy knew it. This was a knowledge shared by no one else.

He wouldn't even try to explain to Gina.

Yes, he had better try to explain to Gina.

In any case he had to telephone her, since it was late: after
7:00 P.M.: he didn't want her to worry about him. By now she had
certainly heard of the further trouble at the Dumont Center; in
Mount Orion, news travels rapidly, and bad news most rapidly. He'd
half expected Gina to call him again at work, but she had not.

Michael called home, from a pay phone, and, after several long
rings, to his surprise, the answering tape switched on. At this hour of
the evening?—but where was Gina? *Hello!* came his own cheery voice,
*This is the O'Meara residence! I'm afraid neither Gina nor I can come to
the phone right now, but if you'd like to leave a message* . . . He was struck
by the forlorn fatuousness of his own voice.

Desperately he said, "Hello? Gina? Marita? Joel? Kenny? Hello,
this is—" But he didn't need to identify himself, surely?

He waited, hoping that Gina might pick up the receiver. There
was someone at the house, of course: Marita was there, tending the
boys. Marita refused to answer the phone at the O'Mearas, however,
with the excuse that her English was poor.

"—Hello? Joel, Kenny? Hey! Can you hear me! This is Daddy—"

In disgust Michael hung up the receiver. Walked away.

For the next two hours he remained in Lee Roy Sears's neighborhood, his car parked, inconspicuously as he hoped, a few doors
up the street from the rooming house. He passed the time by looking
through some of the papers he'd brought home pertaining to the

\$50 million Peverol suit. (The light from the street was just barely
adequate for reading.) And by sipping wine. (On an impulse, he'd
bought a bottle of inexpensive, cloyingly sweet Gallo wine at a
neighborhood store: the very store at which Lee Roy Sears would
probably make his alcoholic purchases, if he was drinking again,
which, Michael hoped, he was not. A small matter, but it might
constitute violation of parole.)

Michael could not recall having had lunch that day—he'd
worked through midday, frantic to clear his desk before the \$50
million Peverol suit swept over him and his staff—but he was not
hungry in the slightest. Hadn't Gina remarked upon that?—no, it
had been Marita, the other evening: Michael didn't seem to have
his old appetite lately. He ate without tasting his food. He wasn't
thirsty at the moment either, and he loathed the Gallo wine. Yet,
there he sat behind the wheel of the stylish white Mazda, near the
shabby intersection of Eighth Street and Graff, Putnam, New Jersey,
sipping now and then from the bottle cloaked in its discreet paper
bag, and frowning over a swath of legal documents and photocopied
material. By the time the Peverol case even came to court, thousands
of pages of such material would have passed through Michael
O'Meara's hands. And brain.

Once, years ago, Michael had happened to overhear two senior
Pearce executives speaking of him, in the executive men's lounge. One
had said, "Isn't Michael O'Meara a godsend?—and he doesn't seem to
know it, or to exploit it!" and the other had said, chuckling, with a
paternal fondness, "That's one of the reasons he *is* a godsend."

Michael, face burning with pleasure, had hidden in a toilet stall
until such time as the coast was clear.

If he's born too soon.
They're what came out.

Legal work of such painstaking kind is arduous but challenging.
You need a zestful commitment. A love of the forest of signs, symbols.
Riddles. Reversals. Ironies, and rewards. In equal measure. Oh yes.

Some temperaments do love the forest, the interior. Daylight
too closely resembles oblivion.

Last Sunday, Lee Roy Sears had come to the O'Mearas for an
early supper, so that the boys could join them. Sundays were traditionally early days. A kind of interim; a daylight sort of day; the

sabbath. Before the meal, Lee Roy, Joel, and Kenny had gone down to the pond, the three of them trotting, calling out happily, a large wiry black dog and two flaxen-haired pups, while Michael and Gina, more proper adults, sipped their drinks on the terrace. It was a brilliant October day, fading deliciously to dusk. The air was fragrant with dry leaves whose very colors—Chinese-maple red, beech-yellow—seemed discernible, as smells. Michael said, with just the faintest tinge of jealousy, "It's wonderful, how the boys have grown so fond of Lee Roy, isn't it?—so trusting."

As if her mind were elsewhere, and she had to draw it back, like a recalcitrant net, Gina said, "—oh yes. I think so."

"You 'think' so—?"

"It's just that they're so sort of—excitable, after they've been with him. And secretive. Marita feels it the most because, I guess, they can be, sometimes, a bit—I don't know—*rude* with her. I've noticed it too, how they talk to each other in code words, the way they used to do when they were little—remember? They fall into these fits of giggling, and then, if I ask them what's funny, tell Mommy so she can laugh too, they just go blank." She paused, sipping her drink. Gina O'Meara's drink was invariably cool dry white wine. "I feel like an intruder in their private lives and I suppose I *am.*"

Michael said, surprised, touched, "Why, Gina, you can't be an intruder in our sons' lives—you're their *mother.*"

Gina laughed, lightly. Saying, "And you're their *father.*"

Michael went down to the pond, to join Lee Roy Sears and his sons. He felt, in that instant, he could not bear to look at Gina, and he did not know why.

In the waning sepia light, the pond looked beautiful. The backdrop of trees was beautiful. How happy I've been, Michael O'Meara thought. For I own this.

As always, the pond, close up, looked much larger than it appeared to be from the house. Now that it had been thoroughly dredged, the choking vegetation torn out by its roots, the black sediment at the pond's bottom hauled away, the pond was flatter, more placid, more mirrorlike than before. Lee Roy Sears, self-conscious in his host's presence, said, mumbling, "The pond looks real nice now, Mr. O'Meara—I mean Michael. I mean, y'know, now you had it dug out—*real* nice."

Michael said, "Yes? Do you think so?"

Lee Roy Sears was gripping one hand in another, unconsciously flexing his biceps. He wore a cheap dark garbardine jacket and a long-sleeved white shirt and a pebble-colored necktie. He glanced at Michael, with his strained grin. Elsewhere, the twins were frisking about, squealing, shouting, pushing at each other. Showing off for Lee Roy Sears; maybe for Daddy as well. They saw Daddy infrequently these days.

Michael said, "I preferred it as it was. Rushes, water iris, cattails. Now it's too manicured. It's suburban."

Lee Roy said, "It's deeper."

It was then that Joel, or was it Kenny, slipped into the pond, or had he been shoved by his brother: shrieking, splashing, flailing about in the foot-deep water at shore. Michael hurried over with as much urgency as if the water were much deeper, and his little boy was drowning.

"Daddy, he pushed me!" cried the enraged child, scrambling to his feet in the pond, and, "Daddy, he pushed *me!*—and fell, himself!" cried the other, indignant, though unable to resist a grin, and, "Daddy, don't listen to him, he's a liar!" and, "Daddy, don't listen to *him*, he's a liar!"

Michael helped Kenny, or was it Joel, out of the water, even as the incensed child wrenched his arm out of Daddy's grasp. He was half-sobbing—he'd been embarrassed in front of Mr. Sears.

"Daddy, you saw!—saw what he did!"

"Daddy, I did *not!* He did it to himself!"

"I did *not*, liar, I did *not*, liar!"

"You're the liar—"

"—fucking *liar!*"

The boys punched and slapped at each other, around Daddy: Daddy, laughing angrily, for he too was embarrassed in front of their guest, held them apart with sheer force. How wild Joel and Kenny could be, at such times!—as Gina had observed, it was as if they regressed to the age of two or three. And how strong they'd grown, in the past few months! Their little bodies sheer energy, muscle. And such obstinacy, such *determination*.

Daddy was profoundly shocked that the boys knew, let alone uttered, a word like *fucking*, but he thought it wisest, in the exigency of the moment (with Gina staring down at them, unmoving on the terrace as if frozen in place), not to say anything. And maybe Lee Roy Sears had not heard.

WHEN MICHAEL O'MEARA WOKE with a start behind the wheel of his car, he was so disoriented initially he didn't know where he was.

The time was 9:02 P.M. He seemed to be parked on the street in a shabby urban neighborhood wholly unknown to him.

A police patrol car was idling up the block: shouts were being exchanged between policemen in the car and several men standing on the sidewalk. It was the shouting that had wakened Michael.

The bottle of Gallo wine in its paper bag had nearly capsized. Fortunately it hadn't spilled on his trousers. There was an ugly stain, however, on a cuff of his suit coat, which he'd tried without success to rub off.

Seeing the stain, Michael remembered where he was, and why. "I'm waiting for *him.*"

He must have dozed off, for a few minutes. (In fact, it had been nearly an hour.) The swath of legal papers had slipped from his grasp and were spread on the seat beside him, and on the floor.

Just down the block was Lee Roy Sears's rooming house: its yellow brick façade looked as if it had been dusted in soot. An obese black man was sitting on the front stoop, fanning himself with a rolled-up newspaper.

Michael wondered, had Lee Roy returned? He dreaded going back into that terrible place, climbing the stairs again, again knocking on the door. This time, the Hispanic man in the undershirt might be violent.

Michael rubbed his neck, which ached from his nap, and regarded himself in the rearview mirror. He had not shaved since before seven that morning and his silvery red-brown beard had begun to push through, like shot in his skin. He felt mildly nauseated from the sickish-sweet wine and could not imagine why on earth he'd bought it.

What an inappropriate neighborhood this was, for a parolees' halfway house! It was more populous now than earlier: there were rowdy jive-talking young blacks hanging out in front of a tavern poolhall, young Hispanics milling about, women and girls in amazing costumes—skin-tight leather skirts to mid-thigh, knee-high plastic boots, sequined or fishnet sweaters that virtually revealed their breasts. Derelicts weaved about on the sidewalks or lay huddled in doorways like piles of old clothes.

A second Putnam Police Department patrol car cruised by, and the driver shot Michael a suspicious, appraising look.

He knew he should go home, it was late, and Gina would be worried about him, if Gina was home. But of course Gina was home.

He was about to start the ignition when he saw, in the rearview mirror, a familiar car drive up behind him, to park about two car lengths away. Whose car it was, why even the license plate looked familiar, he could not say, at first.

He was instinctively hunched a little, head lowered. Watching in the mirror as a woman got out from behind the wheel of the trim little Volvo, and, with some effort, as if he were ill or very tired, or drunk, a man got out from the other side. A man with Indian-black hair, a pasty face—Lee Roy Sears.

Who was the woman?—Michael couldn't see clearly. She was speaking with Lee Roy Sears earnestly, as if giving advice. A well-dressed youngish woman, not plump, but solid-bodied; with a high, healthy color; shining wheat-colored hair. A woman in her mid-thirties who resembled his sister, Janet.

The woman and Sears were walking to Sears's rooming house, Sears unsteady on his feet, and the woman helping to support him. They were of a height but seemed an ill-matched couple. As they approached the building, the black man sitting on the stoop gazed up at them, and the lower half of his face was split by a grin.

Michael O'Meara stared, appalled: it *was* Janet.

He turned just as the couple was entering the building, their faces obscured.

MICHAEL DROVE BACK TO Mount Orion. He had no wish to wait, to see when Janet would emerge from the house she had so freely entered.

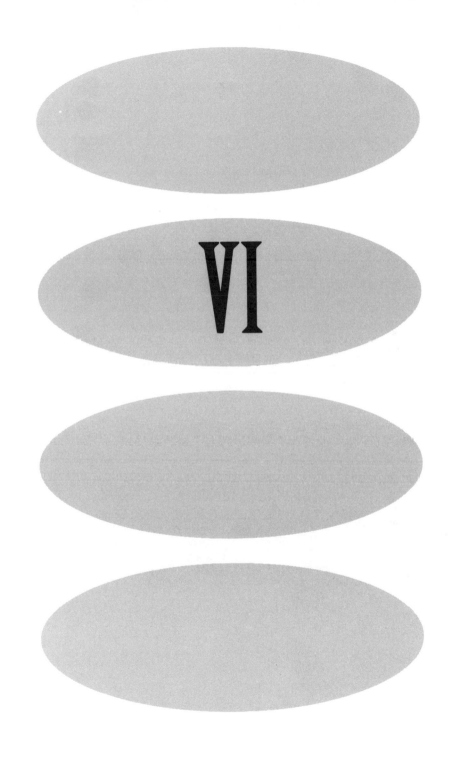

VI

1

SWIFTLY SHE IS WALKING along the upstairs corridor of this semi-public place, heels rapping smartly on the polished oak floorboards like a Spanish dancer's, when the arm reaches out, without warning, to encircle her waist.

What place *is* this, and which evening?—one of Mount Orion's "historic" renovated mansions, a damp blowsy October night, smelling of wet leaves.

Why does autumn, gusty autumn, swirling leaves and wind hammering at the windows, make her want to make love?—just the *idea* of it, that is. Not *really*.

The arm claims her. An arm in a dark sleeve, impeccably tailored tux, dazzling white shirtfront with golden studs. No, don't touch! I said *don't!*

Below, the sound of voices, laughter. Happy sounds. Gay festive mildly intoxicated sounds. The party she has been going to all her life.

Even a string quartet, off in a corner, to which no one is listening.

She is struggling with him, the bastard, following her upstairs like this, or—had he been waiting for her?

She doesn't want to think he's been waiting for her. Upstairs, knowing she'd get restless and follow. Knowing her? Does he?

Damn you I said *don't!* you don't know me you don't have a clue to me how dare you?

She isn't drunk either. Don't think it, you son of a bitch.

Taking advantage. But it won't work!

She is one of those persons who drinks prudently, carefully, gauging ounces. Measuring ounces against a party's duration.

Her drink is the very best white wine: cool, dry, tart, exquisite. And champagne, of course. If it's very good champagne.

Which she has been drinking tonight—moderately.

It's a celebration, is it?—the inaugural reception of whatever this is, fall-winter. Which year?

Before she'd actually seen, and felt, the arm snaking out to encircle her slender waist, before she'd felt his hard hungry teeth against her mouth, her throat, her breast, she had maybe, just maybe had a premonition—the way you do when there is something at the periphery of your vision you can't exactly *see.*

So, she might have paused and turned back; might have hurried back down the elegant old circular staircase. Poised, very beautiful. Mysterious smile on her lips.

So, her husband might not have vaguely, perhaps not at all consciously, sensed her absence. Glancing about, in the midst of talk, smiles, handshakes, hearty greetings.

Descending the staircase she would have been confident that the black jersey sheath snugly fitting her almost-too-thin body is a success, worth its cost. Ah, she'd known at once, seeing it there on its plush cushioned hanger, in The After Five Salon, Henri Bendel's. Some things, you simply *know.*

The shoes, she hadn't had such luck. Shopped for days before locating them at Milady's—but they *are* exquisite.

They are stumbling together in a clumsy dance, quick urgent breaths, widened eyes, and, God damn him, he's stepping on her *toes:* which means her new *shoes:* son of a bitch this isn't funny, will you please *stop!*

Kisses tasting of champagne.

Faint undertaste of oysters, parsley butter. Garlic?

Laughing he walks her into one of the exhibit rooms, walks her backward, sideways, unceremoniously, nudges the door only partway shut with his elbow.

Why should I stop? Hmmmm?

Not *here*, not *now*—

Then where, when?

—what if someone comes in—

—hmmmm?

—oh! you're crazy, you're—

—like this!—

—I said *stop*—

—why, when you like it so?

Hiking her dress rudely above her knees, above her thighs, up to her waist, and the black silk slip with the lace hem, yes and he's tugging down her black silk panties, his fingers hard, hot, thrusting so she's astonished she's clutching at him desperate to keep from falling, damn you you crazy bastard, laughing he nuzzles her, I'll take you where you didn't know you wanted to go just hang on honey, like this? like this? *this?* unzipping his trousers in this shadowy place smelling of dust and furniture polish, lifting to position her recklessly across one of the glass display cases, thank God it's a sturdy piece of furniture, where *are* they?—in an exhibit room solemn as a tomb housing Northern New Jersey history, aged diaries, frayed ladies' fans, snuffboxes, derby hats, yellowed newspapers with banner headlines at which no one has glanced with more than cursory interest in one hundred years, on the faded-wallpaper walls are portraits in massive gilt frames of stiffly posed gentlemen, bewigged, bewhiskered, a beet-faced general in full regalia lording it over the others from his vantage point above the fireplace mantel. Oh! she is struggling to keep her knees together, the muscles of her groin are clenched tight, her jaws clenched tight, she happens to be wearing a black satin garter belt from Edith's (when did such fetching female paraphernalia come back into style?—and why?), gossamer-sheer

smoke-colored stockings, there are hot furious tears beneath her eyelids she is digging her manicured nails into his wrist she is protesting
she is serious she is helpless forced atop the glass display case his
weight pinning her, her head thrown back her lovely mouth contorted as a fish's gasping for air Oh! I said *stop!* please I mean *stop*—
   Too late.

2

T<small>HAT</small> AUTUMN. T<small>HAT</small> WINTER.

Something unknown and monstrous was happening, and Michael O'Meara could not control it, nor even gauge its dimensions; even as, in nightmare logic, he felt himself somehow responsible.

Yet, how?—how was *he* responsible? For these deaths were like accidents, unrelated to him as, apparently, to each other:

Early in the morning of November 3, Mal Bishop died in a blaze that gutted the tenement in which he rented a single-room apartment, in Newark, the consequence, it was believed, of his having dropped a lighted cigarette in his bed; and,

In the afternoon of November 16, on the eve of her eighty-fifth birthday, Julia Sutter was discovered dead, having been viciously beaten and stabbed by an intruder, in the basement of the lovely old colonial on Linwood Avenue, Mount Orion, in which she'd lived alone for many years.

Mal Bishop's death passed virtually without notice in Mount

Orion, but Julia Sutter's death, which had been murder, profoundly shocked the community. Not only was Julia Sutter a prominent, much-revered figure in Mount Orion, a woman with literally hundreds of friends, acquaintances, and associates, but, yet more significantly, there had been no violent death in Mount Orion in many years. The *Mount Orion Courier,* a weekly, prepared a special edition devoted to Julia Sutter: the police case, a lengthy obituary, reminiscences and comments by friends and neighbors, photographs of the dead woman and snippets of her poetry. (Julia Sutter had been a woman of many talents, it was revealed.)

There were only two senior detectives in the Mount Orion Police Department, and both were assigned to the Sutter case: the motive for the killing, if not for its viciousness, was believed to be robbery, since there were a number of valuable household items missing, and Julia's wallet, emptied of cash and credit cards, was found in an alley a few miles away. And there was at least one immediate suspect—of whom police were unwilling to speak at first, save to say of him, tersely, cryptically, that *he was not a resident of Mount Orion.*

Of course, Michael O'Meara thought of Lee Roy Sears at once.

Knowing too, to his shame, and horror, that others must be having the identical thought.

"WHAT A TERRIBLE, TERRIBLE thing!"

"What a tragedy!"

"Poor Julia!—to die like *that!*"

"And her grandchildren were planning a birthday party for her, the very next day!"

"Whoever did it—what a *beast!*"

The First Congregational Church of Mount Orion, to which Julia Sutter had belonged for fifty-two years, was packed with mourners at her funeral service. The atmosphere was hushed, appalled; there was a good deal of weeping; even Gina O'Meara, who had not known Julia very well, surprised Michael by dabbing at her eyes several times during the ceremony. Gina claimed to have felt a "daughterly affinity" with the older woman—the first Michael had heard of this sentiment, though he did not doubt its sincerity.

Though shocked and sickened by the crime, and very sorry for

Julia Sutter, Michael O'Meara did not feel so personally threatened by it as Gina and other women in Mount Orion seemed to feel. He understood that they were responding less to the actual death than to the brutality of the attack leading to the death: multiple stab wounds to nearly every part of the body, a crushed skull and larynx. The murderer had used both a blunt weapon (one of Julia's pewter candlestick holders) and a butcher knife (from Julia's kitchen), both left behind in the basement, covered in blood; but yielding no fingerprints. Police did not release the information, yet it was generally known that poor Julia's body had been so hacked and lacerated that one of her breasts was attached to her chest by only a flap of skin. The murderer, who must have been crazed, or on drugs, even took time to splatter and smear blood on one of the basement walls!— unfortunately without leaving finger- or handprints.

Had he been trying to write something, or indicate something?—or was it simply madness, slinging about his victim's blood?

A madman. Michael thought. But a madman with an agenda.

"POOR, DEAR JULIA!—WHAT a way for her, of all people, to die! I can't bear to think of it," Gina said, shuddering. "Don't talk about it, please, Michael. Unless to tell me the murderer has been found. The monster . . ."

Gina set down her drink and pressed her hands against her ears in a naive childlike gesture.

Michael stroked her thin shoulder, and her ashy-pale hair that felt, to his touch, surprisingly brittle, dry. He said gently, "Honey, it's possible that Julia died at once. Whoever did it—might have killed her, at once." His words sounded weak, unconvincing. His mouth was so dry, that must be to blame.

Gina was squinting up at him as if wanting to believe him, but then she spoke ironically, and shrugged off his touch. "Some comfort!" she laughed. "I hope *I* can expect as much!"

NATURALLY, MICHAEL O'MEARA WAS not the only resident of Mount Orion to have thought at once of Lee Roy Sears, when Julia Sutter's death became known: many others, knowing of the dispute at the Dumont Center, had made the connection immediately and had notified police. As it turned out, however, Lee Roy Sears had an alibi—provided, to Mount Orion's amazement, by Valeria Darrell.

He could not have killed poor Julia, Valeria said, because he had been with *her.*

In fact, Lee Roy Sears had been with Valeria Darrell, both insisted, on November 14, 15, 16, at Valeria's cottage (which was in fact a spacious split-level house) in Cape May, New Jersey, on the ocean. The house was isolated, but there was evidence, indisputable evidence, that the two were together on the night of November 15, for it was that night, at precisely 10:40 P.M., that Lee Roy Sears had driven Valeria, in Valeria's black Porsche, to the emergency wing of the Cape May General Hospital, for treatment of "minor facial injuries"—a fractured nose and lacerations suffered, Valeria said, when she'd fallen from the steep wooden stairs leading from her cottage down to the beach. The medical report noted a mild degree of intoxication.

Hospital records showed that Valeria had been in the emergency room for only forty-five minutes. It was her—and Lee Roy Sears's—claim that, during this time, he was waiting for her outside, in the car; when she left, she simply walked out, to join him. No one at the hospital could swear to having seen Lee Roy Sears after 10:45, and there were conflicting opinions about whether, in fact, he had actually been seen at the time. (The emergency room reception was very busy at that time of night.)

Michael could not help but calculate: it is approximately two hundred fifty miles from Cape May to Mount Orion, on the Garden State Parkway; a four-hour drive. Julia Sutter had died in the late morning of November 16.

Michael could not help but think, though the thought sickened him, Sears *could* have done it.

But, how unlikely!—that, granted Lee Roy Sears had been in Cape May at all, he would have driven back to Mount Orion that night, for the sole purpose of killing an elderly woman. Certainly, *he* denied it. And Valeria Darrell, most adamantly, in the eyes of Mount Orion most shamelessly, denied it.

Lee Roy was questioned by police, however. But not detained. For what evidence was there linking him to the crime?—to even the vicinity of the crime? After police released him, he spoke with Michael O'Meara on the phone, upset, tearful, "Fuckers!—trying to blame *me!*—persecuting *me!*—*I* wouldn't hurt no old lady, not even *her!*—damn *her!*—calling me 'obscene'!—'cause I'm an ex-con, huh?—'cause I ain't lily-white, huh?—fuckers!" Lee Roy spoke in this vein for some minutes, breathing hard, and Michael, deeply moved, simply let him talk. He was relieved to have heard from Lee Roy, with whom he hadn't spoken in two or three weeks, for, now that Lee Roy had his own studio, of sorts, in a loft in a former warehouse in North Putnam, and was no longer associated with the Dumont Center, Michael saw him less frequently; though he continued to think of him almost constantly.

Even when Michael wasn't thinking of Lee Roy Sears, he *was* thinking of him. Somehow, it had to do with the dryness in his mouth.

Lee Roy talked, incensed, indignant, and finally said, as if he had been leading up to this question, somewhat timorously, yet, as it came out, belligerently, *"You* believe me, Mr. O'Meara, don't you?"

The question hung in the air for a brief moment.

Then Michael said, almost explosively, "My God, Lee Roy!—do you have to *ask?* And please, I've told you, call me 'Michael.' "

(HE DID NOT TELL Gina, he would not have wished to tell Gina, that, so constant was his worry about Lee Roy Sears now, coupled with his more reasonable worry about the Peverol suit, he had gotten in the habit of taking Liloprane nearly every day, sometimes twice a day. A temporary measure, a mere expediency—but, to his annoyance, his mouth *was* dry.)

DESPITE MICHAEL O'MEARA'S EFFORTS on his behalf, with both Clyde Somerset and Julia Sutter, Lee Roy Sears was no longer "artist-in-residence" at the Dumont Center.

As Clyde said several times, it wasn't just the obscene art—"I can't, and I *won't,* have anyone that volatile on my staff."

Yet, at Michael's suggestion, the severance terms were not ungenerous: though Lee Roy had taught the art-therapy class for only six weeks of the fall semester, he would receive his full stipend, through December. He was allowed to keep any and all art supplies with which he'd been working. More importantly—and this, Michael O'Meara had insisted upon, with lawyerly sagacity—the exact reasons for his dismissal were not to be aired. The issue was to be, publicly, a disagreement over aesthetic principles.

What is "art," and what is "pornography"; how do we define the "obscene"; is an institution like the Dumont Center to be guided by "community standards"; and what, in fact, *are* "community standards"?

For weeks, the *Mount Orion Courier* published columns of passionate letters from readers, under the headlines PRO and CON: the PRO readers stoutly defended the right of the artist to determine "art," and the CON readers stoutly defended the right of the community to determine "obscenity." The *Courier* tried to maintain an editorial equanimity, for Mount Orion was, oddly, both a conservative community *and* a liberal community, depending upon the specificity of issues. The editor requested an interview with Lee Roy Sears to balance an interview with Clyde Somerset, but, following Michael O'Meara's advice, Lee Roy declined.

It would be wiser, more prudent, Michael said, for Lee Roy to simply withdraw, with dignity—"Since, after all, they're fulfilling the financial terms of your arrangement."

Lee Roy shrugged and didn't disagree. Since that outburst of his at the Center, he was unusually taciturn; sober. He'd confessed to Michael that he must have blacked out, since he could remember smashing the clay figures only vaguely: as if he'd watched someone else smash them, in a bad dream.

Michael said, "I wouldn't tell anyone else that, Lee Roy. Mr. Sigman, for instance. He might not understand."

Lee Roy laughed mirthlessly. "Like, shit, I'm gonna tell *any*body *any*thing!—except you."

When Lee Roy's art-therapy class was canceled by the Center, his students were given the prerogative of switching into other, more conventional art classes there; but their questions regarding their former instructor were not answered. The official statement was, Mr. Sears was no longer on the staff.

Ned Fiske demanded to know, from Clyde Somerset, if Lee Roy had had a breakdown, or if he'd been sent back to prison. Clyde said, diplomatically, "He hasn't been sent back to prison."

To Michael O'Meara, Clyde said, "Don't you think that man should have a psychiatric evaluation?" Michael said, "He has. He will. It's part of his parole regimen." Was this true? Michael had no idea, really. The thought had simply flown into his head. "He's under medication, too." Clyde said, "Something like Lithium?"

Michael said, "Something like Lithium."

FORTUNATELY FOR MICHAEL, IT had not been necessary for him to drive to Putnam, to see H. Sigman in person. He'd talked with the parole officer on the phone one day, and the conversation had gone unexpectedly well.

Michael told H. Sigman, who'd heard of the incident from Clyde Somerset, that Lee Roy had been dismissed because of the complaint of an elderly woman who was a benefactor of the Center. If the woman had not been a wealthy benefactor, Clyde Somerset would never have dismissed him.

"It's politics, then?" H. Sigman asked shrewdly.

"It's politics," Michael said.

"Something about nekkid ladies—'sculptors'?"

" 'Sculptures,' " Michael said. "The old woman was just shocked, seeing nude figures. You know—*nudes*. Common subjects for art."

"I know, I know they're common." H. Sigman spoke quickly, enthusiastically. It was clear that a call from Michael O'Meara was a special event in his day, and he did not mean to take it lightly. "In the old days—I mean, ancient Greeks, Romans—*they* did nekkid statues all the time. That was the style."

"That's right," Michael said, pleased. "It's the style now."

"That's what I'm saying. Lee Roy Sears is in that tradition."

"Lee Roy Sears *is* in that tradition."

"He told me, he was almost crying, they hadn't given him much of a chance there. Poor bastard."

Michael was nodding, as if H. Sigman, or Lee Roy Sears, could see him. He said, "That's so. But they'll regret it."

MICHAEL O'MEARA HAD VISITED Julia Sutter, on the Sunday following the Friday of Lee Roy Sears's outburst: he believed that, could he persuade her to withdraw her complaint, Clyde Somerset would reinstate Lee Roy. "She isn't a vindictive person—a woman of her age, and class. A Christian woman."

Had he spoken aloud?—a low, contemplative murmur, harmonious with the sound of the fine-tuned engine and the soothing *thrum thrum thrum* of the blood pulsing through his veins.

"A bad habit: talking aloud. So *stop.*"

Michael O'Meara had never been one to talk to himself, even when he was indisputably alone.

For how can one be certain, that one *is* indisputably alone?

He'd telephoned Julia, and, hospitable as she was, she immediately invited him to tea—"That most civilized of customs."

Michael would have preferred a drink, but he was grateful to be invited, entering the house on Linwood Avenue with a young man's sense of deference, courtesy. Neither he nor Gina had ever seen the inside of the Sutter house, which was a well-known Mount Orion landmark, an early eighteenth-century house to which additions had been built over a period of many years. The outside boasted a historical marker; it was local legend that George Washington had in fact spent some time in this house, preparatory to his battle in the Great Swamp. In an old cemetery close by, a number of American soldiers of the Revolution lay buried with their Hessian enemies, all killed in the battle of Mount Orion, 1780. Julia Sutter alluded to such events as if they were not remote and of a time hardly contiguous with our own; in her household of meticulously preserved antique furnishings, in her elegant if rather dark drawing room with its tall narrow windows, faded velvet drapes, Currier and Ives engravings, these episodes did not seem in fact remote.

Michael O'Meara had frequently wondered, during the past few years when Gina had become actively involved in Mount Orion organizations—how is it, the preservation of historical things, old landmarks, old furniture, local lore, seems to have fallen into the province of women?—well-to-do philanthropic ladies, like Julia Sutter? Don't these good ladies know that history is mainly battles among men, and battles among men are mainly carnage? What *are* the good ladies celebrating?

Julia Sutter seated her visitor in a hard-cushioned Federal chair beside an unlit, just slightly drafty fireplace, and seated herself, wrapped in a black knitted shawl, on a settee facing him; she served him, almost immediately, Earl Gray tea so strong it left a scrim of bitterness in his mouth, and rock-hard, very sweet "biscuits" out of a Harrods tin, which shattered into crumbs when he bit into one. "Thank you!" Michael was saying repeatedly, and, "Delicious!" and "No, I don't think I'll have more!"

He was uneasy, maybe a bit anxious; he saw on the mantel, beside a pair of heavy, handsome pewter candlesticks and a vase of dried and dusty wildflowers, an antique clock with a beautifully carved cabinet, its pendulum swinging slowly, somehow ponderously, and its ornate hands at 12 and 7: and he could not think, for a moment, what time it actually was—7:00 A.M. or P.M.; or 12:35 A.M. or P.M.

Elsewhere in the room, antique clocks were ticking, occasionally chiming the hour, the half-hour, the quarter-hour. Each of the clocks told its own time—seemed to inhabit, quaintly, and stubbornly, its own time. Michael glanced covertly at his watch and saw that it was 4:45: *his* time. Strapped tightly to his wrist.

Elderly Mrs. Sutter regarded her young visitor with grave, gray, bemused eyes. She was a handsome woman, if a bit thin-lipped; with a cap of white hair, white eyebrows and -lashes; sharp cheekbones; an air both imperial and kindly. She had powdered her face for the occasion and was wearing an odd, yet attractive, outfit—a crimson Tartan-plaid dress that fitted her frame loosely, and youthful high heeled shoes. Over her shoulders the black net of the shawl lay cozily. Julia Sutter was an heiress and the widow of a man many times a millionaire. Her voice was unexpectedly loud, like that of a judge speaking to an entire courtroom. "Young man, you appear— you won't think me rude?—a bit distracted."

Michael smiled. "I don't think so, Mrs. Sutter. I—"

"Please call me Julia."

"—I don't think so, Julia. I know why I'm here. I'd like to—"

"Yes, yes, I know, I know why you're here," Julia Sutter said, as if sympathetically. "You're here to defend that vile, loathsome, disgusting man, that 'Seals'—'Sears'—and his utterly filthy 'art,' and it won't do, young man, it won't do."

As Michael opened his mouth to speak, Mrs. Sutter said another time, still sympathetically, *"It won't do."*

Michael stared at the woman, dismayed. A china cup trembled in his fingers.

"But, Mrs. Sutter—"

"I've told Clyde, and he is totally in agreement—the Dumont Center must preserve standards. Mount Orion has always been a community of standards. So don't hand me that persiflage, young man, of 'the freedom of the artist.' I don't buy it! Your artist-friend's freedom ends where my freedom begins, and his freedom to commit filthy, unspeakable pornographic 'art' ends where my pocketbook begins! You know that—now, don't interrupt!—this is my house!— and I know that, and *he* knows that, now. And, as I've said, Clyde is *totally* in agreement." Mrs. Sutter drew her shawl more tightly about her shoulders. In a different tone of voice she said, "Clyde and Susanne—they're so *very* nice, don't you think?"

Michael stared, blinking. He might have been struck on the head—yet he managed to smile, if weakly. He said, "Yes, they are. I—"

"And your wife—is it Jean?—Gina?"

"Gina—"

"That pretty girl with the lovely hair—*my* color, once. It *is* natural?"

"Natural—what?"

"—very close friends, are you, of Mr. Schatten?—that bright young—is it attorney?—developer? I see you so often together, it must be very nice."

Michael tried to think. Schatten? Dwight Schatten?—a Mount Orion man of young middle age, with a reputation for being a very sharp lawyer. But Schatten was not in the O'Mearas' circle, and neither Michael nor Gina knew him well. Michael didn't even know if he was still married.

Michael cleared his throat and said, cautiously, "Mrs. Sutter, I think—"

" 'Julia'—please! You make me feel old as the hills!"

"—if you knew Lee Roy Sears better, you—"

"Lord forbid!" Mrs. Sutter laughed.

"—would be sympathetic, I think, with—his situation. He has had many disadvantages—"

"So have we all, but we don't go around committing obscenities, do we!"

"—he was in Vietnam, and he—"

"He was in prison, I know *that.*"

"—is trying to begin a new life, to redeem—"

"They don't put a man in prison, and they don't sentence a man to death, for doing nothing, I know *that.*"

Michael drew breath to speak, but Mrs. Sutter added, puckishly, "Anyway, it's no excuse for committing obscenities. That's what I say."

"But the issue isn't so clear-cut, Mrs. Sutter—Julia. Under our law, federal and state—"

"Oh, nonsense! I know, and you know, and everybody with any sense knows, what obscenities are. That's all!"

The word *obscenities* rolled off Mrs. Sutter's tongue with a harsh and somehow sensuous sibilance. Clearly, it was a word the elderly woman enjoyed.

Michael set his tea cup carefully down. He said, as firmly as he could manage under these trying circumstances, meaning to establish a space in which he could speak, "Excuse me, Julia, but—there truly *are* differences of opinion on this—"

"Well, I hope so!" Mrs. Sutter said brightly. "There is *your* opinion, Michael O'Meara, and there is *mine!*"

"—issue. And the artist himself, in his eyes, his art isn't—"

" 'Obscene'—? But of course it is: why else would he *do* it? Like one of these ghastly serial murderers who kill women, hack up their bodies, and when they're caught act as if butter wouldn't melt in their mouths!—*and their attorneys are just as bad.*"

"Mrs. Sutter, surely not!—you don't mean—"

"Oh, everybody knows this! It's hardly a secret."

Michael gazed at this astonishing old woman. A hot flash of anger irradiated his nerves but was dissipated by the tranquilizer before it could take flame. How stubborn, how opinionated, how obdurate!—how unshakable! On the mantel, the antique clock was chiming a smug, throaty sound.

He smiled, and said, as if nothing were wrong, as if he might simply take up their discussion again, "As I was saying, in Lee Roy Sears's eyes, his art is not 'obscene.' It is—"

"Oh, what do we care what *he* claims! More tea?"

"N-No, thank—"

"They're all alike, anyway!"

"Who?"

"Them."

Michael tried to smile. His heart was beating very quickly.

"Who is 'them,' Mrs. Sutter?"

"You know them when you see them," Mrs. Sutter said. "Won't you have more tea? It's had a while to steep."

"I'm afraid I really don't—"

"Another biscuit, then? You do look distracted."

Michael saw his hand reach for one of the rock-hard cookies, which he did not want. Another clock, on an ornate ivory-inlaid table some feet away, had begun a sequence of peremptory chimes.

"I find," Mrs. Sutter said, wiping crumbs off her bosom, "that people know what others mean when they say self-evident things; people know a damn sight more than they let on." The word *damn* was uttered with zest. Mrs. Sutter was smiling. "Even you, Mr. Michael O'Meara! (I *do* like that name: so melodic!) *Even you.*"

Michael, seeing that he had failed in his mission, that he had let Lee Roy Sears down, and that, had this been a courtroom hearing, he would have been thoroughly routed, eviscerated, suddenly laughed—sat back in the hard-cushioned chair, and laughed.

He said, shaking his head, boyish in surrender, "Well, Julia, you may be right."

"Hmmm! Michael O'Meara, I know I am."

The remainder of the visit went quickly and affably. Seeing Michael to the front door, Julia Sutter linked her thin but strong arm through his, and said, warmly, "You *will* come see me again, will you?—and bring that lovely wife of yours?"

Michael said, "I'd be delighted to, Julia."

As if Michael were a boy, and she a doting grandmother, Mrs. Sutter pursed her lips and tapped his wrist with a forefinger, saying, almost coquettishly, *"Promise—?"*

"Promise."

TWENTY-SIX DAYS LATER, JULIA Sutter was dead.

When Michael O'Meara heard the news, he felt as if he'd been struck in the stomach. His knees seemed to dissolve; he had to lean against a doorway. It was Gina who told him, speaking in a low, breathless voice. At this point she knew only that Julia Sutter had been killed by an intruder, a robber—she knew none of the bloody details. Her eyes were wide and damp and her manner urgent, as always when she had shocking news, or scandal, to tell Michael.

"What!—Julia Sutter!—my *God!* When?" Michael cried.

"Shhh!" Gina warned, pressing a forefinger against her lips.

(She did not want the twins, elsewhere in the house, to overhear. They had become, in the past several months, increasingly susceptible to disturbing dreams, which woke them both at the same moment, terrified and gasping for air; and led them to flee to their parents' bedroom for comfort. Nightmares of struggle, drowning, giant snakes?—Michael and Gina were dismayed, but could find no specific cause for the dreams. Michael thought it particularly ironic, and sad, that, now that he seemed at last to have grown out of his own guilt-ridden dreams, his young sons should be victims of their own.)

Gina was looking at Michael in such a way, clearly anxious, dreading, as to suggest that the identical thought had come to her, as came to Michael immediately: had Lee Roy Sears killed Julia, to revenge himself upon her?

Yet neither uttered his name. As, shortly before, having heard of the death of Mal Bishop, in what the *Newark News* described as a "flaming holocaust," they had not spoken his name aloud either.

IN THE FIRST SHOCK of Julia Sutter's death, Michael O'Meara relived the visit he'd had with her in that beautifully preserved if rather airless house. Shutting his eyes, calling back the drawing room, the drafty fireplace, the mantel—seeing with eidetic clarity the carved antique clock firmly chiming its inaccurate time; the china vase (Wedgwood?) of dried wildflowers (asters?) beside it. He tasted again the bitter tea and the stale, sugary, cloying yet delicious cookies. (Why did the English call cookies "biscuits"?—was it Anglo perversity?)

He saw Julia Sutter, ramrod straight on the settee, a teacup in her very slightly palsied hand, gazing at him, her naive, audacious petitioner, with her air of kindly bemusement. Twice Michael

O'Meara's age, how must she have viewed him?—from what lofty perspective of Time? She had reminded him, not of his detached, evasive mother, who seemed so rarely capable of, or willing to, look into his eyes, but of his paternal grandmother, now long dead. *She* had liked him, hadn't she?—had seemed to forgive him.

Michael thought it a melancholy irony, that, having visited the prominent Mount Orion dowager for the first time, and having been invited back, he would never return. And poor Gina—*she* would never visit the house at all.

Ironic too, that, that Sunday afternoon, Julia Sutter could not have known she would die soon. She might have thus set aside her vindictiveness and out of the bounty of her Christian heart forgiven Lee Roy Sears.

THEN THERE WAS THE matter, the utterly baffling matter, of Janet O'Meara.

Though Michael had seen his sister in the company of Lee Roy Sears on the evening of October 18, she categorically denied it. Standing in Michael's study, in his house, a glass of Bloody Mary mix, sans gin, in her hand, Janet absolutely denied it—"My God, Michael, if you're spying on Sears, at least don't involve me!" Janet spoke incredulously, with an air of indignation that grated against Michael's sensitive nerves.

Michael smiled, or tried to smile. Saying, in a reasonable voice, "I'm not *accusing* you, Janet. I'm just *stating* what I saw. Expressing my concern—I think it's a legitimate concern!—that my sister is involved with a man of problematic character. However persecuted he himself has been, however victimized, Lee Roy is—"

"But I wasn't with him that night, Michael. I was in New York: I was home. *Are* you spying on him?"

"Janet, I'm sure I saw you. The two of you, Lee Roy looking a bit unsteady, entering his rooming house on Eighth Avenue, Putnam. It was only a few hours after the blowup at the Center, and you appeared to be comforting him; you seemed on very close terms." Michael spoke quietly, regarding Janet with the patient, slightly reproachful air of a lawyer of good character who knows a witness is lying under oath: knows, and knows that the witness knows he knows. Yet the protocol of the courtoom, as of all civilized discourse, forbids direct accusation, let alone denunciation. "And I'm not spying on the man. Hardly!"

"Sitting there in your car, waiting for him?—for *hours?*"

"I've explained, I was anxious to—"

"And, when he appeared, not talking to him after all?"

"Because, Janet, you were with him. I was"—Michael paused; did he want to say "shocked"?—"appalled"?—such reactions Janet might find amusing, as symptomatic of her older brother's stolid, unimaginative bourgeois life—"*concerned*. Just too taken by surprise to react. And then—the two of you were gone."

"You say you saw my face?"

"I may not have seen your actual face—I mean, clearly. But I saw you, and I saw your car. I recognized your car at once, even out of context like that."

"What does my car look like, then?—tell me!"

"It's a nineteen eighty-nine Volvo, a darkish color, blue, I think—very dark blue. And there were the New York State license plates."

"And do you know the license number, too?" Janet asked ironically.

"In fact, no. Of course not."

"You recognized me, with Lee Roy Sears, on the evening of October eighteenth, in Putnam, New Jersey!—that long ago! and you recognized my *car!* How amazing!" Janet stared belligerently at Michael. Her skin, flushed with indignation, was coarse-pored; her eyes, damp, blinking, were smaller than Michael recalled. "But why haven't you mentioned it, until now? If you were so concerned, why did you postpone inviting me out, like this, to show your brotherly concern?"

Michael winced at the loudness of Janet's voice: Gina was in another part of the house, and, knowing that Michael and Janet had something crucial to discuss, something presumably between them, she was keeping her distance, tactful, not wanting to become involved; yet Janet's voice rose to an adolescent pitch, and Michael judged it too late to shut the door. He did not want to antagonize her further.

He heard again that defiant whining note of adolescence he'd virtually forgotten, in Janet. Over the years, encountering her as a fully mature adult, he'd gradually lost his memory of her behavior at home, her willful, somehow seemingly involuntary, tormenting of their mother.

Janet was one of those who had come of age in the early 1970s: when rebellion was so frequently flaunted for its own sake, in the children of affluent suburbanites; an aftereffect of the more legitimate rebellions of the 1960s, when Michael had come of age.

Janet repeated her question and swallowed a large mouthful of her tart red drink.

Michael was thinking how to answer—for he did not want to say what was uppermost in his mind, that it was now, so crucially now, with Julia Sutter dead and her murderer not yet discovered, that he most worried about Janet and Sears; that, earlier, he had not liked the situation, but had been determined to tolerate it—for his sister was after all a grown woman, hardly dependent upon his counsel. He did not want to explain any of this since, in fact, he did not seriously believe that Lee Roy Sears had killed Mrs. Sutter.

("*You* believe me, Mr. O'Meara, don't you?" Lee Roy had begged; and Michael had said, "Yes, yes, yes." He had given up trying to get Lee Roy to call him by his first name.)

Janet glanced over her shoulder and said, her voice dipping, "I will admit I've seen him a few times, since June. I've told you—there's nothing secret about it. I've been researching a story on him, in depth." She paused. Belatedly, she shut Michael's study door; she appeared less certain of herself, evasive, and yet appealing to Michael, with childlike directness. "I *will* admit too that I find—I did find—him attractive, in that way of his. That way that's so difficult to—explain."

Michael said, embarrassed, "Yes, I'd suspected so."

"But there hasn't been anything serious between us."

"I see."

"—I mean, I haven't"—Janet spoke slowly, frowning, not meeting Michael's eye—"slept with him." She paused, and, blushing fiercely, added, "Not that it's anyone's business but my own."

"Janet, I know."

"I'm thirty-five years old—my life is my own business."

Michael took Janet's hand, a bit awkwardly. He found it surprisingly cool, the fingertips cold—as his own.

"I'm not in love with him."

It was so bold and impetuous a statement, Michael did not know how to reply.

He said, "I wasn't spying on you, Janet, that night. If I happened to see—"

"But you *didn't!* Not me, not that night!"

"Have you been with him, other nights?"

Janet politely withdrew her hand from Michael's. She seemed not to have heard his question. "It must have been some other woman, that night," she said, as if indifferently. "Lee Roy has other women—I know."

Michael felt a stab of pain, somewhere behind his eyes. He said, evenly, "Does he!"

He would have liked the conversation to end, now. They were at an impasse—Janet would not tell the truth, and Michael had no heart to force it out of her. *What does it matter, so long as I know.*

But Janet had more to say. She fumblingly set down her glass on Michael's desk and gazed at him, not defensively now, but with searching eyes. "I don't love him, but—there's a weakness in me that draws me to him. When I'm with him, I believe in him utterly; it's only when I'm away from him, I'm not so sure. I don't think he could have had anything to do with that poor old woman's death, but, in Hartford, I've made some inquiries, with people who knew him back in nineteen seventy-eight, or claimed to—and it's all very—confused."

Michael said guardedly, "What have you learned?"

"I don't know if I've 'learned' anything. I've studied the trial transcripts, as I guess you did, but so much is left out, the trial turns out to be a sort of simulacrum of what might have happened. Is courtroom procedure always like that?—my God! Outside the court, you can learn more, a lot more, but one 'fact' tends to cancel out another. For instance, something you probably didn't know, since you restricted yourself to the trial records—at the time Lee Roy Sears was arrested for killing the drug dealer (if the man *was* a dealer: even that wasn't one hundred percent clear), he'd also been charged with two other killings. These charges were later dropped, so, who knows, maybe they were fabricated, by police, to force him into plea bargaining. At the trial, there was evidence the prosecution wanted to present that was ruled inadmissible by the judge—the police claimed to have had a list of 'hits' in Lee Roy Sears's handwriting, the names of men who had already been killed, and the names of others still living. I know, Michael, I know," Janet said quickly, laying her hand on Michael's arm to prevent his interrupting, "the evidence *was* inadmissible, and that must have been for a reason. What most upset me, though—and this I got from a woman who was a friend of the victims, or said she was—was the way Lee Roy kidnapped a woman and her twelve-year-old daughter, trying to escape Hartford. According to this account, Lee Roy held a gun to the woman's head, made her stop outside town, raped her, beat and abused her daughter, all the while high on cocaine. He—"

Michael interrupted, "Janet, none of that was ever proven, it's impossible to know if it happened or not. In the trial—"

"—he threatened to kill them both, which is why, I was told, the woman decided not to testify against him, and the charges were dropped."

"—in the trial, the charge was murder, and the evidence was problematic, the police witnesses obviously lying—which is why, eventually—"

"Eventually, the woman committed suicide; the daughter became a drug addict, and—"

"—the capital sentence was set aside, and—"

"—and disappeared. Probably died."

"—he's alive today. His life saved."

Janet and Michael had been speaking quickly, hotly.

Michael regarded his hands, which were trembling. Something monstrous was happening, but he did not know what.

In a less impassioned tone, Janet said, "All right. It's 'hearsay.' The charges *were* dropped. But did you and the others in The Coalition investigate?—did you *care?* Or, because these were female victims, did they not seem to count, in your zeal to get justice for Lee Roy Sears?"

Michael rubbed his face vigorously with both hands. He did not want to say, *This happened a long time ago.* Nor did he want to say, *I meant only well.* He said, instead, quietly, "But why have you seen Lee Roy, if he's a rapist and murderer?"

"I haven't seen him since finding out this information."

"Of course you have."

"I have *not.*"

"You've spoken with him on the phone, then."

Janet's gaze wavered, irresolutely. But she said, "No. I'm afraid of him."

"How will you write your story, then?"

"I'll talk with him one more time," Janet said. "I owe him that much—to hear his side."

"But why?" Michael asked ironically. "If the man's a rapist, a murderer—would you expect him to tell the truth?"

Quite seriously, with no apparent sense of the egotism of her remark, Janet said, "Oh, I'm sure Lee Roy has always told the truth to *me.*"

AND TO ME, MICHAEL O'Meara thought.

Feeling wonderfully vindicated, and relieved, when, a few days later, he learned that Mount Orion police had arrested a suspect in the Sutter case—a former lawn-crew worker employed by Julia, who answered descriptions of a prowler seen by neighbors in the vicinity of Julia Sutter's house the day before the murder; and who, most damningly, had household items and credit cards belonging to Julia in his possession when police picked him up.

"Someone Julia knew," Gina said, frowning over the newspaper article, shivering, "someone she *trusted.* From Newark, and he's black—isn't that just what you'd expect?"

3

Laughter up ahead?—loud, raucous laughter?—Michael O'Meara paused, and listened, on the stairs to Lee Roy Sears's studio, on the third floor of a shabby warehouse in North Putnam. He would not have come if he'd known there would be other visitors.

It was late Saturday following Thanksgiving. A chilly, diaphanous day. Though Lee Roy had been working in this place for several weeks now, the rent being paid (so Michael assumed: Lee Roy naturally had not said) by Valeria Darrell, Michael had not had time to drop by and visit, as Lee Roy had suggested.

Nor had Gina, to his knowledge.

Relations between the O'Mearas and Lee Roy Sears seemed to have subtly but unmistakably altered, from what they had been before Lee Roy's dismissal from the Dumont Center. Gina avoided the very mention of Lee Roy's name and found excuses for not inviting him to dinner; Lee Roy himself was reticent in Michael's company. He thinks I didn't try hard enough to keep him on at the Center, Michael thought guiltily.

He imagines I have much more personal power than I have.

The battered-looking door to the studio stood open, and Michael rapped on it and entered. He saw to his disappointment that, with Lee Roy, were Valeria Darrell and two aggressively loud companions, whom he was certain he'd never seen before. Valeria was pouring drinks, with a good deal of ceremony and chatter; seeing Michael O'Meara, she stretched her lips in a grimace of a smile and said, mock-graciously, "Why!—*do* come in! But where is your lovely *wife?*"

Michael winced.

He was fairly certain Lee Roy Sears winced too.

Michael sensed how his presence was unwanted, unwelcome. But he concealed his unease with his usual hearty smile and shook hands all around. (How tentative and fleeting, Lee Roy's handshake: though the man himself had grown quite muscular, and his fingers were certainly strong!) Valeria introduced him to her friends from New York "Vargas" and "Mina"—the one huge, fleshy, a man in his sixties with a round bald head, a yellow satin shirt and red suspenders straining over his belly, pink gums leeringly exposed as he grinned, the other tall, thin, storklike, a "girl" in her thirties with thick glossy lips and eyelids painted frosty blue. "Vargas and Mina own the Avanti Gallery on Greene Street," Valeria said excitedly, "where Lee Roy will be represented." Vargas laughed as he shook hands with Michael, exclaiming, "Michael O'Meara!" as if there were something amusing in the name; Mina lisped, "Oh!—hel*lo!*" widening her protuberant eyes at him and blinking rapidly. Was she flirting, so openly?—was she drunk? What *was* this?

The bizarre thought crossed Michael's mind, and was immediately dismissed, *These are not human beings, these are demons.*

And there stood Lee Roy Sears, Michael's friend, staring at him with a vague blank grin, as if he scarcely knew him.

The men locked eyes, for a brief instant.

Michael's eyes searching, open—Lee Roy's glassy and opaque.

Valeria splashed bourbon into a cloudy-looking glass and pressed it into Michael's hand. The woman was so excessively made up, her brunette hair so extravagantly streaked with gold, she was hardly recognizable as the person she'd been, for years, in Mount Orion society. *She too is a demon. A demon-whore.*

Valeria's fractured nose was mending, presumably. But it looked raw and bruised beneath its thick patina of makeup.

Valeria raised her glass, loudly proclaiming a toast: "To Lee Roy's new studio! To Lee Roy's new *career!*"

"Cheers!" cried Vargas, and "Cheers!" cried Mina, raising their glasses high.

"Cheers!" said Michael, trying to fall in with their mood.

Lee Roy screwed up his face as if in embarrassment, or anger. He said nothing, merely drank.

It was only mid-afternoon, and Michael O'Meara assuredly did not want to drink bourbon, but, what choice had he?—among these people.

Valeria began at once to talk of something—a party, an excursion, planned for the following weekend—about which Michael knew nothing, except, of course, that such talk was aimed to exclude him; to make him feel pointedly unwanted. Very well, he thought, I understand. He glanced again at Lee Roy Sears, who ignored him too.

He drifted off, drink in hand. The room was an immense, drafty loft, in crude repair; with high ceilings, exposed girders, windows of grimy square panes. In a farther corner there were stacks of boxes and cartons. Lee Roy's work area was crowded into a small space at this end of the room, near a window. There was a filthy double sink in a corner and, behind a battered screen, plainly visible from the door, a filthy toilet. A Pullman refrigerator, hot-plate burners, a cluttered worktable, benches, chairs, boxes of hastily packed art supplies, sheets of paint-splattered newspaper spread out on the floor—everything harshly illuminated by the chill November light, as if overexposed. And how strong the smell of oil paint and turpentine, assailing Michael's nostrils.

Michael saw that Lee Roy's original clay figures, the humanoid males, were positioned on the windowsills, like lizards about to spring into life. And where were the "obscene" females?—had Lee Roy smashed every one of them?

They're what came out.

What comes out.

Since moving to Putnam, Lee Roy had returned to painting, which he'd done, or tried, in prison, with limited success. Michael saw several very messy canvases lying about, as if discarded in anger; on a brand-new easel was a large canvas partly untouched and partly layered in swaths of black, gunmetal gray, and bright arterial red, in a manner suggestive of Jackson Pollock. This work appeared, to Michael O'Meara's uncritical eye, as somewhat more controlled than the discarded canvases. Yet, what *was* it?

A tangle of machinery, perhaps. A blood explosion in its midst.

More of the Vietnam nightmare?—which Michael O'Meara, who had never served his country, had never worn a United States Army uniform, had been spared.

On the floor beside the easel was a stack of sketches, some in paint, others in charcoal. Michael squatted on his heels and looked idly through these, as, behind him, talking as if he were not present, their conversation interrupted by peals of laughter, the others continued their celebration.

Casual sketches of machines, helicopters, humanoid figures. Sketches, in charcoal, of more realistically depicted men, and women. What to make of these?—there were dozens of sketches, most so hastily, or so unskillfully, executed, as to be without identity, just bodies, naked and unappealing. Yet their very quantity suggested Lee Roy Sears's commitment to his art.

Near the bottom of the stack, as if hidden away, were several that made Michael pause and draw in his breath sharply.

A porcine figure, male, with tiny genitalia and a round, smug face—was this Clyde Somerset, crudely transformed?

An obese creature, also male, with close-set piggish eyes, writhing horribly in flame, and dripping globules of fat?—was this Mal Bishop?

An elderly female, rail-thin, naked, on her back, with white hair, tightly shut eyes, upper torso hacked and bleeding—was this Julia Sutter?

A fleshy, big-breasted and -hipped woman, naked, lying on a bed, smiling insipidly, plump knees parted—was this Michael's sister, Janet?

And, this—this horror—*could it be Michael's wife, Gina?*

Michael stared. His vision blurred with moisture, and he

blinked to clear it, holding the drawing in fingers that shook so badly the stiff construction paper rattled. He was desperate to see, to know—was this female figure meant to be Gina?—or merely a woman who resembled her?—clumsily drawn, as if in anger, yes it looked as if the charcoal crayon had broken in several places, gripped tightly in the artist's hand. Thus the woman's thin snaky nude body was smudged, and her beautiful masklike face smudged, giving it a leering, leprous appearance.

"Gina. My God."

The next sketch portrayed the same woman—skeletal-thin, yet with sizable breasts, grotesque erect nipples, pudenda boldly displayed, with features comically suggestive of her own face. The next sketch showed the woman lying on her back, wrists and ankles bound, arms and legs outspread so that her vagina was a raw, gaping O; her head thrown back, mouth an O too, of agony. The next sketch, at the very bottom of the stack, showed the same woman, standing, naked, arms lifted toward the viewer as if in a mock embrace, her face a horrifying mass of cross-hatchings (scars? burns? fresh wounds?) out of which, nonetheless, she smiled lewdly, the tip of her tongue protruding from between her lips.

The tip of her tongue had been colored in, in bright pink.

This dash of bright pink, shocking to the eye, was the sole color in the entire stack of sketches.

THE MAN IS A *madman.*.
    A murderer?

No. THESE ARE WORKS *of the imagination. Fantasies.*
    Perhaps he put them there deliberately, to test me?

As, DREAMING, WE *are* the dreams we dream, and cannot escape from them except by the metaphysical impossibility of becoming someone other than ourselves, so too Michael O'Meara, on that appalling occasion, found himself behaving as if—almost!—nothing were wrong. Rising shakily to his full height, leaning for support on the edge of a table; and, in the process, nearly knocking over a bottle of turpentine into which paint-stiffened brushes had been thrust. He saw too, though not with much awareness, a curious sort of razor-instrument, for what function he couldn't guess—it looked as if a razor blade had been secured by layers of adhesive tape to the handle of a broken paintbrush. The blade glinted, sharply.

The others saw Michael O'Meara set down his glass of bourbon, which had been scarcely touched, and turn to leave. Lee Roy Sears stared as if stricken. Valeria, Vargas, lisping Mina—they were looking after the departing man with expressions of—surprise?—curiosity?—derision?—but he did not turn back, except to wave over his shoulder, a friendly sort of farewell.

Lee Roy Sears called, quickly, "Mr. O'Meara!"

Michael was descending the stairs briskly. He did not want to speak with Lee Roy Sears; he did not want to speak with him, nor even look at him, ever again.

But Lee Roy persisted, following him down the stairs. "Mr. O'Meara—how come you're leaving so soon? You just got here, huh?"

Michael's heart was pounding dangerously. The Liloprane in his blood removed what would have been "anxiety" and replaced it with a purely physical and visceral response, as if Michael's body were a mechanism, begun to accelerate, over which he had no control, and about which he felt detached, even indifferent. His revulsion for Lee Roy Sears was wholly mental.

Michael had stopped on the second-floor landing, and Lee Roy limped down quickly to join him. The men regarded each other with cautious eyes.

Lee Roy repeated, with an effort at smiling, "Well, uh, Mr. O'Meara, I mean 'Michael'—what d'you think of my new studio? Real nice, huh?"

Michael said quietly, "Very nice."

He saw that Lee Roy Sears had not only grown thicker-bodied, but, oddly, taller: an inch or two taller, now, than Michael O'Meara.

He saw that the dark, gold-spangled mark on Lee Roy Sears's left forearm *was* a tattoo: a snake: partly visible beneath the man's carelessly rolled-up shirtsleeve. What kind of snake, what sort of posture it was in, he could not see; and did not care to see.

How could you. My wife. My sister, and my wife.

How could you betray me.

Michael stood tall, composed, listening politely as Lee Roy

Sears nervously chattered about his new studio, his new work, the Avanti Gallery, which was going to represent his work—"Gonna make me a millionaire, says Valeria, and I says, 'Shit, all I want is to pay my own way!' " Michael said nothing, or murmured a vague assent. Lee Roy pulled a paint-stiffened rag out of the back pocket of his trousers, and drew it roughly beneath his nose. His eyes too were damp; his skin was mottled, as with teenage acne. Now his hair was longer, it fell in greasy tangles over the collar of his shirt; its fine sheen was gone, and there were streaks of gray in it, as in Michael O'Meara's own hair. *How could you. After I saved your life.*

Not anger, nor even a sense of horror, but simple childlike hurt—as a boy might feel, betrayed by his brother. That was what shone in Michael O'Meara's eyes.

Lee Roy Sears was saying, "Uh—I heard they found the guy who killed the old lady? That's a break, Jezuz! Now the fuckers don't have to try to blame it on *me*."

Michael said, quietly, "You didn't do it, Lee Roy, did you?"

"Huh?" Lee Roy grinned stupidly.

"You didn't kill Julia Sutter, did you?"

"What are you saying?"

"What I'm saying."

"—I *told* you: no." Lee Roy screwed up his face and seemed about to wink; then thought better of it. "You're kidding, huh?—I get it."

Michael said, "Of course I'm kidding, Lee Roy. We both know that."

To Lee Roy's astonishment, Michael was about to turn and descend the rest of the stairs, and leave him there, gaping after. Lee Roy said quickly, "Uh, wait—you're mad at me, or something?"

Michael said, in the same quiet voice, "Of course not, Lee Roy. Why would I be mad at *you*."

"You're asking me if I killed that old lady, *I'm* the one that's got a reason to be mad, insulted, huh?—what about that?"

Michael shrugged. He glanced at his watch and made to move off. Lee Roy shyly touched his arm to retain him.

"I got lots of reasons to be mad at *you*, but—I'm not!"

" 'Lots of reasons'—?"

"You fucked up with Somerset, didn't you?—you know you did."

Michael's face burned. "I did my best."

"And the old bitch Sutter—you fucked up plenty with *her*, I guess." Lee Roy chuckled angrily. "They kicked me out flat on my ass and you said you'd help and what did it come to?—*shit*."

"Lee Roy, I told you I did my best. You exaggerate my power in Mount Orion."

"Yah, I guess I did!"

"Yes, you *did*."

"Okay, fuck it, I *did*. So what? I got a new place now, and I'm on my way. Valeria is commissioning me to paint a picture for her house, and she's got friends who want to buy my stuff, and, like I said, the Avanti Gallery, in New York—"

Michael interrupted, calmly, saying, "Lee Roy, my sister, Janet, has been seeing you, is that right?—she's doing an article on you?—is that right?"

"Article?" Lee Roy's eyes narrowed, as suspiciously. "What kind of an article?"

"*Isn't* she doing an article?—interviewing you?"

"I told her, Jezuz I don't want more crap said about me—it always turns out wrong. Mis-leading."

"But you've been seeing her, haven't you?"

Lee Roy shrugged. Nervous, edgy, yet defensive, he stood on the balls of his feet, as if anticipating an attack; he gripped his left hand with his right, exerting tension, clenching his arm and shoulder muscles. Michael estimated Lee Roy had gained as much as forty pounds since he'd begun working out at the gym. He must have been consuming huge amounts of calories daily.

"*Haven't* you been seeing her?" Michael asked. "Just tell the truth, Lee Roy."

Lee Roy's mottled face darkened. "What's this, an interrogation?—who wants to know?"

"*I* do. *I* want to know."

"So, shit, who're *you?*" Lee Roy asked. Then, at once, guilty, he said, "Okay, you saved my life. Okay, Mr. O'Meara, yah you did, and I'm grateful—you and Mrs. O'Meara both, you been real nice to me. Yah, I been seeing your sister, sort of. Not much."

"How much?—how seriously?"

Lee Roy glanced up the stairs, as if fearful that Valeria might overhear. He said, in a lowered, solemn voice, "Uh, your sister's a real nice woman, y'know? Real nice, classy. Except, she's always asking *questions*. Like, I'm supposed to give her *answers.*"

"Do you see each other often?—are you lovers?"

Lee Roy winced. He looked away from Michael's face. He said, as if not having heard, "I told her, I says, 'Janet, you're too good for me.' I says, 'You don't want to get messed up, get your hands dirty, on a guy like *me.*'"

"You said that?—really?"

"Sure I did."

"Like a—gentleman."

"Hell, I just told her what's what. She's a nice woman, like I said, *I* don't want to screw her up."

"But are you lovers?"

Lee Roy shook his head ambiguously. "You want to know, ask her. She wants you to know, she'll tell you."

"Then—you *are* lovers?"

"I said—*ask her.*"

Michael was gripping the stairway railing, hard. He saw again, fleetingly, in his mind's eye, that image, crude, dreamlike, of his sister lying on her back, legs spread. Insipid smile. The O'Meara smile.

And what of my wife. Have you dared touch my wife.

As if reading Michael's thoughts, Lee Roy Sears lurched away, backward, colliding with the wall; saying, in a whining, childish voice, "You got no right to ask me questions all the time, Mr. O'Meara. You, and everybody else! Just 'cause I'm an ex-con, I'm on parole, nobody's got the right to treat me like some kind of *freak.* Like, Mrs. O'Meara, she—"

There was a pause. Michael said, calmly, "Yes? What about Gina?"

"—the way she looks at me! Used to look at me," Lee Roy mumbled. Then he laughed, harshly. "Haven't seen her in a while, huh!"

"Gina has been very nice to you, Lee Roy. I don't understand what you mean."

Seeing again, in that mirrored surface. Gina, in this man's embrace.

But no: it had never happened. He'd imagined it. Had he?

How have you dared.

Lee Roy was saying, in his whining, aggrieved voice, "—had Thanksgiving with Valeria. Her kids couldn't make it, so"—he paused, sniffing. His eyes glared up at Michael's, defiantly. "We had a big turkey dinner at her place. Just us two."

"Did you!—how nice."

But Michael was frowning, to show his disapproval of Valeria Darrell.

Frowning too, to think that Lee Roy Sears must have expected to have been invited to the O'Mearas' for Thanksgiving dinner: as if he were part of the family.

Michael said, not apologetically, simply as a statement of fact, "*We* had Thanksgiving with Gina's family, in Philadelphia. It's a tradition with us."

Lee Roy grunted something that sounded like "Huhh!"

From upstairs in the studio there came an outburst of gay, inebriated laughter. Heavy footsteps—no doubt Vargas's.

Valeria's voice, high-pitched, playful, as if she were calling a child, "Oh, Lee Roy!—Lee Royyy!"

Michael turned to leave, and Lee Roy, perspiration showing on his face, blocked his way. He was clenching and unclenching his fists. His eyes had a dark, lustrous glare. He said, "*You* tell your sister to keep her distance!—*I'm* not the one! And she better not be digging up dirt about me 'cause I don't like people spying on me, you got it?—huh? My life's my own! My own fucking business! *You*, looking at me like I'm shit!—you got no right!"

Michael was about to protest, he certainly wasn't looking at Lee Roy in any derisive way, in fact he was maintaining an extraordinary composure, when, again, there came Valeria's wavering soprano, which grated against his nerves—"Lee Roy, where are you, oh Leee Royyy, we're waiting!"

Another voice, Vargas's, joined hers, calling something unintelligible, and immediately swallowed up by laughter: words insulting to Michael O'Meara, he knew.

It was this, this insult, that sparked the argument between Mi-

chael and Lee Roy, for, suddenly, Michael was saying, careless of
how loud he spoke, what loathing in his voice, "Those people up
there!—those creatures!—how can you allow yourself to be taken up
by *them!* A woman like Valeria Darrell!" Michael felt his mouth
twist, as he said her name.

Lee Roy said, stunned, "Huh?—what the fuck?—now you're
trying to tell me I can't have my *friends?*"

For months Michael had vowed he would not say such things
to Lee Roy. Yet, now, in the heat of the moment, his words came
tumbling out.

"They're not friends, Lee Roy. They're—demons!"

"Huh?" Lee Roy leaned toward Michael, as if he hadn't heard.

"You know very well: *demons!*"

Lee Roy, panting, sweaty-faced, stared at Michael for a moment
in outraged silence. His nostrils were wide, dark, dilated. He seemed,
in that instant, like Michael himself, relieved, no, elated, that the
tension between them had at last taken a palpable shape: here was
something the men could quarrel over, and hotly.

But Michael was on his way out, he'd had enough.

He started down the stairs, and Lee Roy followed after him,
seizing his arm, pushing him against the railing: which was not a strong
railing: saying, furiously, "who are *you!*—who are you to tell me what
to do!—*you* let me down, didn't you!—you and *her!*—I'm not good
enough for you, huh?—Mr. Hot-Shit Lawyer!—Mr.-and-Mrs. Hot-Shit
Lawyer!—Cunt!—trying to tell *me* who my friends are!—how to live
my life!—like you give a shit about me, huh!—*you and her!*"

Michael tried to defend himself, to seize Lee Roy to keep from
falling, but the other man was too strong, with a sudden maniacal
strength, and there came springing up at him *a snake: a dark-gleaming
gold-spangled snake* in the sinewy muscle of Lee Roy's left forearm.
Overhead, a woman screamed, as Lee Roy Sears, teeth clenched and
bared, shoved Michael against the stairway railing so violently that
the wooden structure broke, broke and shattered with a shriek of its
own, and Michael O'Meara, suddenly helpless, utterly astonished,
arms and legs flailing, fell—into space.

HE DIDN'T MEAN IT, *it was an accident.*
   He meant it: my enemy: at last.

"My god, Michael!—are you all right?"

Valeria leaned over him anxiously, her aging girl's face dead white beneath her makeup: it was Valeria, and not Lee Roy, who hurried to him, to help him to his feet.

Michael had fallen a distance of perhaps fifteen feet: to land, on his side, ignominiously, further insulted, atop a stack of used cardboard cartons on the landing below. Had he struck the bare floorboards he would surely have injured himself, but the cartons, slipping, sliding, capsizing on all sides, had broken his fall.

No skull concussion, no limbs broken, no ribs cracked, yes he was certain. No internal injuries.

Only the injury to his dignity: his O'Meara pride.

Mr. Hot-Shit Lawyer, landing on his ass, on a stack of grimy cardboard boxes.

Lee Roy Sears had pushed him through the railing without meaning to push him to his death, had he?—or *had* he?

And charged back upstairs.

Charged back upstairs and left Michael where he lay.

It was Valeria Darrell, breathless, terrified, smelling of bourbon and Arpège, who came to Michael to help him: teetering in her suede heels and nearly falling herself: Valeria, whom Michael had just now maligned.

She was suddenly sober, responsible. Peering into his face with a wife's concern.

"Michael, my God!—*are* you all right? Is anything broken?"

Michael would recall, afterward, how, for these flurried minutes, he and Valeria Darrell, Mount Orion residents, were linked as blood kin. The animosity between them had vanished.

For Valeria knew, surely she knew, now, that Lee Roy Sears was a madman, and dangerous. As, reluctantly, some months from now, she would volunteer testimony to the district attorney, describing this incident.

Michael assured Valeria that he was all right, he was perfectly all right, his teeth clenched in fury, even as, with nervous plucking fingers, she brushed at his clothing, even at his hair, following him the rest of the way downstairs—"Oh, Michael, it *was* an accident, wasn't it?"

Panting, disheveled, Valeria lurched after Michael as he slammed out of the warehouse, and strode to his car parked in a puddle-strewn driveway. She said, begging, shameless, her eyes snatching at his, "You won't report him, Michael, will you?—will you?"

Michael said, "Lee Roy Sears can go to hell."

My Enemy. At last.

MICHAEL DROVE AWAY FROM the warehouse and did not glance back; and did not report Lee Roy Sears to his parole officer.

Thinking, I'm done with the man, now. I can forget him, now.

Thinking, I need never see him again.

How strangely, ecstatically free he felt, that Saturday afternoon in late November, having narrowly escaped death, but having escaped it!—his senses alert, adrenaline coursing through his body. He felt strong, virile, as he had not felt in months. He felt as if a loathsome weight, up to now unsuspected, had fallen from his shoulders. He felt innocent as a child's balloon lifting off into the sky.

Again he uttered these words, which must have been preparing themselves for a long time: "Lee Roy Sears can go to hell."

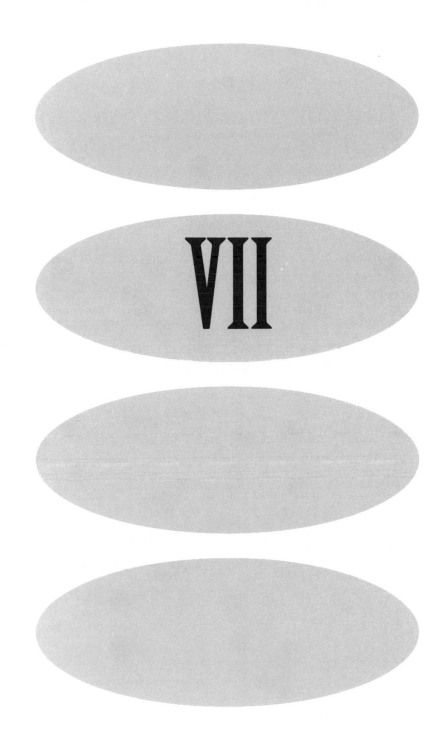

VII

How MISTAKEN YOU ARE, *Michael O'Meara!—and what a fool.*

Can you really not know how intimately, how relentlessly, I will track you?—to your very place of refuge?

Now, AS DECEMBER DARKENED, as winter came on, the nightmare acquired ever more palpable dimensions.

As if in defiance of Michael O'Meara's euphoria, that day.

As if to mock him, where he was most vulnerable.

Frequently, yet in no pattern, the telephone began to ring with no one on the line: no one willing to identify himself. Very early in the morning it might ring, and very late at night. Disturbing the twins' sleep. Disturbing Michael's sleep.

Yet, oddly, not Gina's: for if one of the mysterious calls came at night, and Michael was able to lift the receiver on the first ring, Gina might sleep uninterrupted, and claim, in the morning, that, surely, the phone had *not* rung.

Michael's own sleep was shallow, frothy, unsatisfying. He seemed to be waiting for the intrusion, the violation. He seemed to know how the other was thinking of him, and of Gina; calculating; tracking. Once, he was reaching for the telephone even as the ringing

began. He sat up in bed, body tense as a bow, listening to the silence
on the other end of the line, listening to his enemy's audible, mocking
breathing, which his enemy made no effort to hide. Yet Michael
O'Meara did not want to accuse, still less to threaten. He knew, as an
attorney, that one does not antagonize an emotionally unstable person.

Saying, softly, "Hello?—hel*lo*? Is anyone there?"

Gina stirred luxuriously in her sleep, but did not wake; when
she'd had several glasses of wine before going to bed, she slept especially deeply. In any case, Michael held the receiver close to his
ear and mouth, turned from the sleeping woman as if to shield her
with his own solid, stocky body. Saying, "Hello?—is that you, Lee
Roy?" A pause. Breathing, and a sense of that breath—humid, sticky.
"Lee Roy, why are you doing this?—*we only wish you well.*"

It was a war of nerves, was it?—but the other could not see
how Michael O'Meara's hand trembled.

Finally, quietly, Michael would break the connection and leave
the receiver off the hook for the remainder of the night.

Shortly, Michael would leave the receiver off the hook every
night before he and Gina went to bed.

Why not change their number and get a private listing with
the phone company?—Michael wanted to do so, but, for weeks,
Gina resisted, for the sheerly practical reason that the O'Mearas had
so many friends and acquaintances, so very many, it would be a
nuisance to give out a new number. Gina said, petulantly, "If it *is*
Lee Roy, acting so meanly, why should we give in to him?—I'm not
afraid of him, and I resent him manipulating us."

Michael said, "It's Lee Roy. It's no one but Lee Roy. And I
think it would be best for us all if we changed the number."

"I almost can't believe he would turn against us, so quickly!"
Gina said. "It's so somehow selfish and short-sighted of him."

"But he hates us, now, Gina, don't you understand?" Michael
said.

Gina shook her head, slowly. Her expression was one of vexed
incomprehension, not fear; not alarm. She said, "Oh, I doubt that
he *hates* us, Michael. Aren't you exaggerating?"

Gina was so beautiful and so poised a woman, so admired by
men, she could not seriously grasp the possibility that there might
be a man who, though admiring her, might hate her too.

For which reason, Michael had to protect her.

That very ignorance, that vanity—Michael had to protect.

And his sons?—Michael had to protect them too.

Michael had told Gina about the scene with Lee Roy in the warehouse, but, in his telling, to minimize her upset, he'd softened the details. In this version, Lee Roy had pushed him accidentally, and he'd fallen because the stairway railing was so old and rotted, it had given way at once. In this version, Valeria Darrell was not present. Lee Roy himself had hurried down to help Michael.

In this version, Michael presented himself as a somewhat comic character, a cartoon oaf, falling onto a stack of cardboard boxes that went tumbling and sliding about. He'd even succeeded in making her laugh.

Not that it was entirely funny: for, now, Michael walked with a slight limp, favoring his right leg.

His knee. He'd banged his knee. That was all.

Was there something evasive in Gina's eyes, when he spoke to her of Lee Roy Sears?—was there, or had there been, a secret connection between them?

No. These are works of the imagination. Fantasies.

What comes out.

If the crank calls came when Gina was home, and if she dealt with them in her own way, Michael could not know, for, at such times, he was likely to be at work. He was well aware of the fact, of course that, popular as she was, involved with numerous charitable organizations, luncheon groups, country club and tennis club friends, and intensive bouts of shopping in both Mount Orion and New York, Gina was out of the house most days, and, in her absence, the answering service was on. Thus, she was spared: for when the caller got Michael O'Meara's recorded message, he hung up abruptly.

One morning, however, when Michael was at Pearce, Inc., and knew that Gina would probably still be home, he telephoned his house, experimentally, to see how Gina would respond. When she lifted the receiver and said, "Hello?—hel*lo?*" his heart pounded, but he said not a word, the palm of his hand pressed tight over the mouth of the receiver. *She will think it is Lee Roy Sears, what will she say to Lee Roy Sears?* Gina was unexpectedly curt, fearless, saying, "Who's there? *Is* this who I think it is?" A pause. Then, "If it is, then shame! Shame! An adult man, like you! Behaving so childishly, like this!'' Michael listened with painful intensity, gripping the receiver tight, seeing Gina's face, those fierce eyes, contemptuous mouth. "I've told you, if this is who I think it is, that I can't see you again and I won't see you again and I am not going to be intimidated do you understand!'' And she hung up the receiver with such passion, Michael winced.

Michael spent much of that morning, at his desk, his head in his hands. Not knowing how to decode what he had heard—or whether to decode it, at all.

IN ANY CASE, NOT long after this, in mid-December, Gina at last agreed to having their number changed to a private number. For suddenly the calls had started coming at times when Joel and Kenny might answer the phone, and sometimes did, though they were instructed not to.

Michael happened to lift an upstairs receiver one evening when the phone rang, and Joel, or was it Kenny, had just answered downstairs, "H'lo?" in a child's expectant voice, and, to his astonishment and horror, Michael heard a responding voice, the silence of weeks was broken by a male voice, obviously disguised, thick, gravelly, lewdly cheerful, "Hey!—hey there! L'il fucker, huh? That's you, huh? Which one of you, l'il fucker? You hear me, huh? You're hearing me, huh? You know who this is, huh? L'il fuckers—''

Yet more horribly, Joel giggled.

Giggled as if he were being roughly tickled.

Michael interrupted, shouting, furious, "Get off the phone! I know who you are, Lee Roy Sears! God damn you, you pervert, you sick son of a bitch, leave my sons alone!''

The next morning, with no further reluctance on Gina's part, Michael made arrangements for a new, unlisted number.

And the loathsome calls stopped. For the time being, at least.

WINTER CAME ON, THE days slid skidding into night, the holidays were a promising distraction, so many parties, so many presents, so many meals, so much good cheer, yet Michael O'Meara's dread deepened.

For, knowing that his enemy was *there*, forever *there*, in the

world, in fact not many miles from him, how could he escape?—
how could he protect his family?

His right knee ached, he walked now with a conspicuous limp,
thus he had reason to think of Lee Roy Sears almost constantly.

When friends first noticed the limp, they professed surprise,
sympathy—"Michael, what on earth happened to you?—are you
actually limping?" Michael made light of it, saying, "Oh, it's nothing—I banged it the other day," or, "Oh, it's nothing—an old football injury, acting up." Asked if he was seeing a doctor, Michael
shrugged and said, "Oh, maybe. When I have time."

Gina too urged him to see a doctor, for such problems only
got worse, didn't they?—as one grew older?

Michael laughed and said, "It's just that, you know, I hate to
give him the satisfaction."

"Him? Who?"

Gina stared at Michael, perplexed. Had she forgotten the source
of his knee injury?

Michael said, relenting, "Of course I'll see a doctor, Gina.
When I have time."

How intimately, how relentlessly I will track you.

To your very place of refuge.

One evening, returning to his car in the high-rise parking garage adjacent to Pearce, Inc., Michael discovered that the tires of his
Mazda had been slashed. And no other cars, anywhere in the garage,
had been touched.

One bright winter morning during Christmas recess Joel and
Kenny came running up to the house, screaming that "something
dead" was on the iced-over pond—the carcass of a dog that had been
struck by a car, and was mangled, and very bloody.

IN EARLY JANUARY, GINA received a telephone call from the principal
of the Riverside School, who told her, worriedly, that Joel and Kenny
were disobeying school rules by wandering off school grounds at
lunchtime and recess. Sometimes they returned late and refused to
say where they'd been; if pressed, they grew angry, insolent. One of
the Riverside teachers had seen them walking in a park a short dis-

tance away, in the company of a "dark man," but, asked about the man, they denied him entirely.

As they denied him, entirely, to their parents.

And there was the mystery of Marita, who quit, suddenly, over a weekend, and refused to return to the O'Mearas' house, and refused to say why.

"It's as if we are in a boat, with no engine, no sail, no rudder, being drawn by the current along some river we don't know," Gina said, her angry agitation giving her a poetic flair not usual in her, "and we're going faster, and it's dark, and—what are we to do?"

Michael said, quietly, "What *are* we to do? As long as he's alive, he's dangerous."

When Michael's car tires were slashed, he had notified the police, of course, and told them who he believed the perpetrator was; but, with no witnesses, and no evidence linking Lee Roy Sears to the scene of the crime, nor even to its general vicinity, the police were powerless.

The same held true with the dog carcass. The O'Mearas called the police at once, and the police came over, and investigated, and, yes, the dog had been dragged to the pond already dead, it had not staggered there on its own, but how could it be proved that Lee Roy Sears had dragged it there, if no one had seen him, and if there was not the slightest shred of evidence linking him to the mischief?

The police detective who spoke with Michael and Gina was sympathetic, and incensed, on their behalf, at this shock to their household, but he could only advise them what Michael already knew: they had better not make any formal accusations, without proof. He said, "In these harassment cases, it's best to wait it out. Sometimes the guy will make a mistake and get caught, but lots of times they just lose interest, and it peters out. Either way, you have to wait."

Gina said angrily, "What about our sons?—do we have to wait until they're hurt, too?"

Joel and Kenny continued to deny having seen Lee Roy Sears— "Mr. Sears hasn't been here in a long time!" they said, wide-eyed, half-accusingly. Michael had spoken with them, separately; he found that the boys were more tractable, less excitable, when they were apart, and each could speak in confidence, without the other hearing. But Joel swore *he* hadn't seen Mr. Sears, and Kenny swore *he* hadn't seen him. Michael asked, gently, who the man was described as the "dark man" by one of the Riverside teachers, and each boy said, unhesitating, "Nobody! There was nobody there!"

Daddy tried to smile, Daddy was being very patient.

"Nobody? At all?"

Joel with his beautiful greenish-blue eyes, thickly lashed as a doll's, his fair hair, his skin hot to the touch, "Nobody, Daddy! No-*body!*" as if Daddy were hard of hearing.

And Kenny with his beautiful greenish-blue eyes, thickly lashed as a doll's, his fair hair, skin hot to the touch, his manner just slightly more antic than his brother's, "Nobody, Daddy! *No-body!*" nearly shouting in Daddy's startled face.

Afterward, Gina reported to Michael that she'd heard the boys shrieking with laughter up in their room: had he mixed them up? Joel with Kenny, Kenny with Joel?

"You really should be more careful about that, darling," Gina said, regarding Michael with affectionate eyes. "You *know* how it sets them off."

So TOO HAD MARITA refused to explain why she was quitting her employment with the O'Mearas. When Gina offered her a raise, and, in desperation, shorter hours, Marita said quickly, "Thank you, Mrs. O'Meara. But it isn't *that.*"

"Then what is it?" Gina asked.

This was a telephone conversation; thus Gina could not see the young woman's face. She sensed reluctance, dread. Distaste.

"Mrs. O'Meara, I got to hang up now."

"Is it—was it—somebody harassing you, here?—following you?—threatening you?"

But Marita only murmured something apologetic and hung up.

Gina came to Michael in tears. He was moved by how distressed she was, at this defection of Marita's: it seemed to upset her more than the other incidents.

She said, biting her lower lip, looking up at Michael appealingly, "It's just so hard to believe, isn't it, that Lee Roy doesn't like us any longer!"

Michael held her in his arms, to comfort her. Poor Gina!— even with such evidence, she could not bring herself to utter the word *hate*.

THIS NIGHTMARE TIME.

When, like any normal man, Michael O'Meara fantasized attacking his enemy, beating him into submission.

Killing him?—maybe.

"To protect Gina, to protect the boys—what *wouldn't* I do!"

As the police had advised, Michael decided to wait it out; to do nothing to deliberately arouse Lee Roy Sears's further animosity. He knew by way of the grapevine in Mount Orion that Lee Roy was still with Valeria Darrell, that the two were often seen together at jazz nightclubs in one or another of the suburban communities spawned by the new corporate industries along Route One, east of Mount Orion; he was told that Lee Roy had sold some of his art— to whom, for how much, wasn't clear. "Good for him," Michael said. Thinking, Maybe then he will leave us alone.

There were further incidents, however: Michael was sure he was followed one evening, in his car, driving home from work: by someone whose face he could not see clearly, in a car of no particular distinction. (Did Lee Roy Sears have a car, now?—a driver's license?)

And, despite their unlisted number, the O'Mearas still received, now and then, mysterious telephone calls, when no one identified himself at the other end of the line. (Of course, maybe the caller was *not* Lee Roy Sears?—who could know?)

Michael kept in contact with H. Sigman, whom Lee Roy was obliged to see every two weeks, and who sometimes made surprise visits to Lee Roy at the halfway house. So far as the parole officer knew, Lee Roy Sears was making a satisfactory adjustment to society; and there was the prospect of his career as an artist. And, importantly, Sears had a stabilizing factor in his life—"This lady friend of his, I believe she has assets?"

This was a telephone conversation. Michael smiled wryly. "She does," he said.

"There's talk of marriage, is there?" Sigman asked.

"*Is* there?"

"Lee Roy has hinted, a few times. He seems okay."

"That's good. That's wonderful. I mean—that he seems okay."

"Thanks to people like you, Mr. O'Meara. In my line of work, I can tell you, there are not many people like you, willing to give these guys a chance. If it wasn't for people like you, Mr. O'Meara," Sigman said, extravagantly, as if moved by his own rhetoric, "these poor bastards wouldn't have a chance!"

"Well," said Michael.

"It's so. The average person, he doesn't want to touch an ex-con, any kind of ex-inmate, with a ten-foot pole. But you know that, I guess."

Michael said, as cheerfully as he could manage, "Maybe, if his career takes off, Lee Roy Sears could move to New York?—him and his new wife, both?"

"Sure, he'd be okayed for that," Sigman said expansively, as if nothing would please him more. "No special reason for him to stay in Putnam, then."

"No special reason!" Michael said.

A fantasy. But a happy fantasy.

LIPS ON HIS!—WAKING him! So delicious.

His eyes flew open, and he saw Gina, lovely Gina, her eyes wide and dilated as a cat's, leaning over him, pink tongue poking out, just the tip of it, between her pursed lips.

"Sweetie, wake up! Your neck must be *broken!* If you're sleepy, why don't you go to bed?—no need to wait up for *me.*"

It was a snowy evening in early February. Michael O'Meara, exhausted from his long day at Pearce, had fallen asleep in his leather chair, in his study, sometime between the hour of nine o'clock and—what was it now?—eleven-thirty.

Gina had had to be out for the evening, unavoidably—she was newly elected to the executive committee, unless it was the fund-raising committee, or the social committee, of the Friends of the Dumont Center—or was it the Friends of the Mount Orion Symphony.

Returning with complaints of exhaustion, herself, though, as always, Gina looked poised, cool, effervescent, lovely. Saying, chiding, with a quick caress of her hand along Michael's warm cheek, "I love you, darling, I hate to see you dozing off like, oh I don't know, like some homeless person, in Penn Station!—let's go to bed."

Michael, sleep-dazed, heaved himself to his feet, and followed after.

It seemed a very long time ago, he'd had supper, prepared by the new girl, Clara, and had helped her put Joel and Kenny to bed.

A very long time ago.

Since his solitary meal, Michael had been working in his study, at his desk, as, most evenings, he worked at his desk, preparing Pearce's elaborate defense in the $50 million Peverol suit; sifting through pages of legal documents, photocopied material, and, tonight, catalogues from mail-order rifle companies, with special annotated material pertaining to the AK-47 assault rifle, the weapon used to kill seven people, and the gunman himself, in Memphis. Michael's vision had blurred, despite new prescription glasses for reading; he must have slipped into sleep, as one might slip into warm, soothing water, with no clear awareness of what was happening.

Gina led him upstairs, fingers clasped through his. "My poor honey!—it breaks my heart to see you look so *tired*," she said. "I hope you aren't thinking about—*him*."

"Not at all," Michael said quickly. "I think the situation is under control."

"Everyone I saw today asked about you and said they missed you. Stan says he never sees you on the squash court any longer, and Jack and Pam are *so* disappointed about next Friday, and—even Marvin Bruns, whom we scarcely know, *he* was asking after you too. So, you see, Michael O'Meara, how popular you are!—even in your absence."

It was true, Michael had all but dropped out of Mount Orion's civic social life, since the previous fall. He did not want to think that he was obsessed with his work, still less that he was obsessed with Lee Roy Sears, for, in fact, he was not an obsessive or com-

pulsive personality: it worried him that others might misunderstand.

"As soon as this Memphis case is decided, I'll be back to
normality again. I promise."

"Of course!—that's what you always say."

But Gina forgave him, and kissed him, with a quick teasing
probe of her pink tongue.

THAT NIGHT, PERVERSELY UNABLE to sleep when he wanted to sleep,
Michael found himself leaving Gina (how blissfully, how like a baby
she slept!) and going downstairs, like a sleepwalker, though awake,
on bare, silent feet, with a need to ascertain something; to hold
something in his hand, out of his past.

He then found himself rummaging through old books, most of
them paperbacks, not glanced at in many years, since his intense
hopeful days at the theological seminary. At the age of forty he was
hungry for moral guidance—he seemed to have no source for it, no
model of it, in the world he now inhabited.

With a quickening pulse, in his pajamas, shivering, in a bed-
room at the rear of the house Gina used as an infrequent guestroom,
eagerly reading through his much-annotated paperback of Tolstoy's
My Religion, last consulted in 1969. How hypnotic to Michael
O'Meara, as to Tolstoy, the wisdom of Jesus as preserved in the
Book of Matthew:

*It has been said unto you, An eye for an eye, and a tooth for a
tooth: But I say unto you, That you resist not evil.*

In compelling prose, Tolstoy explains how, encountering this utterly simple, direct verse in Matthew, at the age of fifty, after thirty-five
years of nihilism, he had experienced a complete conversion of his heart.
The direction of Tolstoy's life, his desires, the very timbre of his personality—all were transformed, violently and irrevocably.

*It has been said unto you, An eye for an eye, and a tooth for a
tooth: But I say unto you, That you resist not evil.*

Michael had been awkwardly squatting in front of a bookshelf,
reading in the book; straightening, he winced with pain—his right
knee seemed swollen.

How like a riddle the verse from Matthew was, teasing, mes-
merizing:

It has been said unto you, An eye for an eye, and a tooth for a tooth: But I say unto you, That you resist not evil.

Michael wondered, What *does* it mean, really? Had Tolstoy himself understood? "Resist not evil."

Next morning, on his way to work, Michael O'Meara locked his copy of Tolstoy's *My Religion* in the glove compartment of the Mazda. He was never to glance into it again, but, then, he had no need of doing so.

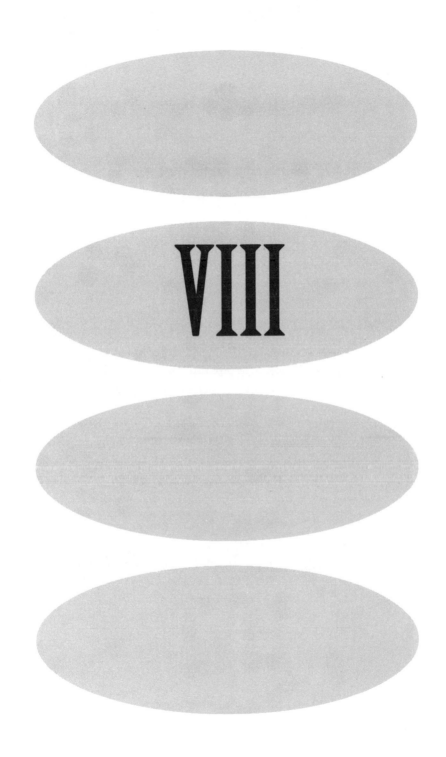

VIII

1

NEVER WILL SHE SEE her assailant's face.

Never will she hear her assailant's voice.

So deft! so quick! an arm snaking around her neck, from behind!

And the blade, the swift terrible blade, the razor blade, or is it blades, many blades, slashing, digging, tearing into her flesh. Oh! oh! *oh!*

Sometime after dark, a rainy dusk mixed with sleet. That smell of wet cement, that urban smell, gritty, yet romantic: as high-rise parking garages adjacent to high-rise luxury hotels are romantic in our time.

So romantic!—her heart fairly faints.

So romantic!—thinking of certain things, fresh memories, she's nearly in a swoon.

I love you, I'm crazy about you, oh God.

And I love *you*.

No but listen, my God I mean it.

I mean it!

Kicking, pummeling, laughing. Like a jackhammer, his hips.

Oh God, that sweet-tingling sensation in her loins.

Even now she could scream, scream . . . *scream.*

Like embers, slow-dying embers, so sweet. It will stay with her, lodged snug and secret up deep inside her, the velvety-silky purse of her, for hours.

Back in Mount Orion, Glenway Circle, home.

Back with *them.* Who scarcely know her.

So, now: walking swiftly, to the elevator.

Swiftly, not at all fearfully, in this deserted place.

Heels smartly rap! rap! rapping! on the stained cement floor.

(Why isn't she fearful, at least cautious?—a woman, alone, a beautiful woman, alone, in a russet-red fox fur, alone, at this twilit hour, rain mixed with sleet, and a half-hour drive on the Parkway ahead?—because her mind is so luxuriantly elsewhere.)

(*And* they'd drunk an entire bottle of French champagne, and devoured a hefty platter of beluga caviar, seventy-five dollars an ounce: and why not? So much to celebrate!)

She takes the elevator (smelly little cube-shaped cage) to level C of the parking garage. The door opens sluggishly: what if she's trapped: dismissing the thought at once, because she *isn't.*

As, in the bath, the fragrant bubbly rosy-tinted bath, she'd glanced down smiling at her white body with its rose-pink blood-pink cast like a shadow in the very same instant dismissed the thought because *she isn't that kind of woman.*

Her pretty watch, slipped hastily on her thin wrist, is upside-down!—thus, glancing at it, wondering what's the time, she doesn't absorb the time, but no matter.

An irony, an oddity, unless of course it's purely chance: never in memory has she slipped any watch of hers on upside-down, until now.

Even in extreme haste.

Oh!—damn you you let me fall *asleep.*

I let *you?*—what about *me?*

I'm the one with a family, not you!

So: whose fault is that?

Her hair is still damp, at the ends. Tendrils of damp. Shivery.

She'd fussed with the blow-dryer, which had seemed always about to fly out of her hand, up into the air. Laughing, his face in the mirror beside hers, an olive-tan skin, good strong grinning teeth. Seizing her around the waist, beneath her breasts, with his sinewy hairy-dark arms.

The two of them in those white terrycloth robes that come with such rooms, in the better newer hotels.

Can you put this on your expense account?

Does a fish swim?—does a bird fly?

Oh, you're—impossible!

You're delicious.

D'you know—in brain research—the latest discovery—it's the left brain that makes up theories, stories—for things that the right brain experiences—so—so!—let's *do* what we want to do, and make up the reasons later!

That, I always knew!

Slipping his hands inside the terrycloth robe. Squeezing her breasts, which are already sore.

Oh, damn you!—that *hurts.*

Does it?

Level C, and only a few cars remaining. It's an open garage and cold damp gusty-exhilarating air touches her face. In the near distance, high-rise lights, headlights of vehicles, in the shifting sky winking lights of airliners: how we love our world, the romance of our world, because it's *ours.*

And that tingling erotic pulsation in her loins, oh God *that.*

That, and the giddy glasses of champagne, have very possibly clouded her judgment.

March 1. She will remember, but only in retrospect.

At the moment, discovering her car (she'd forgotten where the hell she'd parked it; when the level is nearly full the space looks entirely different), she could not have said the date, the time, oh who *cares,* her husband won't be home when she gets there anyway.

Working late. Working working late. Late, *late.*

He's a great guy, I really admire him. I mean, hell—he's *nice.*

Yes. He is.

You love him I guess?

I love him. I guess.

You've been married—how long?

All my life.

Approaching her car, yes that *is* her car, parked at the very rear, in a corner, she'd sort of forgotten parking it in a corner but she'd been in a hurry, panicked at being so late.

Just a coincidence—she isn't really thinking of this—keys in her gloved hand, stooping to unlock the door (but *did* she lock the doors?—can't remember) her breath steaming faintly about her mouth, just a coincidence, and no connection, she finds herself thinking of poor Clyde Somerset, who'd been mugged the week before in the parking lot behind the Dumont Center, shocking! incredible! a mugging! in the very heart of Mount Orion!—what bad luck for Clyde that there were no witnesses, the poor man so savagely beaten his jaw was broken, teeth knocked out, ribs cracked, Clyde, who isn't in the very best physical condition (so ruddy in the face, you can see he has high blood pressure, can't Susanne make him diet?), thus lucky to be alive, lucky the heart attack wasn't fatal.

No. Unfortunately. He didn't see his assailant's face.

Didn't hear his assailant's voice.

Poor Clyde, unable to identify the mugger.

(Yes, of course, the police were provided with the name of a likely suspect, a suspect who might have wished revenge upon Clyde Somerset, but how to connect the suspect with the crime if there is no evidence?—if, apparently, he was somewhere else at the time, and someone will so swear?)

But she isn't thinking of this really. Not in her happy floating mood.

Why not, look, I deserve some happiness too for God's sake, I am not just a wife and a mother, if that's what you think you don't know *me*. And I'm still young.

She slides into the driver's seat, loves the aroma of the new car, sleek black leather seats, she'd wanted a Mercedes for years and, now: her Christmas present from Michael here it *is*.

They'd traded in the Honda hatchback, so suburban-boring.

If that's what you think all of you you don't know *me*.

Oh!—beautiful. De-li-ci-ous.

Scooping up caviar on the pale stoneground crackers, laughing, greedy. Licking the tiny jelly-eggs where some had fallen, on his chest. *His* nipples too.

Always makes her giggle, shivery-giggle, that men have nipples too. That, there, inside their bodies (their bodies that are so *nice*, sometimes), there they *are*—just like us.

So sort of—trapped?

Let's say defined.

Does the body define?

Flesh, bone, blood—*us*?

If not the body, then—what?

She is fumbling to fit the key into the ignition, not that she's drunk (she is *not* drunk!—though they will find a high alcoholic content in her blood) but her damned kidskin glove makes it awkward, and she isn't completely adjusted to the new car, and she is, but isn't, aware of—someone in the back seat?—rising as if to embrace her?—as if he'd been waiting a very long time to embrace her?—and were she to glance astonished into the rearview mirror she would see only what appears to be a masked face, a head exotically concealed in something dark, possibly woollen, a long scarf wound turban-style about the head covering most of the face including most of the eyes, only peepholes for the eyes, the eyes!—damp-glaring with hurt! with rage! with elation! with resolve!—but she doesn't have time for it begins at once and will end within sixty seconds, the quick deft terrible arm snaking about her neck choking her pinning her to the seat, the flash of the razor, the cutting tearing digging slicing razor blade, her cheeks, her forehead, her chin, her nose, her screaming mouth, the agonized O! of that mouth, and the hot blood everywhere, she thrashes from side to side tries to move her head from side to side but he has her pinioned, no escape, the bloody razor leaps, flies, flashes, tears, slicing into her flesh like a lover's caress gone mad, maddened with lust, and then, and then, and *then*—the splash of the turpentine into her face, into her gouged-bleeding wounds, into her eyes, as if to cleanse—?

WHAT COMES OUT.

So it happened: his enemy had struck.

Michael O'Meara half-knew, as, entering his house by way of the kitchen, at approximately 7:45 P.M. of March 1, seeing the new girl, Clara, speaking on the telephone, and Joel and Kenny white-faced beside her—seeing her, seeing his boys, oh God: something has happened to Gina: he knew.

Clara was a sturdy-bodied girl, ordinarily a hearty cheery competent girl, but now her eyes widened at the sight of him, and she cried, "Oh, Mr. O'Meara! Thank God!" and she handed over the receiver to him, as if it were on fire.

So, he knew.

It had been a tightly scheduled day. One of his rather skillfully managed days. A day to keep, for a while, the nightmare at bay.

He'd flown to Boston on a 10:00 A.M. shuttle. Had his luncheon meeting, a fairly satisfactory meeting, and returned, to Newark Airport, on the 3:00 P.M. shuttle. A car was waiting to take him to Pearce, Inc., where he had another meeting, or was it two meetings, and then he hid away in his office, as others left he hid away in his office and he worked, and left at about 7:00 P.M. taking work home with him, driving home on the Parkway he could not recall— had Gina said she would, or would not, be home when he got there; had Gina said they were, or were not, going to have dinner together that evening; thinking of the work he had to do, feeling, perversely, an odd angry pride in the very fact that *I can do it: I will do it: God damn it, yes!*

Michael O'Meara knew that the top executives at Pearce, Inc., were watching him very closely these days. Him, and his team of energetic young lawyers. They were keenly aware of him, uneasily aware of him (for, loyal as he was to Pearce, Inc., Michael was occasionally approached by other corporations with tentative offers of employment: his reputation had never been more bankable), both dependent upon him and anxious to extract the last drop of effort from him—oh yes. And to bear up under this ceaseless pressure, this omniscient eye from above, Michael had discovered that, taken prudently, in very small doses, Pearce's popular "mood-adjuster" Euphomine was very helpful. Very!

Not that he believed in amphetamines—he didn't. And not that he'd abandoned the Liloprane, which was so soothing, comforting, like an old friend—he remained faithful to the Liloprane. But now and then, never more than a few times a week, when, for instance, he needed to be really up for a meeting, like, today, at the office before 8:00 A.M. at the shuttle by 10:00 A.M. required to be as fully awake and alert and as optimistic and as *zestful* as Michael O'Meara's reputation required—well, at such times the Euphomine was helpful.

So, ironically, this day had not been one of Michael O'Meara's more painful days. Like a fast-moving stream it had its own urgent rhythm, carrying him along, propelling him along, with virtually no time to think of the danger to his family; no time to brood upon the fact that Lee Roy Sears was his enemy and wished him harm.

Then, dumbfounded, he was standing in his kitchen being informed by a stranger at a medical center in Ridgewood, New Jersey, that Gina was undergoing emergency surgery there; that she had been savagely attacked by an unknown, as-yet unapprehended assailant; slashed in the face and hands with a razor, robbed of her cash, credit cards, and jewelry, and left, unconscious, to bleed to death behind the wheel of her car, in a high-rise parking garage attached to a Marriott Inn just off the Parkway in—but why Ridgewood, so far away?

Michael could not, at first, comprehend what he was hearing. Neither the words themselves, nor their meaning.

Weakly he asked, "Ridgewood?—are you sure? *Ridge*wood?"

Yes, the voice informed him: Ridgewood, New Jersey. Did he know how to get there?

He thought he did, more or less. Yes. Of course. He had a map of the state, he could find it.

About thirty-five miles away, north and east of Mount Orion.

A suburban town of no special distinction, north of Paterson, just a name on the map. Michael O'Meara had never been in Ridgewood that he could recall but, no, of course he'd have no trouble finding it.

Hanging up the phone, dazed as if he'd been struck a blow to the head, Michael still had enough fatherly presence of mind to comfort his badly frightened sons, who had begun crying softly, helplessly, pressing themselves against his legs, plucking at his sleeves. Of late, Joel and Kenny had grown into husky little boys, but now they seemed very small, very young, vulnerable. "Is Mommy hurt?— is Mommy going to die?—where is Mommy?" they whimpered. Michael squatted, and hugged them, one in the crook of each arm, hugged them hard, blinking back tears, telling them that Mommy would be all right—"Daddy will take care of her, and Daddy will take care of you, don't be afraid, ever again, I *promise.*"

HE DROVE TO RIDGEWOOD, exiting from the Parkway, taking Route 208 north, thinking, repeatedly, over and over, again, again, Don't let her die, don't let her die, God don't let her die, I will always then believe in Your mercy.

Thinking, But I'll kill him. *Must* kill him.

Fumbling as if unconsciously to extract from his pocket, and to place on his tongue, one of the chunky Euphomine capsules—but it slipped from his shaking fingers and was lost.

So, he let it go. In the state he was in, he didn't need further stimulation.

"TURPENTINE? *TURPENTINE?* HE SPLASHED *turpentine* on her?"

Repeatedly, in disbelief, Michael O'Meara asked the emergency room physician this question. He was perceived to be in a state of such extreme emotion as to require medication himself.

The doctor suggested a sedative, but Michael O'Meara backed off, saying, "No! No thank you, Doctor! Not me! Not now!"

While Gina was undergoing surgery, to repair, or attempt to repair, her savagely mutilated face, Michael O'Meara waited, not impassively, but on his feet, pacing, limping, grimacing with pain (because of a bad knee?—though he limped, he seemed scarcely conscious of it); his head lowered, eyes rapidly blinking, sightless. He was perceived to be a professional man, well-dressed, in a gray pinstripe suit, but slightly disheveled, his necktie loose, and his shirt collar unbuttoned; he might have been in his late forties, his face drawn and ashen with fatigue. His skin had a dry, mottled appearance, as if it might be hot to the touch. He gave off a frank odor of masculine sweat, frustration. And, as he paced, he kept clenching and unclenching his fists.

Each time someone in hospital whites appeared—no matter if it was only a very young nurse, or an orderly—Michael O'Meara looked up, fearful, urgent. Licking his parched lips, asking, "Is she—?"

Gina O'Meara would be in the operating room for two and a quarter hours.

During this time, Michael O'Meara made only two telephone calls, both to his home. He spoke with his sons, assuring them that "Mommy is going to be all right, yes really and truly she *is.*"

Three police officers questioned Michael O'Meara, and he managed to speak with them politely, if distractedly. He tried to recall which of her several watches Gina was likely to have been wearing, tried to describe her wedding and engagement rings, and to identify which credit cards she routinely carried in her wallet. (The assailant-thief had taken money and credit cards out of Gina's wallet and left the wallet and the purse behind, in the back seat of the Mercedes. Both were covered in Gina's blood.) It was noted by these police officers that Michael O'Meara behaved as the husband of any so viciously assaulted and robbed woman might have behaved, except, on the matter of the assailant-thief's identity, he was peculiarly laconic, resigned. Thus far, there were no witnesses, nor any suspects. The attack had taken place on level C, the highest level, of the parking garage, at a time in early evening when the garage was relatively deserted; the attendant on duty, on the first level, could recall no one suspicious or out-of-the-ordinary entering, or leaving, at the time of the attack. (Gina had been found by a couple returning to their car, approximately twenty minutes after the attack. By then she was unconscious, in shock from loss of blood, sprawled in the front seat of the Mercedes where everything—her fox fur coat, her clothes, the cushioned-leather car seats, the carpeted floor of the car—was soaked in her blood.) Told these stark, not very encouraging facts, Michael grimaced, and said, flatly, "Of course. No witnesses. *He* would not have tried to kill my wife, if there had been witnesses."

The police were naturally under the assumption that the attack had been more or less random and anonymous, the primary motive being robbery. Michael O'Meara seemed to acquiesce to this theory; at any rate, he did not object. Certainly he did not mention the name "Lee Roy Sears."

MICHAEL WAS TOLD BY the surgeon, after the operation, that Gina had sustained countless deep cuts to her face—cheeks, forehead, chin, nose, mouth; her lower lip had been nearly sliced away, and her left earlobe severed. Yet the razor-wielding assailant had been careful, apparently, not to cut her throat. Nor had he cut her eyes—though he'd badly burnt them with the turpentine.

The surgeon, younger than Michael O'Meara, spoke somberly; he appeared somewhat shaken.

Perhaps he was wondering if the woman upon whom he'd performed emergency surgery had been attractive.

He would recall afterward how intensely the husband, Michael O'Meara, listened; yet how glazed his eyes, how compulsively he kept licking his lips. Several times he asked, in a voice just barely controlled, "But she *will* live, Doctor, won't she?—won't she?" The surgeon said, "Yes, Mr. O'Meara, she'll live. But she'll require further surgery. Reconstructive surgery. Her face has been so"—he paused, searching for the most discreet word—"injured." And Michael O'Meara said, with the same barely controlled urgency, "But the main thing, Doctor, is her *life.*"

Immediately following the operation, Gina had been taken to the intensive care unit, where she had yet to regain consciousness. When a nurse led Michael in, and he saw her—saw the grotesquely bandaged figure she'd become—he gave a cry of horror, stricken to the heart.

Her head (which was shaven) was completely swathed in white, like a mummy's head—mere peepholes for eyes, nostrils, mouth. A transparent plastic tube ran into one of her nostrils, distending it; another tube ran into a vein in her arm. Though her head appeared swollen in its lengths of gauze, her body appeared small, flat, diminished, like a sick child's. And how still she was, except for her hoarse, labored, soblike breathing.

Michael clasped her cool, damp, lifeless hand in his. Whispering, "Gina?—darling? *I love you.*"

She would not regain consciousness for hours. By then Michael O'Meara would have been made to leave, for the facility was closing for the night.

RESIST NOT EVIL.

 AND AGAIN! AS IN a dream! the big-bellied Hispanic in the soiled undershirt burst out of his room, eyes glaring in his swarthy face, when Michael O'Meara banged his fist on Lee Roy Sears's door!— this time, seeing what was in the other's face, retreating back into his room without a word.

And shutting the door.

Quietly.

HE'S RECKLESS ENOUGH, ARROGANT enough, to be there.

And so he was, God damn him: the lights on the third floor of the warehouse were on.

Midnight. A dull glow from within the building, illuminating the panes of grimy glass.

There. Waiting.

Michael O'Meara's heart was pounding hard, fast, steady. He seemed to have no fear. He seemed even to have no plan for what he would do; and what, having done that, he would do next—if there was *next*.

So, running up the stairs. In the dank airless dark barely illuminated by a single bare lightbulb.

From Lee Roy Sears's studio there came the jarring sound of a radio—rock music, shrill and raucous. And that smell, that taunting stink, of turpentine.

Michael O'Meara pushed the door open. There stood Lee Roy Sears, at his easel, paintbrush in hand, a cigarette clenched between his teeth and half his face screwed up against the smoke. As the men locked eyes, Sears stiffened; Michael O'Meara hesitated for a fraction of a moment, simply staring. He was not thinking, *There: my enemy.* He was not thinking, *This is the man I must kill.* Since leaving Gina, he had had no thoughts, in the usual sense of the word, at all.

He had driven from the Ridgewood Medical Center to Putnam, and to this warehouse in a derelict neighborhood in North Putnam, without knowing what he did; with no clear plan, or consciousness.

Knowing only that he was fated to kill his enemy, or, at last, to be killed by him. And not even knowing this fact so much as sensing it, groping for it, as a blind creature, burrowing in earth, might nonetheless burrow upward toward light.

"You!—fucker!—what are *you* doing here!"

Lee Roy Sears faced Michael O'Meara defiantly, guiltily.

The paintbrush he wielded glistened crudely with an oily red, a plasticine red, mock blood. Behind him, the canvas on his easel was a lurid cobwebby swirl of reds, grays, black: a stylized grimace: like the loud rock music that continued to blare from the radio, as if jeering at Michael O'Meara's grief and rage. Sears threw the brush onto the floor, and the red paint splattered. He spat out his cigarette, made a sound somewhere between a laugh and a yodel, *he* wasn't afraid, *he* meant to enjoy himself, seizing a chair and brandishing it like a weapon, advancing upon Michael O'Meara, saying, taunting, "You're here, huh?—and where's *she*?—how's the cunt, huh?—Mr. and Mrs. Hot-Shit Lawyer-Cunt, huh? Okay, asshole, come and get it!"

Was this the man Michael O'Meara had helped bring to Mount
Orion, and welcomed into his and Gina's life?

Sears was heavier than Michael had ever seen him, especially
in the upper torso. Thick with muscle, his neck appeared foreshortened so that his head seemed merely to rest upon his shoulders. His
eyes were glassily bright in their mockery, as if he were drunk, or
drugged. His hair, Indian-black singed with gray, had been tied back
carelessly from his face into a drooping ponytail, secured by a length
of twine; his sleeves, rolled up, bared sinewy forearms, and exposed
the lewd coiled snake, oily black spangled with gold, on his left
arm—how vivid, how pulsating, how springy with malevolent life
the tattoo was! Michael was staring at the thing, transfixed, and
would have remained rooted to the spot as Sears brought the chair
down on his head except, at the very last instant, by a violent
wrenching of his will, he broke free.

Broke free, and jumped aside, with an alacrity he hadn't known
he still possessed: he might have been on the football field again,
jumping aside to elude being tackled.

The chair came crashing down beside him, to shatter on the
floor.

Sears grunted and wheeled upon him.

Again the men locked eyes. Each was breathing harshly.

Michael whispered, "Why—why—why did you do it!"

Sears said, sneering, "*What?*—what the fuck?—I do what I
want to do, man!—what *I* want to do!—got it?"

"My wife—"

"Fuck your wife! The cunt!"

Michael leapt wildly at Sears, who swung at him with a round-
house right, missing him by inches, the momentum of his blow
carrying him forward, and off-balance, so that Michael, not knowing
what he did, merely reacting, had only to bring his own right fist
up—a clumsy uppercut that, as if by chance, caught the other man
on the point of his chin and sent him staggering backward.

The easel, the lurid cobwebby painting, the blaring radio—all
went flying. Abruptly, the raucous music was cut off.

Sears seemed genuinely surprised by the blow and momentarily
stunned. "Fucker!—God damn you!—gonna kill you!" He seized an
empty beer bottle, swung another time at Michael, who ducked,

and again rushed at him, pinioning him around the shoulders as both men staggered backward.

They fell against Sears's cluttered worktable, knocking things to the floor; fell against a pile of canvases stacked against a wall; crashed into the flimsy plywood screen in front of the toilet, and sent it toppling. Sears kneed Michael in the belly and groin, hard enough to make him cry out in pain, but not hard enough to loosen his grip. "Let go!—damn you!—you're crazy!" Sears grunted.

Was Michael O'Meara mad?—his face had gone deathly white, as if the blood had drained entirely out of it, and his eyes were shut tight, his entire face contorted as a gargoyle's. And he would not let go of Lee Roy Sears, locking him in a fierce squeezing embrace.

Sears's hair had come loose from its ponytail and straggled into Michael's face as well as his own.

The one man in paint-splattered (blood-splattered?) clothes, snake tattoo lurid and throbbing with life on his arm, the other in a lawyer's gray pinstripe suit, now badly torn, stained.

Cursing, grunting, half-sobbing.

How many minutes?—faces contorted, eyes leaking tears. Except for the sounds of their struggle the studio was silent, the warehouse empty, and silent. As if no city, no world, existed beyond these walls.

Sears grabbed one of the humanoid clay figures off a window sill and slammed it against the side of Michael's head: it broke into fragments at once, but stunned Michael, who loosened his grip on Sears long enough for Sears to wrench away.

Sears ran to his worktable, opened a drawer, rummaged in the drawer wild-eyed, desperate, then found what he was looking for: a razor blade taped to a broken-off paintbrush: this he brandished at Michael, waving it wildly. It was a sinister instrument, the blade stained with something red, rust-colored.

"You want it?—you want it?—you want it? Come and get it!"

Was it possible?—Michael O'Meara rushed forward.

Head lowered, face grim, distorted.

Incredulous, Sears swiped at him with the razor, slashing him on the forehead, but had no time for a backhand blow. Michael tackled him about the waist, knocking the razor from his hand, and again the men careened drunkenly backward.

Sears was screaming like a madman. "You're crazy!—let me go!"

They were struggling against a wall—near a window—near a door to the fire escape. Sears managed to get the door open, shove himself out of Michael's embrace, and stagger out onto the fire escape, as Michael lunged blindly after.

What happened next, precisely—Michael O'Meara would not recall.

For had it happened to him, by way of him, or to another man, and by way of another man?—whose face he could not recognize as his own?

It *was* his own, of course. Yet he could not have recognized it, in the exigency of those terrible moments.

It appeared that Lee Roy Sears wanted to kill Michael O'Meara, and yet, at the same time, he wanted to escape him: for he tried to choke him, and banged his head violently against the iron railing of the fire escape, but, a moment later, when Michael proved too strong or too stubborn or too inured to pain to succumb, he released him and began to climb down the ladder.

The fire escape leading from the third floor of the old warehouse to an unpaved alley below was old, derelict, rusted.

As Sears climbed frantically down, Michael O'Meara tried to grab him from above, his hair, his shirt, his arm.

Their breaths must have steamed about their mouths, for it was bitterly cold that night. This, Michael O'Meara would not remember.

Nor would he remember whether Sears was still cursing him, or whether, intent now upon escape, he'd gone silent.

What he would remember—vaguely, teasingly, like something glimpsed through wavy glass, or water—was the rung of the ladder breaking suddenly under Sears's groping foot; the white-knuckled grip of Sears's hands on the ladder; the look of, not terror, but baffled outrage on Sears's sweaty face, as his legs swung free, helpless as dead weights.

"Help me!"

Instinctively, Michael grabbed at Sears's wrists, to keep him from falling: but Sears's weight was too much for him, and Sears slipped out of his grasp, and fell, with a high-pitched childlike wail, to the ground two storeys below.

WHERE HE STRUCK EARTH, but also rubble, and sharp-edged chunks of concrete.

Where he lay flat and unmoving as a rag doll, obscured by shadows.

Where, breath faltering, blood streaming out of a wound to his skull, he must have died at once: for by the time the ambulance arrived, approximately eight minutes later, Lee Roy Sears was dead.

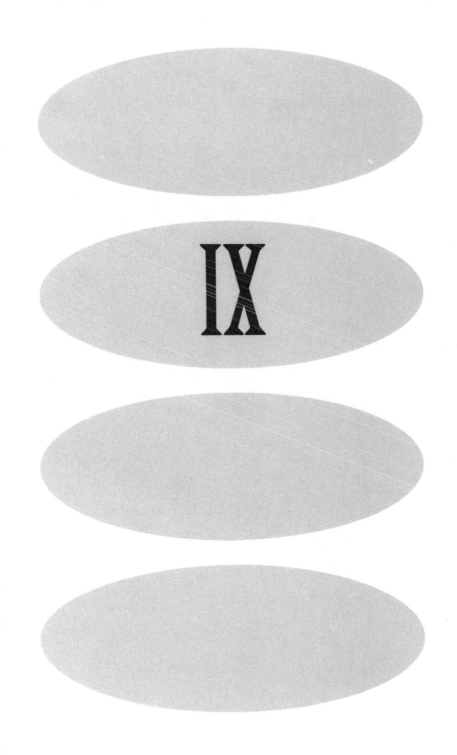

IX

JANET O'MEARA TRIED TO keep the exasperation, still less the alarm, out of her voice. Knowing, from experience, how little good it did.

"But, Mother, why do you say you want to visit them if you *don't?*—why did you fly here, if you can't bring yourself to come with me fifty more miles, to Mount Orion?"

"I—I do want to see them. I will."

"Yes, Mother, but when? You've been here five days now."

Mrs. O'Meara's small, damp, close-set eyes brimmed with sudden tears, as if Janet had struck her. She said, hurt, "Oh!—do you want me to go back home?—is the apartment too small for the two of us? Is that what you're saying?"

In such a way trying to deflect Janet from the true subject of their conversation.

"Mother, I am not saying that, and you know I am not saying that. I *am* saying—"

"Oh!—you sound like that interviewer self of yours, on television!"

"—am saying that it's very strange, that's all. And how can I explain, to Michael?—how can he explain, to Gina?"

Mrs. O'Meara searched for her purse, which was never quite where she left it.

"Tell them—oh, please tell them—explain, dear—that I'm not feeling well. I'm—I am—feeling so weak, in the chest. My migraine—"

"They will think you're avoiding them, you know. I'm not a very good liar."

"Would Gina really see me, if I did go?—we've never been very close. Would the poor woman let me see her?"

The frail question hung suspended, as if unanswerable.

Janet said, drily practical, "There's Michael, Mother. There are your grandsons."

"I—I do want to see them. I've said."

"Yes, but when? Saturday?"

This was a Wednesday: March 27. A day of high-scudding clouds. A glowering-pale sky beyond the windows of Janet O'Meara's thirtieth-floor apartment on East 86th Street, New York City.

"Maybe. Yes. Saturday."

"Good! I'll call Michael and tell him, then. We'll be out Saturday."

Mrs. O'Meara was tugging a handkerchief out of her purse. Her eyes shone dangerously bright with tears that, if allowed to spill over, would damage the carefully powdered façade of her face.

Murmuring, almost inaudibly, in her babyish, petulant voice, "Oh, but don't promise."

THIS WAS THE VISIT, this, the mysterious and frustrating interlude, when Janet O'Meara's mother fussed so much with one or another of her monogrammed handkerchiefs.

No disposable paper tissues, for Constance O'Meara: these were genuine Portuguese linen handkerchiefs, dazzlingly white, edged with lace, and embroidered with the initials CJO.

Fortunately, Mrs. O'Meara laundered and ironed the handkerchiefs herself, as she personally laundered and ironed all her delicate things.

When Mrs. O'Meara so dabbed at her eyes, which were pink-lidded and curiously lashless, it was with an extravagant gesture, as if the handkerchief were a magician's and might be useful for making things disappear.

So Janet O'Meara was led to think, watching her mother—her mother watching *her* around the borders of the Portuguese linen handkerchief.

She wishes I'd disappear. Or, at least, stop asking her questions she doesn't want to answer.

SUCH AS: WHY WAS she behaving so oddly; so excessively oddly, even for *her?*—at sixty-seven, a woman of eccentric, willful habits.

Why, having made the effort (and for Mrs. O'Meara it was indeed a considerable effort) of leaving her comfortable Palm Beach condominium, and flying to the wintry North, with the intention of visiting her son, Michael, and her daughter-in-law, Gina, in Mount Orion, New Jersey—*why* now make every excuse not to see them?

At first, it had seemed quite plausible: Mrs. O'Meara had been "exhausted" from travel.

Then, a day or so later, she'd pleaded "shortness of breath."

The next day, a "queasy stomach."

And always there was the old reliable "migraine."

(In Mrs. O'Meara's self-absorbed cosmology, it was *"my migraine"*—a special gem in her collection.)

Janet said, sighing, "I don't understand you, Mother. I never have, and I guess I never will."

How wounded, how stubborn in her innocence Mrs. O'Meara looked at such times!—turning her pale-powdered, softly creased, moon-shaped face up to her daughter, who superficially resembled her.

Turning up her face, widening her eyes, as if, though wounded, perhaps even insulted, she would not rise to such bait: *she* was a lady.

Quietly she said, with the air of one imparting venerable maternal wisdom, "It isn't the very worst thing, always, to not understand another person. One day, dear, you'll see."

* * *

AND WHAT, JANET O'MEARA thought, does *that* mean?

ON SATURDAY MORNING, MRS. O'Meara complained of shortness of breath, queasy stomach, and "my" migraine. So, driving into New Jersey with Janet was out of the question.

So Janet set off alone, in her Volvo. It was true, though she could hardly so much as hint at the fact to her mother, that the two-bedroom apartment was seeming rather cramped, with the two of them there together so much.

Janet enjoyed driving, when she could drive out of the city, on interstate highways that allowed her a modicum of speed, thus the illusion, and comfort, of significant forward motion. In her professional career, as, sad to say, in her personal life, such significance was frequently lacking.

Jocosely, if with an air of wistfulness, Janet O'Meara had lately cultivated the custom of introducing herself as a "bachelor girl": in this way she placed herself bravely and accurately in a demographic category, yet, by dint of her attitude, defined herself against it, in opposition to such categories. For, after all, was she not *herself*? Janet Elizabeth O'Meara, smart, upbeat, industrious, ambitious? At the age, now, of thirty-six, still youthful, and devoted to her career?

("My" career, Janet thought, wryly. A bit like "my" migraine.)

However, she did value her work in television highly, less for what it was at the present time than for what it might be, one day, when she was offered a position commensurate with her ability and intelligence; as a producer of her own program, for instance. A coordinating director of a series of programs.

What dreams, what girlish hopes she still harbored!

Yet, such offers failed to materialize. Janet O'Meara worked, she worked harder than virtually any of her colleagues, and, yet—!

It's the competition, Gina had said, sagely. *A thousand times worse than in life.*

If Janet did receive offers, or those tentative proposals that, if pursued, might lead to offers, they came from sources in outlying regions of the country where she did not much wish to move . . . such cities, unknown to her, as Omaha, St. Louis, Minneapolis, Portland, even Anchorage, Alaska. Where Janet O'Meara knew no one, of course, and where, surely, she would be doubly isolated and lonely; made to feel distinctly *un*married.

As for love, romance, "relations" with men—even before the ugly episode with Lee Roy Sears, Janet had known herself strangely and unfairly deprived.

Lee Roy Sears!—"Janet, please. Not *that.*"

She had spoken aloud, reprovingly.

For why spoil her drive to Mount Orion, the most spectacular leg of which was her crossing, on the wind-buffeted upper level, of the George Washington Bridge?—where at this moment she sped along in her dark blue Volvo, sunglasses shielding her eyes?

HAD SHE LIED, WELL she had *not* lied—in her heart.

Insisting to Michael that she and Lee Roy Sears had not been lovers.

In the technical, most clinical sense of the word.

Yet it was almost true, for Sears had been so quick, so crude, so selfish, so physically threatening in his lovemaking (but you would not call it lovemaking), and Janet O'Meara so terrified, the incident, which had occurred in August in an anonymous motel room in a Quality Inn outside Mount Orion, quickly seemed, in retrospect, not to have happened to *her.*

He had never so much as kissed her. Nor held her hand.

He had said nothing of an affectionate, even a placating nature.

He had pulled and tugged at her clothes and would have ripped them if Janet had not quickly taken them off.

Thinking, her heart pounding against her ribs, *My God: what am I doing?—and why?*

On a sticky-humid August night, near-drunk, or was she in fact drunk, alone in a motel room with a man she knew not at all; a man she'd naively imagined to be shy, boyish, self-conscious, thus easily maneuvered.

A man she'd naively imagined to be not a murderer, but a victim.

Oh yes: Janet O'Meara had imagined Lee Roy Sears to be *sweet.*

Wasn't that the word, the insipid self-deceiving word, Gina had so frequently used in speaking of him?—*sweet?*

Janet had been fascinated by Lee Roy Sears. The man himself, and his background. For no one she knew was like him in the least. She wanted to write an article about him, but fundamentally she wanted to *know* him; as if *knowing* him would allow her possession of a kind.

A wild creature, he'd seemed. Like—what was that German folklegend?—the tragic tale of Kasper Hauser of Nürnberg?—the lost, untamed boy, the orphan without speech, uncivilized, and uncorrupted?

Very likely, this was what had drawn her brother, Michael, to Lee Roy Sears, too. Michael O'Meara and others in The Coalition. Liberals, good and decent people, well-intentioned people, devoting themselves to the salvation of others. Seeing, in others, mirror-images of themselves, in need of salvation.

Janet had said, warmly, "Let me tell the world your story, Lee Roy: trust me!"

And, "No one else can understand you as *I* do: you'll see!"

Shivering, when he'd touched her.

The weakness beginning in the pit of her belly and spreading rapidly to all the parts of her body, leaving her faint, breathless.

He'd removed his shirt, grinning, thrusting his forearm in her face—"Here's Snake Eyes, sweetheart."

The dreamy smile faded from Janet O'Meara's face. She took a step backward.

"What's wrong, sweetheart? Don'tcha like Snake Eyes, sweetheart? Huh?"

Several steps backward. Staring at the thing on this man's forearm, the snake, a living snake, an oily black sheen spangled with gold, and gold-glaring eyes, eyes fixed on *her*—as she backed away, suddenly very frightened.

Lee Roy Sears's voice rose, in mock anger, derision. "What's the matter, sweetheart, don'tcha like him?—think you're too good for him? White bitch, huh? White cunt? *Huh?*"

In nakedness Janet had imagined herself, at first, *in control;* imagining that Lee Roy Sears, poor Lee Roy Sears, would be overwhelmed with her female beauty, her specialness, the gift that was *her.* How smug and superior she'd felt, how thrilled with her own bounty!—without quite realizing it.

Until now.

When it was too late.

Seeing not admiration not awe not love not affection not even a warm and companionable regard in Lee Roy Sears's hard glassy eyes, seeing only mockery there, and contempt.

Thinking, *He's going to hurt me.*

Thinking, *Is this why I am here?—to be hurt?*

"Think you're too good for Snake Eyes?—nah, nobody's too good for Snake Eyes!"

Lee Roy Sears grabbed Janet by the arm as she'd never been grabbed in her life, pushed her down onto the bed, atop the bedspread, thrust his hard knee between her knees as if prying her open as a shell is pried open, its feeble resistance overcome, its spine broken with a snap—and jabbed, and jammed, and sank his erect penis into her, with no more sentiment than if he'd shoved her aside going through a doorway.

"Oh!—*oh!*"

The pain of it, the dry thrusting pain!—she bit her lip to keep from screaming.

His muscular forearm across her throat, with the threat of increasing its pressure.

His quick staccato thrusts, like an animal's, pragmatic, wholly without romance—or what might be called "mind."

His face contorted in orgasm, chunky discolored teeth bared in a grimace terrible to see.

"Oh!—oh!—*oh!*"

Janet O'Meara had not resisted, Janet O'Meara had been mesmerized, as if with the prospect of her own dying.

She had not screamed. Not once. Not wanting to anger her lover. Not wanting to call attention to herself.

His penis, engorged with blood, an instrument of pain!—and the weight of him, his pale sweaty body, knots of muscles, suffocating her!—and what if quite deliberately he *did* strangle her, and left her in this anonymous room, spreadeagled, lifeless, on the stained bedspread! Janet O'Meara's soft fleshy womanly body she'd always wanted to believe was a beautiful body, breasts, belly, hips, thighs—simply left behind, discarded, as one discards a bone from which the flesh has been gnawed.

But it had not happened that way, he'd spared her.

In his indifference, he'd spared her.

Swiftly and efficiently fucking her (you would not call it love-making), and rolling off her, and falling into a drunken-snoring doze; and Janet, terrified of her life, eased off the bed by cautious degrees, threw on her clothes in a corner of the room, and fled.

No WONDER, THEN, SHE had not wanted to confess to her brother, Michael, that, yes, in the strictest most clinical sense of the term Lee Roy Sears had been her lover: that they'd had a "love affair" of a kind.

"I'd die of shame—I couldn't bear it."

So she had lied, but very awkwardly. And he'd known. (Hadn't he?) Regarding her with his quizzical, searching eyes, brown eyes like her own, sensitive to the most subtle modulations of her voice.

For they were sister and brother, after all: Janet O'Meara and Michael O'Meara. Apart from their mother, who did not seem to be, quite, a mother, they were all that remained of their family.

Yet how odd it was, how profoundly disturbing, that Michael had insisted he'd seen her with Lee Roy Sears weeks later, at a time when Janet had assuredly *not* been with Sears.

She had wanted to complete the article on him, that's true. Even after the humiliating episode in the Quality Inn, she'd been determined, if not fanatic. Like a good reporter she'd accumulated many notes, documents, taped interviews with Sears and others who had known him. The article kept shifting its focus, however. At one time it was to have been "Lee Roy Sears: From Death Row to Mount Orion, New Jersey." Later, it was to have been "Lee Roy Sears: From Death Row to SoHo"—when it had looked as if Sears was indeed an artist with a future.

Now, its title would be " 'Snake Eyes': An American Romance."

THE AIRY EXHILARATING PASSAGE over the George Washington Bridge was the high point of Janet O'Meara's drive: the remainder was simply driving, primarily on the Parkway, with a sensation of dread that mounted as she approached her destination.

"Poor Gina!—and poor Michael!"

What condition *was* Gina in, twenty-six days after the assault?—the last time Janet had seen her, in a manner of speaking, in the Mount Orion General Hospital, her head had been swathed in bandages; her mutilated face completely hidden. Even her eyes had been protected from the light by gray-tinted plastic lenses affixed to grotesque wire frames. She had endured a second operation to "repair" some of the damage. (The word *restore*, Janet noticed, seemed not to be used. In subsequent months, depending upon the condition of the scar tissue, and Gina's mental state, there would be further cosmetic surgery—so Michael said.) Gina, sunk in upon herself, had replied in vague monosyllables to her sister-in-law's resolutely upbeat conversation. Afterward Janet had wondered whether Gina had even known, or cared, that she'd come to visit, with a big pot of spring azaleas. She'd felt an intrusive fool.

Michael had been grateful to see her, as he was grateful for the many well-wishers who came to the hospital, to commiserate with him, and to indicate their support of him: for this was the strained interim when he had had to await a decision by the county prosecutor's office whether, outrageously, charges (first- or second-degree manslaughter?) should be brought against him in Lee Roy Sears's death.

Just a formality, such procedure. So Michael O'Meara was assured. But he was worried, and more than worried, telling Janet repeatedly, as she suspected he was telling others, in his calm, reasonable, yet wondering voice, "It was all I could do, defending myself against him. I had no choice. I had to protect my family. I had no choice."

Tears in her eyes, Janet had hugged her brother, hard. "Oh, God, Michael, of course! Everybody knows. You did what you had to do." She'd considered, and rejected, telling him of Snake Eyes.

THE SUSPENSE HAD NOT been prolonged: no charges were brought against Michael O'Meara, on the grounds that he'd acted to save his life; and that Lee Roy Sears had died of "misadventure."

Forensic evidence substantiated Michael's description of what had occurred in Sears's studio that night: there was the rusted ladder rung that had snapped under Sears's weight, and Sears's lacerated hands that indicated how he'd gripped the ladder as he started to fall. Of course, there were Michael O'Meara's injuries: the deep razor slash on his forehead, a swollen eye, cracked ribs, a broken finger.

And the evil razor-instrument, stained with Michael's blood, found on the floor of the studio.

In addition, a police search of the premises turned up, wrapped in a filthy rag and hidden in the toilet tank, Gina's missing wristwatch, her engagement and wedding rings, and her numerous credit cards.

A number of persons acquainted with Lee Roy Sears were questioned by police, including H. Sigman (who spoke quite harshly of his parolee-client, as if the man had personally betrayed him) and Valeria Darrell (who seemed, according to Mount Orion gossip, both "devastated" and "relieved" by her lover's sudden death), and, after brief deliberation, the county prosecutor, who was in fact a member of the Mount Orion Tennis Club and an admiring acquaintance of Gina O'Meara, declined to press charges against Michael.

The black man arrested in the Julia Sutter case had claimed from the start that he'd never so much as entered Julia's house, but had found the stolen household items and credit cards in an alley a few miles away; apart from these items, there was nothing linking him to the murder, and public sentiment, in Mount Orion, was strongly inclined to see Lee Roy Sears as Julia's murderer—for who, after all, had a motive?—a *personal* motive? As for the vicious assault upon Clyde Somerset, from which Clyde was only now recovering—Clyde had not seen his attacker, but insisted it was, it must have been, Lee Roy Sears, too.

In time, the police investigations into these mysteries would be abandoned. For very likely the authorities knew, as all of Mount Orion did: Lee Roy Sears was the man.

Now, as JANET O'MEARA breathlessly climbed out of her car in the O'Mearas' driveway, her brother, Michael, hurried to greet her and to hug her. How happy he was to see her!

How disappointed, to see she was alone.

Janet kissed him, sensing both this disappointment and his resistance to showing it, and said, faltering, "Mother sends her sincere apologies, Michael. It's such a shame! She wanted to come, she was all ready to come, but—she isn't well. She—"

Michael said quickly, "I understand, Janet. It's all right."

Yet Janet persisted, as if a falsehood compounded were less unconscionably false, "She *did* want to come, and she asked me to ask you if you'll telephone her, tomorrow."

"Of course," Michael said. He was smiling at Janet; and, except for the drawn look in his face, and the scar on his forehead, and his hair, which had turned a bristling metallic gray, he was his old affable self, or nearly. He even managed to laugh, a bit sadly. "I'll be happy to call Mother, sure: but not until tomorrow!"

They entered the white colonial house by a door at the rear, talking, bemusedly, of their mother; as a way, perhaps, of not yet talking about Gina. In the kitchen, Janet gave a nervous start at the sight of a woman's figure in the farther doorway: but the woman was the O'Mearas' new au pair, Clara, who, short, plump, dark-haired, resembled Gina not at all.

They then sat together, sister and brother, in the family room (a beautifully decorated brick-and-teak-paneled room with a white metal fireplace and a view, through glass doors, of the woodland pond below the hill), and talked, earnestly, about many things: yet not, somehow, the most crucial things: for which, at least at the moment, Janet was grateful.

The O'Mearas' house was unchanged, in its material surface. But its atmosphere, its intangible being, was wholly changed—somber, tense, undefined, disturbing.

Like a haunted house, Janet thought. If there could be such a thing really.

And it was discomforting, to anticipate Gina hurrying through a doorway to join them, with bright, insincere apologies for being late, while knowing that Gina was *not* going to do so.

After an hour had passed, and Michael and Janet had covered any number of relatively safe conversational topics, Janet asked, hesitantly, "And how is Gina?—does she want to see me?"

Michael said immediately, "She does. She certainly does. She's been telling me, in fact, she misses you." It was an unexpected thing to hear, for Janet and her sister-in-law had never been close; rarely had they confided in each other.

"Is Gina—well? I mean—generally?"

"Oh yes, yes she is. Her face is—mending. The vision in one of her eyes has been affected, and we're doing all we can to save it. She was supposed to begin seeing a psychiatrist this week, but it's hard for her to leave the house, right now. (I drive her, of course, to the doctors. She isn't quite ready to drive a car yet.) We don't want to push things—there's plenty of time." Michael spoke carefully, as if uttering a prepared statement. He tried to smile. "The important thing is, Janet, Gina is *alive.* For that, I'm infinitely grateful."

Janet, who had been sipping a glass of club soda, pressed the cool glass against her forehead, in a gesture of resignation and horror. "Oh, God, Michael! I still can't believe it! Him! Lee Roy! How could he! Such a terrible, terrible thing!"

Michael had a glass too in his hand: club soda as well: which he set down on a table, carefully. Janet saw that his hand was trembling; she regretted speaking out as she had, so impulsively.

"Yes. It was terrible. *Is* terrible. But he's dead, and we're alive, and we're *not* defeated. Gina is scheduled for another skin-graft operation in six weeks, at the Kessler-Macon Clinic, in Chicago. Have you heard of it?"

"I'm not sure," Janet said, seeing that Michael was eager to talk on the subject. "Tell me."

So, speaking animatedly, almost aggressively, Michael told Janet of the extraordinary cosmetic surgery done at the Kessler-Macon Clinic; "miraculous" work done on patients who were hideously disfigured, in vehicular accidents, or fires—"Even more tragic cases than Gina's."

It was a matter of skin grafting, primarily. Removing "devitalized" tissue and replacing it with "living" tissue. There would always be some scarring, of course. That was inevitable, where the face had been so damaged. But, still, they did work wonders; and Gina's psychological state would surely be improved if some of her old appearance could be restored.

Janet knew, without having to be told, still less without having to ask, that Gina O'Meara was suicidal. Sequestered at home, refusing to see most visitors, turned inward upon herself and on a regimen of numerous medications, how could she fail to be otherwise?

Beauty is only skin deep, the old cliché insists.

But, as Wilde has said: *Those who go beneath the surface do so at their peril.*

As her brother spoke of a future, for Gina, of what could only be pain, pain, and yet more pain, Janet thought of the alarming rumors that had spread in Mount Orion and as far away as Manhattan after Gina's near-death. The most obvious was that Gina and Lee Roy Sears had been lovers, and that Sears had calculatedly mutilated her, out of jealousy or spite; to punish her for her involvement with another man. In one version, the other man was Marvin Bruns, a Mount Orion businessman whom Janet recalled having met, in June, at the Dumont Center reception: a strong personality, with a sexually insinuating smile, but, yes, an attractive man. (It was said that Marvin Bruns had taken a room at the Marriott Inn that day, under another name.) In other versions, Gina's lover was Clyde Somerset, or Stan Deardon, or Jack Trimmer; or an attorney named Dwight Schatten, a local resident unknown to Janet, reputed to be a "charismatic, sinister character."

At first, Janet had been incensed that such ugly gossip was being circulated, in the very wake of Gina's hospitalization: for surely it had no basis in reality?

Then, as the rumors were compounded, overlapping and bolstering one another, Janet had had to consider that perhaps there was some truth to some of them . . . but not, she hoped, to the rumor that Gina and Lee Roy Sears had been lovers.

Unthinkable! Lovely Gina O'Meara, Michael's wife, and "Snake Eyes"—!

No, Janet did not want to think of *that*.

As Michael spoke of Gina's prospective surgery, he unconsciously touched his own scar, which was about four inches long, a raw pink wavering horizontal crease just above his eyebrows. Another inch, and Lee Roy Sears would have sliced his eyes.

Janet wondered, but had not the heart to ask, if the scar would be permanent.

For how, eerily, like a snake it looked, in miniature. The realization made her shiver!

Michael excused himself to go see if Gina was prepared for a brief visit; went away upstairs, and came back fairly quickly, to say, apologetically, that she wasn't, quite. "Maybe after lunch, Janet? You *are* going to stay for lunch?"

"I'd love to, yes," Janet said. "Of course."

Her brother had been looking at her anxiously, as if fearing she might want to slip away from this somber household.

Her heart went out to him, in that instant. Janet O'Meara's so-successful older brother, needing, now, *her.*

"H'LO, AUNT JANET."

"H'*lo*, Aunt Janet."

Joel and Kenny spoke in small, subdued voices, encouraged to greet Janet, and even to submit (and how passively they did so!) to her energetic hugs and kisses.

"Aunt Janet has come to visit Mommy and us," Michael said, "—isn't that nice, fellas?"

Joel murmured a near-inaudible assent, and Kenny murmured a near-inaudible assent. Their eyes dropped shyly, or sullenly, away from their aunt's smiling face.

Janet had brought the twins a newly released children's video, which they accepted from her, with mumbled thanks. Their interest was so minimally tactful, so merely perfunctory, as to suggest that the video was too young for them, or already familiar.

The tragedy in their household seemed to have aged them, about the eyes.

Joel and Kenny had apparently been up in their room all morning and came down reluctantly for lunch when Clara called them. It was clear that Aunt Janet's presence was a mixed occasion for them, at best; ordinarily, they would not have had to sit down to anything so formal as a midday meal in the dining room. If they were too well-behaved to show their resentment outwardly, their carefully neutral expressions and their failure to smile at Daddy's and Aunt Janet's remarks signaled their feeling.

Clara, the darkish-skinned dark-browed au pair, who might have been eighteen years old, or twenty-eight, very sweet, shy, abashed, was prevailed upon by Michael O'Meara to sit at the table with the family and was very ill-at-ease.

She jumped up from the table frequently, to bring in more food, or to take away used dishes. The luncheon was oppressively elaborate, rather more like a dinner. When Janet offered to help, Clara said, startled, "Oh, miss, *no.* You are the guest."

Through this, Joel and Kenny sat docilely, neutrally. Had their eyes welled with tears Janet would not have been at all surprised.

Michael was a loving, attentive father; too loving, and too

attentive, perhaps, at close range. He seemed unaware that he was making his sons uncomfortable, by continually asking them questions, trying to draw them into the adults' conversation. How was school?—how was their space-science project progressing?—could they tell Aunt Janet about their new friend, Tikki? The boys replied in monosyllables, ducking their heads toward their plates and eating quickly, eager to escape. Janet was struck by how *identical* they were in both appearance and affect: sitting side by side, never so much as glancing at each other, they nonetheless mimicked each other, in their facial mannerisms, the very slant of their eyes, the way they chewed their food.

They were growing, physically. Their once-delicate faces had filled out. Their eyes looked sunken in their sockets, with a premature befuddlement and sorrow.

For Gina, convalescing in the bedroom upstairs, rarely saw her children, Janet gathered. And never saw any of her Mount Orion friends.

What terms the elder O'Mearas were on, precisely, Janet of course did not know. On the telephone, Michael was always optimistic, upbeat. Gina was "progressing." Gina was "doing just fine."

Of course, it was very early, still. The maniac had assaulted her less than a month ago.

And now the maniac was dead, removed utterly from the world—*that* might be some solace.

"Daddy, c'n I be excused?" and, "Daddy, c'n I be excused?"

It was a palpable relief when the twins left the table, with scarcely more than a mumbled "G'bye!" for Aunt Janet. They ran away to another part of the house with the happy abandon of young animals released from captivity; Janet saw one nudge the other gleefully in the ribs as they rounded a corner. Their footsteps were percussive on the stairs.

They'd left Aunt Janet's video gift on a table in the hall, forgotten.

Michael, drawing his fingertips unconsciously across the scar on his forehead, said, "It's been very hard on them, of course. Gina was always such a devoted mother, so much a part of their lives, and now it's as if she were"—he paused, sobered by his own words—"gone. But only temporarily gone, as I've tried to make them see."

Janet said, bravely, "Michael, I think they're bearing up very well. And so are you."

"HONEY?—JANET IS GOING to have to leave soon. She'd just like to say hello."
Silence.
"Gina? Are you awake?"
Silence.
Upstairs, at the door of Gina's bedroom, Michael stood leaning in the doorway, speaking softly. Behind him, Janet did not try to peer in; but could see shadowy contours, indistinct shapes, the filmy outline of curtains over a window with its venetian blind drawn tight. Apparently Gina was in bed, or propped up in bed, unmoving. There came to Janet's nostrils a sad stale scent of something medicinal overlaid by a resolutely cheerful lavender air freshener.

How sad, Gina O'Meara, so lately beautiful, vivacious, social, hidden away in this darkened room!

If Janet had even felt a womanly prick of jealousy, or dislike, for her brother's wife, she regretted it now. And did she really want to see Gina's scarred face?

She whispered, embarrassed, "I'll come another time, Michael. Let's not disturb her."

"But Gina *does* want to see you, I know."

"Oh, but—"

There was a stirring in the darkened room, a low, throaty voice murmuring something inaudible. Michael said, eagerly, "Yes?" and hurried inside, to Gina in her bed; the two spoke together, in an undertone, and Michael came away again and shut the door. Michael seemed very moved. He said, "Gina says she just isn't up to talking with anyone, today. She had a bad night last night. And the main thing, Janet"—Michael was now steering her back to the stairs, his hand on her elbow, warm, solicitous, emphatic—"Gina says not to pity her. 'Tell Janet not to pity me,' she said. 'That's the one thing I can't bear.' "

Janet said, faltering, "Oh—of course. I know. I mean I don't— pity her. I—simply feel very sorry for her." Janet surprised herself by starting to cry. Michael quickly slid an arm around her shoulders. "I feel so sorry for you all."

Michael said, "But, really, *why*, Janet?—when you think of it, every one of us—Gina, Joel, Kenny, yes even you—and me—we're damned lucky to be alive."

Janet shuddered. She had not quite been thinking of it that way.

IT WAS TIME FOR Janet to leave, and Michael walked her to her car. Now the difficult visit was over, Janet felt both relief and regret. In full daylight, Michael did look older; his genial, earnest face was thinner than Janet had seen it, since boyhood. And how quickly his red-brown hair had faded, to that harsh metallic gray.

Still, he was smiling. Saying, philosophically, "Well!—it's lucky Mother didn't make the trip out here, after all. Gina wouldn't have felt strong enough to see *her*, certainly." Janet, who had been think-ing the same thing, at the same moment, said, "Maybe next week . . ." Her voice trailed off unconvincingly. Michael laughed.

It was a sun-splotched windy day, still winter, yet with a faint taste of spring. How immature the elder Mrs. O'Meara seemed to her children, with her hypochondriacal obsessions!

At Janet's car, they paused, suddenly shy with each other; as if there were more to say, unsaid. (Janet had forestalled asking Michael about his situation at Pearce, Inc.: she dreaded hearing he might lose his job. But now was not the time to ask.) Michael squeezed her hand and said, frowning, in his earlier, more somber tone, "I had no choice about it, Janet. I had to—confront the man. To put an end to it. I—"

Janet threw her arms around her brother, saying, passionately, as if the point had been contested, "You did what you had to do, Michael, and everyone knows it. You're a *hero.*"

THAT SHARP CLOYING-SWEET SMELL, what was it?—*cognac?*

And why, mixed up with her sleep, her wayward dreams, some-thing so unexpected as—*cognac?*

Janet was asleep. Yet not quite. Recalling how, some time ago, it seemed now like a very long time ago, she had had a romance of a kind with a Lebanese gentleman; a handsome, courtly, cultivated man in his forties attached to the Lebanese delegation to the United Nations. The romance, a typically New York sort of romance, had come to nothing, as Janet had anticipated; the man was married, *must* have been married; and, in any case, would not have married her. He had taken her to astoundingly expensive restaurants, however, and he'd bought her curious gifts, though they had never been lovers, nor even friends. One of the gifts he'd given her— surprisingly, since he, a Moslem, did not drink—was a bottle of Courvoisier "Very Special" cognac. Years later, the bottle was still quite full.

Waking from a dream in which a face floated near, a net of scars through which blind, vacant eyes stared, Janet found herself smelling cognac. How was it possible?

She switched on a bedside lamp: the time was only 2:30. She'd thought it much later.

She'd hoped it was much later, her sleep had been so restless.

Drawn by the faint cognac smell, she went out into the hall, barefoot, in her flannel nightgown: seeing, to her amazement, her mother sitting in the living room, a single lamp burning. Mrs. O'Meara held a glass in her hand; the shapely green bottle of Courvoisier was on the table beside her.

"Mother, what on earth—?"

Mrs. O'Meara turned her bland moon face toward Janet, unsurprised. She had rubbed a whitish cream into her soft, flaccid skin, and her eyebrows, unpenciled, seemed to have disappeared. But her mood was agreeable. "It's just as well, dear," she said. "I have something to tell you."

". . . IT WAS AN ACCIDENT. An accident. It *was* an accident, in two feet of water. I always believed that, and your father always believed that. To his dying day. We simply didn't wish to speak of it, that's all.

"There are some things you don't talk about, no one wants to hear. It happened on August ninth, nineteen fifty-three. A long time ago. The sand flies were biting. The sun was so very *hot*. I've never gone on any beach since then, that's my prerogative. And we moved away, to Darien, within the year, and *never* looked back. I had friends there, in Manchester, young mothers like me, they were heartbroken for me (they said!) but I broke off all contact with them. It's what you must do. It's like cauterizing a wound. Make a decision and stick with it. You see, little Sean drowned; and little Michael did not drown. That was a fact. That *is* a fact. Sean is buried in Manchester, New Hampshire, but we moved away. I don't believe in the immortality of the spirit so he would not know. Michael does not know—he has forgotten. We encouraged forgetfulness, it's what you must do. They were two and a half years old and *so* close. One of my memories is of them sleeping in their crib, that intense sleep of infants so you think almost they will never wake again. One would quiver and twitch in his sleep, and the other would quiver and twitch, and their skin was clammy, but hot; like something white-hot; and strange to touch. (*You* were so different, when you came along: a happy child! And only one of *you*.) Never had there been twins in my family, but we discovered afterward there were twins, identical and fraternal both, in your father's family, through the generations—oh yes! Not that I blamed your father, of course I did not. There could be no warning. In those days you were not prepared. No X rays, I mean. 'Am-ni-o-cen-te-sis': is that how it's pronounced? And no abortions either. In those days, no. Certainly not. It's a different world now for women, isn't it? Oh, but, as I say, *why* look back. It was an accident, they were two and a half years old, why dwell upon the past, and sorrow. My eyes could not see what I was looking at because of the sun, I was blinded. The lifeguard too had not seen. And if we'd seen, would that have brought the poor baby back to life?—it would *not*. The other was playing, splashing. Oh, that yellow plastic seahorse! If only that had been *twins!* But, well, in my circle of friends now, widows like myself, do you suppose there is a single one of us without sorrow? hurt? heartbreak? tragedy?—in Florida, I mean. In Palm View Villas. At our age. And I'm not old. In our bridge set, they treat me like a baby sometimes—so scatterbrained at cards. Well, you know. We all have our weaknesses. I dwell upon happy memories, for there *are* many. You, on television, don't you suppose I'm proud of *you*. And Michael, and his lovely family. It *was* Michael, we believed. Of course it might have been . . . Sean. The survivor. Oh, poor Sean: in two feet of water, only imagine! The children's swimming area was roped off. There were others there, or I'd thought so. And, of course, the lifeguard. I was up the beach, I hadn't gone far. I looked, and my eyes saw, but didn't see. They hadn't any names really—when they are born, when they shove out of you, all bloody and gasping, they have no names: even, when you name them, later, it doesn't change them. That was what I think I was seeing in the water amid the splashing. The lifeguard saw too at the very same moment. I was screaming, and he blew his whistle, so loud. The one baby was floating facedown in the water (such shallow water!) and the other was close by him and there was the yellow plastic seahorse big as they were, they'd been pulling at it, fighting over it . . . no, not really *fighting:* playing with it. I looked, and I screamed.

"My feet were burning on the sand. I could feel the sun beating down like fire on my skull. That was why I'd gone up the beach. I screamed, but it was too late. He just kept playing there by his twin, with the seahorse. The lifeguard ran over to them, but it was too late. Everyone stared. There was one of those helicopters overhead with an advertising streamer behind and I swear the pilot was staring too! We ran over, and pulled the child out, and the lifeguard started mouth-to-mouth resuscitation, but it was too late. I was running on the fiery sand, but it was too late. I'd thought I was so pretty in my two-piece bathing suit, oh my!—twenty-eight years old and a nice, shapely figure and curly hair like yours, I thought I was someone special, the way you do at that age. Later, you learn. Quickly, you learn. Oh in my dreams even now it happens so differently: I would see clearly, in spite of the sun, and I would run to the water, and I would pull him out of the water, two feet of water, such shallow water, and so *warm.* You can drown in six inches of water. The most tragic accidents happen right in the home. In broad daylight. You can't know. You can't be prepared. You *must* be prepared. If only we'd bought a second seahorse. If I hadn't left my straw sandals at the cabana. Then maybe . . . oh God, maybe. I don't know, and it's better not to know. We never talked about it. Your father and I. He had his business, and it was a good business, but it took up his time. It ate up his life. The way the tanners strip those poor beautiful wild creatures of their furs and hides, to make them into coats, that's the way your father was stripped of his life . . . like his soul was on the outside of his body and unprotected. But what am I saying? Am I drunk?—well, shouldn't I be? We never talked about it, afterward. It was a good move, from New Hampshire to Connecticut. It turned out so. I gave up my friends, but what are friends?—friends pass away. You can't depend on them, and they shouldn't depend on you. We never talked about it out of consideration for the one who survived. Michael, that was. The other was Sean. In those few minutes, in two feet of water, and gone forever. It doesn't seem possible, does it? It's like missing a plane I suppose. A matter of minutes. Maybe of seconds. Like when they extract blood from your arm and can't find a vein, and when they finally find a vein, and it's twenty seconds, the nurse says: twenty seconds: a long time. You don't think so, but it is. I was twenty-six when they were born, and twenty-eight when they died.

"I mean, when Sean died. Michael survived. Michael did not come close to drowning. He was a good swimmer afterward, a good athlete, on the football team. It scared us to watch him, running on the field. Your father never said so, and I never said so, but I knew. That look in his face. In his jaws. You see it in their jaws. A high school boy, and so sweet, except on the football field, then you could see. Then you knew. Oh, what *am* I saying? (Am I drunk?) (I am *not* drunk!) We are all strangers, in time. To ourselves I mean. I don't remember that woman who was twenty-eight years old and she would never have guessed me: so old! So changed! But I am not old really, am I old?—sixty-seven? Is that old? My face, my hands. They give you away if you're careless. If you're not clever. *He* is very clever, your brother. Which is why he is a lawyer. Forty-one years old, and his poor brother is only two. The dead are always dead. The dead never age. They are all they can be while we, who are living, are never all we can be. Isn't that strange? Why is that? Of course, *he* has forgotten. Maybe he never knew. It must have happened quickly. Or, without much struggle. In six inches of water it can happen. The depth of the water doesn't matter. Only the intent. Years later there was another accident, in junior high school, in the swimming pool, but the other boy did not drown. He and Michael bumped heads, I think. It was serious, but not fatal. Michael himself may have helped pull the boy out. No one was to blame really. They both swallowed water—ugh, that nasty chlorine water! (Did you know, boys swim naked together in school pools, at that age? Girls wouldn't swim naked at any age, would they?—*I* would not.) The gym coach punished him by dropping him from the team. That was unfair, but we didn't protest. He went out for football in high school, and he made the team. He grew fast, put on weight. He was very strong. He's stronger than he seems. You can see it in

his jaws, and sometimes in his eyes. Not always, but sometimes. If
you know the signs. *You* don't, of course. And neither did Gina.

"It seemed to have begun at about the age of eighteen months.
Something I couldn't name then, and I can't name now. Where they
had been peaceful together sleeping, eating, taking their bottles, playing and laughing together, now there was something else. You might
say 'hate' but it was not 'hate.' You might say 'evil' but it was *not*
'evil.' Just one twin seeking dominance over the other, and that
other resisting. Sometimes it was Sean (we thought it was Sean!)
who was dominant, and sometimes it was Michael (we thought it
was Michael!)—but they were identical, they were mirror-twins, and
most of the time we could not tell. Of course, I pretended to know,
I was their mother, I loved them both, how very queer it would
have seemed to everyone if I hadn't known one child from the other!
They say that men fight one another simply because one thinks he
can win. Nations go to war because one thinks it can win. There is
no other reason. Oh, yes, there are *reasons*, but only this single
reason. We needn't ever speak of it, dear, after tonight. The yellow
plastic seahorse might not have mattered. August ninth, nineteen
fifty-three, might not have mattered. For there would have been
another day. (Your father believed so. We never spoke of it, but he
spoke of that, just once, to me. And then, never again!) When the
one who had not drowned saw his brother's body on the sand, and
the lifeguard giving him mouth-to-mouth resuscitation, when he saw
me, my hysteria, he seemed to forget who he was too. Of course,
he was so young. At that age, they don't understand about death—
its finality. They can die, and they can cause another to die, but
they don't understand about death. It might have been Sean who
died, and it might have been Sean who was taken away. I was
screaming—hysterical. Why did anyone take my word? I screamed,
'Sean! Sean!' So it *was* Sean, on the death certificate. So the other
was Michael. What difference would it have made?—they had the
same face, they were the same child, both pushed out of my body
and I loved them both. I was screaming, and had to be sedated."

IT WAS THREE O'CLOCK in the morning, and then four o'clock. As
Mrs. O'Meara spoke to Janet in her even, unemphatic voice, like a
boat bobbing in placid, sheltered waters. As Janet listened, numb

with horror. Hearing what she could not believe. Unable to believe what she heard.

For a very long time, Janet O'Meara listened and did not interrupt. She had never heard her mother speak in such a way, nor even at such length.

Her icy toes curled beneath her, on the sofa. Her long flannel nightgown fanning about her. As, outside the window, the city at night resembled vertical hives of winking lights, a chill stellar beauty. As, from time to time, she heard her mother draw in her breath sharply as if to forestall a sob, or a hiccup. And there was the occasional touch of the green cognac bottle against Mrs. O'Meara's glass.

Janet had fetched herself a glass too and was drinking. By slow degrees. Thinking, If we both get drunk, maybe we'll forget.

Finally, Mrs. O'Meara seemed to have stopped. Her last words trailed off into a silence that melded with the night beyond the window. She'd rummaged about in the pocket of her quilted bathrobe for a handkerchief and was vigorously blowing her nose.

Janet said, louder than she intended, "Let me see if I understand this, Mother. My brother Michael had a twin—*was* a twin—and has forgotten? You really think he has forgotten?"

Mrs. O'Meara said, naively, "Why would he remember?"

"And his twin, Sean, drowned?—in a swimming accident?—at a lake in New Hampshire?—in nineteen fifty-three?"

"It *was* an accident." Mrs. O'Meara nodded grimly.

"And you don't really know—I mean *really* know—if my brother is Michael, or the other?"

" 'Michael' and 'Sean' were just names, dear. We give our children names to domesticate them, like pets. Sometimes it has that effect, and sometimes it does not. Shall we share this last ounce of cognac?"

"Wait," Janet said. She spoke carefully, with the air of one gripping a ledge with weakening fingers. "They were identical twins—absolutely *identical?*"

"I identified Sean as the boy who drowned. The name simply leapt from my lips, and everyone assumed, as of course they would assume, that a mother knows her own child. Even a hysterical mother knows her own child." Mrs. O'Meara took up the cognac bottle and poured a small portion into her glass and an equal portion into

Janet's glass: Janet was holding the glass out to her, with slightly
trembling fingers. "And so, the boy who did not drown has always
been 'Michael.'

"And no one doubted?—*he* did not doubt?"

"He was two years old. When his twin drowned, half of himself
drowned. You could argue that both 'Sean' and 'Michael' drowned that
day, in two feet of water. The one who survived was someone else."
Mrs. O'Meara spoke slowly, reasonably. She was resting the nape of
her neck against the back of the sofa; the flesh beneath her chin was
revealed as soft and raddled, and the sockets of her eyes were lost in
shadow, as if in calculating thought. "When your father arrived, I
screamed at him that Sean had drowned. How could I have said, 'One
of our sons has drowned!'—as if I hadn't known?"

There was a brief silence. Thirty storeys below, on Second
Avenue, a siren wailed, followed closely by another. Janet realized
she'd been hearing sirens much of the night, in the near-distance,
and in the distance. For this was New York City after all.

Quickly, she drank down the last of her cognac. There!—the
fiery liquid spread up into her sinuses, through her lungs, her very
bloodstream.

She stared not at, but toward, the window. Her gaze was as
sightless as if she were blind.

The thought that glimmered on the threshold of consciousness—*No. It's unthinkable.*

Janet laughed, lightly at first. Then, she was on her feet. She
could bear this no longer!

"Why are you telling me these hideous things, Mother?—why
now? Are you trying to be rid of them, yourself?" she asked. Her
voice rose sharply. Her hair seemed to be lifting from her head,
crackling with static electricity, appalled. *"What do you expect me to
do about it?"*

NEXT MORNING, JANET O'MEARA systematically destroyed it all:
every one of her notes, drafts, documents, taped and transcribed
interviews for " 'Snake Eyes': An American Romance."

EPILOGUE

AND THIS, THE FIRST morning of the first day.

So many mornings over the past several months, he has felt so!
And why, he can't say. Why, he can't know. *But he knows.*

"MICHAEL?—ARE YOU THERE?"—the question is faint, plaintive,
barely audible.

He is down below, on the beach, whistling, briskly raking leaves
and other debris from the previous night's thunderstorm, when,
glancing up, shading his eyes against the sun, he sees her, unexpectedly, on the threshold of the doorway: a thin, wavering figure, in
layers of clothing, a pale gauzy scarf knotted about her head, oversized dark glasses disguising much of her face. She wears loose-fitting
summer clothes, white trousers, a shirt, a bulky sweater in pale pink,
one of those currently stylish sweaters so deliberately big the shoulders slump halfway down to the wearer's elbows, and the sleeves
must be rolled up conspicuously at the wrists. Something of the old

Gina remains, in such touches: but then of course all her clothes had been bought before the slashing.

Her thin fingers grope about the doorway, grip the doorknob of the screen door as she steadies herself there, peering toward him. He is only about thirty feet away, can't she see him?

It is early August. In the Poconos. Where, at Swarts Lake, one of the smaller, more isolated, more private of the mountain lakes, Michael O'Meara has rented a spacious A-frame cottage for his family, for the month. He can't be there all the time, since he has a new, and challenging, job with a law firm in Newark, but he is there much of the time, and always on weekends. The Swarts Lake rental is not exactly a secret, but neither has Michael advertised it much, in conversations with Mount Orion friends. So far as most of them know, the O'Mearas are on Cape Cod, where, until this summer, they've always gone.

For it isn't just Gina who must heal, and convalesce: it is the entire family.

And how restful, how peaceful, how *convalescent* here at Swarts Lake amid tall stands of pines, sharply etched clumps of white birch, a welter of deciduous trees!—simply to breathe in the mountain air, to feel it fill, and expand, one's lungs, is deeply satisfying. Scattered about the angular lake are perhaps a dozen handsome, custom-built cottages—*cottages* is perhaps too modest a word, but it *is* the word of choice—like the O'Mearas', but they are discreetly hidden from one another by foliage, and by the steep hills and wedgelike rocky crevices of the terrain. There is boating on the lake, but, by implicit common consent, no intrusively loud outboard-motoring; and no boating at all after dark. Joel and Kenny were lonely at first, and resentful of being sequestered in so remote a place, but, these past few days, have become more adventurous about exploring the lake, and are gone for long hours at a time. If any of the O'Mearas' neighbors on the lake are aware of their identity, Michael has detected no sign, no hint. When he drives in to the village of Swarts Lake for provisions, he's careful to keep conversations at a minimum. Indeed, Michael judiciously arranged for the cottage rental by way of his father-in-law, so that the name "O'Meara" might not be officially associated with it.

Her voice lifting in concern, not quite in fear, Gina calls again, "Michael?—where are you?"

Michael replies quickly, "Right here, Gina. On the beach."

Gina turns, startled and blinking, in the direction of his voice, and now she sees him, or gives that impression. She may be attempting a smile—Michael isn't sure. This is a delicate moment, for it is the first time in the nine days she has been at Swarts Lake that Gina has ventured out onto the redwood deck before dusk.

"Is anyone else there, Michael?"

"No, darling. I'm alone. Raking."

"Are you sure?"

Michael glances about, as if to confirm the fact. Of course, he is alone: the twins seem disinclined to spend much time with Daddy and have gone off exploring on their own.

"Reasonably sure," Michael says, cheerfully.

"But—along the lakeshore? Can you be certain?"

Michael resists the impulse to answer too abruptly, thus to make light of Gina's dread. He squints out at the lake, where, perhaps a quarter of a mile away, someone is sailboating. On a farther stretch of the shore, where rock gives way to pebbly sand, thus to an appealingly rough, undomesticated beach, there are sunbathers, swimmers.

Gina continues, nervously, "If there's anyone there, they could look through binoculars, couldn't they, and see me? The deck is so exposed." The deck is not much exposed, but shaded by evergreens on either side. Still Gina lingers in the doorway, fussing with her scarf, her dark glasses, her shapeless pink sweater drooping to mid-thigh.

Michael's heart leaps at the prospect of Gina actually venturing outside, by daylight; sitting on one of the deck chairs, or lying on the canvas lounge chair, as he'd hoped she would. He says, "There's no one in sight, darling, there's no one watching, I *promise.*" Like a flamboyant young suitor he lets the rake fall, bounds up the steps to the deck, takes Gina's thin hands in his, before she can shrink back inside, and urges her out into the sunshine.

"Come, sit down. I'll bring us something to drink," he says.

He'd bounded up the steps so effortlessly, he seemed to have forgotten his stiff knee.

Gina doesn't withdraw her hands from his immediately, though, since that terrible evening in March, she often shies away from being touched, even, so gently, by her husband. (Her physicians' examinations are nightmares for her—she has to take a tranquilizer before submitting.) She frowns doubtfully, squinting toward the lake. Is the elegant white sailboat with its billowing sails defined for her, or is it a mere blur?—is the farther shore, vibrantly defined to Michael's eye, entirely lost to her? The vision in her left eye has so severely deteriorated, she is legally blind in that eye; the vision in the right eye is marginally stronger, but unreliable. Behind the thick lenses of her glasses, which weigh cruelly on the delicate bridge of her nose, and give her a bizarre insectlike look, Gina's eyes are hidden from Michael's close scrutiny.

Gina says, "But, if anyone knows we're out here—"

Michael says, "But who would know, darling? Really!"

"—they could even take photographs, couldn't they?—with a telescopic lens?"

"But *why*, Gina, would they? We're not that important."

"People are cruel," Gina says vaguely. Now she does withdraw her hands from Michael's, politely. As if she has only now thought of them, she asks, concerned, "Where are Joel and Kenny?"

"Out in the woods, or down by the lake, playing."

"By themselves?"

"They may have found some other kids to play with, but I don't think so. The last I saw of them, they were going 'exploring.' "

"Not swimming?"

"The shore's too rocky at this end."

"Are you sure?"

"Am I sure—?"

"That they're not here."

"Do you want me to call them?"

"No, they don't want to see me, outside like this. They don't want me to be *seen*, I terrify them."

"Gina, that isn't so," Michael says adamantly. "Joel and Kenny are not 'terrified' of you. They love you, and naturally—"

Gina nods slowly, distractedly. She isn't really listening: she is more concerned with the possibility of strangers spying on her from the direction of the lake, which is so open, and flooded with light.

"They just want you to be well, Gina. And happy. As I do."

Gina allows herself to be urged gently down, to sit in one of the gaily striped red-and-white canvas chairs. Since the assault, she moves her body with excessive care, as if needing to calculate each minute shifting of position and balance; as if her limbs, and not just her face and head, had been injured. Her surgeon at the Kessler-Macon Clinic told Michael that such caution was normal in cases of severe psychophysiological trauma, where the victim's position-sense, or proprioception, had been threatened.

The surgeon went on to say that each individual views the world through the perspective of his or her own physical self, and where that physical self had been injured, the perspective was natu-rally altered. Michael asked, dreading the answer, if Gina's "per-spective" would ever revert to normalcy, or near-normalcy, and was told, yes, perhaps, there was the distinct possibility, with time.

And assuming no further trauma.

Gina sits; stiffly, and anxiously; arms folded tight beneath her breasts, as if she's cold; her disfigured face lifted bravely to the sun. Michael squeezes her shoulders as one might squeeze a child, sig-naling pleasure and approval. "I'll get us some fruit juice, all right? Stay here!"

He hurries inside, into the kitchen. How ravenous he is, with thirst!—he'd been raking debris on the beach for an hour, quite enjoying the physical exertion, the satisfaction of sweating in a useful cause.

Always at Swarts Lake he wakes early, and rises early, at dawn.

His sleep here, and back home in Mount Orion, is less dis-turbed than one might expect: the old guilt nightmares are gone, perhaps forever.

Now that his enemy is dead, and he knows himself morally blameless, out of what reasonable source might guilt spring?

His tragic involvement with Lee Roy Sears belongs to the past. Why then should he not be a reasonable man for the remainder of his life?

Whistling under his breath, in the kitchen. *Must* be happy.

He pours himself and Gina tall cold glasses of grapefruit juice and brings them back outside.

(Now that Gina is on more or less continuous medication, she

isn't allowed to drink alcohol, nor, out of sympathy with her, does
Michael. And he has stopped taking drugs of any kind, except,
sometimes, aspirin—all *that* is safely behind him.)

When he returns to the deck he sees, to his disappointment,
that Gina has shifted her chair so that her back is to Swarts Lake.

Michael pretends he hasn't noticed. It isn't for him to pass
judgment. "Here you are, honey," he says, smiling, handing her her
glass. But not watching her lift it to her lips—she's self-conscious,
about being watched.

THINKING, IT *IS* A considerable accomplishment. For Gina to have
ventured outdoors at all, in her condition, exposed to pitiless daylight.

SINCE MARCH, THERE HAVE been numerous changes in Michael
O'Meara's life. Some of them easily measurable, others not.

He has had a new job, for instance, since mid-May. With a
private law firm in Newark, specializing in civil cases.

No more defending Pearce, Inc., against grieving plaintiffs. No
more "wonder" drugs for him.

He'd turned the massive Peverol documents over to his succes-
sor, with heartfelt good wishes.

(Had Pearce, Inc., eased Michael O'Meara out, embarrassed
by local publicity, or had Michael O'Meara simply eased himself
out, with enormous relief?—even Michael's long-standing Mount
Orion friends didn't really know.)

Another recent development (if it *is* a development of the Sears
episode, and not something wholly unrelated) is the unexpected behavior of Michael's sister, Janet, with whom he believed himself
close; and of whom he was very fond. For, abruptly, with no warning
at all, Janet telephoned Michael one day in April to tell him, somewhat evasively, that she was accepting a position in Portland, Ore-
gon, as program director of a public television station; and would be
moving away so quickly, she wouldn't be able to say goodbye to him
and his family in person!

And Mrs. O'Meara, true to form, had abruptly returned to
Palm Beach, without having come out to Mount Orion to see the
O'Mearas at all.

Michael tried not to show his surprise at such peculiar, yes such rude, and cruel, behavior. His own sister!—his only sibling! Hadn't they felt genuine affection for each other, not just as sister and brother, but as friends? Michael had certainly thought so, the last time Janet had come to visit. What had she said to him, in the drive: "You did what you had to do . . . You're a *hero.*"

Gina, who referred all things to herself, was less surprised. Saying, with a resigned sort of bitterness, "Your sister and your mother never liked me, *before.*" She paused. "Now, they're frightened of having to see me, and having to say I look 'good.'"

Adding, sadly, "In their places, I would probably behave the same way."

Michael, with his lawyerly sagacity, wasn't so sure that this was the explanation. Or the entire explanation. He seemed to know, and to be baffled by the knowledge, that Janet was frightened of *him.*

"Well. So be it."

His only sister. His only sibling.

MICHAEL RECALLED THAT, IN medieval England, a jury could bring in not one of only two verdicts, but one of four: in addition to *guilty* and *not guilty* there were *ignoramus* ("we do not know") and *ignorabimus* ("we shall not know")

The latter two verdicts, especially the last, seemed to him supreme, in this matter of living with other, so very inscrutable, human beings.

AND THERE WAS JOEL, and there was Kenny.

Whom Michael O'Meara persisted in *not* calling "the twins."

(Though everyone else did, of course. It was maddening!—"the twins," or, at the very least, "the boys." Why did this so infuriate Daddy?)

Only eight years old now, Joel and Kenny were husky, energetic, restless boys, who looked older than their age—they might have been ten, even eleven! In a single year they'd grown considerably; wearing out shoes, clothes, toys, at a rate to astonish and amaze. As the O'Mearas' pediatrician said wryly, They were *healthy.* Michael was mystified rather than alarmed. It disappointed him that their pale blond hair, so like Gina's, was steadily darkening, by iden-

tical degrees; soon, it would be dark as his own had been, before it
had grayed. Their eyes, formerly a beautiful blue-green, of the exact
hue of Gina's, seemed to have darkened too, to a very ordinary
brown. How was this possible, and so rapidly?—within a year, or
eighteen months?

Michael knew that Joel and Kenny had been profoundly affected by the hateful presence of Lee Roy Sears in the O'Mearas'
lives: but how, in fact, *had* they been affected? Since his death, they
had never spoken a word of him; before his death, during those
terrible weeks when the O'Meara household had been under siege,
they had not spoken of him to their father directly, nor to their
mother, but Michael had overheard them (he was certain he'd overheard them) whispering and giggling together about "Mr. Sears."

No doubt, Sears *had* enticed them into leaving the school
grounds with him and going to a nearby park: Joel had denied it
vehemently, and Kenny had denied it vehemently, but Daddy suspected otherwise.

Yet he knew better than to interrogate them, frighten them.

Daddy was *not* one of those hysterical-paranoid parents, of
whom one hears so much recently, who suspect "child abuse" on
the slightest provocation, and terrify their children.

So, he'd let it go. But he knew what he believed.

He knew what he *knew*.

True, Joel and Kenny had been terrified of the bloody dog
carcass dragged onto the iced-over pond. They'd even dreamt of it
afterward, or of something mangled and bloody—nightmares from
which Daddy had to wake them, to give comfort. Yet, inexplicably,
maddeningly, they'd also transposed the ugly incident into one of
their "codes," to be spoken of in secret, to be thrilled by, reduced
to spasms of giggles.

And the harsh sibilant whisper, never quite audible, which
Daddy could nonetheless hear: *Mr. Sears. Mr. Sears. Mr. Sears.*

Michael had discovered, in the boys' room, hidden away at the
back of a closet, their comic-book epic, which they'd been drawing,
and giggling over, for years. He had leafed quickly through the loose
sheets of paper, some of it construction paper, most merely tablet
paper, to get to the more recent pages: these, covered in crudely yet
cleverly drawn figures, human, animal, human-animal, involved in

various action-antics, of a kind common to television and children's movies. There were children (Joel, Kenny?) who towered over adults (Daddy? Mommy?); there was a mysterious black-haired man (Lee Roy Sears?) who had a snake wrapped about his arm, and sometimes around his neck, and sometimes even protruding from his mouth, who caused destruction of a cheery comic book nature.

The drawings both impressed and worried Michael, for he believed that they did show talent; at the same time, there was something malicious and cruel about them, granting even, as one must, the instinctive need of the child to unleash his imagination, free of adult restraints and inhibitions.

Of course, it *was* fantasy, wholly. And Daddy had no business intruding.

More worrisome, because more public, were complaints by teachers of Joel's and Kenny's behavior at the Riverside School: they were "hyperactive," they were "bullying, threatening, physically rough" with other, smaller children, they were "unsocial."

Not all the time, of course, but some of the time.

Their grades, including grades for deportment, had steadily declined.

With this, Michael O'Meara would concern himself in September, if the problem persisted into third grade.

Gina, convalescing, could not be told of such family problems, for they would only upset her, and to what purpose?—there were days when the poor woman had but the vaguest consciousness of the fact that she was a mother, at all.

And when she did, it was with a wincing, shrinking gesture, her fingers over her face. "Oh!—don't let them look at me, oh please!"

For it was true, though Michael would not acknowledge it, that Joel and Kenny, though they loved their mother very much, and missed her household presence enormously, were frightened of her, and did not want to see her; just as, for the time being at least, she did not want to see them.

Of course, this would change, in time. Gina was scheduled for further surgery, in the fall. And that would make a difference.

Shortly before he'd brought his family to Swarts Lake, Michael had happened to poke his head in Joel's and Kenny's room, to discover that Joel was lost in childish concentration drawing something, in ballpoint ink, on Kenny's left forearm; even as Kenny was lost in childish concentration drawing something, in ballpoint ink, on Joel's left forearm. So rapt were the boys, so engrossed in their artwork, in blue, green, black, and fluorescent-red ink, they were unaware of Daddy's presence until he stood above them, and spoke, louder than he meant to speak.

"My God!—*what* are you doing?"

Wide-eyed, scared, guilty, they gaped up at him, each dropping his pen, cringing as if fearful of being struck.

"I said, *what* are you doing? Giving each other tattoos?"

Michael seized the boys' arms and examined them: the drawings were childish in conception, but fastidiously executed: on each boy's forearm was a snake, of numerous cross-hatchings in blue, green, and black, coiled, about four inches long, with red eyes and a red forked tongue. Already some of the ink had begun to smear, and the "tattoos" looked unintentionally comical, silly.

Michael managed to keep parental disapprobation out of his voice, nor did he smile at his sons' art.

"Is this something you've seen on TV?—on a video?"

Joel nodded and mumbled, "Yes, Daddy," as Kenny, at the same moment, nodded and mumbled, "No, Daddy." Then Joel shook his head vehemently, and said, "N-No, Daddy," and Kenny, at the same instant, nodded his head vehemently and said, "Y-Yes, Daddy!"

Now Michael O'Meara *did* laugh. Ruffling the hair on both his sons' heads, saying, "Okay, guys: *wash it all off.*"

AND THIS: THE FIRST morning of the first day.

At Swarts Lake, this place of convalescence and peace, the first day Gina O'Meara has ventured out onto the redwood deck of the handsome A-frame cottage her husband has rented for the family for the month of August; the first time since the assault, apart from isolated moments in their home, she has seemed to trust him.

Whispering, "You're sure no one is watching us?"

Michael squeezes her hand. "Gina, I'm sure."

"And the boys—?"

"They've wandered off."

Gina loosens the scarf, timidly. Shaved for surgical purposes, her hair has grown back thinly and unevenly, and more silver than blond; her hairline has receded, exposing her forehead, which is a lurid cross-hatching of angry red scar tissue, where the razor slashed both horizontally and vertically. On the lower part of Gina's face, the razor did not merely slash but gouged, dug, sliced, like a spoon. The effect is pathetic, grotesque: Gina looks like a porcelain doll whose face has cracked in myriad pieces, inexpertly mended, about to crack apart again at any moment. The surgical attempt to restore missing flesh to her left nostril and her lower lip has been only partly successful, as if porcelain has been mended, and crudely, with putty.

Poor Gina has had three skin-graft operations thus far and is scheduled for a fourth, in September. If she is strong enough to endure it.

Suddenly she cries, "Oh, God, Michael!—I'm horrible! Will you let me die?"

"Gina, I've asked you not to talk that way! I love you."

Michael grips Gina's hands firmly, so that she can't spread her fingers over her face, to hide it.

He knows that, when she is alone, she touches herself constantly, tirelessly. Even in her sleep.

He says, urgently, "You mustn't despair, Gina. Think of our sons, think of me. We love you. Everything will be all right."

"But—"

"Oh, Gina! I'm your husband, I love you more than ever."

A tear runs down Gina's mutilated cheek, and then another, and another, though she is not crying, really; her mask of a face remains stiff and inexpressive. What is she thinking, behind that mask?—who *is* she, now? She has lost so much weight, her body has a look of having been mutilated too; her breasts have shrunken, yet are slack; her collarbone, ribs, pelvic bones protrude. Thus the layers of clothing, on even this warm summer day.

Michael contemplates his wife lovingly, yet with a practiced detachment; almost, a sense of satisfaction. For the woman *is*, now, his. His alone. Regardless of the miracle surgery to come, regardless of the bouts of hope, courage, pain, no other man will ever look at her again.

If she'd had a lover, or lovers, back in that other life—who among them would seek her out, now?

But Michael O'Meara is not thinking of such things really.

Just as he does not think of, in fact does not quite recall, what happened between him and Lee Roy Sears in Sears' studio. And on the fire escape.

That entire day, that nightmare of a day, its infinitesimal moments, and the interstices between those moments, so synchronized, so like clockwork: all, now, a blank in his memory. A vacancy. An erasure.

Michael leans to kiss Gina, and, instinctively, though she must know better, she stiffens just slightly.

Gently he touches his lips to hers; he is careful to exert no pressure, to cause no pain. To show the woman that he is not revulsed, as another man would be, by that disfigured lower lip.

Murmuring, "You know I love you, don't you? don't you? darling Gina, *don't* you?"

Until, as if the words are being squeezed from her, small cries of distress, helplessness, dread, she says, finally, her face shimmering with tears, "Yes. I know."